Avengers
of
Blood

A Cass Elliot Crime Novel

Gae-Lynn Woods

Dead Head Press

Copyright

For Martyn, with love in big doses.

And if he thrust him of hatred, or hurled at him, lying in wait, so that he died, or in enmity smote him with his hand, so that he died; he that smote him shall surely be put to death; he is a murderer: the avenger of blood shall put the murderer to death, when he meeteth him.

Numbers 35:20-21, American Standard Bible

Blood will have blood.

Macbeth, **William Shakespeare**

PROLOGUE

IT WAS A BEAUTIFUL night for a killing. One of those gorgeous Southern evenings that occur only occasionally as summer draws near, cool and clear, nearly devoid of humidity. Overhead, the stars sparkled in a vast expanse of velvety sky, their shimmering brightness dimmed only by the whisper-thin gauze of smoke that hung in the nearly motionless air.

Despite the smell of terror and charred flesh, the clearing retained the cheery, slightly crazed atmosphere of a traveling carnival. The crowd had at first been pensive, watchful, but once the killing was done a sense of relief swept through the watchers. Women gossiped and tittered, drinking soda pop from bottles dotted with condensation. Children played chase through the forest of legs and took turns reenacting the murders they'd witnessed only moments earlier. Men smoked pipes and cigarettes, talking in low voices and tapping dried mud from their tired work boots.

The sheeted men nearest the fires took off their hoods and their damp faces gleamed in the flames. People pulled back to give the photographer room and a bright burst stung the night. At last the crowd drifted away, women calling children and fussing at their husbands to hurry home. A few engines cranked in the still air, but most left on foot.

The men in sheets lingered until the last of the crowd was gone and then congratulated themselves on how quickly justice could be served. A rustling startled them and one man took long strides to the side of the clearing and parted two azalea bushes bearing papery violet blooms. A filthy figure gazed up at him, face tear-streaked and snotty, a broken pencil and tattered paper clutched in one grimy hand.

It took a moment, but at last he recognized the child. He leaned over and snatched the paper, calling to his companions. They towered over the tiny body, muttering to one another and turning the drawing to the firelight to see crude representations of the horror they had wrought. At last one of them lifted a foot clad in a pointy-toed cowboy boot and nudged the child toward the road.

"Get on home, now," he said. "And don't you ever talk about what you seen. You understand? Don't draw no more pictures, neither." The child looked up at him with dark eyes that pierced his soul. He blustered on. "What happened here tonight can just as easily happen to you. Easier, even. 'Cause there ain't nobody to look out for you now."

He watched as the child scurried away. Once out of reach, it turned and looked back at them with a burning gaze, searching their faces. He lifted his foot again and the child fled, swallowed quickly by the night. The laughter of the others was at first hesitant, as if they too had felt the intensity of the child's hate. But the sound swelled and gained confidence and at last he joined in, hoping to obscure the vague uneasiness settling in his gut.

CHAPTER 1

Wednesday

CASS ELLIOT GROWLED AS she strained against a crowbar wedged between the wall and a stubborn two-by-four. "I hate these things."

"Easy now," Bruce coaxed, leaning around her to slide a piece of half-inch plywood between the crowbar and the wall. "You'll dent the sheetrock."

"I'll dent *your* sheetrock," she huffed, giving another mighty heave. The cabinet shrieked as three-inch nails screeched from their stud beds. She dropped the crowbar in the cabinet cavity, turned the volume down on the police scanner, and swiped Bruce's freshly opened soda from the table. Sucking a long gulp, she eyed his broad frame, dark features, and – she frowned – clean clothes. "Where're you going, my favorite brother?"

"I didn't know I was your favorite."

"You're my favorite when you're helping me rip out the kitchen." She watched as Bruce added a newspaper clipping to a collection beneath a magnet on the refrigerator. "I wish you'd stop that."

"Let me be famous vicariously." The clippings from the Forney Cater – featuring photographs of Cass, her partner Mitch Stone, or the smoldering remains of a cabin in the Sabine River bottoms – fluttered as Bruce tugged gingerly on the refrigerator's duct-taped handle. He grabbed another soda.

"I just wish it was over. Where're you going?"

"School."

"You don't teach on Wednesday night."

"Some of the students need time in the shop to finish their final projects. I told them I'd open up today."

3

"Those aren't teaching clothes, Bruce. Those are date clothes."

"I might have a little something planned for later on. And speaking of dates, Sam McGee called while you were hauling trash to the dump."

She winced.

"Come on, Cass. He's nice enough. The McGee's are a good family. The two of you would make pretty babies."

"What is it with men?" she asked, raking loose strands of hair, darkened by sweat to the deep red of a merlot, into her ponytail. "I went out with him once and declined every time he's asked since. Surely he's got the message by now."

Bruce lifted an eyebrow. "You gave him hope. He'll think it's possible that you'll say yes again."

"How do I get rid of him? Nicely?"

"It'll take mean. You can do it. I've got the scars to prove it."

"And every one of them was well deserved."

"Or you could start dating somebody else. That's a good way to get the message across."

"Yeah, and there are so many options in Arcadia."

"Tom Kado's one."

Cass groaned. "Don't start."

"The man has a thing for you." He cocked his head to one side. "But, it might be a conflict of interest if you went out with him, right? Since you both work for the police department?"

Do I work for the department anymore? she wondered. "Haven't thought about it," Cass lied. "Besides, his wife died about a year ago. He's in no shape for a relationship."

"Everybody grieves differently," Bruce said. "I don't know why you don't go out more –," he held up a strong hand when Cass tried to interrupt. "And that's your business. But if you're looking for a decent guy, I think Tom Kado might be one."

"Message received. Where's Harry?"

"Upstairs. The almost-ex-wife called and there's an emergency with a client." Her shoulders slumped and Bruce shrugged. "Daddy's not due back from this morning's delivery until tonight, so you get

4

the crowbar and sledgehammer all to yourself. Paradise, if you ask me." Bruce knelt to examine the hole in the kitchen floor revealed when Cass removed the cabinet under the sink. He stuck his hand between the jagged edges and pulled out bits of a mouse nest. "I always wondered why it was so drafty when I was washing dishes."

"I said I'd help." Cass wiped the day's sweat from her brow with a forearm. "I didn't think I'd have to do the whole thing myself."

"It's good experience. Fixing the roof and leveling the porch was hard work. But tearing out a kitchen? That's plain fun. Hey," he continued, plucking his keys from the table, "when you get that one out, start on the cabinet in the corner. Might as well get it all done today."

Cass watched him stride across the tired linoleum floor, boots crunching over the grit and rubble strewn across its surface. The screen door banged shut behind him. Silence, followed by the cranking of a pickup's engine, filled the late afternoon air.

"Fine," she muttered, turning the scanner's volume back up and reaching for the crowbar. "I'll do it myself. But you're not my favorite anymore."

CHAPTER 2

GOOBER JERKED THE RED riding mower's steering wheel and managed to avoid an armadillo trundling across the county road. Scowling, he stomped on the little mower's gas pedal, urging the machine to move faster. Sunset wasn't for another two and a half hours, but the narrow lanes between his small trailer and The Whitehead Store were already crowded with shadow from the massive trees flanking the road. In Goober's world, darkness in any form was bad. Goblins lurked in the dusty gloom beneath the bed; vampires needed the night; and zombies, who could function during the day, vastly preferred terrorizing simple villagers while hiding beneath a cloak of darkness. Goober was a sudden expert on all things monster because, in a moment of insomnia driven weakness, he had flipped on the horror channel last night and watched, trembling, until the wee hours when he fell asleep on his sofa.

The mower's engine whined with the strain, but Goober pulled the tip of his baseball cap down over his forehead and kept his foot on the pedal. He briefly wondered how much gasoline was left in the little machine but pushed the thought away; he'd leave her on the side of the road if he had to. This trip to the store wasn't just for fun. Goober was out of snacks. Although he ate a fairly healthy diet, today's craving for salt and crunch would not be denied. Hence the venture out along Forney County's small, eerie roads in spite of the sun's continuing decline.

Goober rounded Church Bend and looked up to see the wink of a tail light in the distance. A thrill of fear raced through him and he patted the pocket in his overalls where he tucked his folding money. He extracted a battered Timex and saw that it read five twenty-nine — this was cutting it too close. The Whitehead Store closed at five-thirty on the dot. He lifted his heavy work boot and stomped on the accelerator again.

A squirrel dashed onto the road, flicked its tail at the red machine, and darted safely to the other side. So intent was he on reaching the store, Goober hardly noticed. At last, the gas station's concrete apron came into view and Goober screeched to a stop at the pumps. He jumped from the mower and charged across the tiny parking lot, relief in his veins: the 'open' sign still hung in the door. He pushed inside with a greeting on his lips and reaching for the Frito display when he skidded across the sparkling linoleum. Startled, he looked down see to a trail of amber liquid on the floor. The smell of gas reached his nose and his ire rose. Most people were considerate enough not to trail gasoline when they came inside to pay. Goober always wiped his feet and if he made a mess, he knew good and well how to clean it up.

He looked for Mr. Whitehead and spotted a puff of smoke floating through the open stockroom door in the back of the shop. Goober gazed at that black abyss and in a move that would later surprise himself and everyone else, he squashed the ripple of terror threatening his legs and ran toward that open door instead of away from it.

A FIGURE IN DARK clothes stepped inside and watched the man in overalls dart to the back of the shop. He took in the neat rows of shelves and gleaming refrigeration units. There was no sign of disturbance, no indication that anything sinister had happened here. *Odd*, he thought. *If there was no one to murder, why would the three of them come here?*

He moved to the counter, avoiding the gleaming streak of liquid on the otherwise pristine floor. Again, nothing was out of place. A yellowed newspaper clipping taped beside a crucifix on the wall caught his attention. He leaned closer and read a short story about the store's grand opening in 1979. When his eyes rose to a picture of the ribbon-cutting, an icy wave of shock froze him in place. The unsmiling face staring from the photograph took him back almost twenty-five years, to his father's death when he was nine years old. *His father's death.* It couldn't be true.

He hurried around the counter to study the clipping more closely. The thick shock of dark hair, the chiseled features that were so similar to his own. There was no mistaking the man who held a pair of scissors over an uncut ribbon. He was a ghost, burned to a crisp in 1978. But he wasn't dead. He wasn't dead at all. In fact, he'd given up his life and his only child, for what? To open a gas station in some mosquito-infested backwater in Texas?

The events of his life and their meaning re-ordered themselves in his mind, and an immense sense of loss and betrayal sliced through him. Tears stung his eyes and he drew a deep breath, tasting a foul smoke. He turned then, gaze coming to rest on the open stockroom door.

―――――――

A LAYER OF TRANSLUCENT smoke greeted Goober as he dashed into the ransacked stockroom. The sight of toppled shelves and a smear of some dark substance across the floor brought him up short. A creak drew his glance to the murky light filtering through the outside door. He went up on his tiptoes and sidled around the mishmash of food and broken containers. A rancid, stinging smell made his eyes water and a faint popping grew louder as he crossed the stockroom. Goober's empty stomach turned and he pulled a yellow kerchief from his overalls, covered his mouth and nose, and stepped out to a small courtyard.

A concrete patio was open to the evening sky and surrounded by a tall wood fence. The small area was a study in contrasts. The north side was orderly and somewhat peaceful. A hand truck rested against the wall beside neat stacks of wood pallets and flattened cardboard boxes. Garden implements and leggy ladders hung in tidy rows from pegs, and a green water hose was wrapped around a reel. A metal gas can squatted beside a weed trimmer leaning against the wall.

The rest of the area was chaos.

A wheelbarrow lay on its side against the southern portion of the fence, alongside a toppled step ladder. Closer to the middle of the courtyard, a misshapen pile of red plastic smoldered. A sycamore tree grew in one corner, its smooth-barked trunk rising gracefully from a patch of scraggly dirt. Goober whimpered as his vision expanded to take in the scene. Only seven feet or so from the ground, the tree's lowest limb sprung outward at a nearly ninety-degree angle, and from it dangled a zombie, blackened and blazing. Tongues of orange flame danced in a mouth stretched wide in a silent scream and nibbled at the rope around the zombie's neck. The concrete beneath him was scorched and heat rose in shimmering waves from its surface.

Goober danced in a tight circle and fought the savage urge to flee as a debate raged through his brain. Everybody knew that zombies were dangerous. They lived on human flesh. But zombies were undead, which meant that they were alive until they were dead. Goober hated to see any living thing hurt, and if this zombie was alive, it didn't deserve to burn even though he knew he'd have to kill it eventually. He wasn't sure he could save a zombie that was already on fire, but – in another surprising move – he decided to try.

He felt for the spigot, never taking his gaze from the zombie as it swayed ever so slightly on its noose. Goober yanked the hose from its reel and flinched away from the steam that rose when the sputtering stream hit the burning body. Suddenly, the rope around its neck snapped and the zombie hit the ground with a smacking thud. It lay motionless for a moment, then stirred.

Goober's released a blood-curdling shriek before dropping the hose and charging into the stockroom. He slammed the door shut and stood trembling, heart in his throat, listening as the zombie staggered to its feet. Goober took a running leap over the gooey mess on the floor and sprinted into the store, where he dove behind the counter and grabbed the phone.

With shaking fingers, he pecked out 911. "Police? This is Goober. We got a burnin' zombie on the loose in The Whitehead Store. Bring the machetes. We gotta cut his head off."

———————

THE MAN RECOILED AT the shrill scream and hid between two rows of shelves. He watched dispassionately as the overall-clad man darted behind the counter and started babbling about zombies. The door to the stockroom was still open and he slipped through it, taking in the toppled shelving and burst food containers. The rancid, smoky scent was stronger here and he sidestepped the mess on the floor to make his way to the outside door. Gently pulling it open, his eyes narrowed as he peered through a small crack and then opened the door more fully.

It seemed the murderous little trio did have a purpose in coming to this remote store.

He inched closer to the form smoldering on the concrete, gaze latching on to a sooty gold ring with a red stone fixed to its dome and then roving the figure more carefully. An unscorched tuft of thick white hair was still attached to the scalp. Although the face was blackened and stretched, its basic structure was still evident: broad forehead, defined cheekbones, angular jaw. Unbidden, his mind recreated the muscular detail that once covered those features.

The scarlet edges of rage crowded his vision and he sucked in a stinking breath, fighting back a scream. Everything he'd believed, all the circumstances of his life – it was a lie. Panic thrummed through his veins and he physically forced himself to study the smoking body, memorizing the horrifying tableau and dipping deep into the well of hate in his soul. His spirit quieted then and the despair morphed inside him, settling into a molten and searing ball of fury.

Without a backward glance, he retreated through the courtyard gate and melted into the woods, dabbing at the sweat beading his upper lip. He trotted at a slow but steady pace toward his car and brought his breathing and thoughts under control.

Until today, he had considered the murderous little cabal his silent partners. Granted, he had no idea why some of the same names had landed on both their kill lists, but between them and the work they had completed so far, the world was a far better place. Since learning their identities several months ago, he had traced them to this slice of redneck paradise and watched, moving with caution to learn the rhythms of their lives. But he hadn't stalked silently; instead, he had poked and prodded into their personal lives to see how fragile they were. If they were made of the right stuff, perhaps he would've approached them, wormed his way into their inner circle. He wanted to understand their motivations and discover who else they had marked for termination. The trio was careful, and that he appreciated. They must've known about this victim for some time, because they hadn't visited this little store since he'd been tracking them.

But any semblance of camaraderie he felt for this odd group of executioners vanished at the sight of their latest victim. In its place sprang the germ of revenge – they had bested him, understanding his own life even better than he had. And from their knowledge, they had taken his father from him. Again. A hope he hadn't known existed, extinguished before it could form. They were now the enemy.

His mind focused on his new prey with an eerie intensity. He would extract payment from each of them for what they had cost him. Payment in full.

CHAPTER 3

CASS WORKED STEADILY, PAUSING only to haul broken sections of cabinet to the backyard and toss them on a growing burn pile. The air conditioner had been off since she and Bruce started work early this morning, and they had left the doors and windows open in hopes of catching a breeze. Instead, the summer heat built as the day wore on, bringing a healthy dose of sticky humidity that caused the dust and grit from their demolition project to hang nearly motionless in the air. Cass stopped to wipe the sweat from her face and take a swig of cold water. It had taken the better part of the day to remove most of the wall and base cabinets from the kitchen, leaving only one cabinet squatting in the corner.

She had no complaint; sweat was her salvation. The physical work cleared her mind and her fears about the future wept out through her pores. She could forget about Mitch Stone and how much pain she'd endured since that devastating night in the spring. Her dreams were still riddled with the image of his face as she remembered it through the small window in the ICU door – pale, motionless, devoid of life. The phantom scent of a burning building caught her at the most improbable of times and alternate outcomes to that night played continuously through her mind. It had been over six weeks since she'd been suspended from the police department, and even though she'd found solace in hard labor and power tools, doubt over the outcome of the Firearm Discharge Board review had taken a toll.

She'd spent the time during her suspension – the banishment, she called it – getting reacquainted with the two of the six Elliot brothers who lived with her in their father's house. Harry, the third oldest, was a recent addition as he and his wife had separated only weeks earlier, a bitter event that left the normally genial Harry in a state of perpetual irritation. Bruce had left home some years ago to study drafting, but had returned after graduation to teach at the local college. Never married, at thirty-three Nell and Abe Elliot's middle child was considered a tasty catch by the local female constituency, and Bruce played that role to his advantage; always interested, never committed. The siblings and their father spent many evenings laughing at the past and dissecting local events, careful to skirt the most painful part of their early lives – the arrest of their oldest brother Jack when Cass was four years old, and their mother's untimely death only a year later.

They also talked about the Elliot home, a ramshackle affair rented by a kindly family to Abe and Nell when they were first married and eventually sold to them on very favorable terms. Cass had to agree that the place needed work, and in fairness to Bruce and his scheme to modernize the house, she could finally see his vision for the kitchen. He'd spent evenings browsing the internet for appliances and floor coverings, and his weekends prowling lumber yards to find perfect cuts of maple for the cabinets. His goal was to create a kitchen that would've made their mother proud. Cass, Harry, and Abe groaned every time Bruce asked for more money, but his excitement was so great that none of them had the heart to shut him down.

Although she still burned over the fact that Sheriff Hoffner was taking his sweet time in signing her back on to work, in a way, she relished the time off. Her early mornings were devoted to exercise and Cass was tighter and leaner than she'd ever been. Solitude on the days when Harry, Abe, and Bruce were away at work was also an odd sort of blessing, as Cass could slow down and think carefully about how best to pursue the man who had raped her six years ago.

The temptation to simply forget what had happened never tugged at Cass. Instead, her life changed course, becoming a methodical hunt for the man who had hurt her. Thinking about that night, even today, brought a rush of anger so powerful it was palatable. But she'd turned that fury into forward motion. Her initial efforts to identify her rapist were rudimentary, involving scanning the newspapers every day. Over time she'd become more sophisticated, utilizing internet search alerts to pull relevant rape cases to her inbox, and trolling the interagency traffic for similar crimes. At least twice each day she checked for results. So far, nothing had popped.

Cass finished her water and leaned the crowbar against the wall, unable to stifle the urge her thoughts had brought on. She climbed the stairs to her room. As usual, her inbox was empty and the spam folder overflowing with offers to make her penis larger. Disappointed but not surprised, she returned to the kitchen and studied the lone remaining cabinet.

She slid the crowbar between the countertop and the cabinet, jammed it home, and levered the top up. It sprang free with a shriek. Cass turned at a giggle to find a tiny ballerina watching.

"Hey, Auntie Cass."

Cass switched the burbling police scanner off and smiled at her niece. Phoebe was swathed in pink, from her ballet slippers and seashell pale tights and tutu, to her fuchsia leotard. Cass wiped the dust from a seat at the scuffed kitchen table and lifted the five-year-old to the chair. "You look gorgeous. What are you up to?"

"Going to jazz class."

"Why are you wearing your ballet outfit?"

"I'm a princess, Auntie Cass, and this is my gown."

"Oh," Cass said, as Harry entered, guilt on his face.

"Can you take her?"

"Bruce said you've got a meeting?"

Harry pulled gingerly on the refrigerator's duct-taped handle. He removed a pitcher of orange juice and poured small glasses for the three of them. "Do you remember the Martins?"

"Sure. Old money."

"We're doing some work for them and they're not happy with what the interior designer is planning." He glanced down at Phoebe, but the little girl was bobbing her head to an internal rhythm, oblivious to the fact that the interior designer was her mother.

"Why don't they talk to her?"

"Drama."

"Ah." Harry and his estranged wife Carly shared an architectural and design business and were known for their innovation. Carly also had a well-deserved reputation as a diva, and the firm had lost several clients over her refusal to change her interior design plans to suit the client's wishes.

"I need to smooth things over and knock the designer off her high horse. Can you take Feebs to town?"

"Sure," Cass said, glancing down at her filthy clothes. "When?"

"Class starts at seven-thirty." Harry leaned down to kiss his daughter's cheek and be kissed in return. "I'll pick her up. Thanks, Cass."

She looked at the dusty kitchen clock as the screen door slammed shut. An hour and a half to go. "Okay Feebs, what's next?"

"Supper."

"Right." Cass ran a finger along the stove top and looked at the grit it gathered. "I'm not cooking tonight."

"Uncle Bruce always cooks."

"Good point. How about a burger from Chubby's?"

"Can I have a chocolate shake?"

Cass considered the fallout that would arise from the inevitable spatter on Phoebe's pink ballet outfit, and decided that Carly's wrath was well worth the price of retaining favorite aunt status. Even if it cost Cass a new leotard and tutu. "It's not Chubby's without a shake." She tried to work her fingers through her tangled hair. "But I need a shower. Want to come upstairs and watch TV while I get ready?"

The little girl nodded and pulled a sparkling tiara from behind her back. "Mommy won't let me wear it outside 'cause I might lose it. But it's okay if I'm with you, right Auntie Cass?"

Cass recognized the crown Carly had received when she was named Fire Ant Queen some years ago. It was a tacky thing made of paste jewels that formed hearts and something meant to resemble a fire ant. Her heart warmed at Phoebe's transcendent grin as she settled the shiny crescent on her niece's head, and she wondered only briefly how much a new tiara would cost.

CHAPTER 4

OFFICER HUGO PETCHARD LICKED his thumb and smoothed his eyebrows down. Fresh from the shower at the police station, he leaned against a lamp post. It was after six o'clock, and rush hour traffic — what there was of it in a town as small as Arcadia — had died off. He glanced around and swiped his arm across his forehead, surreptitiously sniffing his armpit and catching only a whiff of Old Spice.

A figure hurried around the corner of The Golden Gate Café's little building and Petchard recognized Junie's slender form. His heart thudded against the cage of his ribs. He opened his mouth to call out but she darted inside before he could muster the words. In only an instant the door opened again and there she was, framed by the apricot hue of the early evening sun. His breath caught in his throat. He found her perfect in every way. Well, except for the height. He was five foot ten and in flat shoes, Junie was a good two inches taller. Otherwise, there wasn't a flaw on or in the woman. Smooth skin, strong arms, narrow hips, gorgeous black hair. Eyes of the purest, darkest brown Petchard had ever seen. A patient, funny personality. And she liked him.

She liked *him*.

He watched as she called a good-bye over her shoulder, adjusted her bag where it hung across her body, and started at the sight of Petchard. A frown creased his brow. His normally composed Junie looked flustered. Something he'd never seen before. A smile found its way to her mouth and she waited while he made his way down the sidewalk to her.

"Hello, gorgeous," he said, kissing her cheek.

"Hello, lover," she replied, her voice a husky purr. "I thought you'd be at home having dinner with your family and getting ready for church. You must be tired after your long day protecting us all."

He preened. "I had to stop and say goodnight. How's your headache?"

"Gone. I managed to take some pain medicine before it got too bad. You're so sweet to remember."

Petchard took her hand and led her to the employee parking lot at the back of the café. "Are you sure you don't have time for a movie tonight? You could come to church with me and we could see a late show. Or we could have dinner. I still want you to meet my family." At her look of panic he added, "When you're ready, of course."

Her features softened and she touched his lips with a finger. "Not tonight. I have to wash my hair."

Petchard suppressed a grin at this display of feminine vanity. Junie's hair was short. Not as short as his own thinning blond crew cut, but short enough that a good toweling would dry it in no time. Perhaps she would use the evening to perform the other mysterious and somewhat terrifying rituals that women thought necessary to maintain their beauty. He watched as she unlocked a battered old Honda, and wanted again to offer to buy her a newer vehicle. Or loan her the money to buy one. But he held his tongue. She'd already rebuffed his offer in the kindest of ways. He cleared his throat. "Maybe tomorrow night?"

"Perhaps," she said, presenting her cheek for another kiss. "Let's see what tomorrow brings."

Junie slipped into the car and the rust bucket turned over on the second twist of the key. Petchard blushed when she blew him a kiss through the windshield. Through a haze of adoration, he watched as the object of his affection backed out of the parking lot and drove away.

CHAPTER 5

THE STENCH OF BURNING flesh was ripe even in front of the store when Detective Carlos Martinez stepped outside to clear his head. Several emergency vehicles cluttered the station's forecourt and spilled onto the county road. Swirling lights bounced around the small area, creating a nauseating psychedelic patina. He was grateful that no sirens pierced the still evening.

He lifted his chin in greeting to the young officer posted at the gas station's front door. The man nodded while pressing a handkerchief over his nose and mouth. Drawing a shallow breath, Martinez looked more closely at the forecourt. Firefighters rolled up their hoses and an officer was stringing yellow crime scene tape in a wide perimeter around the store. Goober sat on the tailgate of the forensics guy's pickup, his mouth slightly ajar, eyes staring vacantly into the shadows crowding the county road. After seeing the torched body in the little courtyard behind the store for himself, the detective considered Goober's means of coping by shutting out the world quite reasonable.

After more than thirty years with the Forney County police force, Martinez thought he had seen the worst that humanity had to offer. From cases of domestic violence where a woman's head was swollen to almost twice its normal size due to a beating, to knife fights, gunshot wounds, smotherings, drownings, and even the aftereffects of a bowling ball slammed into a skull.

But this, what had happened to the man who died behind The Whitehead Store, was an exceptional kind of evil.

Martinez blew his nose to try and force the smell of seared flesh from his sinuses. As a fire truck growled away from the scene, he noticed movement near a patrol car blocking the road. A small man paced in the gloom cast by the setting sun, speaking quietly into a handheld recorder. He changed direction when he caught sight of Martinez. As he drew nearer, the detective groaned inwardly. Wally Pugh, the Forney Cater's roving reporter, had the pointed features of a weasel. His beady black eyes darted from Martinez' face to the store's door as his narrow body moved in a sinuous, almost hypnotic stroll toward the gas pumps. He wasn't a bad guy, Martinez knew, and had supported the police force after The Church of the True Believer debacle several weeks ago despite the negative coverage the major news outlets had provided.

He met the reporter just past the gas pumps, ran his strong hands over his face and steely crew cut, and crossed his massive arms over his broad chest. "Hey, Wally."

"Detective Martinez. What happened back there? It smells like somebody barbequed a skunk. Goober's almost comatose and won't say a word."

"How'd you hear about it?"

"Scanner. They said something about a burning zombie. Did somebody get roasted?" Wally held the recorder out between them and pushed a button.

Martinez considered his words. Dealing with the press was Sheriff Bill Hoffner's responsibility and a chore the man seemed to relish, but Hoffner was out of town and the Forney Cater needed something to print. Martinez steeled himself for a dance around the facts. "We have one dead body."

"A zombie?"

"Yeah. *Night of the Living Dead* does Forney County. Come on, Wally."

"Who is it?"

"We don't know."

"What happened?"

"We're not sure, but the body is burned."

"How badly?"

"Pretty severely."

"Accidental?"

"We're still investigating."

Wally's delicate eyebrows shot up. "Murder?"

"Like I said, we're still investigating."

"Who found the body?"

Martinez hesitated. "Goober."

"Is he a suspect?"

Are you kidding? Martinez thought. "No. That's all I've got for you right now, Wally. I hope we'll have an ID later tonight. Check with the ME's office or give me a call before you go to print."

Wally eyed Martinez, nose twitching as he sucked his teeth. He switched the recorder off. "Any chance I can get back there and take a photo?"

"Not tonight. How about one of the front of the store? Keep Goober out of it. And leave him out of your story. I don't think he could handle attention like that."

The reporter nodded and wandered away, tucking his recorder into a pocket and lifting a digital camera from around his neck. Martinez watched him go, then turned to the little red mower parked near a gas pump. A two-gallon can was bungeed to a platform behind the seat and Martinez snapped a paper towel from a nearby holder and loosened the cap to peer inside. Maybe one-quarter full. He unscrewed the cap on the mower's gasoline tank and bumped the little machine. From the sloshing and glint of light on liquid, Martinez guessed the mower was almost empty. According to the cash register, the store's last transaction was conducted at five eighteen. A purchase of three gallons of gas for cash. Probably used to barbeque the guy out back, who must be the store's owner, Calvin Whitehead. Or perhaps an employee. Martinez tightened the gas cap and turned to focus on Goober, who was wringing his baseball cap between his hands.

The detective shook his head and wondered where to start.

GOOBER WAS A MYSTERY. He'd appeared one morning about forty years ago, nestled in the gnarled roots of the ancient hanging tree on the courthouse lawn, abandoned in the middle of the night. In spite of announcements on the local radio station and in the newspaper, the toddler's parents never came forward to claim him. An elderly widow took him in and over time, Goober became a fixture in Arcadia. The odd man was probably closer to forty-five than to forty given the silver that peppered his nearly black hair. People said that Goober wasn't truly retarded, but Martinez wasn't so sure. Goober hadn't finished high school and his ability to read and write was limited. Granted, he was always polite and seemed eager to help, but there was a slowness about the man, almost an innocence, that Martinez thought reflected some sort of mental challenge.

He stiffened as Forney County's Forensic Examiner, Tom Kado, came through the gas station's front door. As Martinez had done, he nodded briefly at the officer near the door and stopped to remove the booties covering his shoes. He shoved them in a plastic garbage bag and rubbed his eyes. Kado was new to the force, having joined only a couple of months ago. Martinez found the younger man arrogant and disrespectful of the last forensic examiner, Hank Comfrey, who had held the job for nearly five decades before dropping dead of a heart attack earlier this year. Kado was full of new procedures and science but didn't seem to trust his gut as old Comfrey had. Martinez wasn't sure the science was all that reliable. The wariness he felt for Kado was justified when a crucial DNA sample in a recent case was found by the state lab to be contaminated. If Martinez was the detective assigned to this murder, and he surely would be because there *were* no other detectives in Forney County at the moment, Kado would have to walk the straight and narrow to Martinez' satisfaction. He met Kado at the tailgate where Goober sat, still torturing the baseball cap.

"You okay, Goob?" Kado asked.

Goober nodded but his gaze was glassy and his face devoid of color. Kado climbed up in the pickup's bed, opened a cooler and passed a root beer to Martinez, then took one for himself and Goober. He took the cap from Goober's hands and replaced it with an open can. "Drink."

Slowly, Goober did. "Thanks," he said, burping quietly.

"You up for talking?" Martinez asked.

Goober nodded.

"Why did you come to Whitehead's tonight?"

"I ran out of potato chips."

Martinez looked at the mower parked by the station's pumps. "Did you pump gas?"

"I was gonna check her after I got the chips."

"What time did you get here?"

"Right about five-thirty."

"You sure?"

He pulled a beat-up Timex from a pocket and held it out. "It was almost five-thirty when I came around Church Bend."

Martinez compared the little watch to his own. It was two minutes fast. "Did you pass anybody on the road?"

"Naw, my mower don't go that fast."

Kado bit back a smile, and the detective's jaw tightened. He tried again. "Did you see any other vehicles on the road?"

"Just some tail lights."

"Where?"

"When I was coming around Church Bend." He turned and pointed into the night. "A car was farther down the road."

"What kind of car?"

Goober shrugged. "All I saw was red lights."

"What happened when you got to the store?"

"I went inside to make sure Mr. Whitehead was still open." He blinked. "There was gas on the floor. And then smoke came out of the door in the back. So I went to see what was burning."

"Why didn't you call the fire department right then?"

"I was scared," he answered in a small voice.

"You were scared but you headed toward the smoke, to the fire?"

Goober nodded, his eyes fixed on some distant, internal point.

Martinez and Kado exchanged a glance. "What happened next?"

"The smoke was bad, but the back door was open. I heard a noise and went outside and saw... the zombie. He was hanging." He

22

shuddered and root beer sloshed onto his overalls. "And black all over."

"Did you see flames?"

"He was breathing fire. Like a dragon. I tried to put it out." Goober's eyes filled with tears and he drew a deep, stuttering breath. "But the zombie fell off the rope and started to get up. I figured he was coming after me. He fell and I ran away."

KADO AND MARTINEZ PULLED fresh booties over their shoes and crossed through the gas station's neatly organized shop and the chaotic stockroom to the courtyard, each trying not to wince as the smell of burned flesh grew stronger. The odor was thick and sickly, like pork in sweet and sour sauce roasted for too long, tinged with sulfur and melting plastic. It clung to the roof of Kado's mouth and coated his sinuses.

His first view of the courtyard had been cursory, simply to photograph the scene and, unfortunately, turn off the hose. Now, Kado examined the space more closely. Water lay in silent pools on the uneven slab that formed the courtyard's floor. Bits of charred matter – skin and clothing, Kado guessed – rested in drifts against the base of a wooden fence. Washed there by the water hose Goober had left running when the body dropped to the ground. A step ladder and wheelbarrow were toppled against the fence, and a smoldering red container was the source of the biting smell of burning plastic. Waves of disgust and despair rolled through Kado in equal measure. He had no idea how long it would take to collect and analyze all the evidence in this case, and he was already stretched thin from a heavy workload. He considered drawing a deep breath to release the tension, but changed his mind and rubbed the back of his neck instead.

Forney County's Medical Examiner, John Grey, and his assistant Porky Rivers were crouched next to the blackened form. A plastic sheet was spread on a patch of dry concrete. They were discussing the best way to lift the body without jarring flesh loose. The victim had landed on his left side, the arms bent over the chest and fingers curled near his neck. Kado looked closer and saw bits of scorched clothing still in place around parts of the body. In others, delicate layers of the epidermis and dermis had blackened and curled back from the man's flesh, exposing red muscle or yellowish fat. A heavy gold ring was barely visible on the corpse's right hand and a lonely tuft of white hair had somehow escaped the flames and clung to the scorched scalp.

"Who would do something like that to Calvin Whitehead?" Martinez asked.

"How do you know that's Whitehead?" Kado responded.

Martinez crossed his arms over his massive chest and thrust his chin forward. "Who else would it be?"

Grey unfolded his lanky form, balancing carefully until he reached his full height of six feet eight inches. "He's too badly burned to be sure it's Whitehead. We'll check for a wallet when we move him, and use dental records or DNA to confirm."

Martinez moved his gaze from Kado to Grey. "I'll find his house next, see if he's home."

"Do you know him?" Kado asked.

"I don't," Martinez replied. "His store is way off my beaten path. Grey?"

"I'd heard his name but didn't know where his store was. Porky?"

The thin man looked up from his squatting position and his gaze bounced between Grey, Kado, and Martinez. Fading sunlight glinted on the studs, rings, and barbells that dotted his nose, eyebrows, and ears and provided the source for his full nickname of Porcupine. Most were silver and contrasted sharply with his inky black skin. "This is too far out in the boonies. I've never even heard of the place."

Kado turned to Martinez. "Is he home grown?"

"I said I don't know him," Martinez replied with an edge to his voice, and Kado responded with a cool look. "He's been here as long as I can remember. We'll check with the neighbors and court records to see when he opened up."

"There haven't been any problems out here?"

"Nothing I've heard about," Martinez answered. "And I would've, through roll call and gossip."

Kado looked to Grey. "Do you know cause of death yet?"

"Looks like barbequing to me," Martinez said, casting a sidelong glance at Kado.

"It depends," Grey answered, "on how long he hung before he was set alight, and on whether he was alive when hung. We'll need to complete the autopsy to confirm COD, but I can tell you a few things now." Grey motioned to Porky who lifted the corner of a flat, blackened mass from the thigh. "The fire burned long enough to char his clothes and burn through the epidermis and dermis in places. In some areas, it looks like clothing and skin have fused, so he might've been wearing a man-made fabric that melted, like nylon. Maybe tracksuit bottoms or trousers with a stretch material."

"Is there any chance he was alive when the rope broke?" Kado asked.

"I doubt it. Why?"

"Goober thought he saw the zombie getting up to chase him after the body fell. That's why he ran and called 911."

"If the hanging didn't kill our victim, the burning finished the job quickly." Grey motioned to the slightly bent elbows, hips, and knees. "When a body burns, the muscles draw in and shorten, creating the positioning you see here. It's called a pugilistic attitude because the body takes on a stance similar to a boxer. Goober might have seen movement as the muscles contracted and with his imagination, thought the man was still alive."

Kado's gaze followed the sycamore's trunk up to the first limb. A length of rope hung there, its end blackened. "Is any rope left around his neck?"

Porky pointed to a narrow section of charring. "I'm not sure it'll survive when we move him."

"Suicide or murder?" Kado asked.

"You have got to be kidding," Martinez stated.

Grey sighed. "You'd be surprised at what people will do when they want to die. This," he motioned at the tree and the charred form on the ground, "is extreme, but not unbelievable. I haven't seen a lighter or matches, but they could be under the body. Or melted. Or burned."

"It's a possibility we need to consider, Carlos. He could've doused himself with gas," Kado said, motioning to the moldering plastic mass, "and jumped or fallen from that ladder." He turned to Porky. "Can I get photos now?"

Porky nodded and asked Martinez to help him bring in a stretcher. Looking grateful to leave the corpse and related stench behind, Martinez followed Porky through the stockroom.

Kado's shoulders loosened as he made his way closer to the body and lifted his camera.

Grey cleared his throat. "Are you and Carlos having problems?"

"We got off on the wrong foot. I was too critical of the last forensics man, Hank Comfrey. When Sheriff Hoffner recruited me, he told me that the last man had died while on the job and that they were looking to bring the forensics department up to date, to use more science to help solve crimes. I didn't realize Comfrey had almost fifty years on the job and had only been dead a few weeks when I came to Texas. That would've been good to know." He moved to the other side of the body and took several shots. "And then there was the whole mess with the corrupted DNA. Martinez and some of the others want to believe that I screwed up. They've been hovering at crime scenes, watching everything I do." He turned and looked up at the tall medical examiner. Grey's bushy black hair was bursting straight from his scalp as usual, and his dark eyebrows were lowered over serious eyes. "Why do you ask?"

"The department is so short of people. You need every ounce of cooperation you can get on this one."

Kado stood, grimacing as his knees popped. "I'll do what I can, but I'm only half the equation." He looked up at the dangling piece of rope. John Grey tilted his head back as well, and they stood silently for several moments.

"What does your gut tell you?" Grey asked.

"I tend to agree with Carlos. I don't like it as a suicide. It's too much. But," he added, "I'll let the science do its job."

CHAPTER 6

TWILIGHT WAS SETTLING LONG shadows over Forney County as the shooter crept into Deadwood Hollow. The overhanging boughs blanketed the Hollow, creating a murkiness that his eyes could not penetrate. But lack of vision wasn't a problem. This trek from the county road to his perch in an ancient oak tree was one he had made several times as he sought to first identify, and then possibly understand, the people who were helping him cleanse the world. But tonight, his journey had a radically different intent.

The shooter was unremarkable, a born hunter with a lethal blend of instinct, intuition, and bland good looks that allowed him to blend into his environment. Of average height and slender build, his hair was short and dark, his face chiseled with high cheekbones and a strong jaw. Only his deep brown eyes hinted at the intelligence and cunning within. He moved down the well-used path without hesitation, stopping to listen for sounds from the drug dealers and partying teens that commandeered these woods after dark. His movements were controlled, deliberate, a careful dance executed many times over the years during a hunt, choreographed to avoid noises that would draw attention.

His heart picked up its pace as he neared the dip in the trail where he would step into the brush, and he shifted the rifle to wipe his sweaty palms on his jeans. For a moment he stood silently, listening to the breath ease in and out of his body, slowing his heart rate, centering his thoughts. Six kills, that was the goal. Three murders tonight and three more to go would mark the last stop on the trail of punishment he had traveled for so long.

No.

Not punishment.

Vengeance.

The taking of lives in payment for the life that was stolen from him all those years ago.

Calmer now, he pushed through the brush and made his way to the old oak in the clearing. The climbing stick was still in place. He scaled it and settled into the sturdy crook of a branch where it met the tree's trunk. He slipped the shooting glove on his hand, adjusted the homemade brass catcher, and lifted the rifle's scope to his eye. It was approximately one hundred yards to the house. Although the interior was dark, he knew the layout of these back rooms by heart. A set of gorgeous windows allowed an unfettered view of the tidy kitchen with its clean appliances and the colorful tile backsplash that created a strutting rooster over the stove. He fiddled with the rifle. This was the longest shot he would make tonight. While he preferred the satisfaction of an up-close kill, ending the life of a police officer was worth the compromise. A cosmic justice of sorts.

He took another look through the scope, adjusted his position, and waited.

———————

MARTHA FRANKLIN BREATHED A quiet sigh of relief as her son unlocked the front door and ushered her inside. Her body could do nothing but ache these days. The doctors promised that the tiredness would fade when the treatments were done, and that her strength would return. But lately, it was all she could do to stand for more than a few minutes at a time. Her appointment with the oncologist and this evening's quilting club meeting had certainly taken it out of her. The meeting had run longer than usual, until seven-thirty, while the ladies twittered over Moses when he arrived to pick her up and helped clear the church hall.

She unwound the scarf covering her head and heard her son removing his tennis shoes. He stood and she caught him watching her in the hallway mirror, worry in his eyes. Martha was tall for a woman. At five feet eleven inches in her stocking feet, she was only three inches shorter than her son. Their body shapes were similar as well. Her mother had always called Martha's figure 'proud', referring to her strong shoulders and erect carriage, the narrow waist that flared gently to slender hips, and her long, firm legs. Reaching up, she turned her son's head to the left and right, and compared her smoothly dark reflection to his. "With my bald head, Moses, we look just alike."

He bent to kiss her cheek. "You're prettier than I'll ever be."

"And ain't that the truth," she laughed. "You go get a shower. I need some tea."

"I'll make it, Momma."

She waved him away. "I may have the cancer, but I can still boil water."

Martha watched as Moses shuffled down the hall, his shoulders rounded forward, hands pushed deep into his pockets. He had moved back home just over two years ago, after his wife of twenty-five years divorced him. It was a bitter affair, that much a mother could sense no matter how hard her child tried to hide his pain. Martha still wasn't clear on the details, but she suspected that a midlife crises and a younger man were to blame. She only thanked the Lord that no children were involved.

Moses had explained his decision to move home as a desire to help during her cancer treatments and to be available for his twin brother, Joseph, when he was released from prison. That had happened only recently and the three were still finding a way to live together again. Martha had re-mortgaged the house to pay for Joseph's defense against some computer crime she didn't understand. Both of her sons had protested loudly, but she wouldn't have had it any other way. Moses and Joseph were her life.

Although the boys were twins, their different natures were evident from the moment they left the womb. Moses basked in the light; Joseph stayed in the shadows. Moses loved people, while Joseph preferred solitude. Moses expressed his feelings; Joseph was a stoic. Moses was sheer emotion; Joseph followed the path of logic.

Moses had always walked the straight and narrow and had a clear definition of right and wrong, deciding early on that he would become a police officer. Joseph turned away from people, choosing instead to live within the mysterious land of computer languages and databases. Martha never understood the work he did, but she knew he achieved great success for a time. Joseph moved to New York and went to work for a big bank while the ink was still wet on his degree from the local college. When they talked on the weekends, he told her how happy he was to live in a large city and do such important work. And she believed him. Until he called to tell her about the arrest. Looking back, she wondered how she had missed the signs that her son was involved in something illegal, and consoled herself with the thought that of the two boys, Joseph had always been the better actor.

As she moved through the dark house, Martha said a silent prayer that Joseph would find a good job in spite of his arrest. One that provided adequate financial compensation, but more importantly, fed his self-esteem. He was playing basketball this evening with a club for teenagers, a program designed to let former convicts give back and hopefully keep youngsters from following in their footsteps. Moses was also a frequent player and said the kids loved trying to figure out which of the Mojos – their lifelong nickname – was the cop and which the robber.

Martha reached the kitchen and leaned her cheek against the cool door, resting and listening to the sounds of water rushing through the pipes to the shower. A smile of gratitude crossed her lips for her children, the convict and the cop. And as happened so often lately, images of both her dead husbands appeared in her mind, deepening her smile. Charles Franklin was the one true love of her life, and she had lost him too early, when the boys were only toddlers. Homer Radcliffe was a solid, reliable man, marrying her shortly after she arrived in Arcadia with her small twins in tow and only a job as a cook in the local school to support the three of them. He'd taken care of her and loved the boys as if they were his own for twenty-three years, until the good Lord took him home too suddenly. A brain aneurysm, the doctors told her. Dead before he hit the floor in his engine repair shop. Although she intended no disrespect to

Homer, she took Charles' name back after her second husband died, wanting to live out her days as wife to the man she had loved so dearly. Becoming a Franklin again had brought her a measure of peace. And in spite of the various tragedies in their lives, she knew that God indeed walked with her family.

Martha pushed through the swinging door and turned on the soft lights under the cabinets. Water spat from the faucet as she filled the kettle. She lit the burner and placed the kettle on it, then reached out a finger and touched the backsplash behind the stove. The hand-painted tiles created a stylized banty rooster and she'd adored him the moment she saw him on display at the DIY center. Homer protested mildly when she asked him to chip out the plain white tiles and replace them with her new friend, but whistled while he worked. She sighed at the memory and glanced at her reflection in the bay window overlooking the dark backyard. In her early sixties, Martha Franklin was still a handsome woman. Her ebony skin was smooth and supple, her athletic body trim and lithe. She smiled briefly at her shapely skull. Her comment to Moses had been true: with each bearing bald heads, she and her sons could be triplets.

The kettle uttered its first low notes and Martha opened a cupboard, reaching for tea bags. Her mind turned again to Joseph and his basketball game tonight. As she grasped a box of chamomile tea and closed the cabinet door, Martha's last thoughts were a peaceful prayer that Joseph could make a difference in those boys' lives, and they in his. She never registered the piercing of glass and the slight retort of a rifle firing the bullet that entered her brain and ended her life.

THE SHOOTER LEANED BACK from his firing position and prepared to climb down the tree. The time spent sighting in the rifle and selecting ammunition had been worthwhile. His breath caught when he spotted movement in the dimly lit kitchen and he jerked forward again, brushing against the brass catcher as he stretched to look through the rifle's scope. A mirror image of the man he had just killed was leaning over the body. He'd never seen the twins together before. The cop was the one he wanted, and this was the officer's night off. Apparently the brother was home as well.

He smiled. Two for the price of one.

He pulled back the bolt to eject the spent casing into the catcher but it hit the tip of the catcher and disappeared into the gloom beneath the tree. Ignoring the hit of anxiety that flushed his system, the shooter used his chin to adjust the catcher, then slipped the bolt forward to push home a new round. He moved to his firing position and raised the rifle in one fluid motion, targeting the distraught man who lurched for the kitchen phone. Adjusting the rifle's angle, he drew a slow breath, released it, and squeezed the trigger. He watched as the second bullet pierced the window pane and ripped through the twin's chest, erupting in a spray of blood, bone, and tissue that blew through the steam rising from the kettle. Motionless, he waited for more movement. The bodies were perfectly still, and he'd even managed to destroy the tile rooster's head. A nice touch considering how much he hated the homeliness of the thing. Satisfied, he stripped the glove from his hand and tucked it and the brass casing into a pocket, then climbed quickly down the ladder. For a moment, he searched for the lost casing before giving up and trotting for the edge of the clearing, the slight mistake already forgotten. In his mind, he could hear the kettle screaming in the house of the dead.

CHAPTER 7

"THIS THING IS TOAST, man," Mark Grove whispered, slapping the flashlight against his palm. The moon was out in a cloudless sky, but its light left only faint patterns as it fell through the forest's thick canopy. Mark squinted into the blanket of night that rested between the trees and he squatted on the narrow trail.

"Why are we whispering?" Matt Grove asked in a low voice as he switched off his flashlight.

"There's freaks out here, man. Druggies. Escaped convicts. Killers."

"You watch too much TV." Matt watched as his brother knocked the flashlight again. "It's dead because you keep banging it around, idiot. Why didn't you bring extra batteries?"

"Why didn't *you* bring batteries? You lost the damn phone."

"That's a dollar for the cuss bucket. Besides, this is your fault," said Matt, aiming the bright beam of his flashlight off the narrow path that wove through Deadwood Hollow.

"My fault?" Mark asked, mouth gaping as he watched the narrow beam of his twin's flashlight dissipate in the deep brush crowding the trail that the high school used for cross-country training. The boys wore their dark blue track suits, and with the exception of their pale faces and hands, were nearly invisible in the gloom. "How can it be my fault that we're out here after dark looking for the cell phone that you lost?"

"You *brought* your phone. If you'd left it in the locker like coach told us to, Katy couldn't have found me."

"Wait a minute. She texted me looking for you, so I gave you my phone. What a nice thing for a brother to do." Mark stood and followed Matt into the brush, tentatively feeling for brambles.

34

"Instead of waiting until after training you text her right back. That's stupid, texting while you're running. Why not call?"

"I needed to keep my time up. You gunned it after you gave me the phone. Unfair." Matt paused, handing the working flashlight to Mark while he pushed aside a mass of thick, twining wisteria vines. "Point it here. Come on man, how could I ignore her? Katy's got bodacious hooters. Have you noticed?"

"Have I noticed? It's amazing she can run cross-country without getting two black eyes." The beam of Matt's flashlight grew dim and Mark shook it. The light brightened. "Why would she text you on my phone?"

"Duh. Because her mother knows my number and checks Katy's phone to make sure she isn't calling or texting me. I told her to send texts to you."

"Why does Katy's mom care if she talks to you?"

Matt shrugged. "I guess she thinks I'm a bad influence and doesn't want Katy to go out with me."

"Why would Katy want to go out with *you*?"

"I'm better looking than you are."

"We're twins, ass-wipe. What did her text say?"

"You're calling me toilet paper? That's the best you can do? And that's a dollar for the cuss bucket."

Mark exhaled deeply. "Her text?"

"She wanted me to meet her at that fork in the trail, before we cross under the highway."

"What for?"

"Sex."

Mark coughed back a laugh. "Katy probably wanted to copy your biology homework. You're the only one passing."

Matt huffed farther off the trail, crashing between two slender pine trees. "She's already copied my biology homework, idiot, so it has to be sex," he hissed.

"Must be your math homework. Speaking of idiots, why didn't you bring your phone tonight?"

"My phone?"

"If you'd brought it, all we'd have to do is call mine and listen for the ring," Mark whispered, shaking the flashlight as he re-crossed the trail, his tall, lanky form bent double as he searched. A quiet hiss escaped him. "Shit. Another honey locust. I hate those things."

"That's another –" Matt stopped short as a retort split the night. Both boys ducked into a crouch.

"What was that?" Mark asked across the trail.

"A gun? It's May. What's in season?"

"Sixteen-year-old dudes, I guess. How should I know? We don't hunt."

A second shot snapped through the trees, and the boys flattened themselves against the forest floor.

"Damn. That one was closer," Mark whispered.

"That's two dollars for the cuss bucket," Matt whispered back, lifting his head to peer over the path as the sound of hurried footsteps drew near, then turning his face quickly toward the ground. "Shit."

A figure sped past on the trail. Wisps of moonlight slithering through the canopy glowed blueblack as they caressed the stock of a rifle cradled across the runner's chest. Air whispered as cloth brushed between thighs and then fell silent as he passed. The boys lifted their heads, watching until the figure was enveloped by the night. Slowly, they stood.

"What was that about?" Matt asked, his voice low as he looked left and right down the trail.

"I don't know, but your 'shit' took everything I said tonight out of the cuss bucket."

"That does not eliminate all your curse words. I'll put a dollar in, or you can back one out."

"Whatever. I'm gettin' out of here. That dude was freaky. You can tell Mom about the phone or we can bring yours out here after school tomorrow and try calling my phone." The faint screech of metal impacting on metal sawed through the night air and Mark lifted his hands to his head. "Oh no," he whispered, bolting down the path. "Don't let that be the car. Not again."

CHAPTER 8

KADO SLICED THROUGH THE rope, careful to preserve the knot that secured it to the sycamore's branch. He was stretched along its length and slowly unwound the rope from the limb and placed it in an evidence bag, then stuck his foot out to try and find the ladder resting against the tree. Down below, Porky and Grey were moving the burnt corpse onto a plastic sheet with Martinez' help.

"Uh oh," Porky said.

Kado looked down. "What?"

"Definitely murder," Martinez said, studying the corpse.

"Why?"

Porky Rivers reached out and traced a figure above the dead man's chest. "Swastika."

"Tattoo?" Kado asked, wiggling along the branch to better reach the ladder.

"Carved," Grey answered. "Want a photo?"

"Yes." Kado nudged the ladder with his foot and felt it scoot against the tree. "Carlos?"

The burly detective looked up.

"Would you hold the ladder so I can get down?"

Martinez ran his tongue along his teeth and sauntered over to the base of the tree. Kado quickly climbed down. "Thanks."

He received a grunted reply.

Kado tucked the evidence bag in his kit and took several photographs of the jagged cuts. "Is this some sort of race thing? A swastika would be used by a white supremacist on a non-white, right?"

"Or maybe on a white dude who was spending too much time with the blacks or browns," Porky said.

Grey and Porky wrapped the corpse in the plastic sheet, slid it into a body bag, and all four men helped lift the form onto a stretcher.

"This is more than a one man job," Martinez said. "It took at least two people to get this body up in the air."

"I think you're right," Kado said.

"Well there's a first time for everything," Martinez muttered.

"I'll call you when the autopsy's done," Grey said. "Or stop by the morgue when you get finished out here." He nodded at Porky and the two men maneuvered the stretcher through the gate that led to the sparse patch of dirt behind the shop, where Kado's flags marked tire treads and shoe prints.

Kado turned to Martinez, who gazed at him with flat eyes. "What's the problem?"

"I don't have a problem," Martinez replied. "Do you?"

"Yeah, I do. I'm happy to be out here doing my job working with you. From what I've seen and heard, you're a good cop. But you don't seem so happy to have me here. Unfortunately, I'm the only show in town. So until you persuade the sheriff to fire me, or find another forensics man to replace me, you're stuck. We can try to get along and make this bearable, or you can keep freezing me out."

Martinez pursed his lips but said nothing.

Kado shifted. "I know that my observations about Hank Comfrey pissed you off. Tact isn't my strong point. But his processes and his lab were poor." Kado held up a hand as Martinez started to protest. "You've told me they held up in court and I've seen the files for myself. All I can guess is that the defendants had stupid lawyers or guilt wasn't really a question."

Martinez crossed his arms and lowered his head, watching Kado from beneath a furrowed brow. Kado thought it made the man look like a bull preparing to charge. "Your record ain't so great, *hombre*."

"Are you talking about the DNA?"

"What I heard, you screwed up. Big time."

"Stop by sometime and I'll show you why it can't be me who screwed up." Kado glanced around the courtyard and pulled his latex gloves off. "Until then, can we call a truce? There's a mountain of evidence here, and it'll take at least two of us to collect and sort through it all."

Martinez studied the ground and seemed to come to a decision. "At least two?"

"Scott Truman is on the front door. Do you know him?"

"Of course."

"He's young, but he's smart and eager to learn. If we can put somebody else out front, I think we can use him back here."

Martinez' phone rang and he snapped it open. Blood drained from his face as he listened. When he looked at Kado, all traces of hostility were gone. "He's with me. We'll be there in twenty, tops."

He snapped the phone shut. "Shots fired at the Franklin's house."

"*Officer* Franklin?" Kado asked, following Martinez through the stockroom.

"Two down. The mother and possibly Moses."

"Oh no," Kado breathed.

"Exactly."

CHAPTER 9

CASS SANG ALONG WITH The Smithereen's "A Girl Like You" as she drove home from taking Phoebe to Chubby's and dropping the little girl at her dance class. True to form, her niece had dribbled chocolate shake in her lap, left a ketchup trail down her leotard when she missed her mouth with a fistful of French fries, and somehow tipped the ends of her tutu with mustard. Cass smiled while washing Phoebe's hands and face, pleased to note that while the ballet outfit might be in ruins, the tiara was still firmly in place.

As Cass was leaving the dance studio, a familiar voice called her name and she'd wound up talking to a high school friend for nearly an hour. She deftly sidestepped questions about why she wasn't back at work and steered the conversation around to gossip about other members of their graduating class. The entire encounter was exhausting. Cass had avoided Arcadia for just this reason, and now wished she had moved faster to get out of town.

Turning onto a two-lane road, she flipped the headlights to bright, cranked the radio's volume up and tapped her thumb on the steering wheel. She was driving an ancient Ford pickup that had passed through the Elliot clan from child to child until returning to their father's possession when Cass finished university. Thanks to Abe's meticulous care of the old vehicle, she was able to crank the Ford's engine on the first try after her suspension. Unable to tolerate a complete black-out about what was happening on the force, Cass purchased two police scanners and with Harry's help, installed one in the truck. The other was on the kitchen counter. She'd turned the volume down in the truck before leaving home tonight, wanting to limit the impact police chatter could have on her young niece.

Her mind drifted back to the events leading up to the banishment. She examined her actions before the shooting for the umpteenth time, searching for something she might've done differently, and found no fault with herself. The local newspaper, the Forney Cater, was steadfast in its support of her and the rest of the force. Cass thought the debriefing immediately following the incident, and her testimony to the Firearm Discharge Board a week later, had gone smoothly. Her only concern was how Sheriff Hoffner might try to tie her actions into what had happened to her partner. But Mitch's accident wasn't her fault. They had followed procedure and things had gone terribly wrong in the way that they sometimes do. Mitch's accident aside, she was baffled as to why the Sheriff refused to put her back on active duty.

A dark mass careened around a tight curve and swerved into her lane. Its form was barely discernable, but Cass caught the outline of a pickup truck. She gasped and yanked the steering wheel to the right, riding the shoulder to get out of the way. She swore as the Ford lost its grip on the asphalt, spilled onto the soft verge, and went up on two wheels. Struggling to regain control, she heard an engine roar and watched as dim tail lights disappeared around the bend. Adrenaline slammed through her veins as Cass stood on the brakes and then gunned the Ford into a u-turn. She screeched to a stop again when two dark figures burst from the tree line and dashed toward a small vehicle parked on the side of the road. One collapsed to his knees by the front fender while the other stood holding his head with his hands.

She drove slowly forward, stopping when she drew alongside the car, an old Chevy Vega bathed a rusty brown in bright moonlight. It was parked with two wheels on the road's shoulder and the other two on the verge, and was partially hidden beneath the overhanging limbs of a Chinese tallow tree. The front fender was caved in and the car's shiny silver bumper flopped awkwardly like a broken arm. Cass looked more closely at the two figures and realized that they were only teenage boys. Neither appeared injured and she bit back a smile as she recognized them. These were the Grove twins, nephews of Officer Ernest Munk.

"Oh man," one of the boys moaned. "She's gonna kill me."

"Evening, guys," she said. "What's going on?"

Her words broke them from their stupor, and their agonized expressions turned to horror. "Oh shit," she heard one boy whisper. "The heat."

"That's a dollar," the other whispered.

"You're Evelyn Grove's boys, Ernie Munk's nephews?" she asked. The kneeling boy braced one hand on the car and stood, nodding slowly. "What were you doing in Deadwood Hollow? It's after eight."

The twins exchanged another glance, and one lifted a chin at the other. He turned rueful eyes on Cass and spoke with reluctance. "We lost a phone earlier today."

"Which one are you?"

"I'm Mark," the boy with the scraggly beard answered. He hooked a thumb at his twin. "He's Matt."

"How did you lose the phone?"

"During cross-country training."

She cocked her head to one side. "You can talk and run at the same time?"

Mark shot a glance at his brother. "No, but apparently you can run and text at the same time. Just not very well."

"Why didn't you look for the phone when you lost it?" Cass asked.

Matt heaved a huge sigh. "Look, it was my fault –"

"Yes!" Mark hissed, smile dying as Matt scowled at him. "Sorry."

"I borrowed Mark's phone because a girl texted me and then I texted her back and then the coach showed up where he wasn't supposed to be and I kind of fumbled the phone and it fell into the brush. But I don't know exactly where I was when I dropped it, and we didn't want to tell Mom that I'd lost it. So that's why we were out here."

"I think I get it," Cass said. She nodded at the car. "What happened?"

The boys exchanged another glance and shrugged. "We don't know."

"A pickup nearly hit me as I was coming around that bend. Could it have been the same guy?"

"Maybe," Mark answered. "Some dude went running past us through the woods, and then we heard a screech and started running after him."

"What dude?"

"Dunno. But he had a rifle," Matt said.

"Yeah, and we heard two shots just before he ran past us," Mark added.

"Someone was poaching?" Cass asked.

Mark nodded. "Maybe."

She opened her cell phone and walked over to the small car. Dark streaks marred the fender's ruddy orange paint. An impatient voice answered Cass's call on the third ring and her heart gave an annoying leap at the sound. They hadn't spoken since her debriefing several weeks ago and she thought she'd mastered the emotions his voice was conjuring. She strained to hear his greeting over the swell of a screaming siren. "Kado?" she asked.

"Cass?" he yelled. "What is it?"

"I've got reports of two shots fired in Deadwood Hollow. Where are you?"

"On my way to Mojo's house. It backs up to the Hollow, doesn't it?"

"I think so. What's up?"

"One of the brothers is dead. So is their mom." She heard tires squeal through the phone. "Who reported the shots?"

"Matt and Mark Grove." She looked at the two boys. "They saw the shooter."

"Get them over to the Franklin's house. We need a description."

––––––––––––

FORNEY COUNTY'S FORENSIC EXAMINER stared at the phone after he snapped it shut and had to yank the pickup back onto the road when his tires hit the rumble strip. He caught Martinez flashing a dark look in the rearview mirror of his cruiser as Kado straightened the wheels and raced close behind the detective.

His blood was galloping through his veins and he knew it wasn't due to the adrenaline rush from being called to a crime scene involving a fellow officer. Cass Elliot had occupied his thoughts and intruded on his dreams non-stop since he saw her last at the debriefing following the cult shooting. He might actually see her again tonight, and in spite of the horrific nature of the crime he was about to investigate, Kado had to suppress the surge of joy threatening to curve his lips into a smile.

Chapter 10

CASS ARRIVED AFTER THE first responders and searched the crowd, looking for Kado. The area was controlled chaos and she realized he would be inside by now, performing the delicate task of collecting and preserving evidence. She itched to join him. Outside, porch lights up and down the street were on, providing welcoming bubbles of light that never quite touched one another. Behind the yellow tape embracing the Franklin house, neighbors milled next to Cass, stumbling with bewilderment and whispering in frightened voices. Uniformed officers stood guard around the perimeter, hands resting on the weapons at their waists, their gazes roaming the crowd and softening at the sight of Cass before moving on. Two ambulances rumbled away from the Franklin house, empty and silent. A heavy van inched into the spot they vacated. The cadaverous medical examiner and his assistant climbed out and opened the back doors. Grey raised his hand in greeting and Porky nodded in her direction before they wheeled two stretchers up the sidewalk to the house. The acidic smell of frustration, grief, and fear rose in the air.

Cass had known Moses and Joseph Franklin as long as she could remember. She knew Moses better because he had worked as a patrol officer in Arcadia for so long, and Joseph had headed north shortly after he graduated from college. They were twins, as identical as were the Grove boys. Their joint nickname of Mojo arose simply because no one other than their mother could tell them apart. They were giants; broad, tall, and muscled, but Cass had always perceived a gentleness when she encountered Moses at crime scenes. The more violent the act, the more empathy the man seemed to exude. She respected him for this, for his lack of cynicism, his willingness to believe in the goodness of humanity. And while she wished neither man ill, she hoped fervently that it was Moses who was still alive.

The thought of twins caused her to turn toward her truck, where Martinez was questioning the Grove boys. The detective was a bull of a man, his wide chest and torso giving way to strong arms and muscled legs. His hair was close-cropped and a steely gray, and in spite of his height of nearly six feet, Martinez looked up at the boys as they answered his questions. A car screeched to a stop and a small woman darted from the driver's door. Cass recognized Evelyn Grove as she raced to the twins, throwing her arms around the boys and pulling them to her. She pushed them away, looked at each face, then pulled them close again. The boys flashed embarrassed smiles at Martinez that faded when their mother pushed away again and popped both hands on her hips. Their heads dropped in response to her words, unintelligible at this distance but recognizable as a tongue lashing to anyone who had ever irked a parent's ire. Martinez sidled away from the trio. Cass moved to meet him in the street.

"Get anything?" she asked.

"Only what you did. Two shots fired and a man running past on the trail."

"Description?"

"White man. Dark trousers, dark shoes, hooded jacket."

"Did they see his face?"

"Chin and hands. They said his hands were very pale. He was carrying the rifle across his chest as he ran."

"Height, weight?"

"The boys said he was thin-ish and shorter than them."

Cass snorted a laugh. "They're what? Six foot five or so? Almost everybody in the county is shorter than them."

"I know."

Cass searched the street. "I saw the pickup that smashed into their car. It must've been the shooter."

"Plates?"

"The light over the back license plate was out. No plates on the front."

"Color?"

"Dark. Probably black. Even the bumpers and hubcaps. Its headlights were off when it came around a curve and nearly hit me. I could hardly make out that it was a pickup. Did anyone in the neighborhood see anything?" Cass asked.

"A few people heard the shots. Nobody saw anything unusual."

"Moses and Joseph are both living here, aren't they? Which one is it?" she asked softly.

The detective turned to look at the house, raising his hands to his temples and rubbing small circles. "He had a towel around his waist, Cass. Both of the Mojo's rooms had wallets, cell phones, and car keys in them. We're trying to find the other brother to make sure."

She looked more closely at Martinez. His eyes were bloodshot and the faint glow of a street light emphasized the exhaustion lining his face. "Are you all right?"

He exhaled slowly. "We need you back. And without Mitch..."

"I know. Where's Danny?" she asked, referring to Martinez' long-time partner.

"His back."

"Again?"

"Still. Dr. Rambo never released him after the last time it went out." He looked out over the crowd. "Did you hear about the murder at Calvin Whitehead's store?"

"No. When?"

"This evening."

"What happened?"

"Goober found a corpse in the courtyard behind the shop. It was hanging and burning."

Cass covered her mouth. "Poor Goob."

"He was pretty upset. But the amazing thing was that he smelled smoke and went to find out what was burning."

"He went toward danger?"

"Brave, huh?"

"I'd say so. Do you know who the victim is?"

"We're pretty sure it's Whitehead, but Grey wanted to wait until he got the body back to the ME's office before he checked for a wallet."

"Why wait?"

Martinez grimaced. "The body's in pretty bad shape."

"I know Calvin Whitehead. I fill up at his station sometimes. He's a big guy, white hair. Nobody else works there."

"Family?"

"None that he's ever talked about."

"This crime was personal."

"How so?"

"Somebody carved a swastika into his chest."

"Good Lord," Cass said. "Any leads?"

"Not yet. That shop is so remote. How did he stay in business?"

"I have no clue. He carried milk, bread, the basics, and his hours weren't great. Maybe he owned the shop outright."

"Maybe. Too bad he doesn't have family." Martinez grinned. "You might get to go to the morgue tonight for an ID."

Cass smiled. "I'll actually look forward to it."

"Any idea when you'll be back?"

"Nope. Was there a lot going on before tonight?"

"Aren't you reading the Cater?"

"Not every day. All the coverage, the speculation, I got tired of it."

"You remember the old lady that went missing a few weeks ago? Iris Glenthorne?"

An image flashed through Cass's memory of Martinez pinning a missing person's photo to the bulletin board. Iris Glenthorne's face was creased in wrinkles as she smiled for the camera, her full head of white hair complementing her sparkling green eyes. Cass nodded. "It was right before The Church of the True Believer stuff went down. You found the car, but not the woman. She had Alzheimer's?"

"Never diagnosed, but her friends said that her memory was going. We found her car with the keys still in the ignition and her purse on the seat. Almost seven weeks later, we've found her body."

"That's good news, isn't it?"

"Yes and no." Martinez glanced out over the crowd and lowered his voice. "We've got a decomposing body, and from what Grey can tell us, there's no sign of foul play."

"But?"

His steely gaze returned to Cass. "We found her in a location that we'd already searched."

"What do you mean?"

"We searched that location the day after she went missing, again three days later, and again, ten days later."

"Who searched it?"

"All three times, it was Hugo Petchard."

Cass took a step back, hot anger coloring her face. "He's back on duty?"

"I'm afraid so."

"I thought...," she started, and then fell silent. Officer Hugo Petchard had been involved with The Church of the True Believer, and while all they could pin on him was stupidity, Cass quietly held him responsible for the entire miserable incident down in the river bottoms. She was stunned to think that Petchard was back on the force while she remained suspended. She swallowed her anger down. "Maybe he missed something."

Martinez shrugged, his eyes flat. "Maybe."

"You don't think so?"

"At best, Petchard is an incompetent fool. But I don't think he could've missed finding her body. Not all three times."

"What do you think happened?"

"Somebody grabbed her and dumped her body when they were done with her." He placed his hands behind his head, huge biceps bulging, and sighed into a stretch. "Sheriff Hoffner hinted that he wants me to drop it, but there's something hinky about what happened to Iris Glenthorne. And with the Whitehead murder and now these two, we don't have people with the right skills. That's why we need you back."

Cass silently accepted his compliment. "Do you know why Hoffner's dragging his feet?"

"I haven't heard –," Martinez began, swiveling at the sound of running feet.

A tall black man in shorts and a Forney County Police t-shirt materialized from the dark void at the corner of the block, feet pounding the asphalt, arms pumping a frantic rhythm in time with his legs, face a mask of fury. Street lights painted streaks of gold across his bald head as he passed beneath them. He wove through the crowd, hurdled the crime scene tape in a single stride, and held up a huge hand to the officer who tried to stop him from entering his home.

The neighbors grew silent as the air filled with the wretched sounds of Mojo's grief. Cass and Martinez exchanged a glance. He walked back to the Grove boys who were watching the house with their mother, her anger forgotten in recognition of what another family had lost. Cass moved to the tape barrier and waited.

———————————

KADO ROSE FROM HIS position near the window at the sound of scuffling. A tall man, identical in almost every way to the two bodies on the floor, forced his way into the kitchen, one uniformed officer clinging to his left arm, another to his waist. The overwhelming power of Mojo Franklin's anguish drove him forward and he seemed oblivious to the men struggling to hold him back. Kado moved to block the opening to the kitchen, but he needn't have bothered. Mojo stepped through the door, looked past Kado to see his brother and mother dead on the floor, and collapsed to his knees, taking both officers with him. Sweat slicked his head and face and huge drops were jarred from his nose when his fell. He lifted his face to the ceiling and uttered a tormented cry. The three men in the room were stunned into silence. Kado glanced at the medical examiner whose hands were suspended motionless over Mojo's mother. Porky had a gloved hand stretched toward Grey, offering a thermometer. Kado blinked at the sight of Porky wiping his wet cheek against his shoulder.

He spoke in a low voice between Mojo's sobs. "Porky, do you know these guys?"

The thin man nodded.

"Grey," Kado said, "maybe if Porky talked to Mojo…"

"Yes," he said, taking the thermometer. "Porky, would you mind?"

The young man stripped off his gloves and stood, unsteadily at first. The small silver studs and barbells rimming his ears and eyebrows glinted in the overhead lights as he moved. Easing around the corpses, he placed a dark hand on Mojo's shoulder and squeezed. "Come on, man."

Mojo's eyes were unfocused when he looked up at Porky, his lips peeled back in a crescent of pain. "My momma…"

"I know. Grey and Kado will take care of them. Come on." Porky placed a hand beneath Mojo's elbow and helped him to his feet. The two men stood, their dark complexions nearly identical, and Porky nudged the larger man from the kitchen, the officers following warily in their wake.

Kado looked at Grey. "Was that Moses or Joseph?"

Grey shrugged. "I guess we have to wait until he calms down to find out."

"Can you work without Porky?"

"With one body, maybe. But with two, I could use help. Who's available?"

"Martinez is outside," Kado offered.

Grey glanced at the gore spattered around the stove and the crimson pools on the floor. "He hates blood."

"But he dealt with the Whitehead scene fine."

"That was roasted meat. No blood, no problem. Who else?"

"Ernie Munk is on vacation. Scott Truman is at Whitehead's store. We were going to use him out there, but do you need him here?"

"This would be his first time to process a body. Anybody else?"

Kado fought the stupid grin trying to plaster itself across his face. "I think Cass is out front."

"Is she back on duty?"

"No."

"Where's Hoffner?"

"At a sheriff's retreat."

"Has anybody called him about Whitehead or the Franklins?"

"I've left a message at his hotel. They said the group went out for some bonding ritual and are on their way back now, but it'll still be a few hours before he calls."

"Why didn't he deal with Cass before he left?"

Kado shrugged.

"The man is amazing. He's short on detectives and won't sign the papers to put Cass back on duty." Grey snagged his earlobe between his thumb and forefinger and began to rub, a sure sign that his substantial brain was working overtime. Suddenly, he smiled up at Kado. "Go get her. The ME's office has a new temp."

CHAPTER 11

JOSEPH FRANKLIN SAT AT the kitchen table while Porky River's girlfriend Stella fussed over him. She was a beautiful, intelligent woman, and Joseph envied Porky's luck in catching her. The rich smell of chocolate rose from the oven and he was surprised to hear his stomach rumble. Stella put a bowl of chicken and dumplings and a glass of milk in front of him. He stared at them mutely.

"You've had a dreadful shock, Moses." It took him a moment to respond to the name. When he raised his head to look at her, Stella cupped his chin. "Your body needs food to recover itself, physically and emotionally. I made those chicken and dumplings fresh today." A loud buzzing sounded and Joseph flinched. She put a soft hand on his shoulder. "That's the laundry. Eat up."

The kitchen door swished closed behind her. Joseph picked up a folded napkin, pressed it to his face, and fought to control the unfamiliar emotions slamming against his brain. Stella was right. Seeing his mother and brother slaughtered like deer had shocked him, unleashing a blinding torrent of rage and frustration he had never known. A desire to do malicious, grievous bodily harm to the person who had ripped his family from him. A burning need to find the man who had coldly pulled the trigger, to find him and deliver agonizing death. And those feelings scared him. Joseph Franklin was always in control of his actions and reactions. *Always*. An innate ability to master his thoughts and focus on the task at hand had held Joseph in good stead and provided the foundation behind his success with computers. Moses, on the other hand, is — *had been*, he corrected himself — pure emotion. Joseph's head throbbed. He closed his eyes and took three slow, deep breaths and forced the sight and smell of the bloodied kitchen from his mind.

He picked up a spoon and ate a bite of chicken and dumplings, his brow furrowed. Moses. Stella had called him Moses. It wasn't a surprise that she was confused. People had a hard time telling the twins apart on a normal day. But Stella hadn't even asked his name. Neither had Porky. No one had, come to think of it. Joseph glanced down at his clothes and suddenly understood. He was wearing Moses' black Forney County Police t-shirt and shorts. He wondered how long it would take Stella and Porky to figure out that he was Joseph, not Moses.

Or *if* they would.

Joseph put the spoon down. *Could* anyone figure it out?

His mind reeled at the thought, and he fought to analyze the possibilities. There was no question that physically, the brothers could imitate one another. They'd done it for years with teachers, girlfriends, and even friends. Now that both kept their heads shaved, their physical resemblance was as strong as when they were infants. Their voices were very close in pitch and speech pattern. Moses and Joseph shared the same sleek manner of movement on and off the basketball court. They even used their joint nickname of Mojo when referring to themselves or each other, to keep people confused. Joseph's left-handedness made him a true mirror image of Moses, who was a righty.

But the most significant difference between them, the one area where Joseph would struggle if he wanted to become Moses, was their mental make-up.

Moses was light and movement. He had the gift of extreme emotion that allowed him to empathize and connect with people and sharpened his senses when he was out on patrol. Joseph was dark and distant. Strong feelings had always crystallized in his brain, becoming objects for analysis and brooding. Joseph had no gift for passion or people. Personality-wise, Moses and Joseph were opposites in every way. Could Joseph fake all those emotions? Convincingly enough that Moses' fellow officers wouldn't question which brother wore the uniform? Could he step into Moses' life and find the person who slaughtered his family? Find them, and kill them in turn?

Joseph swallowed hard. The realization that he was considering adopting his brother's life, effectively murdering himself and becoming Moses, was startling. It wasn't too late to back out now, but by tomorrow, no one would believe that he was in shock. Joseph tried again to think about the differences between them, to decide whether he could really pull it off. But the image of Moses' body covering their mother's, of their blood blown across the stove, the counter, the floor, snapped through his brain over and over. He lost precious moments to bewilderment at this inability to control his thoughts, struggling to shove the images down to that remote part of his brain where unprocessed emotions were imprisoned.

Joseph realized that he was holding his breath, and slowly released it. He looked down at the table, surprised to see that the food was gone. The kitchen door whooshed open and Stella stepped into the room, followed by Porky, who wore fresh orange scrubs and carried a floral overnight bag. Stella glanced at the empty bowl and glass and refilled both, then filled another bowl and glass for Porky, who put the bag by the outside door.

"Now Moses," she said, sitting at the table between the men. "You're going to stay here for at least a few days." He opened his mouth to speak but she cut him off. "You can't go back to that house tonight, and probably not until the police finish whatever they have to do. We have a guest bedroom that has its own bathroom. It's comfortable and private."

"I can't impose, Stella."

"No, you can't. Because we want you here. Porky *and* me. I have to go see about my aunt. She's having surgery tomorrow and I told her I'd be there this evening. I'll be back in time for the funerals." A chime dinged and Stella took a cake from the oven, tested it with a toothpick, and poured dark chocolate icing from a saucepan over the hot cake. The pan sizzled as the liquid hit its sides and a rich aroma rose into the air. Joseph's eyes watered when he realized this was the same recipe for chocolate cake his mother always used.

He dug his fingers into his eyes to clear his blurry vision and then glanced at the clock on the stove. "It's ten-thirty. How far do you have to go?"

"She's on the south side of Watuga County. No more than an hour and a half." Stella placed the saucepan in the sink and filled it with warm water and detergent, then stuck a fork in the cake and scooped a bite out. Her eyes rolled as she chewed, and then she resolutely dropped the fork in the sink. "I've left food in the fridge and you're welcome to use the washer and dryer if you need them."

Porky drained the last of the milk from his glass and carried his dishes to the sink. "I have to get to work."

"Will you be the one to autopsy," he hesitated, and then the decision was made, "Joseph and Momma?"

"Maybe. But it's been busy tonight. When did you finish your last shift?"

Joseph thought back to when he'd last seen Moses. His brother had worked the night shift, slept during the day, and then taken their mother for her afternoon doctor's appointment and on to her quilting club meeting. Joseph ate breakfast with them, then started out for several interviews in Shreveport. "This morning. What happened?"

"Somebody was murdered at Calvin Whitehead's store. We're pretty sure it was Calvin."

"Shot?"

"No," Porky answered. "He was hanged and set on fire."

Joseph blinked hard and cleared his throat. "Dear God. That's downright evil."

"And there may be others that have come in. I don't know if I'll work on Martha and Joseph, but their autopsies should be quick." Porky stopped, watching the other man. "Are you okay?"

Joseph sucked in a deep breath and his eyes cleared. "I've been trying to figure out who would want to kill Joseph, but I can't think of anybody who had it in for him. It can't be my momma they were after. She's never done nothing to nobody. So it's got to be me. I know I've pissed off some folks over the years, but I can't think of anybody who would want me dead." He looked up suddenly. "You think they'll let me come back to work tomorrow?"

"Maybe, Mojo. The police department is so short on detectives they'll probably need help, which means the patrol pool will be running short and they'll need every officer available," Porky said. "But there may be a policy about having to take time off when a member of your family is killed. Or you might have to see a psychologist or something. We'll find out tomorrow." He took a key ring from a hook and gave it to Joseph. "For the doors. I'll take you to your house tomorrow morning and you can get your car and whatever else you need. I won't have my cell phone on in the autopsy room, but leave a message if you need anything and I'll call you as soon as I can."

Joseph rose and hugged Stella, then shook Porky's hand. "I don't know how to thank you."

"It'll be thanks enough if you eat that chocolate cake before I get back, Moses," Stella said with a smile. "I love it, but it's hell on my hips."

CHAPTER 12

CASS STEPPED OUT OF the shower at the medical examiner's office, skin glowing from a good scrubbing. She had followed Grey's orders as carefully as possible while helping him process the Franklin's bodies at the scene, but still managed to end up bloodied. At the morgue, she'd quickly changed into a spare pair of scrubs and assisted Grey with the autopsies, unsurprised to see his pent up emotions released with precision into the intricacies of taking x-rays, opening the bodies, removing and dissecting organs, and recording his observations. He was patient as they worked, describing the instrument he needed from his cart and explaining where to place her hand or direct a scalpel when her unfamiliarity with the interior of the human body slowed her down or caused her to fumble.

From the moment they entered the ME's office that evening, they were assaulted by the odor of charred human flesh that hung in the air. When the call about the shooting at the Franklin house had gone out, Grey and Porky had brought the torched body to the morgue and slid it into a mortuary refrigerator. Cass and Grey managed to avoid wincing at the smell as they worked on the Franklins, but Cass knew it would be some time before she could eat barbeque.

She had listened while they worked, hoping to hear the exam room door open and see Porky walk through. From the way his eyes flicked toward the door at every creak and groan of the old building, she knew Grey was waiting, too. They needed to know which Franklin brother they were working on, Moses or Joseph. Not that it mattered in the end, but simply to help answer the questions no one had yet dared voice: had someone targeted Moses Franklin because he was a cop? And even if it were Joseph who was dead, would they have the answer they needed? The men were so similar in appearance, was it possible the killer had shot the wrong man?

They had nearly finished the Franklin autopsies when Grey found a stopping place and asked if she would help him with the corpse from The Whitehead Store. Cass smeared more Vick's under her nose while Grey pulled the shelf from its unit, unzipped the body bag, and peeled back the plastic. Cass held her breath and leaned in. The face was a study in agony. "I can't tell; the burns are too bad. But Calvin always wore a ring on his right hand. Kind of like a college ring with a red stone. Did you find it?"

Grey eased more of the plastic apart and Cass peered closely at the blackened chest. She could just make out the carved swastika. She and Grey exchanged a glance, and then he exposed the right hand. Although sooty, the gold was very yellow, probably eighteen karat, and worn almost perfectly smooth over the years. A richly red stone topped the dome. Cass nodded. "That's it. This must be Calvin."

"Help me look for a wallet."

Gingerly, they eased the body onto its left side and Cass teased a lump of moldering material away from the corpse. "You think this is it?"

Grey examined what she held. "Kado can dig through it and see if anything survived."

The thunk of the shelf sliding home in the refrigerated unit stuck with Cass as she stepped into her panties and pulled her jogging bra over her head, gently shaking her breasts into its cups before pulling on a fresh set of clothes. She chose not to wipe steam from the mirror over the sink. She didn't think she could bear the sight of the scar tonight; too much anger was humming through her veins at the thought of such senseless killings.

During the weeks she'd been away from the police department, she thought she'd gained some distance from the crimes she was charged with investigating. But given the surge of helplessness that rolled through her body, Cass realized the job could still crawl under her skin and leave her aggravated at the uselessness of procedure, the sluggishness of process. She heard voices and hurried into socks and boots. Opening the door, she ran her fingers through her hair, damp and the deep color of drying blood, and stood facing Kado and Grey.

Kado's eyes skimmed her body and she was surprised to feel a fluttering in her stomach, similar to the response he'd provoked the first time they'd met. She had believed that simply deciding Kado wasn't suitable relationship material would've helped control her reaction to him. Apparently not. Their contact at the Franklin house had been minimal, with Kado hurrying her inside to help Grey, then largely ignoring her while he examined the fractured window and collected the little evidence available. He seemed unable to resist the sight of her now, and as Cass looked more closely at him, she could see the stress the last few weeks had placed on him. His smoky gray eyes were weary and dark hair curled over the collar of his shirt. She thought his hair looked good when it was longer, and she bit her lip to stifle the urge to smile at him.

Grey covered his mouth and yawned until his jaw popped. "Kado needs you to go with him to Deadwood Hollow."

"Are we done here?"

"Porky's coming in. He can finish with the Franklins. Bernie's on his way to help me with Calvin Whitehead."

"He's still in town?"

"Bernie Winterbottom is infatuated with Elaine. He met her at the courthouse a few weeks ago — before you were suspended, I think — and fell in love. I don't know what she sees in him," Grey groused, "but there it is. He was scheduled to fly home to England this week, but the Caddo Indian Mounds dig got the go-ahead and he's staying."

"Where's Minnie?" Cass asked. Minnie Peck was Grey's long-suffering, chain-smoking administrative assistant.

"Visiting her sister in Florida. I'm worried she's thinking about retiring."

"She's probably old enough."

Grey raised an eyebrow. "I was raised better than to ask a woman her age. But I'd guess Minnie's at least eligible to draw Social Security." He frowned at Cass. "Those aren't the same clothes you had on, are they?"

"You are observant. I keep a spare set in the truck, just in case."

"Some habits die hard, huh?" Grey asked.

White lights pulsed outside the ME's office, and the exterior door opened and shut quickly, muffling the sound of shouted questions. Porky Rivers stepped into the administrative area, blinking.

"Press?" Grey asked.

Porky nodded. "A few. They know what happened at The Whitehead Store and the Franklin house. It's gonna be ugly."

Grey examined the thin man. "Are you okay?"

"Yeah. It's just hard."

Cass asked the question: "Who is it?"

"Joseph is dead," Porky answered slowly. "Moses is staying with me for a while."

She breathed a quiet sigh of relief. "How is he?"

"For now, all right. I think his training is taking over and he's trying to stay analytical, to figure out who would've targeted him."

"He thinks this is about him?" Kado asked.

"He thinks it's possible." Porky leaned a thin shoulder into a filing cabinet, his smooth face lined with worry. "Y'all will have to talk to him, he knows that. But he said he couldn't think of anybody who would want to kill his momma or Joseph."

Grey snagged his earlobe between his thumb and forefinger and rubbed gently. "Joseph recently moved back to Arcadia, didn't he? He was in prison up north."

"For some white-collar crime." Porky's teeth tugged gently at a silver stud in his lower lip. "You think somebody came after him?"

"It seems odd that he comes home and gets killed a few weeks later."

Porky's eyes filled with tears. "Why his momma, man? She was an old woman."

"Maybe," Cass said, "because they looked alike."

"They didn't look nothin' alike," Porky protested. "Joseph was huge; his momma was a tiny thing."

"She might've been small compared to Moses and Joseph, but she was a tall woman."

61

"And there wasn't much light in the kitchen when the first officers got to the house," Kado said. "With her bald head, the three of them look very similar to one another."

Grey nodded. "From the way the bodies lay, she was shot first. Joseph must've been in the shower or just gotten out, grabbed a towel, and ran to the kitchen. He fell on top of her. If she was in the kitchen alone, it could be a case of mistaken identity. Someone shoots her, then realizes his mistake when Joseph appears."

"Did you find the slugs?" Cass asked Kado.

He nodded. "They were buried in the tile behind the stove. One more mangled than the other. Large caliber, .308, maybe"

"That explains the damage to Mrs. Franklin's skull," Grey said.

Porky straightened. "Did you finish the autopsies?"

"Almost. Cass helped, but Kado needs her for forensic work. Can you help me finish?"

"No problem. What did you find?"

"Not much more than we saw at the scene. Martha Franklin suffered one gunshot wound to the head, and Joseph one to the chest. Both shots went through the bodies."

"If Moses is right that he's the target, the killer could've shot the other two in error," Cass said.

"You think he's in danger?" Porky asked.

"Until we know better."

"Can you get protection for him?"

She gave him a small smile. "In my official capacity with the Medical Examiner's office, I can't do anything. But I'll call Detective Martinez and see what he can do." She paused. "Porky, is Moses going to give us trouble?"

He frowned as he considered her question. "You mean with the investigation?"

Cass nodded.

"I don't think so, but y'all better talk to him. Moses is a good guy. If you lay it out for him, the rules or whatever, he'll abide by them."

"How do you know the Franklins?" Grey asked.

"Same church. We sing in the choir. Joseph sings bass and Moses sings tenor." His smile was wistful. "That's about the only difference I ever saw in those two. I can't believe I'll never hear Joseph's voice again."

CHAPTER 13

JOSEPH FRANKLIN LAY PERFECTLY still in Porky River's guest bedroom. The sheets were so crisp they had practically crackled when he slipped between them, but they were incredibly cool and smooth against his skin. Light from the parking lot snuck between the blinds and slashed the ceiling with thin white stripes. Joseph focused his attention on the void between two bright bars and allowed his thoughts to roam free.

The murders were his fault, no doubt. Joseph Franklin was a master of the computer break-in, the type of nefarious hacking wizard they dubbed a cracker. His first intrusion into a protected system came when he was still a teenager. Joseph had decided to take a look at the payroll for the college where he was enrolled, and found that worming his way through the network of systems was ridiculously simple. He took a peek, found the salary details he wanted, and then waited to see if anyone would notice. They didn't. So he checked out the accounting and finance systems, and finally hacked the database that housed information on the students and their class schedules. He discovered more than he'd bargained for: Social Security numbers, home addresses, phone numbers, and birth dates. And that was when the seed was planted. Joseph realized that the potential for identity theft was virtually unlimited, but also recognized that their lack of credit history made his fellow students extremely poor targets. He considered dipping back in to the payroll database to purloin a better quality of information, but questioned the wisdom of stealing from his own backyard. Instead, Joseph pushed that germinating idea to a remote section of his brain, and then finished his studies and graduated with honors.

He worked for years as a respected programmer for an international bank based in New York, but in spite of his academic and professional achievements, had been unable to find work when his job was outsourced to India ten years ago. Joseph was nearing the end of his emergency cash stash when the seed planted those many years ago sprouted in the fertile soil of his brain. From it grew a black market business in which Joseph traded in identities and, in some cases, blocks of credit card data. It was lucrative work and competitors were few. In fact, Joseph knew of only three other crackers who could supply the same quantity and quality of data. The hacking community itself provided few threats. It was the people who purchased the data who were dangerous. Although they rarely met, the buyers were shady characters; some simple entrepreneurs, others with links to organized crime.

And that's why the murders were Joseph's fault.

Greasy Lou Spitano, a front man for the big players in the information game, put down a deposit on a credit card database. And while the job was simple enough for someone with Joseph's talents, he put it off for one day too long. The police came for him in broad daylight, and to this day he didn't know how they found him. They'd charged him with a list of cyber crimes as long as his very long leg. While Joseph recognized some of the jobs as his, he also realized the prosecutor was fishing to try and clear his case backlog. It was only thanks to his mother and the money she raised from mortgaging her house that Joseph had been represented by such a powerful lawyer.

The State of New York was hungry to make an example of Joseph and wanted a high-profile case that would garner media attention. But his attorney managed to avoid a legal circus and instead wrangled a three-year stay for Joseph in a minimum security facility, along with a $10,000 fine, long-term restrictions on his computer usage, and a whopping $2.5 million in restitution to the various banks he had invaded. The sum still boggled him. In return, Joseph confessed to the hacks on the district attorney's list that were his, but refused to roll over on anyone else.

That left Greasy Lou Spitano and his shadowy associates. Was it possible that they knew Joseph was out of prison, and wanted a refund?

The mantle of guilt lay heavy on his chest, threatening to smother him into paralysis. His bottom lip trembled, and Joseph gave in, letting tears roll down his temples and onto the pillow. He cried for the loss of his family, the choices he had made, and perhaps even more for the possibility that he had brought this brutal end on them. In truth, he knew the punishment for his hacking crimes was light, but he was shamefully grateful to be free. He also recognized that whoever had murdered his mother and brother might not receive a full measure of justice under the law. And that thought burned him.

By the time his reservoir of tears was exhausted, Joseph was resolved to his new life as Moses. Not only would he have full run of the law enforcement systems, but a new identity solved a world of problems for Joseph. The struggle he faced as an ex-con trying to find work would be over. Parole would end. Restitution? The court couldn't collect money from a dead man. As a cop, Joseph would have a steady source of income, something he hadn't experienced in years. And most importantly, he could begin the search.

Joseph was ready to find whoever had killed his mother and brother, even if it was Greasy Lou Spitano and his network. And from that knowledge would spring a plan for vengeance. *The details will come*, he thought as he drifted into sleep.

In Joseph's logical mind, they always did.

CHAPTER 14

Thursday

OFFICER SCOTT TRUMAN STUDIED Calvin Whitehead's cash register. He pushed a button and the drawer popped open with a bang, exposing stacks of bills resting undisturbed in their slots. Martinez was crouched by the stockroom doors taking photographs of the mess within.

"No robbery," Truman called. He had wrapped a bandanna over his nose and mouth and his words were muffled. "Money's still in the register and everything is orderly."

"Balance it with the tape," Martinez replied.

Truman took photographs and then balanced the drawer. "Checks, cash, and credit card receipts all add up."

He slipped the money into an evidence bag, snapped his latex gloves off, ran his hands over his blond crew cut, and yawned. It was past midnight and his hazel eyes were red rimmed and his fair skin paler than normal. He had worked the day shift but was still in uniform and having dinner at home with his parents when the call went out about the murder at The Whitehead Store. He hopped in his patrol car and headed over to the remote little gas station, and although he'd been here for over six hours and could feel exhaustion clawing at his brain, was glad he had responded.

Martinez stood and stretched his burly arms over his head. "Well, that's one motive gone." He examined the frames hanging on the wall behind the counter. A photograph of Calvin Whitehead, standing in front of his store on the day of its grand opening. A certificate of appreciation from the Boy Scout Troop. A note of thanks from the Little League. And a crucifix. He fingered the smaller version hanging on a chain around his neck. "I didn't know Whitehead was Catholic."

"He didn't go to church?" Truman asked.

"I'm not at mass regularly, but I've never seen him."

"Maybe he backslid."

"Yeah, maybe. Seems strange that he'd keep a crucifix on the wall to remind him, but to each his own."

Truman glanced around the tidy store. "You'd never even know a crime was committed here."

"What do you mean?"

Truman shrugged and yawned again. "Calvin Whitehead keeps a really clean store. There's no dust on the shelves, the glass doors to the refrigeration units are clean, and the floor mostly sparkles. Except for that little puddle of gas by the door this afternoon, nothing was disturbed in here."

"Unlike the storeroom," Martinez said.

"Yeah. Whoever did this either caught him off guard back there, or he knew them and was comfortable going to the storeroom with them."

"Makes sense."

"What now?"

"We dust for prints and collect evidence from the courtyard." He glanced around the small grocery store. "Let's wrap up and get out here in the morning when Kado's available."

Truman followed Martinez outside, removed the bandanna, and tested the air before breathing deeply. "What happened at the Franklin's house?"

"Sounds like the shooter was in the woods behind the house. Probably used a rifle."

"Was it Moses or Joseph?"

"Joseph. Cass called to confirm."

"Rumor says John Grey hired her tonight."

"Yup," Martinez answered. "I figure the sheriff will stroke out when he hears, but I'll lay odds that Grey will win this round. You want to put some money on it?"

A sly grin crossed Truman's weary face. "No way. But I'd like to be a fly on the wall when Sheriff Hoffner hears that Cass is back at work. That's one stroke that would be worth seeing."

CHAPTER 15

CASS, KADO, ROBERT GROVE, and two uniformed officers followed the Grove twins into Deadwood Hollow and listened as the two bickered over where they'd been when the shooter ran past. When Cass had called their house at eleven-thirty, Evelyn Grove was reluctant to allow the boys to assist with the investigation but relented after her husband volunteered to take the boys out and bring them home.

Deadwood Hollow was a maze of trails worn over the years by students in the athletic programs and citizens who preferred to jog on dirt rather than concrete. The trails themselves were maintained by the City of Arcadia who owned this sixty acre section of woodland. Beyond the boundaries of each path, however, the woods closed in quickly. The space between the tall pines, massive oaks, elms, and the occasional willow were almost impassible due to thick brush growth. During the day, the Hollow was too busy to tolerate much nefarious activity, but at night, drug dealers and their clients were known to frequent the area to exchange cash and product.

It was almost twelve-thirty and the boys were using fresh flashlights provided by Kado to scan the brush beside the narrow path, looking for spots crushed while they had searched for the missing cell phone. Up ahead, both lights stopped moving.

"Here," the brother with the scraggly facial hair said.

Mark is the one with that sad beard, Cass remembered.

"Are you sure?" their father asked, shining his own flashlight off the trail.

Mark squatted and peered into the brush. "Yeah, I scratched my head on that honey locust tree when I was bent over looking for my phone. The one my idiot brother lost," he added, looking up at Matt who opened his mouth to protest.

"Tell us how it happened," Kado interrupted, handing his forensic case to one of the officers and crouching to look farther along the path.

"I was over here," Mark said, pointing down into the shadows.

"And I was over here," Matt added, pushing aside brush on the opposite side of the trail. "We were looking for the phone when there were two shots."

"How close together?"

The boys looked at each other. "Seconds," Matt answered. "Four, maybe five."

Mark nodded.

"And then?" Kado asked.

"And then we ducked our happy asses –"

"Mark," Robert Grove warned.

"– down in the brush. I laid flat but was looking up at the trail."

"I was looking that way," Matt added, pointing deeper into Deadwood Hollow. "I saw him coming."

"What did you see?" Cass asked.

"This dude. He was carrying a rifle, like this." Matt crossed his arms as if to hold a baby. "He wore dark clothes, maybe a track suit, maybe jeans and a hoodie. His hood was up and I barely got a glimpse of his face."

"Eyes, nose?"

"Chin and neck."

"How do you know it was a guy?"

Matt tilted his head to one side. "Adam's apple. And he had broad shoulders and narrow hips, like a guy. But it could've been a butch chick with no boobs."

"*Matt*," Robert Grove growled.

"Sorry, ma'am. Breasts."

Cass hid a grin. "Did he have a beard?"

"There was nothing obvious like a full beard, goatee, chin puff, or curtain. But he could've had a chinstache or soul patch."

"You are such a dweeb," Mark muttered.

Kado cleared his throat. "How do you know so much about beards?"

"I did some research before I grew mine. It was too itchy, so I shaved it off."

"Thorough. Did you notice anything else about the guy?"

"His hands were really white."

Kado held his hands out and motioned for Cass, Robert, and the two officers to do the same.

Matt and Mark squinted. Mark pointed at Cass's hands and those of a fair skinned officer. "Dad's hands and the other officer's are too hairy, and your skin is darker than his."

"Good. You said you were looking up, Mark. What did you see?"

"Same thing as Matt. Tall dude, dark clothes and shoes, rifle in his arms, almost no skin except his chin and hands."

"How do you know he was tall?"

Mark shrugged. "He looked tall, but not as tall as us."

"You're what, six foot five or six?"

"Five."

Kado looked at Cass and asked a question with his eyes. She coughed a small laugh and said, "We need to know."

"Let's try something," Kado said, turning to Mark. "Get down in the brush, where you were."

Mark's mouth fell open. "You're kidding, right? There are brambles down there, not to mention a honey locust tree, mosquitoes, and probably ticks."

"Stop whining, you weenie," Matt said. "We could catch a killer."

Mark continued grumbling but folded his long frame in on itself and slipped down the side of the trail, scooting deeper until he found the right position. He craned his neck to look up at the group. "Now what?"

"Twist your head at the same angle you held it when the shooter ran past." Kado had Matt, Robert, Cass, and each officer stand where Mark could see them. "Anybody the right height?"

"Dad is close. Maybe a little taller than the killer."

Kado turned to Robert Grove. "How tall are you?"

"Six foot one."

Mark started to crawl to the path but stopped, groped deeper in the brush, and gave a triumphant yelp as he held up a cell phone. "Found it."

"O brother of mine," Matt said as Mark brushed debris from his track suit. "You rock."

"And you owe me," Mark stated. He turned to Kado. "That'll help you catch him?"

"It will," Kado said. "I know it's late, but thanks for coming. Can you get back to the cars by yourselves?"

Robert Grove held up his flashlight. "As long as we can keep these. I'll drop them by the courthouse tomorrow, if that's all right."

"Perfect. Would you bring the boy's shoes with you? We need them for exclusion purposes."

"No problem. We'll stop by before school."

"School? Seriously? Come on Dad, it's past midnight. Matt needs his beauty sleep."

"So do you, Mark, but you'll both be in school by eight."

The three Grove men started through the woods, the boys arguing quietly.

"That's another dollar for the cuss bucket."

"What are you talking about?"

"You said 'ass'."

"Ten second rule."

"There's no time limit on the cuss bucket."

"*I* found the phone. So now we have a time limit. Dig?"

CHAPTER 16

THE MIDNIGHT SKY WAS free of clouds and the pale moon shimmered in a velvety sky sprinkled with bright stars. The shooter parked on the tiny dirt road and sat in the truck, watching the dark house across a freshly planted field and keeping an eye on the silent road. When nothing changed – no lights, no vehicles – he slipped on his shooting glove and grabbed his rifle, closed the driver's door with a soft click, and walked beneath the moonlight across the field.

The expansive farmland around the house was owned by one of Forney County's wealthiest families and worked by a crew of Hispanics. Illegal, no doubt. At night, the fields were vacant except for the silent husks of the tractors used to plow, spray, and harvest during the day. The hills and furrows in the freshly planted field slowed him, as did the slippery clay that caked his shoes. No matter. He would dispose of them later and no one in Forney County would look twice at a muddy pair of old boots. He stepped over a low stone wall and into her backyard. It was covered in thick St. Augustine that needed mowing. He scraped the muck from his boots, and then crept toward the house.

If her nighttime routine remained consistent with what he had observed over the last few weeks, she would be sound asleep in the master bedroom at the rear of the house. Her bed was a massive four poster with a pale headboard that looked as if it were covered in fabric. She slept propped up on pillows, almost in a sitting position, which he found unusual. Her bed faced uncurtained floor-to-ceiling windows and as he eased closer, he realized that the moonlight had penetrated deeply enough into the room to illuminate her doll-like form. This was easier than he'd dare hope.

He stepped back from the window, raised the rifle to his shoulder, aimed, and fired. The retort bounced back from the window, making the shot seem louder than it really was. He peered through the spiderwebbing caused by the bullet's impact and spotted the spatter of blood, bone, and brain matter across the wall behind the bed.

"Magnificent," he whispered.

He checked his watch: barely twelve-thirty. Three down, one to go. Not bad for a night's work. With a small salute at the corpse, he ejected the spent casing into the catcher and shoved a new round home, shouldered his rifle, and strode back toward his truck.

CHAPTER 17

CASS FOLLOWED KADO FARTHER along the path, deeper into Deadwood Hollow. She couldn't help but feel grateful that she wasn't leading this expedition as she drank in the way his strong shoulders tapered to that narrow waist. His jeans fit perfectly, tight enough to outline his buttocks and thighs, but loose enough to allow movement. She stumbled over a tree root and bit her lip to hold back a giggle. She seriously had to get a grip before this man caught her drooling over him.

"Ma'am? Is everything okay?"

Cass started, then remembered the two officers trailing them. Kado had requested back-up for their venture into the Hollow, and dispatch sent two extremely young officers out to meet them. She vaguely recognized them as new hires who joined just before her suspension. When introduced earlier, they greeted her with a mixture of awe and fear. Kado flashed a querying look over his shoulder. "Everything's fine," she said.

They walked to either side of the curving dirt path, flashlights playing over the dry, packed ground, looking for shoe impressions. Kado squatted and shone his light toward the middle of the path at an angle. "There's literally nothing here. It's so dry, the dirt is like concrete."

"The shooter had to be off the trail and closer to the Franklin's house. Maybe he left tracks as he came out of the forest," Cass said.

They continued silently forward, using their flashlight beams to sweep the trail and probe the dense brush beside it, looking for a sign that someone had earlier passed this way. Kado stopped and crouched several times, identifying potential impressions in soft sand. He marked them with a flag and took photos.

Cass moved past him and shone her flashlight along what looked like a hog run worn in the dense brush between two towering pine trees. Kado joined her and peered at the thin dirt trail. "Those could be shoe prints. Let me take a quick look before we all come through here."

He disappeared into the gloom and was gone for several minutes. When he returned, his face was grim. "It's the perfect spot."

They followed him around the pine trees and pushed through heavy brush to avoid trampling the hog trail and any evidence it contained. Within moments they arrived at a small clearing. A tall oak stood alone, surrounded by thin swells of grass and wildflowers. A barely discernible path had been worn between the edge of the clearing and the tree's base. Kado instructed the officers to begin searching the brush along the clearing's edge, and then inched forward, marking potential impressions as he went. He put his case down and stood at the base of the tree, examining a narrow pole attached to its trunk with a series of cam buckles and black nylon straps. Small metal bars stuck off to each side of the pole at regular intervals. "What is this?"

Cass joined him. "It's a climbing stick. They come in short sections, four foot or so. Hunters use them as temporary ladders if they don't have time to put up a full deer stand." She leaned closer. "This one looks pretty new."

"He must've been out here a few times," Kado said. "There are a lot of imprints here. It looks like they're all from the same boot."

"Are you sure this is the right tree?"

"Not entirely, but the Franklin's house is in that direction," he pointed north. Kado studied the tree, then looked out toward the trail. "I guess that explains how Matt and Mark Grove heard the shots, even though the vegetation is pretty dense here."

"What do you mean?"

"The path curves around in an 's' shape, so the distance as the crow flies between where the boys were standing and this tree really isn't that far." He bent over to open his forensics kit. "No more than forty yards, fifty at most."

Kado checked for trace and dusted the climbing stick for prints, holding his flashlight in his mouth and stepping up the narrow ladder to reach higher rungs until he was at the top. "Nothing. He wore gloves or wiped the climbing stick down," he called. "I'm going to check out this branch. Pour casting mix in those impressions, Cass, and check for brass."

She examined each of the flagged impressions with her flashlight, selected three, and took the casting materials from Kado's forensics case. The two young officers watched from the clearing's edge as she worked, holding their flashlights to provide illumination. "Stop your flashlight right there," she called.

The men froze and watched as she left the imprints and squatted to eyeball a scraggly patch of weeds near the tree. Cass slid the end of a pen inside a metal cartridge and held it up to the light. "You were right, Kado. He's shooting .30-06 rounds."

"Brand?"

"Nothing special. It's Winchester."

One of the officers cleared his throat. "How do you know that's from the guy who shot the Franklins?"

"Good question." She held the brass cartridge up into the beam of his flashlight. "For starters, it's still shiny so the case hasn't been exposed to the elements for long. It was nestled in the weeds, not mashed into the ground, which means it hasn't been here long enough for someone to step on it. And if Kado can prove this is the tree he fired from, chances are pretty good this came from the rifle that killed the Franklins." Cass studied the ground. "I wonder if we can find the other casing?"

The officers adjusted their flashlights, and Cass glanced over at them. They had identical crew cuts, square jaws, and bulging biceps. "Ready to do some real detective work?"

They nodded in unison.

"Go back to Kado's truck and get the flood lights. Stay off the trail."

The two held a short conference before one turned and disappeared. Cass was pouring mix in the last impression when

Kado's phone rang. He was sitting in the crook created where the branch met the tree and directing a laser pointer out through the woods. He cursed, reached to pull the phone from his back pocket, and dropped it. "Answer it Cass, would you?"

She picked it up and brushed debris from the cover. "Tom Kado's phone."

"Who is this?"

Cass closed her eyes as Sheriff Bill Hoffner's voice barked from the earpiece. *What a great start*, she thought. "It's Cass, sir."

A pause. "Elliot? Where's Kado?"

"In a tree trying to find the shooter's line to the Franklin's house."

"What are you doing at a crime scene?" he sputtered.

"John Grey hired me as a temp. Apparently the county doesn't have enough officers to handle three homicides in one night." The words came without thought, and it was only when she glanced up in the tree to see Kado staring down at her, his gray eyes amused, that she realized what a smartass she'd sounded like. "Sir," she added into the phone.

Hoffner's breath came in short gasps. "I'll deal with you and Grey when I get back. Give the phone to Kado."

She raised it toward him but Kado waved her away. "Brief him. I've almost got it."

"Kado can't get down from the tree, sir. I can give you an overview, if you'd like."

Silence.

"Sir?"

"Start with Whitehead," he grunted.

"From what I understand, Calvin Whitehead was hanged and gasoline used to set him on fire. Grey doesn't have a time of death, but Martinez assumes it was some time after the last sale at the gas pumps, a little after five o'clock."

"Who's working with Martinez?"

"Scott Truman."

"Who found Whitehead?"

"Goober."

Sheriff Hoffner sighed. "I should've guessed. What happened to the Franklins?"

"Two shots fired from Deadwood Hollow through the kitchen window at approximately eight o'clock. Mrs. Franklin was hit first, and then Joseph when he came into the kitchen to check on her."

"You're sure it's Joseph? Not Moses?"

"Yes, sir. He confirmed his identity with Porky Rivers earlier."

"Where are you now?"

"In Deadwood Hollow. Ernie Munk's nephews, the Grove twins, saw the shooter run past. Kado put out a BOLO on a dark truck, but we don't have a license plate for it. Thanks to the Grove boys, we think we've found the shooter's tree."

"Any ideas on motive?"

"Joseph was recently released from prison in New York for some sort of white collar crime. That could be a link. Or someone could be after Moses and simply mistook Mrs. Franklin or Joseph for him."

"Where is Mojo?"

"Staying with Porky."

"Ask Detective Martinez to arrange protection for him."

"Already done."

She heard him grunt. "Fine. I'm on my way to Texas but can't get a flight until early morning. I won't make it to Arcadia until tomorrow afternoon. I'll call Kado when I'm on the ground in Dallas." He hesitated and Cass heard the phone shift. "Has the press shown up?"

Typical, she thought. "Yes, sir, but only a few local reporters so far."

"Have Martinez and Kado hold them off until I'm back."

"I'll tell them."

She shut the phone and watched as Kado came down the climbing stick. "Anything?"

He looked north. "It's close to a hundred yards to the Franklin kitchen from here. I'll have to check the angle where the bullets penetrated the window, but I think this is it. The laser indicates the shooter had a clear line of sight to the kitchen. It's a narrow path through the canopy, but there's nothing to block a shot from that branch."

"Why didn't the kitchen window shatter?"

"Bullet velocity and the distance between the entrance holes."

She looked over her shoulder at the sound of the returning officer. He stopped at the clearing's edge and the two men began assembling the lights. "The casting mix needs another twenty minutes," she said. "I'll ask the officers to look for the other casing. Can I do anything else?"

"We'll take photos when the lights are up. It's almost one o'clock. That's about all we can do tonight and we might as well get a few hours sleep." He turned to the two officers. "Grab some crime scene tape and flip a coin to see who searches for brass and who tapes the path."

One of the officers lifted a roll of yellow tape from Kado's forensics case. "How much of the path, sir?"

"All of it."

"All of it to where?"

"All of it from wherever it begins to wherever it ends." He looked at the half-used roll in the officer's hand and offered a small smile. "You'll need more than that."

CHAPTER 18

THE SHOOTER STEPPED FROM the pickup's cab and scanned the neighborhood. His final target's house was dark, and the old lady who lived to the left slept without her hearing aids. The house to the right was up for sale and empty; the next family down the line was on vacation. Beyond that distance and this late at night, he doubted anyone would stir at the sound of a rifle's retort.

The moon's fat face was out fully now, bathing the neighborhood in a clear white light and spilling deep shadows beneath the trees. The shooter took his rifle from the truck and moved along the driveway's edge to the house, pausing to inspect the carport. Still only one vehicle. This was a relatively new arrangement for the couple; through his periodic visits to the backyard in the late evenings, he had learned that some sort of tiff had the wife staying with her mother. Which suited him perfectly – his quarrel was with the man.

After checking the houses and the woods on the opposite side of the street again, he crept past the small pickup and into the wide backyard. Celia Hedder was a stickler for keeping the bedroom curtains tightly closed. Although the house backed onto the golf course, she must have a fear of peeping toms. A reasonable apprehension, given her appearance. But it seemed that in Celia's absence, her husband Emmet wasn't as particular about who might be watching. All to the good.

The master bedroom was at the far end of the house and the thick grass helped muffle his movements. He reached the windows and was gratified to see the curtains still tied back, exactly as they'd been since Celia left. He lifted the rifle to his shoulder in a smooth movement and sighted on the motionless form in the couple's bed.

A chill flush of paranoia swept up his spine as his finger moved from the guard to the trigger. Tonight had been easy. Almost too easy. It was only earlier this afternoon that he'd decided to murder three people, and he was about to achieve that goal. All that remained of their unholy trio was this man. And he was about to die. No hunting trip had ever gone this smoothly.

His unease intensified as he applied pressure, pulling the trigger steadily toward his shoulder. He wasn't sure which happened first – whether the round left the barrel or the man rolled over. Regardless, once the round was discharged everything moved in slow motion. A neat hole surrounded by a halo of cracks appeared in the window, blood flared up and out, and the headboard splintered with the slug's impact.

HE'D BEEN A LIGHT sleeper since his days in the military, drifting in that hazy world between the conscious and unconscious and able to snap from one to the other in an instant. Emmet Hedder rolled over and felt a searing heat in his upper right arm. The disturbing sensation of being watched had interrupted his dreams moments earlier, and the fire in his arm brought him to full wakefulness. He reacted instantly, shoving his left hand under the pillow, grabbing his Glock, and rolling out of the covers to the floor in a smooth movement. Ducking his head under the bed, he looked for feet and legs, saw none, and fired high through the window, the bullet piercing a top pane.

A scrambling sounded from outside. Emmet tightened his stomach muscles to raise his upper body and peek over the window sill. No one was visible in the moon-drenched backyard. Adrenaline screamed through his body and his left hand trembled as he reached up and ripped two extra magazines from the bottom of the bedside table drawer, then found his wallet on the table itself. His tennis shoes were near the bed and he slipped his bare feet into them, then pulled the small duffel from beneath the bed with his uninjured arm.

Again, he looked over the window sill and saw no movement. He breathed deeply and then rolled onto all fours, hissing against the pain, and crawled to the bedroom door, standing only when he was away from the windows.

The hall seemed to bend out and away when Emmet gained his feet, but he rested against the cool wall to let his vision clear before hurrying toward the kitchen. He crouched as he passed the open bathroom door so as not to be seen through the small window. Emmet stopped at the end of the hallway and poked his head into the kitchen for a quick look through the windows above the sink. Nothing.

Squatting, he duck-walked across the linoleum floor, wincing as his tennis shoes squeaked against the clean surface. A cool sweat bathed his face and he took a steadying breath, then grabbed his keys from their hook, yanked open the outside door, and dove for his truck.

———

THE SHOOTER DROPPED WHEN the shot exploded from the bedroom and crab-walked along the house to a shadowy cluster of trees, a startled smile on his face. As quietly as possible, he ejected the spent casing into his homemade brass catcher and slipped a new round home. This was an unexpected turn of events, but a strangely exhilarating one.

He heard a door bang open and the pickup's engine roar to life. Running through the carport, he lifted the rifle to his shoulder and aimed, following the little truck's tail lights as it careened out of the drive, bounced over the curb, and sped down the road. Slowly, he lowered his weapon and watched to see if lights went on in any of the nearby houses. All was still and dark.

He trod quietly to his truck, placed the rifle in its special compartment, and drove away. The smile was still on his lips, for the hunt was on.

"You want to play, Emmet? Let's play. Run, little rabbit," he whispered, "run."

CHAPTER 19

HER HEADLIGHTS FLASHED ACROSS three sets of tail lights and an unusual lump by the front porch. Cass looked closer and a riding lawn mower materialized from the gloom. Her brothers and father were home, and it looked as if Goober had come out for a late night visit. She wondered what in the world could've brought Goober out after dark. It was a time of day he studiously avoided, due to his fervent belief in the monster-world. She climbed from her pickup's cab and waved at the solitary figure marching back and forth in front of the house across the road. The shotgun Herman the German carried bounced on his shoulder as he lifted a hand in salute without breaking pace.

She stretched and admired the Elliot's porch roof. During the first few days of the banishment, Cass was in a state of perpetual motion, running and lifting weights first thing in the morning; pacing the house as she scoured the newspapers; and doing some long neglected deep cleaning, stopping only in the evenings to devour Bruce's collection of thrillers by Daniel Silva, John Connolly, and an indie author called Russell Blake. It was only when Bruce came home and found his bedroom spotless, his closet arranged by color and season, and the books on his shelves organized by author and subject matter that he took drastic action. He borrowed tools from the college and as soon as Cass came in from her run the following morning, the two of them started work on the sagging front porch. Together they leveled it with a jack and rebuilt worn supports; pried out rotted lumber and replaced it with pressure-treated wood; laid shingles; and finally, sanded the rough spots where paint was peeling, used caulk to fill the seams, and covered the entire area with fresh paint. Although Cass had played the role of apprentice, she felt some pride of ownership for the work. And if she focused only on the porch, she could imagine a normal, functional family living here.

Unfortunately, the rest of the place looked like a well-dressed chicken coop. The house and land were originally owned by the Craven family who, out of pity, had rented the two room shack on the northern edge of their vast property to a very young, very pregnant, and very poor couple – Abe and Nell Elliot. Over time, Abe had purchased the house on surprisingly favorable terms. He added rooms to hold his expanding family, the severity of tilt of each new room against the old in direct proportion to his degree of inebriation at the time of construction. Bruce planned to tackle problems with the large house one at a time. After the front porch, his eye turned to the kitchen, a project he had shelved in the spring. Once the kitchen was done, Cass wasn't sure what would come next, but she enjoyed the processes of destruction and creation that were remodeling, and planned to help as much as her job – whatever it turned out to be – and brother allowed.

The front door swung open and Abe Elliot motioned her inside. She crossed the yard and enjoyed the satisfying thunk of her boots against the now sturdy porch, stepped into her father's embrace, and sniffed surreptitiously; there was no smell of booze on his clothes or skin. Although she felt a twinge of guilt at using his display of affection to determine whether he had been drinking, her shoulders relaxed. "How long have you been home?" she asked.

He released her and leaned toward the living room door to check the DVD player's display. It was one-thirty. "About two hours. You're not usually out this late. Are you okay?"

A surge of pleasure rushed through her. "I'm back at work."

Abe lifted a hoary eyebrow. "Hoffner signed the papers?"

"John Grey hired me as a temp."

"The medical examiner? What happened?"

"Three murders tonight."

His expression changed to one of concern and he motioned her to the living room. "I'll get milk and cookies," he said, acting out the immutable Elliot tradition of feeding in times of trouble. "Bruce went to bed but Harry and Goober are still up."

Cass sat on the sagging couch next to her brother, who was bent over the paperwork and cloth swatches spread across and around the scarred coffee table. Goober was cross-legged on the floor in front of the television. The volume was low and he leaned forward to catch the actor's voices. He was oblivious to anything but the world inside the glowing box, and Cass wondered if that wasn't for the best considering what the man had been through this evening. "Hey, Goober."

He looked up at her with glassy eyes. "Hey, Cass," he said, and returned his attention to the "Gilligan's Island" re-run.

Cass nudged her brother. "Hey."

He ran his hands through his cottony-white hair, already in a considerable state of disarray. "Thanks for taking Phoebe to dance class. And I should thank you for distracting Carly."

"What are you talking about?"

Abe stopped to give a glass of milk and some cookies to Goober. "You diverted Carly's wrath from Harry. And given that woman's temper, he *ought* to be grateful."

"She's mad about the tutu?" Cass shrugged. "It's not like I could've cooked with the kitchen all in an uproar."

"Cass, you can't cook in any kitchen," Harry said.

"There is that."

"She was more pissed about the crown. Phoebe told her that Auntie Cass said it was all right if she wore it to dance class."

Cass took a glass of milk from her father and reached for the cookies. "Yes, Auntie Cass did. If Carly's mad about it, then Phoebe must have gotten home with the tiara still on her head, right?"

Harry bit into a cookie and nodded.

"So what's the problem? The tiara's home, Phoebe was princess for a day, and I'll buy a new tutu and leotard if she wants. Everybody's happy."

"That crown is her most prized possession."

"Paste jewels in the shape of a fire ant? Harry, how did you manage to marry this woman?"

"Temporary insanity that lasted fourteen years." He finished his cookie, a wistful smile on his face. "What can I say? She had a crown."

Cass grinned. "Too much information, man. So," she motioned to the colorful mess on the coffee table, "what's this?"

"I'm redoing the interior decorating for the Martins."

"Isn't that Carly's job?"

"Technically, yes. But she refused to budge when the Martins explained the changes they wanted, so I got her out of the house before she could argue and told them we'd get a new plan to them tomorrow morning." He glanced at the clock. "Which is now today."

"What's the big deal?" Cass asked.

"They want rustic, Carly wants country chic."

"And the difference?"

"Rustic is big, dark, and simple with clean lines. Country chic is whitewash, florals, and frilly edges to everything."

"Oh."

"Yeah."

"Your sister's back at work, Harry," Abe said, glancing at Goober and keeping his voice low.

"Really? When did that happen?"

Cass drew a deep breath. "Tonight. Martha and Joseph Franklin were shot in their home."

Harry's jaw dropped. "Mojo's mom and brother?"

She nodded.

"Man, she was my favorite lunch lady. She always brought me extra dessert if there was any left. I can't believe somebody could kill that woman. Was it a break-in?"

"No. They were killed from a distance with a rifle."

Abe cleared his throat. "You said there were three murders tonight, Cass. Who else?"

She motioned her father and brother into the kitchen. "Calvin Whitehead was murdered at his store. Goober's the one who found him."

"What happened?"

She rubbed the bridge of her nose and considered how much to reveal. The swastika was one detail that might be useful in the investigation and should be held back. Except for that, it didn't matter how much she told them; the story was already weaving its way through Arcadia's vast and efficient grapevine and would be on the Forney Cater's front page in the morning. "The body was burned."

"Whoa," Harry said. "Did the store burn, too?"

"Just Calvin. He was hanged and then set on fire."

Harry and Abe digested this. Their father wiped a thin film of dust from the kitchen table and placed his milk glass on its worn surface. Abe's eyes, the color of honeyed oak, were clouded. "Calvin Whitehead was a grumpy old man, but who would want to kill him?"

"What do you know about him, Daddy?" Cass asked.

"Not much. He moved here in the late seventies or early eighties and bought that shop and house. Both had been deserted for years and he put a lot of work into them."

"Where did he come from?"

Abe considered her question. "Out east somewhere. Or maybe up north. He didn't talk about his past much. Never, that I can recall. He talked a lot about guns and hunting."

Either topic would've caused her father's eyes to glaze over. "Did he have any friends?"

He shrugged. "I think he was Catholic. There was one of those Christ-on-the-cross things hanging on the wall when he first opened."

Cass usually paid at the pump when she stopped at The Whitehead Store. She tried to remember if she'd noticed the crucifix on those occasions when she had gone inside. "Was it still there last time you bought gas?"

"I think so, but I can't be sure. It's one of those things that become part of the environment. Once you accept that it's there, you don't really notice it again."

"Harry, did you know him?"

Her older brother shook his head. "I've only started filling up there since I moved back home in March. He knew I was an Elliot, but we never talked except to say hello or about the drought."

"Let me know if anything about Whitehead comes to mind, or if you hear anything tomorrow." She washed their glasses in the makeshift sink Bruce had rigged up. "What's Goober doing here?"

"He was on the front porch when I got back from taking Phoebe home," Harry answered. A grin played across his lips. "He said you told him that he could stay with us if he found another dead body."

She cringed at the thought of the crucified man Goober had stumbled upon several weeks earlier. "I guess I did, but I didn't really think he'd find another one." She shuddered. "Seeing Calvin Whitehead like that must've been pretty dreadful. He'll probably have nightmares tonight. I would."

"Goober's no bother. I've put him in Bobby and Mack's old room," Abe said with a reproachful glance at Harry. "It's got the least amount of high school crap in it."

"Sorry, Pop. I'll clear out my stuff one day. But now, I've got to finish these plans."

Cass checked the time on her phone. Almost two o'clock. "I need to get to bed. I'll be up and out early tomorrow." She grinned at her father. "Tell Bruce the crowbar and sledgehammer are all his."

BEFORE GETTING INTO BED, Cass checked her email and found no notifications of new search hits. She turned the computer off and tried to sleep, but her mind was buzzing with random details from the Franklin's autopsies, Calvin Whitehead's murder, and her time with Kado. At last, after trying desperately to focus her thoughts on work, she allowed herself to think about the man.

There was no point denying it: she was attracted to Kado in a way that she hadn't known in years. Cass had been a reluctant dater since the rape, willing to endure society's mating rituals only to preempt the gossip that would arise if she didn't date. Somehow, she'd managed to avoid finding any man so attractive that she was unable to resist getting to know him other than on a surface level. Any physical attraction died as soon as the guy in question opened his mouth and revealed his IQ. But what she felt for Tom Kado was different. Sexually visceral, yes, but there was a mental connection struggling to develop as well. Cass couldn't determine whether Kado felt the same way, and regardless, there were good reasons to steer clear of him.

While she was honing her internet skills in the search for her rapist, Cass also dug into Kado's background. He'd joined the police force as Forney County's Forensic Examiner back in March, coming from Oklahoma. With only his name and home state as a place to start, she soon learned more than she wanted to know about the circumstances that brought him to Arcadia.

Kado was full-blood Caddo Indian, which explained his last name, ruddy complexion, dark hair, and the flat planes of his high-cheekboned face. His name, and occasionally his photograph, had popped up in various news articles about crimes committed in western Oklahoma. His forensics department was lauded by the local sheriff and various state agencies for their exacting attention to detail. These comments probably helped persuade Sheriff Hoffner to hire Kado after old Hank Comfrey died. But his name also appeared in an online death announcement from a funeral home in Ada, Oklahoma, identifying him as the husband of a Caroline Kado. She had died a little over a year ago. The photograph accompanying the announcement showed a beautiful black-haired woman with mischievous eyes. In an article detailing the service, Kado's eulogy was poignant and indicated a deep-seated love for the woman.

If Bruce was right that people grieved differently, there might be a chance that Kado was mentally healthy enough for a relationship. But they worked together, and Cass wasn't sure whether Forney County had a policy on office affairs. She *was* sure that once Sheriff Hoffner learned about her involvement with Kado, whatever policy emerged would not be friendly to her desires.

And then there was the scar. Cass always wore jogging bras to work. They were practical in case she ended up chasing a suspect on foot, but their full coverage also hid the scar completely. As an added precaution, Cass never left more than the top two buttons on her blouse undone. But once in a physical relationship with Kado, she wouldn't be able to hide the scar, or the cause of it, from him. Lying about its source wasn't an option for Cass, and besides, she'd never be able to conjure up a plausible scenario for an accident that left such a deliberate mark. Bottom line: she wasn't ready for the level of vulnerability that a relationship would create.

Cass expelled a deep breath and knuckled her eye sockets. All of this was wasted energy. Whether Kado reciprocated her feelings or not, she wasn't about to step outside the perimeter of mental protection she had so carefully constructed. Her mind – and her body – would just have to accept that fact. She reached for the alarm and with a small groan that settled into a grin, set it for five o'clock.

———————

NEAR DOWNTOWN ARCADIA, KADO tossed and turned on the lumpy bed that folded out from his sofa. Despite a long shower, the smell of roasted meat and burned plastic still permeated the air around him. But that wasn't what was troubling him. Guilt tweaked his guts as he tried to recall Caroline's face and then gave in and glanced at the framed photo on his bedside table. And there she was, fully formed in his mind again. He closed his eyes. Since Cass's suspension, his dead wife had eased herself from his dreams, as if offering him the emotional space to go on living, but he clung to her. He struggled with the thought of releasing her but Cass occupied his waking thoughts and his dreams with more and more frequency, seeming to squeeze Caroline from his mind. At a primal level, Kado was terrified that he might forget her and all that their life together had meant. For if he could forget his beloved so easily, who was to say that he couldn't pass from this world and just as easily be forgotten? As if he had never existed.

Kado shook himself. This was part of the grieving process. Finding a way to move on after so much time and love was hard. But people did it. He would have to do it, or wither and die emotionally. And he wasn't prepared to go that route. Not without giving life another chance. He mentally apologized to Caroline and imagined her memory settling into the recesses of his mind, but to a place not so far removed from his consciousness that he couldn't recall her at a moment's notice. He tested his hypothesis, calling her smiling face forward and allowing it to ease back into its corner. Satisfied that Caroline was still within reach, he finally allowed that stupid grin to roll across his face.

Hearing Cass's voice over the phone tonight had stirred him in ways that he hadn't felt in ages. The jolt he got from seeing her outside the Franklin home had been downright dangerous given the circumstances. He craved the feel of her face beneath his fingers and the taste of her lips against his, and he had fought mightily to still that urge. He'd managed to keep his back to her while she worked on Martha and Joseph Franklin with Grey. Thankfully, his focus on the shooter's position in Deadwood Hollow kept his thoughts occupied while they were together in the woods.

But now, alone, he could replay the image of Cass as she stepped from the medical examiner's shower room, her red hair darkly wet, violet eyes troubled, creamy skin paler than normal. She was even leaner now, whether due to exercise or stress Kado couldn't tell. He was amazed at how badly he wanted this woman. To know her body, and her mind. The attraction was powerful and, he suspected, mutual. After living for more than a year in a state of frozen grief, he was thawing. The realization was frightening and exhilarating.

Thanks to the catastrophe of the compromised DNA from their last significant case, Kado's future was uncertain. But he wanted Cass as part of that future, and not just as a colleague.

Kado felt the pleasure of his smile again as sleep closed in, and the woman with fiery hair stepped into his dreams and touched her lips to his.

CHAPTER 20

THE SHOOTER PULLED THE pickup into the old barn that served as his garage and cut the engine. He sat in the truck's dim interior and listened to the engine tick, breathing quietly. After several moments, he flicked on the bank of fluorescent lights and ran a finger along the bumper. Thankfully, this truck was an older model, built when pickups were meant to last, and it bore the brunt of the encounter with little more than lost black paint and an added streak of burnt orange.

He checked his watch: two-thirty Thursday morning. Heaving a weary sigh, he took a can of black spray paint from a nearby shelf. With short, even strokes, he applied a thin layer of paint to the bumper, working steadily until the damage was covered. He removed the stolen license plate from the back of the vehicle, screwing the originals back in place and tightening the light bulb over the rear plate. Finally, he lifted the truck's bench seat on the special hinges he'd installed, removed his rifle case from the narrow compartment, and dropped the seat back into place. He left the barn, pulling a chain through the handles of the double doors and snapping a padlock closed.

The little farmhouse was dark. As was his custom, he walked its perimeter checking doors and windows before working a key into the old lock in the kitchen door. He'd found the place when he first came to Forney County several months ago to discover more about the unusual threesome that seemed to share his view of the world. The old house was in passable condition, with only a few soft spots in the floor and one corner of the ceiling where the roof leaked. The overstuffed furniture was dust-logged, and he'd taken each cushion outside and beat most of the dust out of it, reducing the powdery residue that could mar his black clothes. But he hadn't rented the place for its creature comforts. It served his purposes beautifully. Located on forty acres in a secluded section of the county, he could come and go without worrying about prying eyes. Although he was away at work for most of each day, the cameras he'd placed in strategic locations on the property revealed that with rare exception, the obese chick who drove the post office vehicle and the well-checkers who visited the gas well on the place were the only people who ventured out this way. He felt safe enough here to take the cameras down and leave only sensors on the doors and windows. The presence of expensive video equipment to protect a place as run down as this would raise more questions than he cared to answer.

The shooter checked that the curtains were drawn before turning on a lamp in the musty living room. He then pried a loose flagstone from the hearth and extracted his laptop. While the machine started up, he headed into the kitchen, lit a gas burner on the stove, and placed a kettle on the hotplate. A wry smile crossed his lips at the irony of his actions, and he opened a cupboard door and drew down a heavy ceramic mug and tin of instant decaf coffee. While he craved a caffeine kick, he would have to show up to work in only a few hours. Decaf it was. He poured boiling water over the dark crystals, added milk and three spoons of sugar, and stirred the tan liquid with quick flicks of his wrist.

Coffee made, he headed to the living room and started at the black cat grooming its whiskers against his laptop's screen. The cat seemed to have a mysterious portal that allowed it to appear and disappear inside the house. The shooter never knew when it — a supposed female given the name 'Sheba' on its tag — would turn up. Sheba never bothered him or begged. Instead, she watched with inscrutable golden eyes as he worked, showered, cooked. One minute she was there, the next gone. He had searched the house's exterior and found no way for the cat to enter. He supposed she must have a secret entrance through a hole in the attic or perhaps a tear in the mesh protecting the latticework over the crawl space. His only complaint was the shedding, but a quick swipe with a tape brush took care of that problem.

He shooed Sheba away. She stretched and hopped onto the couch, curling in on herself. He fired up his wireless internet access card and sat in the soft chair by the window, propping the laptop on a pillow in his lap to catch the faint satellite signal, then opened the GPS tracking program. Moses Franklin and Donna Moore's cars were right where he expected them to be – still parked at their houses. Although Moses and Moore were Satan's business now, he left the trackers active in case he decided to retrieve them. Emmet Hedder's truck, on the other hand, was moving. The shooter sipped his coffee and watched as the GPS system updated. Finally, the little dot stopped outside Arcadia's city limits. He jotted an address on a scrap of paper, then shut the computer down. He slipped the equipment into its hiding place and headed to bed, praying for deep sleep. The charade at work would start in a few hours, and the day wouldn't end until the evening's stalking and killing was complete. Although Emmet Hedder had no way to see him coming, the former Marine would be on high alert, adding a thrill to this chase. Through his weariness, the shooter smiled.

CHAPTER 21

THE SUN WAS ALREADY up as Joseph Franklin thanked the officer driving the patrol car and said that he wouldn't need protection any longer. When the driver protested, Joseph thanked him again and said that he would clear it with Sheriff Hoffner. The young officer looked doubtful but drove off, probably grateful to be released from baby-sitting duty.

Joseph stood on the sidewalk, feeling sweat pop out on his skin. He was wearing the same t-shirt, shorts, and tennis shoes he'd worn last night, clean from their run through the laundry at Porky and Stella's. Today, he needed to get into Moses' closet and figure out what a cop wore when he was off-duty. Something lightweight, hopefully. It was barely six o'clock and the temperature was already touching seventy-eight degrees. Considering that it was early May and technically still spring, things did not bode well for East Texas this summer.

As he looked at his mother's home, Joseph realized that the lawn needed mowing and her adored roses a good watering, and his heart ached. He trudged up the path to the porch and reached for the clipboard held out for him by the sweat-slicked patrol officer. He was a slight man, easily six inches shorter than Joseph, with fair skin, thinning hair, and a problem with acne. Joseph read his expression as a combination of pity and wariness. He'd probably heard how Joseph had blasted through the police perimeter to get inside the house last night and was wondering if the big man would give him problems today. Joseph looked down at the paper on the clipboard. It was a crime scene log with signatures in one column. He signed with his indecipherable scrawl, wondered briefly what Moses' signature looked like, and handed the clipboard back, realizing that his decision to be Moses could not be undone.

Here we go, Joseph thought. *The rubber meets the hot ol' road, boy, and we find out how well you knew your twin.*

He moved to lift the yellow tape wrapped around the front porch and the officer cleared his throat. "Sorry, Mojo, but I have to go in with you." He shrugged, the thin material of his summer uniform sighing with the motion. "Procedure."

Joseph lowered his gaze and caught sight of the officer's badge. Petchard. He rolled the name around silently and at last it registered in his memory. Officer Hugo Petchard had been the man allegedly working undercover to find child molesters that were part of a cult. The whole thing exploded just before Joseph arrived back in Arcadia, and the fallout was bad. Several people had died and the police department received serious flack from the regional and even the national media – until the next big story came along a couple of days later. Moses told Joseph that he wasn't sure the Sheriff would recover from all the negative publicity. He also confided that he didn't think Petchard's role in the whole affair held water, and he had actively stayed away from the younger officer to avoid becoming tainted with the man's stink.

"Let's get it over with," Joseph answered.

Petchard lifted the tape and moved aside, letting Joseph duck under first. Joseph's hand hovered for a moment before he grabbed the brass knob, twisted, and pushed past the stubborn spot in the door frame. The coppery smell of death stung as he drew his first breath inside the house, bringing involuntary tears to his eyes. He blinked them back and turned to Petchard. "I need to change clothes and pack some things. Is that okay?"

Petchard stepped into the entrance hall, flinched at the smell, and retreated to the porch. "I'll wait here. Give you some privacy."

The door closed, leaving Joseph alone in the dimly lit foyer. His memory of the previous night's events had morphed into a surrealist image of the violence that had torn his life apart. It tugged at him, pulling him silently across the small space and down the short hall.

Using only his fingertips, he pushed through the swinging door and stopped. From this position, looking straight across the kitchen, past the dining table and out the large window into the backyard, Joseph could imagine that nothing had changed. It was only when he focused his gaze that he spotted the small holes in the window, their stress fractures radiating outward like crazed rays from some aberrant sun.

He stepped inside and turned his head to take in the darkened pool of blood on the floor and the spatter covering the stove and wall. Someone had moved the kettle from the stovetop and a patch of white was visible; a void in the space behind the kettle and up onto the stove's control panel. The backsplash was covered with blood spray and bits of bone and tissue. He leaned closer and looked through the gore at the tiles. The head of his mother's beloved rooster was shattered and the bullet's impact had forced cracks into several surrounding tiles. A vision of his mother and Moses' lifeless bodies flashed across his brain. A surge of bile seared his esophagus and Joseph squeezed his eyes shut, swallowing convulsively until the bitter, burning taste receded. He stepped out of the kitchen, forcing images of them in life into his thoughts.

Joseph walked to his bedroom and opened the door. Everything was as he had left it when he went to play ball last night: his desk, its surface bare; cell phone, wallet, and his brother's car keys on the dresser by the window; bed crisply made and clothes folded on the seat of an old rocker in the corner. He grabbed the keys, phone, and wallet and slipped them into his pockets, then opened his closet to extract a duffel bag and clothes. A creak sounded from within the house and his massive hands, full of shirts, stopped, suspended over the duffel. An expression of surprise crossed his face. He was being Joseph.

But Joseph was dead.

In this hideous new reality, only Moses was alive.

He turned and glanced at his open bedroom door. No one. Quietly, he returned the clothes to their drawers and hangers, and put the duffel away. He placed the cell phone and wallet on his dresser, but kept the car keys since he had borrowed Moses' car yesterday, leaving Moses to use their mother's car. He walked across the hall to Moses' room. The light scent of his brother's cologne hit him as Joseph opened the door and he gave in to the rush of grief, stumbling forward and crumpling onto the unmade bed. Bracing his elbows on his knees, Joseph buried his face in his hands and let the hot tears burn a trail down his face.

Quick footsteps stopped at the open door.

"Oh," Petchard said, eyes wide as he took in Joseph's tear-stained face. "Sorry, man. I heard a noise. I'll, uh, go wait outside. Take your time."

As Petchard retreated, Joseph quieted his breathing. He lifted the tail of his t-shirt to wipe his nose and eyes and had to stifle a reluctant chuckle at the sight of his brother's room. In contrast to Joseph's tendencies toward utilitarianism, Moses' bedroom was always cluttered. The desktop was covered in papers, and a pile of clean clothes was heaped on a chair. The bed itself was a tangle of sheets. A forest of used coffee cups sprouted from the bedside table, and Joseph lifted a leather wallet gingerly from between them. His brother's grinning face stared at him from the driver's license, a sharp stab in the heart. The wallet held thirty-seven dollars and three blank checks from Moses' bank account. Plastic cards were slipped haphazardly into slots. Joseph extracted them and examined the little rectangles that represented his brother's financial life: health insurance; a blank card that must be an electronic key to the police station; grocery store loyalty card; his Forney County Police ID; one debit / ATM card from a local bank; and two credit cards from national banks. Joseph had hacked each in his time, and he wondered if his brother's account information had been compromised thanks to his nefarious activities. Too late to dwell on that now. He turned the cards over and smiled at Moses' signature; a meaningless scrawl, impressively similar to his own.

Business cards were packed in one end of Moses' wallet. Joseph tugged them free and spilled the pile onto the bed. He started to shuffle them together when a startled breath caught in his throat. He used one finger to pull a photo from the stack. It was a shot of Moses with a white woman unfamiliar to Joseph. She was small, very short, and thin. Petite, they called it. Her hair was dark and thick, her skin luminous and pale as the moon. The woman and Moses were standing side by side, their arms wrapped around each other. To this degree, the photo didn't surprise Joseph. Moses was the touchy-feely of the two brothers, hugging and patting freely, which was one reason people responded to him so easily. No, this proximity between the white woman and Moses wouldn't have caused him alarm if it hadn't been for the looks on their faces. They were gazing at one another, Moses looking down and the white woman looking up, their expressions intimate and full of joy.

"Oh, Moses," Joseph whispered. "What did you get into?"

CHAPTER 22

CASS PUSHED OPEN THE door to The Golden Gate Café and felt a physical wave of relief wash through her. Same mouth-watering smell of coffee and maple syrup. Same lawyers arguing at the same table in the same corner. Wallace and Wilbur Pettigrew almost motionless in their customary booth. A singer crooning bad country from the jukebox. Cass was in her regular uniform of button down blouse, Dockers, and cowboy boots, and her thick red hair was pulled back in a French twist. The only things missing were her gun and badge. She was exhausted from the physical labor of removing the kitchen cabinets yesterday, her late night working, and the early run this morning, but a small sigh of pleasure escaped her.

Almost all was right with the world.

Heads swiveled in her direction. She lifted her chin and, same as always, waved her folded newspaper at the lawyers and the Pettigrew brothers. The lawyers nodded in reply. Something that might've passed for a smile touched the weathered faces of the Pettigrew men.

She crossed the café and slipped into the burgundy vinyl booth she and Mitch had used so frequently over the years she was sure their butt-grooves were worn in the soft seats. It tugged at her heart to sit here alone, with no Mitch grinning at her, waiting for his double-helping of pancakes. But she opened the Dallas paper and spread it across the table as usual, skimming the crime reports. There was nothing that resembled the details of her rape six years ago. Quick footsteps sounded across the linoleum floor and Cass looked up with a smile that vanished when she realized that it wasn't Stan or Sally Overheart, the owners, who had come to take her order.

The woman who stood beside Cass's table was taller than Cass, close to six feet, and wore her dark hair short and her make-up skillfully applied. Her face was angular, her mouth wide, her painted lips full. Fine lines webbed from her tired eyes, but her aura was of youth. A soft blue scarf was tied at her neck and she sported jeans and a black shirt that exposed a narrow strip of creamy flat stomach.

"Oh," she said, stepping back from the table. Her voice was soft and husky. "I was expecting someone else."

Cass blanched at the thought that a stranger had appropriated her booth. "I haven't been in for a while, but I usually – I mean me and my partner, used to eat here in the mornings."

"The person I expected usually isn't in until later. But nobody sits here," she glanced around toward the kitchen, "maybe because it's so far in the back. So when I saw someone, I assumed it was my other customer coming in early." She lifted her order pad and smiled. "What can I get for you?"

Skinny Stan Overheart bustled from the kitchen carrying several plates. He placed them in front of the Pettigrew brothers, who pointed in Cass's direction. Stan turned with a jerk and twisted quickly between the flock of empty tables crowding the floor before sliding into the booth across from Cass and taking both of her hands in his. "How are you?"

"Hey Stan," Cass croaked, and her eyes burned with tears. She cracked a watery smile at the faded skull tattoo peeking from beneath the sleeve of Stan's Grateful Dead t-shirt, and the tiger rippling down his hairy forearm. Both felt like home. Cass pulled a napkin from the dispenser and blew her nose, struggling to loosen the knot in her throat and the tightness in her chest.

The waitress moved away to greet a new set of customers. Stan tossed his silvery ponytail over his shoulder, patted her hands, and sat back in the booth. "We've missed you," he said, motioning to his wife, Sally.

She bustled over with a tray of steaming coffee mugs and plopped two down on the table, then reached out a bony hand and stroked

Cass's cheek. "You haven't been in since that horrible business with those church people. Don't stay away so long next time, you hear?"

Cass nodded and reached for another napkin as Sally moved on to the table of new customers. "Don't know why I'm such a crybaby today. Sorry."

Stan snorted. "It's that jerk, Hoffner's fault. Anybody who's lived with so much uncertainty over the last six weeks, eight hours, and," he glanced at the clock over the cash register, "twenty-three minutes, give or take, is bound to be a little frayed around the edges."

She chuckled. "I thought I was the only one keeping count."

"It's not just me. You'd be surprised how many people are pissed that Hoffner's taken so long to bring you back. Is this your first day?"

"Yeah, but technically, I'm working for John Grey as a temp at the ME's office."

"Seriously?"

"Yup."

Stan grinned. "Stickin' it to the man. I can dig it."

Cass grinned back. Stan and Sally Overheart were aging hippies and loved nothing more than the chance to fight the establishment, especially in small ways. The country singer's voice died and the liquid bass line from Lou Reed's "Walk on the Wild Side" oozed from the jukebox.

"Did I ever tell you that Herbie Flowers is playing upright bass *and* bass guitar on this track?" Stan asked.

"I think you left that part out of my musical education."

"He overdubbed the bass guitar. It's brilliant, and so subtle." His eyes closed and his head bobbed in time until Reed started to sing. "Are you working the Franklin case?"

She nodded.

His eyes opened. "I saw it in the paper, and some officers who stopped in for coffee were talking about it. It's terrible. And that man at the gas station." He shuddered. "Was it as bad as it sounds?"

The phantom odor of burned flesh hit her nostrils along with an image of Whitehead's blackened, contorted body. "I imagine so."

"With all this going on, it's good that you're back." Stan patted her hand again. "I'll get you some breakfast. What do you want?"

"Fruit and yogurt. A little granola if Sally has any."

"You're too skinny," Stan stated, eyeing her. "You can have eggs, turkey bacon, nine-grain toast, and a whole wheat pancake." Cass started to protest but Stan held up a hand. "Sally's testing a new recipe, so you're obligated."

Cass stopped him as he slid from the booth. "Who's the chick?"

"Junie. We hired her when the media people were here after, well, you know."

"She's not from around here, is she?"

"Her driver's license said Tennessee. She's worked out pretty well."

The café's door opened and Kado, Martinez, and Truman walked in. All three looked as ragged as she felt and Cass struggled to keep her smile at only a quarter-megawatt when she realized that Kado's bleary grin was meant for her.

"Hey," Kado said, putting a copy of the Forney Cater down on the table as Cass refolded the Dallas paper. He scooted into the booth beside Truman.

Martinez sat beside Cass. "Where's your gun?"

"Seems that folks from the medical examiner's office don't carry."

A thoughtful expression crossed his face. "The image of John Grey and Porky Rivers carrying weapons is disturbing."

Junie appeared beside the table, coffee mugs and a full pot in hand. She looked at Cass with wide, dark eyes. "Stan got your order?"

Cass nodded.

"Anybody else?"

The men ordered and Kado unfolded the Forney Cater. "The Franklins and Calvin Whitehead made the front page," he said. Photographs of Joseph and Martha Franklin were above the fold and smiled out at them. Calvin Whitehead's death was reported at the bottom of the page, accompanied by an image of The Whitehead Store's forecourt swathed in crime scene tape.

"They have any details?" Martinez asked.

Kado and Truman scanned the articles. "Just speculation."

"Good. Hoffner's back today?"

"He told Cass he'd be back this afternoon."

Martinez twisted in the booth to look at Cass. "What did he say when he found out you're working for the ME's office?"

"He wasn't a happy bunny. Said he'd deal with me and Grey when he gets back today."

"Well, in case he blows a gasket and does something stupid like re-suspend you, we'd better get as much done this morning as possible." He flicked a glance across the table. "I need Kado out at Whitehead's store to dust for prints and figure out what to collect as evidence. Are you okay at the Franklin house by yourself?"

"No problem. Then I'll go to the station to start looking at Joseph's criminal records and Moses' case files to see if there's a connection from either angle."

Kado folded the paper, straightened from his slouched position, and said, "This is too much work for the four of us. Why don't we call Munk back from vacation?"

Motion at the table ceased.

CASS GLANCED AT TRUMAN, whose mouth gaped, and at Martinez, who glared at Kado. She placed a hand on Martinez's arm and said softly, "He doesn't know."

"How can he not know?" Martinez snapped.

"Carlos. He's only been here, what? Six or seven weeks? How *could* he know?"

"Know what?" Kado asked.

Martinez slumped against the booth. "You tell him."

She drew a deep breath and released it slowly. "Ernie Munk and his wife Gabrielle have a daughter."

"They *had* a daughter," Martinez muttered.

"As far as we know, they still do," Cass retorted. "She was snatched in 2003 while Ernie and Gaby were in Galveston at Gabrielle's family reunion."

Kado covered his mouth with one hand.

"The Galveston and Houston police responded quickly. They brought in tracker dogs, helicopters, issued an AMBER Alert, and put up road blocks all around the area. Munk and Gaby stayed for almost two months looking for her. Forney County cops joined them on their days off."

"Why couldn't they find her?" Kado asked.

"She was taken in the middle of a massive *Cinco de Mayo* celebration. Munk said there were literally thousands of people there, along with a carnival and all the usual beach-side stuff. They were waiting in line for an ice cream cone when his daughter, Angel, disappeared."

"My God."

"Every year they go back and stay for the two weeks around *Cinco de Mayo*."

"Looking for Angel?"

"He takes a photo of her at age three, and an age progressed image estimating what she would look like this year. He, Gaby, and her family put up posters all over the area. His sister Evelyn Grove, and her husband and the twins, they go some years, too. Angel's in the national missing kids database and in Texas' DNA database."

"No sightings?"

"Nothing that has panned out."

Kado sat back as Stan brought their plates to the booth. "I can't think of anything more terrible for parents to deal with."

"Talking about Ernie Munk's daughter?" Stan asked.

Cass nodded.

"We'd only been here a few years when she disappeared. I've never seen a man so utterly destroyed. He must be in Galveston now, right?"

"He should be back later this week."

"Good luck to him," Stan said, sliding the empty tray under his arm. "Anybody need anything else?"

They shook their heads and Stan hurried off. Kado slowly picked up a fork. "Does this have anything to do with why Munk isn't a detective?"

Martinez answered around a mouthful of pancake. "He'd make an excellent detective, but he won't even take the test. He's afraid that if she comes back to Arcadia and he's not out on the streets, he'll miss her."

"That explains why he won't consider coming to work with me in forensics, I guess," Kado said, smearing butter on toast. "I've asked him about it a couple of times. He never explained why he wasn't interested. Just said that he wouldn't be any good doing forensics full time."

"Maybe he doesn't like you, *hombre*," Martinez said.

"Maybe he isn't a detective," Kado countered, "because he doesn't want to be partnered with you."

"*Touché, mi amigo*," Martinez responded with a salute of his knife. "*Touché*."

Kado ate a bite of toast. "Back to the Franklins. Has Moses arrested anybody who would want revenge bad enough to kill him?"

"He's been involved in several big arrests," Martinez said. "He stopped that car that was packed with cocaine, remember?"

Cass chuckled. "That was sheer luck."

"Why?" Kado asked.

"They were Mexicans carrying drugs north. Somebody in the car got the munchies and they went through the Dairy Queen drive-thru off the Loop. Moses got them as they were coming out of the parking lot. One of their headlights was out."

"What gave him probable cause to search the vehicle?"

Martinez choked a laugh around a sip of coffee. "After they got ice cream, they sat in the parking lot toking up. When they rolled down the window, Moses got a beak full of *mota*."

"Pot and ice cream?" Kado shook his head. "Where are they now?"

"I don't know, but we'll find out. Who else?"

Cass snorted. "There's Rob Conroy. He'd sure have motive."

Truman's young face lit up. "I remember that."

Kado cupped his hands around a mug. His gray eyes were dark as storm clouds this morning, and Cass kicked herself for noticing. "What did he do?" he asked.

"Drugs again," Martinez announced, mopping egg yolk with toast. "Conroy has the distinction of being Forney County's first meth cooker. Unfortunately, he made the mistake of setting up shop in Deadwood Hollow."

"Behind the Franklin house?"

Martinez nodded. "It's not the most discreet place to cook, but lots of pushers hang out there because the vegetation is so thick and there's a warren of trails to move around on."

"Tell Kado what happened," Cass prodded.

A small smile crossed his lips. "Moses worked second shift and went for a run in the Hollow at about two o'clock. Conroy was shakin' and bakin'."

"All the chemicals go in a soda or juice bottle that gets shaken and then burped until the chemical reaction is complete," Kado said. "I processed some labs in Oklahoma. Cooking meth is a dangerous business, but shake and bake takes the risk of explosions to a new level."

"Conroy got caught because Moses smelled something like ammonia and went to investigate."

"Burping fumes?"

"Yup," Martinez said. "Conroy was in the middle of a juggling act. He had several soda bottles cooking, and he was hopping from one to the other, trying to keep up with the gas build-up in each."

A grin spread across Kado's face. "What did Moses do?"

"Pointed his gun at Conroy and told him to keep burping. Moses called for backup and they managed to neutralize the bottles."

"No explosions?"

"Nope," Martinez confirmed.

"Why didn't Rob Conroy run?" Cass asked. "I never understood that. Moses couldn't chase him. He would've had to stay and deal with the bottles or he'd have had multiple explosions on his hands."

"Moses snuck up behind him – if you can picture someone that big sneaking – and got close enough to put his gun to Conroy's head and tell him to keep moving. I think the thought of a big black man with a gun against his head scared the *mierda* out of Conroy. That's the way Sheriff Hoffner and Mitch found them. Moses and Conroy moving in a dance from bottle to bottle. Hoffner doubled over laughing from what I heard."

"I guess Conroy didn't know that Moses can barely hit the side of a barn at ten paces," Cass said.

"Or that he still had the safety on."

"Ouch," Kado said, grimacing.

"It all came out at trial when Conroy's lawyer tried to assert that Moses acted recklessly by holding the gun to Conroy's head."

"Where is Conroy now?"

"He should be in prison," Martinez said. "He got convicted on a first-degree felony for manufacturing meth with an intent to distribute, and was sentenced to twenty years plus a $10,000 fine."

"He could be out, Carlos," Cass said. "Moses arrested him about twelve years ago."

Martinez sipped his coffee. "That sounds right. Conroy had trouble early on in prison, but I heard he sorted himself out." He heaved a satisfied sigh. "If he was released, he could be in a residential treatment center, halfway house, or out walking around on parole."

"Do you think he'd be mad enough at Moses to try and kill him?" Truman asked.

Martinez shrugged. "Conroy is a classic blowhard – all hat, no cattle. The way Moses took him down embarrassed him in front of his boys."

"He had a distribution network?"

"He must've. There was too much product for him to deliver alone. But there was only one runner we were sure of."

Cass started to giggle.

Martinez tried to muster a stern expression. "It's not funny."

"It's natural selection," she protested, giggles dissolving into outright laughter.

"What happened?" Kado asked.

"I guess Darwin would be proud," Martinez conceded. "The morning after Conroy's arrest, we got a warrant to search his house, but before we could execute it –"

"The whole thing blew up," Cass gasped through her laughter.

Martinez grinned. "Conroy had money, which is part of what makes the whole thing so sad. He inherited the family home on the golf course when his parents were killed in an automobile accident."

"Along with a ton of insurance money from the company whose truck flattened them," Cass said, calmer as she wiped her nose with a napkin.

"It was a big place, an old one. Two stories, old-fashioned wood frame. Anyway, word got out about Conroy's arrest and one of his runners, a guy named Eddie Houston, decides to cook off the ingredients they've worked so hard to obtain. We're not sure what went wrong –"

"Oh, no," Kado said.

"Oh, yes," Cass told him, biting her lip to suppress more laughter.

"– but the house blew up as we were turning down the drive," Martinez said.

"You were there?" Kado asked.

"You bet. The front corner of the house blew off, windows, walls, front porch, everything, and the house started collapsing in on itself and burning. The fire trucks went out with us – we had all that hazmat gear, too – they managed to keep about a third of it from burning, but the house wasn't livable."

"They must've had quite the cooking operation. Did Houston live?"

"Long enough to tell us what a big *honcho* he was and that we could all go perform various physically impossible acts on ourselves before he'd give up his friends."

"Houston wasn't one of Arcadia's favorite sons, nor one of the brightest we've produced," Cass said. "And that, along with his trying to hurry the cooking up, probably caused the explosion."

"Conroy couldn't have been too happy about losing his house," Kado said.

Martinez swallowed a bite of pancake. "When Sheriff Hoffner interviewed him the night of the arrest, he kept going off on Moses. He was amped on some of his own product and threatened Moses. It was a lot of hot air and his lawyer told us to let him sleep it off." Martinez sipped his coffee. "So the sheriff did. The next day Conroy was hurting from withdrawal and couldn't keep his mouth shut."

"Did he threaten Moses again?" Kado asked.

"And everybody else he had contact with. I think he threatened his lawyer, too."

"Did anybody take it seriously?"

"The guy's a windbag."

"But now that he's out?"

Martinez rocked his head from side to side. "I don't see Conroy changing his personality in jail. Or growing the balls to kill a cop."

"Still, that's a pretty big grudge," Kado asked.

"True," Martinez agreed. "We'll find out where he is and go from there. Best case, he's still in the joint."

"Worst case," said Cass, "he's learned a whole new skill set from his fellow inmates."

Martinez took in the empty breakfast dishes and rubbed his hands together. "Okay people, *ándale*. Let's get these cases solved before Hoffner gets back and throws a monkey-wrench in the gears."

CHAPTER 23

THE TOMATO JUICE JUMPED in its plastic cup as the airplane shuddered through an area of turbulence. Sheriff Bill Hoffner dabbed a blood-red drop from the seatback tray, then drained the cup and placed it precisely in the middle of the small table. He folded the napkin to hide the stain and arranged it so that its edges neatly aligned with the tray's corners.

Leaning out of his seat and into the aisle, he glanced down the narrow passage toward the cockpit. The door was closed and although the logical part of his brain knew that this was a security measure, the part of him that needed control grumbled at his inability to see what was happening.

Of the many activities that Bill Hoffner hated, flying was up there at the top of the list. The thought that human beings could actually leave the ground, go hurtling through the air in a metal tube at some absurd speed, and return safely to the earth was sheer arrogance. This fear, based in a fundamental lack of logic in the whole process, had never kept him from flying. But no matter how many times he got on an airplane, at take-off and landing his fingers still dug into the arm rests separating him from his coach class neighbors, leaving neat little fingernail crescents in the cushioned material.

He shifted his long frame, searching for a comfortable position in the seat. The damn things were built for anorexic dwarfs, not for men over six feet tall and approaching one hundred and eighty pounds. Thankfully, the airplane was quiet, travelers drowsy despite the occasional bounce. The chatty stranger in the middle seat was dozing, her head nearing her shoulder, a clear strand of drool snaking from the corner of her mouth. The rambunctious child seated behind him had finally stopped kicking his seat when Hoffner turned around after take-off and stared. The little boy grew still in the heat of the older man's gaze and hadn't moved a muscle since. Another job well done.

It was satisfying, this ability to shut another human being down with just a look. Long before he reached his current age of fifty-eight, Hoffner had mastered the art of the glare. But it might have been the sheriff's appearance that caused the toddler's enthusiasm to wane. Bill Hoffner was a vulture of a man, eyes set close to a long, hooked nose, his snowy hair cropped short, Adam's apple hung high in a long neck. His thin lips were perpetually pursed and his bushy eyebrows drawn together, making him look as if he had tasted something foul. His icy blue eyes were bloodshot this morning, his features worn from sleeplessness. Since the call to Tom Kado's phone last night, Hoffner's mind had been alive, struggling to comprehend what three deaths in the span of one night would mean. Not for the victims or their families. Not for the little town of Arcadia or Forney County. But for himself, especially once the press showed up and latched on to him with its gnashing rows of pointed little teeth. And he had even bigger problems than the Franklin and Whitehead murders.

Alone and somewhat settled at 30,000 feet, Hoffner turned inward and thought. His youngest detective, Cass Elliot, had side-stepped her suspension and was working for the Medical Examiner's office. The moment he had received her application to join the department, he knew she would cause trouble. But he hired her for the sake of public relations and in a moment of weakness he attributed to his past with her mother. And having another woman officer on the force did demonstrate openness. She'd dogged him persistently for eighteen months until, with Detective Mitch Stone's encouragement, Hoffner finally promoted her to detective as Stone's partner.

Despite his initial assumptions about the cult shooting all those weeks ago, Cass's description of events had tied exactly to the evidence Kado collected at the scene. The debrief and subsequent Firearm Discharge Board review had gone without a hitch, concluding that Cass's actions demonstrated levelheadedness and sound judgment, surprising Hoffner. She saw a psychologist as required by department policy, and the shrink cleared her to return to work.

Sheriff Hoffner could have signed her back to work after receiving the psychologist's report, but one thing after another seemed to keep him from finalizing her file. Thanks to John Grey's actions last night, Hoffner had no choice but to put his John Hancock on the form that would return Cass to active duty. But he would drag the formality out as long as possible, ensuring that Grey and Elliot felt his wrath.

Hoffner rubbed his face with both hands and then nodded at the silent flight attendant who refilled his tomato juice. He sorted through all the leadership mumbo-jumbo they'd tried to fill him with this week to find a nugget that fit this situation. *Objectivity* sprang to mind, and he decided to give it a test ride. If he looked at the Cass problem objectively, the department needed her. They were seriously understaffed. And if what Cass had told him last night was accurate, the coming days would bring a storm of work and media attention. Murder was never easy. But working two murder scenes at the same time, with such limited staff, was nearly impossible. Hoffner would simply have to find a way to cope with her presence. Objectivity wins this one.

Satisfied that he'd made a decision, if not with the decision itself, Hoffner drained the tomato juice and squirmed in his seat, unable to avoid his biggest problem. All of this rumination over Elliot was a ploy to avoid addressing what was truly difficult about this trip back to Texas. Hoffner glanced again at the woman in the middle seat and confirmed that she was still asleep. Slowly, he pulled the folded letters in their clear plastic bags from his jacket pocket and spread them across the tray. They'd arrived, one a week, for the past four weeks. Each was brief, the individual letters that formed the words snipped from newspapers or magazines and glued to the page. They were in hand-lettered envelopes delivered by the United States Postal Service, and each escalated in intensity:

How well do you know Moses Franklin?
Where is Moses Franklin?
Why do you trust Moses Franklin?
Moses Franklin is not a nice man.

At first, Hoffner thought the letters were a joke. And then that they were an attempt to smear Franklin's name. But when he received the third letter, Hoffner wondered if this was something more than a nasty prank. At that point, he slid each into its own plastic evidence bag. The last letter arrived the previous Friday, just before Hoffner left for the retreat. He had avoided dealing with them, dodging the possibility that they represented an unsavory side to one of his preferred officers. But now, with Mojo's mother and brother murdered in a potential case of mistaken identity, Hoffner had to look into Moses Franklin's activities, if for no other reason than to protect the man from whoever had killed his family.

If his personality had held the capacity for guilt, Hoffner might have felt responsible for not acting sooner on these four letters. These four notices that something wasn't right with Moses Franklin. But the writer hadn't said that he wanted Hoffner to do anything about his concerns over Moses, and he – because the writer must be a he – hadn't added threats to his messages, as in: *You'd better do something about Moses, or else I will.* But Sheriff Bill Hoffner was not a man who questioned his own actions, certainly not when they could lead to something as distasteful as guilt.

He folded the plastic bags together and put them in his pocket, then leaned his head into the seatback and closed his eyes. He set his immensely logical brain to work, trying to find a way to investigate one of the department's favorite officers without setting his already frazzled force into an uproar.

Chapter 24

JOSEPH SHUFFLED THE BUSINESS cards together and shoved them, along with the photograph, into Moses' wallet. His heart was pounding and a sickly sweat slicked his forehead. If Moses was seeing a white woman, this opened a whole new world of possibilities in terms of murder suspects. A surge of anger shot through him: was it Moses and his colorblind pecker who had gotten their mother killed?

He yanked open the drawers on Moses' desk and rifled the clutter of paperwork they contained: ancient Christmas cards, 'thank you' notes from school kids, seemingly meaningless clippings from the Forney Cater, and at last, credit card bills and bank statements. He dug and found the most recent of each. Moses owed about fifteen hundred dollars on the two credit cards and had just over two thousand in the bank. Regular deposits totaling almost five thousand per month went into his account from the Forney County Sheriff's Office.

He snorted. *Not a bad chunk of change for a guy who gets to wear a gun and ride around in a car all day,* Joseph thought. *So where did all that money go?*

He looked at the account's debit history and remorse closed his throat. In addition to paying a hefty sum in alimony, Moses was making at least half of the mortgage payment on their mother's house, along with contributing to the other household bills. The account also reflected regular payments to a local pharmacy. Probably to cover the drugs his mother needed during her chemotherapy and radiation treatments.

A good guy, Moses. Joseph blinked back tears and shuffled the papers together. *Better than I've ever been.*

The closet door opened with a puff of Moses' cologne, and Joseph changed into a pair of his brother's jeans, a yellow polo shirt, and leather loafers. He found a duffel bag on a shelf and packed Moses' uniforms, work shoes, duty belt, work-out gear, and some casual clothes. He hesitated a moment before packing his brother's guns. One was silver and although he tugged at the bottom of the handle where the thing that held the bullets went, for the life of him, Joseph couldn't figure out how to open it to see if it was loaded. The other was a little black revolver and he could see the bullets' shiny butts in their housing. He also packed belt and ankle holsters and two boxes of each type of ammunition Moses kept in a drawer. This was one area where Joseph could seriously screw up at being Moses, and he thanked God that his brother was a marginal shot. Joseph had never fired a gun. Their heft and cool surfaces had a wicked feel that made the chicken skin of his testicles crawl, and he was relieved to stuff the guns in the duffel. He'd have to find somewhere remote and figure out how the things worked.

Moses' wallet went in his hip pocket. Two cell phones, identical in color and design, were on the dresser. One had a metal band with a serial number on the back, clearly a county phone. It had received no calls since early yesterday morning.

The other phone was off. Joseph pushed the power switch and saw the icon for voicemail flashing in one corner of the screen. He accessed the account and tapped in the first four digits of their shared birthday, snorting in frustrated amusement at his boneheaded brother when the password was accepted. "Call me, man. It's Wednesday, no, it's Thursday morning. Call me as soon as you get this."

A car's engine gunned behind the caller's strained voice and the message ended abruptly. Joseph looked at the phone's screen. No name, just a number. Prior to this last call, the phone's history showed outgoing calls, all to this same number. Incoming calls were from a different number, but from that number only. Moses had no mobile phone bills in the desk. Unease settled at the base of Joseph's skull and he flashed on the photograph of the white woman in Moses' wallet. This must be a burner, a pay-as-you-go phone. Not a good sign. His finger hovered over the send button, but Joseph wasn't sure if he was ready to deal with whatever hidden life this phone represented.

He turned the volume on both phones to vibrate and pocketed them. His mother's keys were on the dresser and Joseph slipped back across the hall, leaving them in his room. Checking the bathroom they shared, Joseph dropped his dirty clothes in the hamper and packed his toiletries.

Stepping back into his brother's bedroom, Joseph stopped short. An unopened box containing a new laptop was partially hidden between the desk and wall, a basketball balanced on top. The brothers had gone shopping this past weekend after Joseph demanded that Moses step into the modern world and connect to the internet. He promised that he would keep his hands off the laptop, but would help Moses learn at least the basics of functioning virtually.

His fingertips itched. The terms of his supervised release from prison stipulated that Joseph was banned from using a computer or the internet for the duration of his parole, plus a further three years. A local parole officer had come by the house twice to ensure Joseph was sticking to those terms. So far, he'd been clean. But abstinence was impossible. Physically impossible. Joseph had spent his adult life, short of two years and some months in prison, parked in front of a computer terminal.

But then he remembered.

Joseph was dead.

And Moses had no restrictions on his computer usage.

A smile flickered at the corners of Joseph's mouth. With a computer, checking out the possible suspects in his brother and mother's murders would be a piece of cake. There was nowhere Greasy Lou Spitano or the white woman in Moses' photograph could hide. Grasping the laptop box in one hand and his duffel in the other, Joseph left Moses' room with something resembling a spring in his step.

CHAPTER 25

KADO'S BRUSH WHISPERED OVER the handle of the pump and he frowned at the smeared, greasy mess the gray powder revealed beneath the gas station's harsh fluorescent lights. It was seven-thirty and the sun was up, but the tall trees that crowded the small station had its forecourt in twilight. He switched to black powder and moved to the keypad. Several usable prints appeared. Since the last gasoline sale at The Whitehead Store was for cash, this part of the exercise was probably futile, but Kado had rather be complete than criticized.

Martinez stood with his arms crossed across his massive chest and watched Kado work. His eyebrows rose as the forensics man dipped a brush in the pot of black powder and worked his way from side to side and up and down the pump's white plastic face. "What are you doing?"

"Dusting for prints."

"I get that part, smartass. Why are you wasting time on those?"

Kado stopped mid-twirl and looked at Martinez. "Pull that nozzle out of the pump I've already dusted."

"What?"

"Just do it."

Martinez moved to the next pump, lifted its handle and held it up.

"Pump."

"Into what?"

"Use your imagination."

He sighed, and then lowered the nozzle to an invisible gas tank. Flashing a smug smile, Martinez leaned toward the pump and placed his palm on its face. "Now what?"

"What are you doing?"

"Pumping pretend gas into a pretend tank."

"And where's your other hand?"

Martinez' grin vanished as he turned to look at his hand where it rested on the pump. He carefully replaced the nozzle. "I'll go see how Truman's getting on in the courtyard and stockroom. Carry on."

"*Gracias.* I will."

CHAPTER 26

THE OLD MAN STEPPED out of his work boots and into the kitchen, passing the basket of freshly washed eggs to his wife. She nudged them onto a counter and finished the call with her sister, hanging the phone up with a smirk. Humming the theme from *The Phantom of the Opera*, she placed a plate laden with fried eggs, bacon, and greasy fried potatoes on the table.

He poured coffee from the percolator. "Is she going to see it?"

His wife jellied toast, her lips pursed. "I told her how wonderful the show was. But it's sold out in Tyler. She'd have to go to Little Rock. It's a shame productions with the New York cast come through East Texas so infrequently," she said with a satisfied smile.

Into their seventies and still the one-upmanship continues, the old man thought.

"Thank you for taking me last night. I know it was late when we got home, but I so enjoyed it." She batted her eyes at him and he saw once again the sixteen year old girl who had captivated him. He melted a bit. He'd caught her when she was young enough to train and his judgment had been sound; she'd become the kind of wife any man would've been proud to possess — an excellent housekeeper and cook, sensitive but strict mother and grandmother, still trim and attractive, still obedient.

"You're welcome, sweetheart," he answered, and reached for the Forney Cater. The faces of two smiling black people stared up at him, and he scanned the accompanying article.

"Terrible tragedy," his wife commented. "The family of one of our very own police officers, murdered in their home."

The old man murmured a reply and unfolded the paper. An image of The Whitehead Store, its forecourt wrapped in crime scene tape, was in one corner. The old man's heart skipped a beat as he studied the picture and then read the article. Coffee sloshed into the saucer when he reached for his cup and his wife tutted as she mopped up the liquid. He barely heard her.

Fear rippled through his bowels. Calvin Whitehead was dead. Another member of The Church of the True Believer gone. The article didn't specify how he died, and the old man would have to dig to find out whether this was a one-off attack, or if The Church's remaining members were under threat. His mind flashed to Hitch, banished from Forney County those weeks ago, and he checked his watch. It was Thursday morning, a little after seven-thirty. His designated time to contact Hitch was fourteen hours away. Ample time to gather the information he needed.

He soothed his wife with a muttered apology and watched as she refilled his coffee and added cream, insisting on carrying the cup and saucer to the living room for him. She placed it on the small table beside his recliner and bustled from the room. The old man dug in his overall pocket and found his pipe. He placed it, cold and empty, between his teeth and let the sweet, sooty taste soothe him. Whitehead was a good man and didn't deserve a violent end. Not long ago, the call would've come directly to him shortly after Whitehead's body was found. He hated that his network had been disrupted, but resigned himself to making the calls. Rebuilding The Church was a slow process, but he was a patient man.

He settled into the recliner and retreated inside his mind; an ancient Venus flytrap, hinged jaws stretched wide, exuding sweet nectar to attract the resources he needed to protect his domain.

CHAPTER 27

CASS HOISTED THE FORENSICS case and stared at the man guarding the Franklin's front porch. Her skin crawled as she recognized Officer Hugo Petchard. He wore a brown short-sleeved uniform that fit his scrawny frame poorly, and his stance — hands on hips, feet spread wide, mirrored sunglasses perched high on his nose – was as defensive as she remembered. Anger boiled in her guts but she strode toward the house calmly, promising herself that she would behave, forcing a half smile to her lips.

He whipped the sunglasses from his face. "What are you doing here?"

"Working. What are you doing here?"

"Sheriff Hoffner hasn't signed you back on."

"I don't have a rich daddy to bribe the sheriff into giving me my job back."

Petchard's chin jutted forward. "Hoffner brought me back because he knows I didn't do anything wrong."

"Bullshit," Cass snapped, her vow of control evaporating. She took a step forward. "He brought you back because your doctor daddy funds his election campaign."

Petchard's pale face colored but he stood his ground. "Sounds like that suspension hasn't improved your language any."

"Sounds like your involvement with that cult hasn't made you any more observant. Heard you missed poor Iris Glenthorne's body three times."

"That wasn't my fault."

"How can it not be? You totally missed a decomposing body. Even the smell. All three times. And still the sheriff keeps you on."

"Yeah, well at least I don't shoot my fellow officers without provocation."

"I should've let him slice you open. We could fill your position with someone competent." He bristled but she spoke first. "When you're signing my payroll check, Hugo, I might be interested in what you think. Until then, you're just the monkey who guards empty houses." Cass held out the temporary ID Grey had printed for her. "I'm working for the Medical Examiner's office, and Grey loaned me to Kado. Where's the log?"

He snatched the clipboard from the porch. She squinted down at the signatures. "Moses has already been here?"

"Yeah, so what?"

"He left in his car?"

"Yeah," he repeated, his tone recalcitrant. "So what?"

"What did he take with him?"

"I don't know. A bag. A laptop box. I didn't search the man when he left."

"You should have, idiot," Cass said as she signed. "This is a crime scene. We need an inventory of what was here when the Franklins were shot."

Petchard's mouth dropped open to protest but Cass jammed the clipboard into his chest. She squinted at his cheek. "Are you wearing make-up now?"

He lifted a hand and wiped his face, looking with surprise at the powdery film and streak of rusty color on his fingers. "My girlfriend…"

"A girlfriend? Really? That shade of lipstick, raven red or whatever, doesn't suit you. You're more a baby pink kind of guy," Cass said. She moved past him to duck under the yellow crime scene tape and felt his eyes on her back as she reached for the doorknob. He remained silent as she put her shoulder into the stiff door and disappeared inside the house.

It took several moments for the coppery smell of drying blood to work its way through her mouth, nose, and sinuses to become a tolerable fug. Cass stood in the foyer, letting the echoes of last night's tragedy wash over her. The bodies were gone, the bustle of crime scene investigation stilled. But remnants of the violence visited upon this house still lingered. It would be some time before even human presence could exorcise these deaths.

She slipped on a pair of latex gloves, took a camera from the forensics case, and made shots of the foyer before squatting to examine a pair of massive tennis shoes. They were a size thirteen, the white leather spider-webbed with cracks, the tread so slick it was almost nonexistent. She hesitated, and then put them in an evidence bag and made a note to ask Mojo whether these were his shoes or Joseph's. It was possible that Joseph had been somewhere or run into someone who followed him home. A long shot, she knew, but it wouldn't take long to examine the shoes for trace evidence and eliminate them as a potential source of information.

The living room was decorated in soft earth tones with quilts folded over the back of a recliner and a couch. A curio cabinet displayed the boys' awards for both athletics and academics. Joseph's diploma from the local college was framed and stood on a shelf next to Moses' certificate from the police academy. Photographs of Martha Franklin and her sons at various ages dotted the white mantelpiece and the walls. Cass stepped closer to the fireplace and moved the frames around. An older photograph, yellowed with age, showed a young Martha Franklin looking down at twin toddlers hugging her legs. A handsome man stood next to her, his broad face smiling directly into the camera. Cass assumed this was Martha Franklin's first husband, a man who had died when the boys were young. She scooted the frames back to their original arrangement before moving to the hallway that led to the bedrooms.

The first door on the left was a small coat closet reeking of mothballs. The door almost opposite opened into a bathroom. From the contents of the medicine cabinet and the towels hanging to dry, it was shared by the Franklin men. The laundry basket held casual clothes and workout gear. If this was the outfit Moses had worn last night and presumably home today, he had also changed when he came home this morning. Another fact Petchard either failed to notice or to share with her. Cass photographed and bagged it all.

Moses' bedroom was through the second door on the right and Cass stood just inside, taking photographs. Reluctantly, she searched the disorganized room, smiling slightly at the faint smell of Moses' cologne when she opened the closet door. She found no evidence of his uniforms or work shoes, badge, or gun. His wallet, cell phone, and car keys were missing.

The room directly across the hall was Joseph's, and Cass was surprised at its neatness. His wallet, a cell phone, and a set of car keys were on a dresser. Cass checked the closet and the drawers in the dresser, bedside table, and small desk and found the paperwork relating to Joseph's release from prison in New York. She took it, the wallet, and the phone, with her.

The master bedroom was feminine without being overtly so, the furniture dark and heavy. Martha Franklin's dressing table was crowded with make-up and perfumes. A plastic box held an assortment of prescription bottles. Cass looked at their labels and found a variety of drugs used to manage the side effects of chemotherapy.

A heavy desk was in one corner. Its surface displayed only a mug holding pens and pencils, a large Bible, and another photograph of a young Martha with the same handsome man from the photo in the living room. They were standing together in front of a wood frame house, its white paint beginning to peel, their arms barely touching. Their eyes were bright and optimistic as they smiled at the camera.

Cass gasped as she tugged open the drawers. It seemed that Martha was something of a paperwork pack-rat. Tightly jammed folders were labeled in reverse chronological order. They went back years and contained all the paper required to live a modern life: utility bills, property tax receipts, a second mortgage on the house, records pertaining to automobile maintenance, receipts and warranties for major appliances, income tax forms, and bank statements. Cass skimmed these and saw regular deposits from two retirement accounts. All of the disbursements were via check, and she reviewed the images included on several statements, finding only payments to the expected places. The income tax records were for both Moses and Mrs. Franklin. They were self-prepared forms and varied little from one year to the next.

The bottom left drawer stuck when Cass pulled on it, refusing to open. She considered using a pocketknife to jimmy it, but decided the risk of damage was too great. Chances were it contained more meaningless paperwork. Cass debated: she could keep fighting this drawer, or get to the station and start digging into Moses' cases and Joseph's arrest.

Her phone rang. "Elliot."

"Cass, it's Carlos. I had one of the patrol officers check into the drug dealer's and Rob Conroy's status."

"Anything interesting?"

"The drug runners are still in prison. But Conroy is out."

"Since when?"

"About six weeks now. Do you have time to go see him? I can send Scott Truman to meet you."

Cass bent and tugged on the stuck drawer once more, then stood, decision made. "Give me the address. I'm on my way."

CHAPTER 28

CASS AND TRUMAN WALKED up the concrete steps and stood facing Rob Conroy's apartment. The teal paint on the door was peeling and the rubber welcome mat disintegrating. A rancid liquid oozed from a split in a bulging garbage bag.

"You sure this is it?" Truman asked. His uniform was sweat-stained. Cass didn't have the heart to tell the usually immaculate young officer that he stank of smoke and burned meat.

"Yup," Cass answered.

"Wow." Truman moved to the metal handrail, drew in a lungful of fresh air, and looked down at the scraggly patch of grass and sagging benches that passed for a courtyard. "It's kind of a step down from his mom and dad's place, isn't it?"

"Yup," Cass confirmed.

Truman took off his mirrored shades and eyed her. "You okay?"

She drew in a cautious breath and rolled her shoulders to fight the stress building in them. "I ran into Petchard at the Franklin house."

"He's out of the station?"

"Guarding the house."

"Guess his daddy's campaign contribution cleared the bank."

Cass suppressed a smile. "That's what I said."

"Sad, but true," Truman stated matter-of-factly. "He shouldn't be in uniform after the stunt he pulled, but money talks. The good news is that everybody knows why he's still on the force, that it has nothing to do with ability." He turned to face her. "And everybody is furious at Sheriff Hoffner for not bringing you back sooner, just so you know. We even sent him a petition demanding that he sign your release papers."

Cass examined Truman's face and found stiff resolve there. "You did?"

"Damn straight." Truman shrugged, the motion causing his tan uniform shirt to pull up from his trousers. He tucked it in and shrugged again, with less vehemence. "I don't know what he did with it, but I took it to him and told him that we had signatures from ninety-eight percent of the force."

She cleared her throat. "Ninety-eight?"

"We couldn't get to everybody who's off sick, and nobody cares what Petchard thinks."

Cass swallowed hard, grateful that she still had her shades on. "Thanks, Truman. I think that's about the nicest thing anybody's ever done for me."

"Nice had nothing to do with it. Everybody's tired of working so much overtime." He flashed a grin and nodded at the sad front door. "Ready?"

Cass knocked. A series of choking barks sounded from inside the apartment. "Sounds like a big one."

"It's probably a Chihuahua," Truman said, hazel eyes wide as he flipped the strap off his holster. "Try again."

Cass pounded on the door. "Conroy? Forney County police. Open up."

A chain scratched against the door and it opened a slit. A bleary eyeball peered out, and a pair of slathering jaws lunged at the opening from knee level. "What?"

"Rob Conroy?" Cass asked.

"What if it is?" he demanded in a slurred voice.

"Step outside, please. We have a few questions."

"About what?"

"Outside, please."

Conroy rolled the visible eye and slammed the door. The dog barked again, then yelped. The chain slipped and rattled and a man inched backwards through the door, poking at the dog to keep it inside. He wore only threadbare boxer shorts, ripped down the middle seam and bearing a brown stain. Cass winced at the hairless cheek that appeared when the fabric around the damaged seam fluttered, and took a short step back at the flash of pubic hair that greeted her when Rob Conroy turned to face them. He wore a grubby wife-beater that strained across his potbelly, and tufts of graying brown hair protruded from his armpits. Cass bit back a grimace at the stale scent of body odor that floated their way.

"What do you want?" Conroy demanded.

"Where were you last night?" Cass asked.

Conroy sucked at his teeth and ran both hands over his dark hair, combing it back from his face and around his ears. He was taller than Cass, perhaps two inches taller than her five feet ten inches. That jived with the height of the shooter the Grove twins had seen in Deadwood Hollow. "What time?"

"From six onwards. All night."

He looked Cass up and down, gaze stopping on her breasts. Truman shifted near the handrail and Conroy's gaze snapped to Cass's face. "I went to a NA meeting at six. No, six-thirty. Talked to my parole officer over coffee at eight-thirty." His teeth clicked as he talked and his eyes bobbed back and forth between her breasts and her face.

Cass resisted the urge to cross her arms over her chest. "After that?"

"Came back here. Had friends over."

"And?"

He stuck a grimy toe in the garbage bag and lifted it. More brown liquid dribbled from the slit. "Watched TV. Went to bed."

"What time did your friends leave?"

"Around eleven, I think. The news was over."

"Their names?"

Conroy's tongue flicked over his lips and he looked from Cass to Truman, who stood motionless near the handrail. "Who'd you say you are?"

"I'm Detective Elliot. That's Officer Truman."

"Why do you want to know who was here?"

Cass raised an eyebrow.

"I need an alibi? For what?"

"Names, Conroy."

Huffing, he ticked the names of three small-time hoods off on his fingers.

"That everybody?" Cass asked.

"Yes."

"Nobody stayed with you?"

"Overnight? Nope." Conroy rubbed at his nose with his forearm. "What's this about?"

"A shooting."

"Who got shot?"

"The shooting was at the Franklin house."

Conroy's face was blank for a moment, then recognition dawned. "That black cop who arrested me? Shit. I thought I might get a chance at him. But if he's dead, I'm not complaining." He picked at a fresh scab on his lip. "I'm surprised nobody's gone gunning for Hoffner. Lots of folks in the joint want a piece of him." Conroy giggled, exposing even rows of white teeth.

Cass realized that he'd probably developed meth mouth over his long period of drug abuse, and received dentures courtesy of the Texas taxpayer. A jailhouse fit explained the clacking when he talked. "Are you threatening the Sheriff, Conroy?"

"Me? Threaten a Do Right Boy?" Conroy shook his head once. "And it wasn't me who killed Franklin, but I sure wish it was. I woulda burned his house down, too. Cooked him to a crisp."

Cass sighed inwardly. They would check with the guy who ran the Narcotics Anonymous meetings and Conroy's parole officer. If his story checked out, Conroy couldn't have killed the Franklins. "What other weapons have you got in there?" Cass asked, lifting her chin at his front door.

Conroy crossed his arms over his skinny chest and Cass spotted old scars and a few newer sores. "I ain't got no weapons."

"That pit bull counts, Conroy. What else have you got? Guns, knives? Have you started using again?"

He swiped at his nose with his forearm and shook his head. "Are you crazy? Fat Frannie'll put me back in if she catches me with a gun."

Cass noted the absence of a denial on the drugs. "Fran Starkowsky is your parole officer?"

He nodded, picking at his forearms.

"You working?"

"Loading lumber every afternoon down at the True Value. Hopin' they'll give me more hours."

"Where's your ride?"

"Black Toyota pickup out in the parking lot."

Cass flipped her notebook closed. "We'll talk to Frannie and your NA buddies. Make sure the meeting chair knows we'll be calling. Let's hope it all checks out, Conroy, or you'll be making a repeat visit to our fine establishment downtown."

CHAPTER 29

CHEWIE RODRIGUEZ BACKED HIS zero-turn mower off the trailer and paused so his jaw could crack open in a wide yawn. He was tired but elated this morning after the birth of his niece the night before. He'd held her just after she was born, a fiery-faced bundle of indignation but healthy and whole – what more could an uncle want?

He aligned the mower for his first pass and his sleepy eyes narrowed at the slender stems of Bahia grass poking above the smooth, emerald carpet of St. Augustine in the front yard. Their presence in this otherwise immaculate lawn was an abomination, an inauspicious start to this otherwise pristine day, and Chewie knew just the chemical to restore order. He shut off the mower and carried a backpack sprayer and jug of weed killer to the garden hose attached to the house, measured and mixed, then hunched the backpack's straps over his shoulders, adjusted his wide-brimmed straw hat, and prepared to do battle.

Creeping through the two acres that surrounded the house, Chewie sprayed judiciously. Although this particular mix was effective at eradicating Bahia, it was expensive. As sole proprietor of his own lawn care and landscaping business, Chewie knew to the drop how much controlling this weed would cost him. And Miss Moore. His father, an exalted landscaper who had passed the family business, along with a love of vocabulary, down to Chewie, would be proud of his son's exacting methods of lawn maintenance.

He started at the property's north edge, near the stone wall, and slowly spiraled in toward the house, circling the flower beds and avoiding the root area of the small trees he had recently convinced Miss Moore to allow him to plant. Her yard was his masterpiece and he took periodic photographs for his website, as evidence of his horticultural prowess for prospective customers. To date, the work invested in Miss Moore's property had brought him three new customers who wanted a similar degree of care for their lawns and beds. At only nineteen, Chewie was already gaining a following. His one fear was the weather. Texas had been short of rain for some time now, and this summer was predicted to be the hottest and driest for nearly a century. His only weapon against such seemingly insurmountable odds was diligence, and he monitored the moisture levels in his lawns as carefully as his sister would watch her new baby's diet.

As he moved around the house and to the western section of the yard, Chewie stopped short. A slick of mud marred the lawn near the stone wall. He drew several deep breaths, counted to ten, and slipped the sprayer from his shoulders, balancing it carefully to ensure none of the liquid spilled. Chewie wished he could levitate as he walked gently across the St. Augustine, inspecting the muddy footsteps. A combination of gray and red clay from the freshly plowed field bordering Miss Moore's property. They drew a map the perpetrator had traveled toward the rear of the house.

A farm worker, he concluded. *Coming into the yard for a drink from the hose.*

Chewie clicked his tongue and walked carefully to the house to unreel the water hose and wash the muck away. It would take a very light spray to deal with the footprints close to the house, more water to deal with the sticky smear by the stone wall. But the heat was intense this morning. Nodding, Chewie decided the entire backyard would be dry by the time he was ready to mow.

A prickle of unease lifted the hairs on the back of his neck, and Chewie stopped, looking up suddenly. The west side of the house was still in shadows and he could see clearly into the bedroom through the tall windows, marred in one spot by a strangely beautiful star resembling a dandelion gone to seed. A mannequin lay in the unmade bed, red paint sprayed on the tufted silk headboard. A chill swept up his spine. Against his better judgment, Chewie stepped closer. He recognized Miss Moore's mass of dark hair spread across the pillow and his mind balked as he focused on the brilliant flower blooming in her forehead.

Vision drawing to a narrow point of light, Chewie Rodriguez dropped to his knees, crossed himself, and fumbled the cell phone from his pocket.

CHAPTER 30

THE OLD MAN ROUSED from his meditation and realized that his wife had refilled his coffee without his noticing. He lifted the cup with a steady hand and took a sip. Perching his glasses on his forehead, he pressed a speed dial number on his phone and inspected his fingernails.

"I thought we were in a total blackout," the man who answered said.

"Unless one of us is murdered, Mayor," the old man retorted. "Then I expect a call. What happened to Whitehead?"

Through the phone, he heard the bite of gravel under tires and the sliding home of a gear shift. "He was hung and burned to death," Mayor David Wayne Rusted answered, his voice brittle. "The police have no leads."

The old man sipped more coffee. "Is this something to do with The Church?"

"I have no idea. Hoffner is on his way back to Arcadia. He won't get in until this afternoon."

"It's just as well; he'll only be another barrier. We're out of resources in the police department, so you'll have to do some digging with his staff."

"Me? I have no business going over to the station side of the courthouse. I don't even have access to that wing."

The old man shook his head at his empty living room. "Then get it, David Wayne. You're Arcadia's mayor. You can go wherever you want."

A car door opened and slammed shut. "I suppose that's true. And Calvin Whitehead was a respected businessman in Forney County. It wouldn't be unusual that I would ask questions."

"It would not. Find out what you can this morning. We need to know if there's a threat to the rest of the members. They'll all have seen the Forney Cater and be wondering if they should take precautions."

"Fine. I'll get back to you."

The old man slipped the phone into his overalls and put the problem aside to focus on his cows. He pulled the cold pipe from its ashtray and slipped it between his teeth, then marched to the kitchen and his work boots waiting outside. Hell might be breaking loose in Forney County, but his cows still had to be fed.

CHAPTER 31

CASS SLIPPED THE TRUCK into park and watched the fat ginger cat as he stalked a chicken pecking her way across the lawn flanking Forney County's courthouse. Constructed in the late nineteenth century from cream-colored Texas sandstone, it was an utterly unique design. Part plantation home and part European castle, the courthouse had steep gables sporting tall windows and shutters. For practical reasons, the building had been modified over the years and two leggy additions splayed to either side of the main entrance, housing improved court facilities on one side and the police department's offices on the other. The lawn was carefully maintained; its grass mowed, shrubs trimmed, and trash collected by the inmates in the Forney County jail located just off the square. She'd been back twice since her suspension: once for the debriefing the morning after the shooting, and again almost a week later for the Firearm Discharge Board hearing. She'd felt like a pariah at the time, as though all eyes were watching her. Today felt no different, although the ginger cat and the courthouse's familiar façade gave her an odd sense of calm.

A hefty figure left its car and walked slowly up the path to the courthouse, stopping to turn and look at Cass as she shut the truck's door. She joined Arcadia's corpulent mayor, David Wayne Rusted, in the portico's shade, bags containing the personal effects she had taken from the Franklin house in her arms. "It's nice to see you, sir."

His smile was hesitant. "You too, Cass. I talked to the sheriff last night, and he told me Grey had hired you as a temp."

"Yes, sir. And kindly loaned me to the Forensic Examiner's office."

Mayor Rusted mopped his round face with a handkerchief and motioned Cass toward the courthouse's front door as a slim reporter rounded the building, paper and pen in hand. "We'd better go inside."

"I wondered when the press would show up. They're usually pretty quick when an officer or his family is killed," Cass said, welcoming the rush of cool air that met them as they pushed open the door.

"You didn't see the news this morning?"

"What happened?"

"Explosion at a gas plant in Watuga County."

"It's a terrible thing to say, but thank goodness for small favors."

Mayor Rusted chuckled, his smile genuine now. "I'm glad you're back, even as a temp." Rusted shifted, his eyes, small in the doughy expanse of his face, searching hers. "Did you visit The Whitehead Store last night?"

"No, sir, I didn't."

"So you don't know what happened to Calvin Whitehead?"

"I saw his body at the ME's office. It was a horrible way to die."

"Any leads? Any idea why someone would target Whitehead?"

She shook her head. "Detective Martinez is out at the store with Kado and Officer Truman. Maybe they'll find something this morning."

"In the sheriff's absence, keep me in the loop, would you Cass? Whitehead was a respected businessman, and I'd like to know what's happening with the investigation."

She nodded.

"And don't worry, I'm sure Hoffner will take care of your paperwork when he gets back from his sheriff's conference today."

He tossed her a wave and headed for his office. Cass felt her breakfast curdle. Hoffner would take care of her all right, she just wasn't sure how.

Cass turned and was met by a flurry of motion. Elaine, the courthouse's long-time receptionist, grabbed Cass in a hug and squeezed. "I'm so glad to see you," she said.

Cass studied the small woman. "You look gorgeous. What did you change?"

Elaine ran her fingers through her dark curly hair, cut at chin-length. "Cut and color from that new place out on the Loop."

"Which one?"

"Holy Rollers." She twisted her head to allow Cass a better look. "Those Pentecostal girls can do some hair."

"I like it. There's a little red in the color and it looks good on you."

Elaine smiled. "How are you?"

"Relieved to be working again."

"I can imagine. Sheriff Hoffner should have taken care of this ages ago." She took some of the bags from Cass's arms. "Do you need to get into the station?"

Cass nodded at the bags. "I've got evidence from the Franklin house for you to check in, too. Is that a problem?"

"Not as far as I'm concerned." She sat behind her desk. "I'll give you a temporary pass and issue a new one when Hoffner gets back."

"We're not using codes anymore?"

Elaine shook her head, curls swinging with the motion. "They've switched to key cards to keep track of who comes and goes. You have to swipe them to open secure doors from the inside and outside now."

Cass leaned against the counter while Elaine worked. "How've you been?"

"Me? Fine. Happy to see you, happy Hoffner was out of town, even if only for part of the week."

"Mayor Rusted said he was at a sheriff's conference."

Elaine laughed, bringing color to her heart-shaped face. "Is that what he's telling people? Hardly. Sheriff Bill Hoffner is getting remedial leadership training."

"He's getting what?"

"They call it leadership development, but let's get real. Hoffner doesn't have an iota of leadership ability in that lanky body of his. There's nothing to develop." She reached for the bags and signed the chain of custody paperwork. "You said this is from the Franklin case?"

"Yes."

"Any leads?"

"Not yet. Truman and I talked to Rob Conroy this morning, and I'm going to go through Mojo's reports to see if something pops out."

Elaine frowned. "They were after Mojo?"

"We don't know yet. Joseph was in jail up north, so maybe there's a link to his crime. I'll check out his records, too."

"I remember when he was arrested. Moses was devastated that his brother was doing something criminal. Hacking, right?"

Cass shrugged and took the white plastic rectangle from Elaine. "All that happened just as I joined the force out here. Have you seen Mojo this morning?"

"No. I don't expect him for a few days, do you?"

"Not really, but I need to talk to him about Joseph."

Elaine flipped to a different screen on her computer, wrote on a sticky note, and handed it to Cass as she reached for the phone vibrating on her desk. "Hey Chewie. I thought you were mowing on Friday."

Cass opened her own phone and dialed the number on the sticky note as she walked to the door that secured the police station. Moses answered on the first ring. "Franklin."

"Hey Mojo. This is Cass Elliot." She waved the card in front of the reader and heard a click as the lock slid back.

The phone was silent for a beat. "Hey, Cass. What can I do for you?"

"Listen, I'm sorry about what happened to Joseph and your mom. And I wish I didn't have to do this today, but I need to talk to you."

"I'm at the funeral home but I can call you later. At this number?"

"Yes. Thanks, Mojo. I'll be available when it's convenient for you."

Elaine caught her attention as she was stepping through the station's door. Cass waited as Elaine finished her conversation.

"That was Chewie Rodriguez," the receptionist explained. "Somebody shot Donna Moore."

Cass searched her memory for the name and came up with a feisty, petite woman who had an accounting office off the square. "Where is he?"

"At her house. The old Knutting place. He went to mow and found the body. I'll get somebody from patrol out there. Can you call Grey and Kado and go?"

Four murders in less than twenty-four hours. Worked by two detectives, one forensics man and a young, if very smart, patrol officer. There was no way they could get on top of it all.

"I wish Mitch was here." The words tumbled from her mouth before she could stop them and Cass felt a physical pain in her heart.

Elaine's smile was rueful. "Me too, honey. Me too."

CHAPTER 32

ROB CONROY STOPPED SHORT as the door to The Golden Gate opened. A woman rushed outside and almost bumped into him. He drifted out of her way, his hung-over head thudding with the movement. And then he got a look at her and the jackhammer beating against his skull slowed. *This definitely improves my morning,* Conroy thought, straightening and smiling. *She's a looker.*

"Oh," she said, dropping the letter she carried. "Sorry about that."

"No problemo," Conroy answered, savoring her silky voice. "Let me get that for you." He stooped, grabbed the envelope, and held it out to her.

"Would you mind dropping it in the box for me?" she asked, pointing behind him. "I'm in a terrible hurry."

"Be happy to. What's your name?"

She smiled and the breath whooshed from his body. "Junie. And yours?"

"Rob," he squeaked.

"Come in for a cup of coffee some time," she said, smiling over her shoulder. "It'll be on me."

"Definitely," Conroy whispered, watching as the door closed behind her. "And I'd like a piece of ass to go with that coffee. *A la mode.*"

CHAPTER 33

A RED DOT BOUNCING on the wall caught Cass's attention and she looked up from Donna Moore's body. Kado stood outside the bedroom, adjusting a laser pointer through the single hole in the window until he found the bullet's trajectory. He glanced over to speak to Truman, who was taking notes, and the two of them turned to follow the trail of muddy footprints across the backyard.

John Grey unfolded from his crouched position over Moore, slowly straightening to his full height of six feet eight inches. He stretched his arms out to his sides, rolled his head on his shoulders, and cracked a wide yawn. Cass glared, then gave in and yawned as well. She couldn't be too angry with him; the bags hanging under his bloodshot eyes told her that he hadn't slept much, if at all, last night. Even his dark hair, normally a natural quiff, was wilted. He checked his watch. "I'll let Porky sleep a few more hours. He didn't leave until four." He exhaled heavily. "I'm done with you for now, Cass, if you want to look at the rest of the house."

"I'd better go talk to Chewie. He's been incredibly patient."

Cass found the lawn care man in the same spot where he'd been when they first arrived. He had refused to tell them how he came to find Moore's body, and instead directed them to the backyard and her bedroom window. He also told them which rock in the front bed was fake and held the spare key. Chewie Rodriguez was talking on his cell phone when Cass approached.

"I've got to give a statement or something. Kiss her for me." He hung up and greeted Cass with a dreamy smile.

"Mr. Rodriguez? Are you okay?"

"I'm great." He motioned her to join him beneath the wide branches of a tree overhanging the county road.

"You just found a dead woman, Mr. Rodriguez. How can you be great?"

The smile slipped from his face. "You're right. My sister had a baby last night, and I was talking to my mom. She's taking care of the baby while my sister rests. What should I tell you?"

"How you came to find Mrs. Moore's body, please."

"Miss."

"Pardon?"

"Donna Moore never married. She was a Miss."

"And you worked for her?"

He nodded and proceeded to tell Cass about how he was on a search and destroy mission with regards to the Bahia when he spotted the abominable smears in the backyard, and then sensed that something was different about Moore's house.

"Different how?"

"This is usually a peaceful place. But when I was in the backyard, it felt sinister."

"You looked through the window and saw her body?"

"Yes, but not from very close. It took my mind a moment to process what I was seeing."

"And then?"

"I prayed. And called Elaine."

"Why not 911?"

Chewie shrugged. "I care for her lawn, too, and know that she works at the courthouse."

"What happened after you found the body?"

He pointed to where he sat. "I waited."

"You were on good terms with Miss Moore?"

"She gave me free rein with the landscaping and always paid on time. Even tipped me on holidays."

"How did she seem to you recently?"

"Fine." He cocked his head. "Happy, even."

"About what?"

"I never asked. But she was more relaxed lately. Perhaps over the last month or so. I wondered if she had a new boyfriend or if her business was doing exceptionally well."

"Do you know anyone who would want to hurt Miss Moore? Anyone who held a grudge against her?"

"No, but I really only talked to her about landscaping. I can't recall a time when she was upset or withdrawn, if that helps. She's always on an even keel, Miss Moore, very controlled. Maybe that's why the happiness was noticeable."

Cass thanked him and let him go. Truman and Kado joined her as she searched the house. The security system was sophisticated, with door and window contacts and infrared sensors in the rooms, all of it linked to a reputable security firm for monitoring. They found her purse, cell phone, and keys on the kitchen counter. Cass checked the phone but the register showed no incoming or outgoing calls since right before noon on Wednesday when Moore called The Coffee Shop. Presumably to order lunch. She bagged it all to take to the courthouse.

Throughout the house, original chunky oil paintings, watercolors, and contrasting charcoal sketches covered the walls. The paintings were abstracts of vivid oranges and reds. The sketches were interspersed between the paintings and contained impressionistic interpretations of objects that were fairly easy to identify: a pair of well-worn work boots; a set of keys on a ring lying next to a tuft of grass; a campfire with its burning logs disturbed. Each piece was signed by Moore.

A loaded 9 mm was in the nightstand, along with a box of ammunition and three full clips. They found a 20-gauge shotgun in the laundry room. Extra shells were in a cabinet above the dryer.

"As small as Donna Moore was, I'm surprised she didn't have an auto-loader," Truman said. He racked the shotgun and expelled six shells from the magazine. "Wouldn't have kicked as much."

"She could handle a 20-gauge," Cass said. "And she wouldn't have been able to rack a shell home with an auto-loader, would she? That sound, accompanied by a screaming woman, would terrify most criminals."

"Good point," Truman said.

Nothing in the house was disturbed, indicating that someone had come here specifically to kill Moore and was familiar enough with the home's layout to know the master bedroom faced the open field. The shooter had either been inside before, or close enough to peer through her bedroom window.

Kado helped Grey moved Moore's body into a bag and onto a stretcher, and then all four of them tugged the massive bed away from the wall. Cass watched as Kado cut the sheetrock away. The tail end of a slug protruded from a stud, mushroomed more than halfway back to its base. Kado carefully removed it. "Looks like another .308."

Cass turned to Truman. "Did you find any brass in the yard?"

"Nope."

"There was only one casing under the tree in Deadwood Hollow. How could he find his brass in the dark?"

"Flashlight?" Truman asked. "Brass catcher?"

"Maybe. Is this the same guy who shot Martha and Joseph Franklin?" she asked Kado.

"Seems a little strange that we'd have murders in two locations on one night from two different guys using the same type of ammunition, but I won't know for sure until I can compare the bullets."

"If they match..." Cass's statement trailed off as she considered the implications of one shooter killing three people.

"Your job gets easier. All you have to do is figure out who knew both families."

"And who would want them dead in one night."

CHAPTER 34

THE BLUE STARFISH STANDING sentinel on the pole by the highway was chipped and faded, a ghost of its former self. *Kind of like me*, Officer Ernie Munk thought as he sat on the edge of the motel's bed, trying to keep from touching the sticky bedspread. He was fresh from the shower and wrapped in a scratchy, tissue thin towel.

In truth, the whole place was crumbling: the parking lot dotted with potholes big enough to swallow a dump truck; the maroon carpet worn so thin in places he could see the dirty pad beneath; the baby blue tiles in the bathroom chipped, their grout grown black from years of mold. It seemed there wasn't enough bleach or anti-bacterial spray to eradicate the faint smell of rot and decay permeating these rooms. He supposed they were rented less frequently now that fancier hotels were sprouting near Galveston's shore.

But The Sapphire Starfish Inn was new when he and Gabrielle had picked it all those years ago, their choice of motel driven by Angel's fascination with aquatic life. At three, she had loved Dr. Seuss's "One fish, two fish, red fish, blue fish" and demanded that Daddy read the book over and over until she drifted into a dreamland inhabited by colorful sea creatures. Munk wished that this was the way he could remember Angel. Snuggled into crisp sheets, dark hair framing her face, brown eyes wide with expectation even though she whispered the rhyming words as Munk read them aloud.

Instead, his memory was seared with the sensations of losing Angel. The sun blistering his nearly bald head because, as usual, he'd forgotten to grab his hat when he and Angel left for the beach.

Friendly jostling as they waited with the crowds in line for ice cream, wrapped in the mouth-watering scent of baking waffle cones. Her beautiful face furrowed in concentration as she struggled to choose between vanilla and chocolate. The feel of her tiny left hand in his right.

Precious everyday sensations, a dulling prelude to the coming horror, that moment, that fraction of a second: his right hand releasing hers and reaching into his back pocket for his wallet and passing it to his left hand. His right hand reaching for hers again and finding only air.

Hand.
No hand.
Hand.
No hand.
Angel.
No Angel.

The sun, the smells, the pressure of her soft hand in his, the vacant space where her hand should be, they bored through his brain like a movie stuck in perpetual replay. With a background track that repeated "if only". If only Gabrielle had taken Angel for ice cream. If only Munk had used his left hand to fish for his wallet. If only he'd kept an eye on his daughter. *If only.* Munk threw his head back and fought the foul stream of bile that burned his throat at the agonizing truth of how he had lost his daughter. Their daughter.

The waking memories were a noxious cocktail of anger, guilt, and regret. But the nightmares were worse. In them, he couldn't control where his subconscious would take him. Or Angel.

Gabrielle, Munk's normally fastidious wife, insisted they stay at The Sapphire Starfish Inn every year, in the same room, regardless of how much the place had deteriorated since their last visit. And for those two weeks Gaby let all the emotions held so tightly in check during the other fifty weeks have their head. Munk adored his wife, loved her with a power that frightened him at times. Perhaps because he had failed her so desperately when he lost their only child. So he listened with patience as she explained her sad logic concerning this ghastly old motel – that if Angel were able, this is the one place in Galveston she would come to find her mommy and daddy. And for moments, Munk would stop the self-flagellation and allow himself to sip from the same waters, imagining his daughter as she would look at age eleven, picturing her smile as he opened the motel room's door at her soft knock.

Many of their friends wondered how much longer they could perform this charade. How long they could grasp the fraying thread of hope that allowed them to believe that Angel was alive and well. Given the depths of his love for his wife and daughter, Munk knew he would come here every year until he and Gaby were no longer physically able. He'd lost Angel once; abandoning her again was not a possibility. With that return of purpose, he sucked in a breath of tepid air and forced his mind to the present.

Munk peeled himself from the sticky bedspread and dressed in shorts and running shoes and tugged on the same t-shirt he was wearing when Angel disappeared. Once a brilliant school bus yellow, it was now a threadbare shade of watery sunlight that barely stretched over his belly, distorting the advertisement for Forney County's annual balloon race. He wore it every day they were in Galveston, washing it each night in the bathroom's chipped basin and hanging it on the crumbling patio. The shirt was stiff this morning from drying too fast in Galveston's oppressive heat, and it scratched as he pulled it on.

His heart leapt at a knock on the door, and he opened it to find one of Gaby's young nieces looking up at him, an open cell phone in her hand. "Hey Alicia," he said softly, fighting the lump of disappointment in his throat as he squatted on protesting knees. Munk reached out and tucked a strand of dark hair behind her ear. Tears stung his eyes at the smell of baby shampoo. "What's up?"

She pecked him on the cheek and held out the phone. "It's your sister, Miss Evelyn. Tia Gaby said to take the dirty clothes with you and stop by the breakfast buffet before you leave."

"Where am I going?" he asked, but Alicia had swirled and was headed down the sidewalk toward her father, who waited at the corner of the motel's main building. Her flip flops smacked the cracked concrete as she ran, her swimsuit cover-up flapping around her knobby knees. Munk watched her go, fear overriding the regret burbling in his gut. He raised the phone to his ear. "Evelyn? What's wrong?"

CHAPTER 35

THE HOUSE WAS UTTERLY still when Detective Martinez stepped over the front door's threshold and into Calvin Whitehead's living room. Already he perceived abandonment. It amazed him how the houses of the dead sensed that their owner's absence was permanent and responded with a commensurate drop in the creaks and groans that made them seem to live.

He moved through the rooms, his footsteps echoing hollowly on the floor supported by the old pier and beam structure. The small frame house showed no sign of disturbance, indicating that robbery was not a motive for Whitehead's killers. Martinez then went through each space more slowly, absorbing the personality of the man who called this sparsely furnished place home.

Calvin Whitehead was fastidious. The few items of furniture he owned were functional and well-maintained. A shotgun leaned against the wall behind the front door. The walls were bare except for the space over the mantle, which was adorned with a large cross made from – Martinez stepped closer – two pieces of charred wood fixed together with baling wire. He sniffed, surprised to inhale the relatively fresh scent of burned wood. Odd.

Other than the living room, the house had only one bath, two bedrooms, and a kitchen with space for a small dining table. Both the front and back porches were covered and screened. Martinez had spotted a metal storage building behind the house when he drove up and he noted several keys hanging from a hook in the kitchen. A .22 rifle rested in brackets above the door to the back porch, and Martinez spotted a 9 mm semi-automatic in its holster taped beneath the kitchen table. The cabinets contained mismatched dinnerware for two, an assortment of aged cooking equipment, and enough ammunition to eradicate the entire population of raccoons, squirrels, and possums roaming Texas.

Whitehead's bedroom closet housed work clothes: jeans, overalls, and shirts for both summer and winter. Several coats, their pockets empty, hung from the rail. Martinez also found three pairs of black polyester / cotton blend trousers and three white dress shirts, 'The Whitehead Store' embroidered over a pocket on each. Worn work and cowboy boots were arranged on the floor. The shelf above the clothes rail was packed with neatly stacked boxes of 12-gauge shotgun shells, .22-long cartridges, 9 mm ammunition, and .38 caliber rounds. He wondered where Whitehead kept the .38 and mentally added armadillos, deer, and hogs to the list of creatures Whitehead could stamp out.

The top drawers of the dresser held briefs and socks. The bottom drawers contained undershirts, pajamas, and sweaters. Martinez peered under the bed and lifted the mattress. Nothing. Not even dust bunnies. A Bible rested on the bedside table, along with a well-thumbed copy of Stephen King's *The Stand*. The narrow top drawer contained a box of tissues, a tube of hand lotion, a tidy stack of *Barely Legal* magazines, and there it was, a loaded .38 revolver.

Calvin Whitehead used the second bedroom as an office for both his personal business and that of the store. A metal desk and file cabinet occupied one wall. The desk surface contained only an old rotary phone. Its drawers housed precisely labeled files for the current year's bills: personal in the right-hand drawers, store in the left. The filing cabinet held paperwork covering the last seven years. Martinez was a high-energy man, and he considered plowing through paperwork – preparing or reviewing the stuff – worse punishment than processing the bloody scene of a knife fight. At least Whitehead only kept seven years worth of information.

"I have been a very good boy lately, haven't I?" the detective said to the silent house.

Two other walls were covered with shelves holding books on a wide variety of topics. Martinez looked closer at their spines. Fiction, astronomy, philosophy, business, and gardening. Many on religion and the occult. Two books lay face-up on a shelf: romances of the bodice-ripping variety, to judge by the covers.

Closet doors were closed over most of the fourth wall. Martinez opened them. The clothes rail and shelf were gone. Instead, the space was packed with cardboard boxes. He lifted one lid and groaned. "Maybe I haven't been as good as I thought."

CHAPTER 36

BERNIE WINTERBOTTOM STRAIGHTENED AS the door to the autopsy room opened. Instead of his customary khaki safari outfit, the Englishman was swathed in a pair of turquoise scrubs. Two huge eyes stared at Cass, the headband magnifier strapped over his unruly blond hair making the gold flecks in his green irises more pronounced. He pushed the visor back, stripped off the gloves, and reached for her. "Cass, my dear. How good to see you."

She caught her breath at the smell of charred flesh and strained to hear him over the death-rattle of the autopsy room's extractor fan. She hugged him, surprised at the surge of affection his English accent brought. "Hey Bernie. How have you been?"

"Very well, thank you. Grey tells me that you're on his payroll now. Although I understand that your appointment is only temporary."

"Unfortunately," Cass said, dipping her finger into an open jar of Vick's and smearing the translucent substance under her nose. "I expect it to last until Sheriff Hoffner gets back today. Then he'll probably fire me and try to fire Grey."

"Shame on the sheriff for putting you and Grey in this position. He has wasted your talent and the taxpayer's money by failing to return you to duty as soon as those gun people cleared the shooting. As I knew they would." He pottered to the table where Grey was stitching Donna Moore's Y-incision closed and peered at her brain where it rested on a small cart. "In the meantime, enjoy the dead. They're ever so much easier to work with than the living, my dear."

"That depends," Grey stated, pointing a scalpel at the burned corpse on Bernie's metal table. "Calvin Whitehead isn't an easy customer."

"True enough, although I am slowly teasing his secrets free." He leaned over to look at Moore's empty skull and the fragments of bone resting near her head. "Quite a bit of damage. The killer used a high-powered firearm?"

"Kado pulled a .308 slug from the wall behind her bed," Cass said.

Grey tied a knot and snipped a bit of twine. "Does it match the bullets used on the Franklins?"

"He's comparing them now. Did you find anything unusual in Moore's autopsy?"

"No. She was a healthy woman in her late forties. Had years of life left." Grey looked over his shoulder at the x-rays on the light box. "The bullet's exit shattered the skull. I took photos. Need anything else?"

"That should do."

"Her personal effects are on the counter."

Cass opened the paper bag. Moore's blue cotton nightgown was neatly folded. Her jewelry was in a plastic bag: diamond stud earrings and a necklace bearing a small gold cross. "Where did she go to church?"

"I wondered that, too," Grey said as he scooped Moore's intestines into a plastic bag.

Cass pointed to the extractor fan. "If that's for Whitehead, it's not working."

"It needs replacing, but there's no budget for it. Whitehead's smelling stronger today, but we're also autopsying the three dead men from this morning's explosion in Watuga County."

"Why doesn't their ME handle them?"

Grey shrugged. "He's been off sick for a couple of weeks now and we're helping out. It hasn't been bad until today."

"What came up in Calvin Whitehead's autopsy?"

Grey glanced at the forensic anthropologist, who had pulled on fresh gloves and was once again bent over the blackened body. "Ask Bernie. He's been muttering to himself all morning."

Cass reached for the Vick's again, refreshing the smear beneath her nose. "How do you stand the smell, Bernie?"

"It is vastly underrated, the olfactory system. One never knows what one might detect if the sense of smell is left unfettered."

"Has it detected anything related to Calvin Whitehead?"

Bernie straightened and scratched his nose with his forearm. "Not yet. But I have drawn some conclusions that might be useful." He indicated the burned section of Whitehead's head. "Notice anything?"

Cass leaned closer. "Goober said the zombie's mouth was on fire when he found the body, and the area around the mouth is significantly more burned than the rest of the face."

"Very good. Grey's autopsy found charring in the esophagus and lungs."

"What does that mean?"

"He drank an accelerant, probably gasoline, or had it forced down his throat," Grey answered quietly. He joined them and studied the man's torso. "It wasn't a lot, maybe a cup or so. The damage to his throat and lungs means that he was alive when he was set alight."

"Good Lord."

"And that means that this was a brutal killing," Bernie said. "Designed to inflict maximum pain. These burns are third degree." He indicated sections of the arms and torso where blackened skin had peeled away or split, revealing the underlying fat and muscle. "The damage to his legs is second."

Cass cleared her throat. "It makes sense that the fire was started after he was hanging, correct?"

"I suspect so. A burning body would be difficult to manipulate."

"If he was breathing when the fire started, the hanging didn't kill him."

"Correct." Bernie pointed to a narrow length of charred rope. "Kado will need to examine it, of course, but we don't believe that a hangman's noose was used."

"That matters?" Cass asked.

"It can," Grey answered. "Death by hanging can occur due to fracture of the upper cervical spine and damage to the spinal cord. For this type of injury to occur, great stress must be placed on the neck, as in falling or dropping from a reasonable height. A correctly tied hangman's noose is designed to add to the stress, snapping the neck."

"As in hanging for judicial purposes?"

"Yes. Another cause of death in hangings is cerebral hypoxia, which occurs when the supply of oxygen to the brain is reduced for an extended period of time."

"Similar to death by strangulation, right?"

Grey nodded. "In Whitehead's case, the spine itself shows little sign of trauma. Presumably, the noose was loose enough around his neck to allow him to dig his fingers beneath the rope and breathe for a short period of time, permitting the accelerant in his throat and lungs to ignite." He motioned to the corpse's burned hands, which were curled into claws.

"So he didn't fall when they hung him," Cass stated. "Or he didn't fall far enough to break his neck."

"Or," Bernie added, "his executioners hung him gently to ensure that he would be alive at the end of the rope long enough to experience the agony of being set alight."

Cass blinked. "Torture."

"If you also consider the swastika that was carved into his chest before he hung, yes, it would appear so."

"This was a calculated murder," she stated. "It wasn't driven by rage."

"A cold rage, perhaps, my dear," Bernie said, looking again at Calvin Whitehead's scorched scream. "Very, very cold."

CHAPTER 37

THE BREAKFAST CROWD WAS long gone and the lunch folks had yet to arrive when Joseph Franklin pushed open The Golden Gate Café's door, Moses' laptop in its original box tucked under his arm. He chose a booth with an electrical outlet nearby, sat facing the door, and rested in the stillness of the little diner. He recognized the sounds of The Kinks harmonizing on "Lola" coming from a jukebox in the corner, and Joseph could hear the soft sounds of silverware jangling from the kitchen. Each was surprisingly soothing after his visit to the funeral home.

In his wildest dreams Joseph had never imagined that he would make burial arrangements for his mother and brother. He'd maintained his composure while discussing details with the undertaker, gratefully accepting the public servant's discount on the cost of the caskets as he realized he had only the slightest idea about his mother and brother's finances. His own were in ruins. It was only when the other man had deftly nudged a box of tissues that Joseph realized his cheeks were wet. The undertaker stood, placing a cool, bony hand on his shoulder before leaving the room. Joseph had cried then, great tears sliding down his cheeks as he mashed his lips together and swallowed the sobs struggling to break free. Control eventually returned, and he found the men's room and splashed water on his face before driving back into town and finding a location with Wi-Fi.

If he wanted to impersonate Moses effectively, Joseph should have chosen to eat at The Coffee Shop, on the other side of the square. Moses ate breakfast there almost every morning; early if he was working the day shift, or a bit later if he was finishing a night shift. But Joseph needed the free internet access offered by The Golden Gate. Joseph glanced up as a woman stopped at his booth, order pad in hand. She was tall and attractive in a small-town sort of way.

She raised her eyes and began to speak, then slapped a hand over her open mouth and took a step back.

"Ma'am?" he asked, trying to remember that he was Moses Franklin, a Forney County police officer who would be polite and helpful, rather than offended that a white person was terrified by a black man.

"I - I'm sorry," she answered, face pale. "You were, I mean, I thought I saw your photo in the paper this morning."

"Me?"

Without breaking eye contact, she leaned into to the next booth and snagged a copy of the Forney Cater, holding it out to him. His mother and Moses stared up at him and Joseph caught his breath, then touched each face. They were good photographs, probably taken for the last edition of the church directory. He should've realized that the press would print the story today. "This is my brother, Joseph," he explained. "We're twins."

Her head lowered as if on a hinge to look at the paper. "And that's your mother?"

He nodded.

"I just saw the photos. I didn't read the article. I'm very sorry about what happened," she said slowly. "You – I mean, the police, they don't know who killed them?"

"No, ma'am. Not yet."

"Well, good luck," she said, and a blush swept over her cheeks. "I mean, I hope they catch whoever did it."

"Thanks. I do, too."

"Can I get you anything?"

"How's the coffee?"

"Pretty good. Stan gets it from Costa Rica. I'll make a fresh pot."

Joseph nodded and she stepped back again, still watching him. He ignored her and the urge to shudder at the sensation of her lingering gaze, extracted the laptop and its associated components from the box, plugged it in, and hit the power button. His mind went to work while the computer guided him through its set-up process. The first two steps were clear: connect with his cracker friends to learn if any information was available through the hacking grapevine, and find Greasy Lou Spitano. The crackers were accessible through various restricted boards and chat rooms around the internet and a bit of searching would be required. For Greasy Lou, he would start with search engine queries and review newspapers for references to the man. If neither of those options provided the information he needed, he would hack the governmental, law enforcement, and correctional systems in various jurisdictions.

His third step was finding the woman in Moses' photograph. She could prove challenging. He might need a scanner and access to facial recognition software. That would come later. Greasy Lou and the crackers were first.

The waitress returned with his coffee. "Cream?"

"No thanks."

"I'm Junie. Shout if you need a refill."

"Sure," he mumbled, but already the outside world was receding. A sensation of warmth and security, as if he were wrapped in the soft protection of the womb, filled him at the sight of an empty search engine. His spine tingled as he rubbed his lip and decided which site to visit first. His fingers danced over the keyboard.

At last, Joseph was back in his element.

CHAPTER 38

CASS SAT AT HER desk and unlocked its drawers, grateful to find that no one had appropriated her space. She had parked behind the courthouse to avoid the three reporters talking on the front lawn, relieved to see such a small contingent from the press. The attempted murder of a cop usually generated intense interest, but Cass was grateful for the small favor of the gas plant explosion, unwilling to be recognized as the woman who had killed a fellow officer only a few weeks ago. She'd experienced more than her fair share of press exposure since then. Her paranoia was in full swing; even walking across the station's parking lot, the small hairs on the back of her neck rippled with the sensation of someone watching.

She pushed a button on her computer and crossed the squad room to fill a coffee mug and doctor it with powdered cream. She returned to her desk, impatiently tapping the blotter as the machine stuttered and whirred to life. It was almost eleven and Cass's urgency to get some work done before Sheriff Hoffner returned was a knot in her stomach. The monstrous computer terminal glowed to life, and then dimmed. She smacked its side and the dark screen blinked back on as Truman, Kado, and Martinez entered the room. Kado flicked a glance at Cass, those gorgeous gray eyes momentarily meeting hers. She looked down and dug into a drawer, swallowing down the surge of heat that ran through her body.

"It didn't smell like gas to you?" Kado asked as he and Martinez wove through the maze of desks.

"No," Martinez said, "and so what if it did? He probably filled up his mom's car for her."

"Who are you talking about?" Cass asked.

"Joseph Franklin," Martinez answered. He hooked a thumb over his shoulder at the forensics man. "This yahoo thinks Joseph killed Whitehead. What a bonehead. He also thought Whitehead committed suicide by hanging himself and then striking a match."

Cass raised an eyebrow at Kado, who looked frazzled. "Before Porky spotted the swastika carved in Whitehead's chest, even Grey agreed that suicide was a possibility." He raised a hand at Martinez' attempted intrusion. "A remote possibility. Joseph's shoes have a red food substance in them and his clothes have some sort of chemical smell."

Martinez snorted. "To you, *hombre*. Not to me."

"We'll let Hazel figure it out."

Cass asked, "Who's Hazel?"

"The man names his machines," Martinez sighed.

"Hazel is a machine?" Cass asked, watching as a blush crept across Kado's ruddy cheeks.

He nodded. "A gas chromatograph mass spectrometer."

"In *your* lab?"

"I've added some equipment since you've been out. You'll have to stop by and see it."

"And you name it all?"

He shrugged. "Hazel is a little more personal than GCMS, don't you think?"

Cass glanced at Martinez. "It is."

"Well, it's not gasoline. So we waste precious time waiting for the machine –" Martinez began.

"Hazel," Kado interrupted.

Martinez glared. "– to do its job. Cass, did you make it over to the ME's office?"

The squad room door banged open to the sound of an indignant squawk. A pair of naked toes peeked around the door frame. The toes disappeared and then rammed the door as a leg in a full brace was thrust into view. A fresh howl sounded and Truman hurried across the room, smile wide. He stood aside as Darla Stone shoved her husband's wheelchair forward with a great huff. Truman took over, wheeling Mitch through the maze of desks.

"Meet 'She Who Must Be Obeyed'," Mitch complained as Truman positioned the wheelchair alongside Cass's desk. She stood and then leaned down to hug him, surprised at how thin his shoulders felt.

"He's been whining to come back since he heard about the shooting at Mojo's on the scanner last night," the attractive, dark-haired woman told them.

"She made me go to physical therapy first," Mitch groused, and Cass gloried in the sound of his voice.

Darla darted into the hall and carried a pair of crutches as she returned. She leaned them against a nearby desk and hugged Cass. "He's not as helpless as he looks. And your homicide statistics will increase if you don't find him some work. Soon," she said, arching an eyebrow. "I'll plead insanity. He's driving me mad."

Mitch sniffed, picking at the fraying cotton where his cut jeans touched the brace riding high on his thigh. "I was injured in the line of duty, woman. I can't help it if my recuperation is lengthy."

"I'll pick him up when he stops obsessing over the mating patterns of the cardinals in our backyard. Not a minute before," she stated, eyeing Kado, Truman, Martinez, and Cass. "Until then, he's your problem."

"We'll put him in the slammer if he doesn't shape up by the end of the day," Kado replied.

She winked at Cass and turned on her heel, leaving the citrusy scent of her perfume in her wake. Mitch watched her go, a woeful expression on his face. It was over four weeks since Cass had seen her partner and it was a shock to realize how much she had missed him. She had stayed away from the hospital after they knew that Mitch would live, simply to avoid the hassle that Hoffner would heap on them if he knew she had violated his orders to stay away until she was back at work. Mitch had always been slim, but there was a leanness to him now that spoke of the severity of his injuries and how hard he still struggled to recover. She wondered if he ever would, fully.

"Eighteen years of marriage and this is how she treats me?" Mitch asked.

"Cardinals?" Kado asked.

Mitch shook the hands of the officers who came to greet him. "I tried watching Jerry Springer, but those folks are really scary."

"A little too close to some of the gems in Forney County?" Martinez asked.

"Way too close. Cardinals are nice. Nobody cares if they have all their teeth."

"How's the leg?" Truman asked, bringing Mitch a cup of coffee.

"Not bad," he admitted. "The last of the pins come out next week."

"How long's it been?" Kado asked.

"Fifteen days, nineteen hours and," he glanced at the squad room clock, "fourteen minutes since the last surgery. I appreciate the miracle of modern medicine and all, but I sure wish the stuff moved faster."

"They say the healing process takes longer the older you are," Cass said.

"I swear," Mitch breathed, "two women working me over. I'm not sure why I missed working with you, exactly."

"Me either," she grinned. "What did they say about your lung and the concussion?"

"They puffed the lung back up and it seems to work. Dr. Rambo said the concussion didn't do me any harm, but it didn't help anything, either."

"Thank goodness there's no brain damage. We can work around your existing shortcomings."

Mitch rolled his eyes. "When did Hoffner sign your paperwork?"

"John Grey hired me last night to help with the Franklin investigation."

"Sneaky ol' Grey. Where's Hoffner?"

"A sheriff's conference," Kado answered, and Cass chose not to correct him. "He should get here this afternoon. Did Dr. Rambo sign you off to come back to work?"

"Desk duty only, but I'll take what I can get."

Kado began filling Mitch in on the investigations as Martinez, Truman, and the officers drifted away. Reveling in the warm glow of having her partner back, Cass pulled a phone book from her desk and dialed the number for the local Narcotics Anonymous fellowship to ask about Rob Conroy's alibi for the night before. As promised, Conroy had called and given permission for the NA meeting's chair to talk to Cass. Her concentration failed halfway through the conversation when a colossal figure swept into the squad room to a salvo of catcalls and whistles. A wide smile spread across the woman's face as she leaned down to encase Mitch in a hug. His head was crushed against an immense breast and he looked at Cass from beneath a wobbling ham-hock of an upper arm, his eyes pleading. She quickly thanked the NA contact and, with some trepidation, walked around her desk to rescue Mitch.

"Frannie?" she asked.

A tornado of crimson burst into motion, releasing Mitch, rising and swirling with outstretched arms to sweep Cass into her embrace. Cass found her face mashed nose first against Fran's mono-bosom and managed to turn her head and suck in a gasp of Elizabeth Arden's Red Door perfume before Fran squeezed her in a rib-crushing hug. Cass squeezed back, as well as she was able, and started the process of extricating herself from this mountain of a woman.

"Cassie!" Fran Starkowsky at last exclaimed. "I can't tell you how glad I am to see you and Mitch back at work. Although you're a little thin, honey," she said, looking Cass up and down. She turned to Mitch. "And you. When are you gonna get that wimpy thing off your leg and do some proper work?"

Mitch started to stutter an answer when Cass interrupted him.

"We're both glad to be back, Fran. You look," she paused for only a fraction of a second, "absolutely stunning, as usual."

Fran beamed and twirled, sending a tidal wave of sparkling blood-colored fabric whooshing through the air. The breeze ruffled Cass's hair. "I made it myself. Sewed all the crystals by hand."

"It's really nice. What brings you to the station?"

"You called about my favorite jailbird, doll. What else?" Fran Starkowsky was one of two parole officers in Forney County. Her age was quite literally a mystery; she refused to fill in birth information on any government form, and although she could've been anywhere from mid-thirties to late-fifties, Cass put her at around forty-five. Ranging close to six feet five inches tall – although in spiked heels her true height was anyone's guess – and carrying nigh on three hundred pounds on her frame, Fran always managed to move with grace. Her skin, smooth as a baby's and with the warm red tones of teak, was always beautiful. Today, her close-cropped hair was jet black. "You saw Robbie?"

"Earlier this morning."

Fran waved a hand the size of a porterhouse steak. It was tipped with talon-like nails the same color as her outfit. They sparkled as they rippled through the air. "Morning isn't playing fair, Cassie. I'm only out before the crack of noon because it was you who called. Tweaking, was he?"

"I think so, but he's not in deep. His skin still looks pretty good, but he was picking at his arms and twitching a bit."

One long red nail tapped a dangerous rhythm on Mitch's desk. "If he's using again, I'll lock him down in rehab so fast it'll knock the blow right out of his sinuses. Your message said you thought he might be involved in this nasty Franklin business?"

"I checked his alibi with the NA chair. Conroy attended the six-thirty meeting last night, but he left early. The chair doesn't remember exactly when he left."

"Why's that? They're supposed to keep an eye on these folks."

"Some sort of tussle broke out between attendees."

Fran raised a pencil-thin eyebrow. "Robbie involved?"

"No, but they think that's when he slipped out." Cass explained about someone leaving Deadwood Hollow in a hurry and hitting the Grove boys' orange Vega.

"Robbie's ride is a heap, doll. It's amazing the thing still runs."

"Scott Truman and I checked it over this morning but the bumper is in such bad shape I couldn't tell if he'd hit anything."

"So the truck doesn't rule him in or out?"

"Correct. But Conroy also said he talked to you over coffee last night. Did you see him?"

The other eyebrow joined the first near Fran's hairline. "Now that's truly creative. Robbie might've been having coffee when he called and left a message on voicemail, but I did not speak to him."

"What time did he call?"

She extracted a bejeweled cell phone from the depths of her garment and tapped with a talon. "Nine o'clock on the dot. Gives him time to do the deed?"

"Theoretically. But Kado said Mrs. Franklin and Joseph were killed with a rifle from about a hundred yards away. If he's using, it's doubtful he could be that accurate," Mitch said.

"There were lots of guns in his family home when it burned, and he knows how to handle a weapon. I'll swing by and check on Robbie today," Fran said. "But I suspect he was partying with his friends last night. If so, it's off to rehab for our little friend."

"Do you want to take Animal Control to help with the dog?" Cass asked.

The phone disappeared into Fran's outfit and her hand reappeared, clutching a set of car keys. "Rosie? She's a pussycat."

"The pit bull?"

"She's a sweetheart in the right hands. If Robbie goes into rehab, I'll take her home and see if I can't find a new owner. Somewhere out in the country this time." She swiveled on a stiletto and sashayed toward the squad room door, speaking over her shoulder, "Thanks for calling, doll. I'll let you know what happens with dear Robbie."

Mitch and Cass watched her go, deflating a bit as Fran sucked all the air from the room. "Where does she keep the phone and keys? Do you think she has pockets in that thing?" Mitch asked.

Cass raised a hand to stop him. "Don't ask me to think about what goes on in Frannie's clothes. I can't afford the therapy."

Truman and Martinez approached, steps wary. "How was Frannie?" Martinez asked.

"Wuss," Mitch said.

"*Amigo*, it's personal safety. I think she cracked a rib last time she hugged me."

"Did she say anything about Rob Conroy?" Truman asked.

Cass filled them in on Conroy's activities the night before.

"He lied to us," Truman stated.

"If Robbie disappeared from his NA meeting last night, he could've driven to Deadwood Hollow and set up in time to kill the Franklins," Mitch said. He looked around the squad room, as if suddenly aware that something was missing. "Carlos, where's your partner?"

"Danny's still out with his back," Martinez answered.

"So it's just y'all? Well no wonder the bad guys are busy. There ain't nobody around to stop 'em." His stomach rumbled. "I can't work without food. Anybody up for Chubby's? Dr. Rambo said something about my cholesterol and Darla's like a rabid guard dog now. I haven't had a chocolate shake in weeks."

Truman snagged a piece of paper and took orders.

"Sheriff Hoffner's no more than four hours out. Every minute counts," Martinez told him. "Pull your badge to get to the head of the line at Chubby's. If anybody gives you grief, arrest them for obstructing an investigation."

Chapter 39

EMMET HEDDER ROLLED ONTO his injured shoulder and groaned. The searing pain brought him instantly awake, and he hacked out a cough, throat dry from breathing the arid stream from the motel room's air conditioner. His eyes were stuck closed with the crusty residue of sleep, and he massaged them to help his eyelids peel open. Edging himself to an upright position, he craned his neck to check his right shoulder. Only a narrow streak of blood had worked its way through the gauze, leaving a rusty brown smear on its surface.

Emmet worked his way to the edge of the bed and lowered his feet to the floor, one at a time. The room spun and he waited for the merry-go-round to slow before he leaned down and snagged his duffel bag with his good hand. Digging inside, he found a digital thermometer and slid it beneath his tongue, waiting in a sleepy daze until the final beeps sounded.

"Shit," he whispered. One-oh-one point seven. Not bad, but not good, either. Emmet stood, swayed, and then inched to the bathroom. After relieving himself, he leaned toward the mirror and peeled the gauze away. A gaping valley of flesh was revealed, fresh blood oozing from it depths. Deeper than a graze but less than a full puncture, its edges were an angry red; an infection was building. He had doused it in alcohol and smeared antibiotic ointment across the exposed flesh before taping the gauze in place last night. Apparently, that wasn't enough. He needed stitches and antibiotics.

After fleeing his home, Emmet had driven for over an hour, watching the headlights behind him for signs that he was being followed. He'd finally stopped at an anonymous motel on the outskirts of Arcadia, struggled out of the track suit he slept in and into jeans and a shirt in his truck, and rented a room for cash. If the clerk thought his request for a room at nearly three in the morning unusual, his face hadn't expressed it. After dressing the bullet wound, Emmet stripped and fell into a dreamless sleep.

He refreshed the bandage and poured water in the tiny coffee pot provided by the motel, slipped a sachet of grounds into the filter cup, and pressed the button to turn the machine on. The plastic packet that contained the coffee grounds was the right size to tape over the gauze, allowing Emmet to bathe without getting it wet. He stepped from the shower with more life in his eyes and rubbed himself dry with the rough towel before pouring a cup of coffee and padding back into the bedroom.

His shoulder was throbbing. Emmet dumped the contents of his duffel bag on the bed and pawed through the suture kits, spare magazines for his 9 mm, road maps, extra boxers and socks, a box of bandages, and the painkillers. He shook the bottle and smiled as he twisted the cap off. One left. He swallowed it with a slurp of coffee and scanned the mess on the bed: no antibiotics. There were none in the medical kit he kept in his truck, either. His wife, Celia, had thought she was developing a urinary tract infection a while back, and he had given her his spare bottle of pills.

Thoughts of his wife brought him back to last night, and he lifted his cup in a grateful toast to God that his wife had moved in with her mother. At least for one day, her absence was a blessing instead of a weeping abscess in his soul. Emmet found his phone and checked for messages. Nothing. He'd broken protocol and called Moses Franklin last night. To warn the man and to ask for help. It wasn't unusual that Moses didn't answer; they rarely carried the spare phones with them and only checked for messages periodically.

He hesitated, then pushed the button for the only number programmed into the phone and waited as it rang. He didn't expect Donna Moore to answer either, but he had to try.

A white triangle on the door mat caught his eye and Emmet recognized a corner of newspaper. He squatted gingerly, keeping his woozy head level, and pulled the Forney Cater under the door, hanging up on the still ringing cell phone. Emmet stared in horror at the faces smiling up at him from the front page and he fell on his butt with a thud. His heart leapt into a wild rhythm, slowing only after he'd read the caption beneath each, confirming that it was Joseph and not Moses who was dead. The article contained scant details; only that Martha and Joseph Franklin were killed in their home the night before and that the investigation was continuing. Emmet's eyes slid closed as a fistful of guilt hit him in the gut. Their deaths had to be related to his shooting. Had to be. They'd known for weeks that someone was after them. But who? And how had the shooter figured out what they were up to? They'd been so careful. He looked back down at the paper. No wonder Moses wasn't answering his phone. But the man needed to keep watch. The murders of his mother and Joseph weren't random. And Donna. She needed to be careful, as well.

Emmet opened his phone and slowly punched in the number for her office, fearing her reaction to his contacting her at work but desperate to warn her.

A wan voice answered on the third ring. "The Moore Agency."

"Can I speak to Miss Moore, please?"

A snuffled breath came through the phone. "I'm very sorry to tell you that Donna died last night."

"What?"

"Donna was killed last night."

"What happened?"

The man's voice broke. "I'm not sure. Her gardener called and said she'd been shot in her bed." He hesitated. "Who's calling, please? I'm sure I can help if you have a question."

"Thank you," Emmet whispered, and closed the phone.

Donna's killing made it definite. The Franklins' murders weren't random, and when the shooter realized that Moses was still alive, he'd come after both of them. Flattening the paper across the floor, Emmet read the short article at the bottom of the page and wondered if everything they'd achieved had been worth the price they were paying now.

The sound of wheels skimming the pavement brought his head up. He struggled to his feet, moved to the window, and peeled the curtain back. An elderly couple stepped from a station wagon and a black pickup cruised slowly past. Emmet lowered the curtain and eased to the bed, reaching for his clothes. He wasn't safe here. He wasn't safe anywhere.

And neither was Moses.

CHAPTER 40

JOSEPH WAS SO DEEP into his search that he sensed, rather than heard, the phone vibrating on the table beside him. It was Moses' personal phone and a glance at the number told him it was the same person who had left a message last night. He reached to answer it, then realized someone was refilling his coffee and he hit the 'ignore' button. He glanced up to see a skinny man holding a coffee pot. The older man flipped a graying ponytail over his shoulder and crossed his arms over his narrow chest, tilting the pot to avoid a spill. Joseph thought back to the time before he left for New York, and to the few visits home he had made since then. Slowly, it came to him.

A small town scandal over the tattoos and long hair; avoidance because this man and his wife came from San Francisco, the epicenter of hippiedom and homosexuality; suspicion over vegetarian entrees and the liberal use of oats and sprouts in the recipes. And then a slow thaw thanks to wholesome food, music with no violent lyrics, and a safe place for kids to hang out on the weekends. The man watching him owned The Golden Gate Café and was in an excellent position to note the addition of new faces to the community and hear gossip.

Moses, Joseph thought. *I am Moses.*

"Hey Stan," he said with a measure of wariness that he hoped the other man would perceive as weariness.

"Hey Mojo. I sure am sorry about your mom and Joseph."

He nodded. "Thanks."

"Something like that should never happen. Let me know if there's anything I can do."

"As a matter of fact, have you noticed any strangers hanging around?"

"Lately?"

Joseph nodded. "In the past few weeks, let's say."

Stan frowned. "There was a gray-haired man who turned up a few weeks ago. Fit, works on a computer a lot. Keeps to himself. Grapevine has it that Sarah Henderson over at the bank picked him up at her last banker convention. Her husband doesn't know yet. Another fellow, kind of Marlboro-man looking with funny yellow eyes used to come in. That's one who looked dangerous, but I haven't seen him around in a while. You think somebody from out of town might've," he motioned to the Forney Cater, the faces of Joseph's mother and brother smiling up at them, "you know."

"It's a possibility."

"Of course. I'll check with Sally and see if anything else comes to mind."

Joseph watched Stan Overheart retreat to the kitchen and suppressed the urge to shudder. During his time in New York, he'd grown accustomed to the abruptness of strangers, the sensation of being invisible on the street because so few people made eye contact. And he'd relished that anonymity, especially once he started hacking. Now, back in Arcadia, the sensation that he was always being watched, that everyone knew his business, was creeping into his bones. True or not, he would have to tread carefully.

The phone vibrated again: a voice message was waiting. The same man's voice told him to lay low and asked him to call, urgently. Again, the caller used no names. Joseph hesitated a moment, then flipped the phone closed. A return call could wait.

The computer screen faded to sleep and Joseph tapped the touch pad. The web browser still held the information published by New York's criminal justice system. Turns out that Greasy Lou Spitano was easy to find. The man was pulling five years at Riker's Island for burglary. Spitano's sentence started about twenty-four months after Joseph's. Before getting into business with Spitano, Joseph had searched the man's online history and hired a private detective to research his tangible life. Joseph learned that Spitano was a small-time hood and conduit for stolen credit card details to the criminal world. Since no one had come to talk to him after Spitano was arrested, Joseph had to assume that either the authorities hadn't twigged to Spitano's nefarious credit card activities, or that Greasy Lou was mute about the source of the card databases he exploited. Barring parole, Joseph had several years before he had to worry about Spitano hitting the streets.

Although he had expected Greasy Lou to be simple to locate, Joseph was surprised at how quickly he found his cracker friends. The chat room they'd used before he'd gone to prison no longer existed, but the email account where each left messages for the others in the drafts folder was still functional. He dropped a short note about his legal status and asked if anyone was looking for him. Three responses came back in a matter of minutes. They knew he was out on parole and back in Texas, but no ripples about him were spreading across the internet. Each thanked him in their own way for not giving them up to shorten his sentence, and he accepted their appreciation with confirmation that he was out of the game for good now.

Joseph sat back in the booth and sipped his coffee, feeling relief slide through his veins and letting his logical brain work. It wasn't his criminal life that had led to the murders of his brother and mother. This meant that either the shootings were random, which Joseph doubted, or that something in Moses' life had gotten them both killed. He thought back over the past several weeks since he'd been back in Arcadia. There was nothing about Moses' behavior that suggested he was involved in anything illegal, or even untoward. Which left Moses' past. His divorce just before Joseph went to prison was ugly; but Joseph thought all divorces were difficult to some extent. To his knowledge, Moses' ex-wife was still in Houston. He checked online and found an address for her in Conroe. She'd never been a violent woman and had no reason to come after Moses or their mother. Her involvement in these deaths didn't make sense.

Joseph pushed her aside. His fingers hovered over the keyboard and he wondered where to start.

In the beginning, he realized, typing in a date. *From the first day that Moses was a cop.*

CHAPTER 41

"FILL ME IN," MITCH said, grabbing a box of fries. "Frannie interrupted Kado's story earlier."

They sat around the table in the dingy conference room, the odor of greasy burgers, onion rings, and the dust of decades worth of crumbling paper permeating the stale air. Mitch had maneuvered his wheelchair to the head of the table, sitting sideways so his leg didn't interfere with his ability to reach the food. While Truman made the run for burgers, two officers stacked the boxes from Calvin Whitehead's closet in a teetering pile that covered half of one wall. A knock sounded and at Mitch's call, Mayor David Wayne Rusted's bowling ball shaped head poked inside.

Mitch started. "Mayor? No offense, but this area is off limits to you."

"I know," he said, shifting his bulk through the door. "But in the sheriff's absence, I wanted to see how the investigations were going. Would it be all right if I joined you?"

Mitch glanced at the others, noted their wary expressions, then slowly nodded. "Please bear in mind that this information is extremely confidential."

"Of course," Mayor Rusted said, and joined them at the conference room table.

"Lunch?"

"No, thank you. I've already eaten."

Martinez cleared his throat and focused on Mitch. "You know about Calvin Whitehead?"

Mitch nodded as he chewed. "Anything new?"

Kado shook his head. "I'm running fingerprints from the store, and we'll work through the sludge from the storeroom and patio where he was killed. Those boxes," he motioned to the long stack, "are his business and personal records. Maybe we'll find motive there."

Mayor Rusted shifted slightly but remained silent.

Martinez spoke again. "How about Donna Moore?"

Mitch's mouth dropped open. "Donna's dead?"

"Last night. After the Franklins were killed. How did you know her?"

"She did our taxes," Mitch said. "She was the sweetest person I've ever met. Almost apologized when we had to pay the IRS one year. Who would want to kill her?"

"Whoever murdered the Franklins," Kado supplied. "The shooter used the same rifle on all of them. The slugs match."

"How are they connected?" Mitch asked.

Mayor Rusted's gaze darted between the speakers.

"We're just getting started," Cass said. "I've been through the Franklin house. Mrs. Franklin did her own taxes, and Moses does, too. So there's not a business link." She cocked her head to one side. "I didn't find any records for Joseph. I'll have to ask Moses about them."

Mayor Rusted's phone rang and he flushed, then apologized and stepped outside.

Mitch watched him leave and exhaled slowly. "That was weird." He turned back to Cass. "Have you talked to Moses?"

"I tried earlier, but he was at the funeral home. He said he would call later today. Kado and I went through Donna's house. I've got her purse and cell phone, but she must keep all her records at her office." Cass sighed. "Frankly, there's so much to do that I'm not sure what to prioritize. We need Donna's office and home phone records. I need to get into Mojo's files to see if anything or anyone pops out, and," she reached into her back pocket and pulled out the papers related to Joseph's release from prison, "look at Joseph's criminal records to see what his arrest in New York was all about."

"I'll do it," Mitch volunteered.

"Do what?"

"Files and records."

Cass frowned. "Mitch, that's paperwork."

"And computer work."

"You hate that stuff."

"I'd prefer to be sweating on a crime scene with y'all, but I'd rather handle paperwork than watch daytime TV." The conference room door swung open and Mitch didn't miss a beat. "And Munk can help me."

The room went silent as Officer Ernie Munk entered, his pockmarked face sunburned, peeling, and etched with weariness. He was dressed in wrinkled shorts, running shoes, and a faded yellow t-shirt that barely stretched across his protruding belly. Munk sat heavily and reached for a box of fries. "I'm starving."

Cass watched as Munk chewed and studied the stack of boxes in the corner. She pushed a cup dotted with condensation toward him. "Want my shake? I haven't started it."

He slipped the top off and slurped.

She bit her lip. "You're not due back until Friday."

"My sister called this morning. Evelyn. She said somebody tried to kill Moses Franklin."

"We're not sure who the shooter was after, but he killed Mrs. Franklin and Joseph. Did Gabrielle come home with you?"

He drew a deep breath, pulled his gaze from the boxes, and motioned to Kado's burger, still in its wrapper. "You gonna eat all that, or can I have half?"

"Half is good with me."

Truman dug a knife from his uniform pocket and passed it to Munk, who stared at it. "Gabrielle is still in Galveston. She had my phone so she talked to Evelyn first, then demanded that I come home." He cut the burger in two, took a huge bite and chewed, then drank more shake. "She's always had a soft spot for Mojo. He took vacation to come and help us when… well, in 2003, and he's been back to Galveston with us a few times. Gaby's family is still there and they'll finish out the week."

"There was no sign of Angel?" Cass asked.

"Same as always. Lots of possible sightings, but nothing definite."

"I'm so sorry, Munk."

He nodded. "Me too. What's in the boxes?"

Chapter 42

THE OLD MAN SHUT his barn door and stood sweating in its shade while he filled and lit his pipe, waiting for Mayor Rusted to speak. The sweet scent of cherry tobacco wafted on the afternoon air and he puffed contentedly, listening to sounds coming through the handset. A door closed and he heard the mayor's breathy voice.

"There's no news."

"How can there not be any news? Whitehead has been dead for almost a day."

"They're working on the Franklin murders. And there was another killing last night. Donna Moore, the accountant. They think she was killed by the same person who shot the Franklins."

"Damn it. Have they pushed Whitehead's murder to the side?"

"No. They have all sorts of debris from the fire and fingerprints from the store to go through." Mayor Rusted's voice dropped to a whisper. "And paperwork. Boxes of it." He drew a quick breath. "I don't think Calvin would've kept anything damaging to The Church. He was too sharp for that."

"As Lenny Scarborough taught us, we can't trust what others will do." The pipe clacked against the old man's teeth. "There's no indication that Whitehead's death is the beginning of an attack against The Church?"

"So far, the police know nothing about why Whitehead was murdered, and in such a brutal fashion." The mayor grunted. "What now?"

"Stay on it. I want to know what's in those boxes as soon as the police do."

"That may be too late."

"I know," the old man said. "I'll see what I can do about getting in reinforcements."

CHAPTER 43

THE SPEEDOMETER'S NEEDLE DROPPED to eighty as Sheriff Bill Hoffner snapped his phone shut. The courthouse receptionist, Elaine, had confirmed that there were no reporters camped out on the front lawn and that calls about last night's murders had slowed dramatically; it seemed a minor miracle that a gas plant in Watuga County had chosen this morning to blow up. Not that Hoffner wasn't sympathetic, but he'd had more than his share of fun with the press lately. He mentally crossed his fingers that nobody would notice the slaughter going on in Forney County.

He took the split from Highway 80 to I-20 at Terrell, set the truck's cruise, and let his mind drift, blind to the wildflowers dying in the median from searing temperatures and lack of rain. Elaine had told him about Donna Moore and the match Kado found between the bullets used to kill the Franklins and Moore. A link between the families seemed remote unless Moore did the Franklin's taxes. He shook his head. Almost as remote as the chance that one killer would randomly shoot the members of two different families who lived across the county from each other on one night. If this wasn't some indiscriminate shooting spree, his detectives would have to dig deep to find a link between these people.

His detectives. What the hell were they up to?

According to Elaine, Cass Elliot was actively working the Franklin and Moore murders. Detective Carlos Martinez was investigating Calvin Whitehead's brutal killing and had pulled Officer Scott Truman off patrol. Mitch Stone was back at the station in a *wheelchair*, for God's sake. The mayor had wormed his way inside the station, telling Elaine that he needed an update in case the press came calling.

And before she signed off, Elaine told him that Officer Ernie Munk, who never ever *ever* worked these two weeks in May, had just walked across the courthouse foyer in a pair of shorts and a t-shirt, flapped his card at the reader, and headed straight into the station.

Good Lord, it was out of control. Thank God he'd gotten that early flight out of Billings this morning. He absently patted the letters about Moses Franklin in his coat pocket. If things kept moving at this pace, the whole force would be upside down before he got back.

CHAPTER 44

"EVELYN SAID HER BOYS were involved in the Franklin shooting. What did they do?" Munk asked as he wiped mustard from the corner of his mouth.

"Your nephews were out in Deadwood Hollow looking for a cell phone," Cass said.

"At night?" Munk asked.

"It had something to do with a girl."

Munk held up a hand. "Enough said. What happened?"

"They heard shots and were smart enough to hide in some brush. The shooter ran past, but they didn't get a good look at him."

"He didn't see them?"

"Matt and Mark didn't think so."

"That's manageable. From what Evelyn said, I thought the boys had taken a shot at the Franklin house." He glanced at Kado. From his expression of almost respect, Cass read that Munk and Kado were on their way to making peace over their differences in forensic techniques. "What caliber was the weapon?"

Kado explained how Martha and Joseph Franklin were killed with shots from a .30-06 rifle. "We found the tree he used out in Deadwood Hollow. He stalked them, but we don't know for how long."

"I can understand how somebody could confuse Moses and Joseph. Nobody could tell them apart. But why did he kill Martha Franklin?" Mitch asked.

"He shot her first. The under-cabinet lights were the only ones on in the kitchen. Mrs. Franklin had cancer and was going through radiation treatment," Kado answered.

"She was bald," Munk stated.

"And would have been almost identical to Moses and Joseph in a dimly lit space through the scope of a rifle at one hundred yards."

Mitch used a fry to scrape the last smear of ketchup from his burger wrapper. "Was she cooking?"

"Making a cup of tea. The neighbors said she and Joseph were just home from her quilting club meeting."

"That might explain something," Kado said, pulling his notebook from his pocket. "Cass brought Joseph's running shoes from the Franklin house. A red substance was in some of the cracks. It smelled like garlic or onions."

"Pasta sauce?" Cass asked.

"I don't know. Maybe they bring food to those meetings and something with tomato, garlic, and onion was on the floor. Martha's shoes were clean, though."

"We can check into it with the quilting club and Mojo," Cass said.

"And we need to look for receipts for gas." Kado turned to Martinez. "Hazel confirmed that there is gasoline on Joseph's gym shorts." At Martinez' stormy expression he quickly carried on. "But it was only a trace. Probably no more than a splash from the nozzle."

"I brought Joseph's wallet and Martha's purse to the station," Cass said. "We'll look for a receipt."

Mitch puffed his cheeks out and exhaled. "Okay, let's eliminate Martha Franklin as a possible target. She was retired from the schools?"

Cass nodded.

"Any enemies?" Mitch asked.

"The neighbors were shocked," Martinez answered. "They said Martha didn't have a mean bone in her body. She lived for her sons, the church, and her quilting club. She was struggling through her cancer treatments, but the neighbors said she was upbeat and her prognosis good."

"A nice old lady."

Martinez nodded.

"There was one drawer in her desk that was stuck," Cass said. "It's probably more paperwork, but it's worth a look."

"I'll deal with it," Munk said. "And if Mojo doesn't mind, I'll bring her paperwork to the station to process."

"So Martha Franklin most likely wasn't the target," Mitch said. "That leaves Moses' case files, Joseph's arrest and incarceration, and anything in their personal lives that could've led to this. I told Cass I'd look into the first two this afternoon. We can talk to Moses about their personal lives later. That's all we can do on the Franklins for now." He looked at Cass, who was sneaking a fry from the box in front of Truman. "Calvin Whitehead. Tell us about his autopsy."

"Bernie's still examining the body," Cass said. "But he confirmed that Whitehead was alive when he was set on fire."

Truman coughed into his fist. "Seriously?" he croaked.

"His throat and lungs are burned. Grey and Bernie said he swallowed whatever accelerant was used, or had it forced down his throat."

"Wow," Martinez said.

"And, from the lack of damage to his neck, it looks like they took care not to let him die when they hung him."

"Are you sure there was more than one perp?" Mitch asked.

"There had to be," Martinez said. "It would be too difficult for one person to subdue a man that big and get him up a ladder."

The room went silent. Kado balled up his burger wrapper and they jumped at the crackling noise. "This was personal."

"Bernie described it as a cold rage. And if you consider the swastika carved into his chest —"

"The what?" Munk interrupted.

"A swastika," Cass said.

"Who would do that?"

"It's a good question. We need to find out if there are other cases like Whitehead's: carving on the body, hanging, and burning."

"Did you find any evidence at the store?" Mitch asked.

Kado nodded. "Fingerprints, tons of debris. I need to load the prints into IAFIS and start on the debris this afternoon. Did you know him?"

"No," Mitch answered. He looked to Cass. "His store was out towards where y'all live, did you shop there?"

"Sometimes, but none of us knew him very well."

"Any idea on motive?" Mitch asked.

"Truman found cash in the register," Kado said, "so it wasn't robbery."

"Calvin Whitehead was ready for trouble at home," Martinez stated. "I found four guns, but I didn't toss the place, so he might have more stuffed between the sofa cushions."

"What about his shop?" Cass asked.

Martinez looked at Truman. "He had a sawed-off shotgun and a baseball bat on the shelf beneath the register. That was it, right?"

Truman nodded.

"Was the shotgun fired?" Mitch asked.

"Nope," Martinez answered. "And the baseball bat was undisturbed."

"So they either caught him by surprise, or he knew his killers and trusted them enough to let them get close." Mitch looked at Kado. "Anything else on Whitehead?"

"No."

"Did you find a cell phone?"

"Just regular phones in the house and shop."

"Well," Mitch said, "that leaves Donna Moore."

"The accountant? *That* Donna Moore?" Munk asked. "What happened?"

"She was murdered last night, with the same weapon that killed the Franklins," Kado said.

Munk blinked. "This keeps getting weirder. How did they know each other?"

"We have no idea," Martinez said, checking the clock on the conference room wall. "But Hoffner's burning up road. Let's get moving in case he loses it and kicks Cass and Mitch out when he gets here."

"I'll go to Donna's office," Cass said.

"I'll head over to the Franklin house and bring their paperwork back, then start on it and the boxes from Whitehead's closet," Munk offered.

"Truman can help with the sludge from The Whitehead Store and I'll work on the fingerprints," Kado said.

"*Gracias, amigos,*" Martinez said with feeling. "No paperwork for me. I'll find Mojo and have a chat with the quilting bee."

CHAPTER 45

SHADES WERE DOWN ON the windows when Cass approached The Moore Agency. It was housed in one of the old buildings on a street adjoining Arcadia's square, its exterior creamy Texas sandstone that matched the courthouse. A flat plaque over the door was carved with the date the building was erected – 1908. The solitary eye of a security camera peered down at her from beneath a green and white awning. She squinted through the grate protecting the glass door, spotted the distant glow from a desk lamp, and knocked. A figure darted through the shadowy office and Cass reached for her gun, finding only her belt. Her breathing quickened. The door buzzed and Cass heard a bolt click. She pushed the door open a crack and a bell tinkled above her head. No one was visible in the gloomy interior.

"Hello?" She hesitated as she chose her words. Somehow stating that she was with the Medical Examiner's office didn't feel right. And even though she didn't have the badge or gun back, she was still a detective. "I'm Cass Elliot, with the sheriff's office. Is anyone here?"

A narrow head popped up over a partition. "I know who you are. Come in and make sure the door catches when you close it. The press was knocking earlier. Thank goodness for that explosion in Watuga."

The office was sleek and modern, and Cass noted the motion detectors mounted in the room's tall corner. A whip of a man had appeared at the swinging gate separating the reception area from the rest of the office. The head that sat atop his thin neck was the narrowest Cass had ever seen, to the point that his eyes appeared to be positioned on opposite sides of his face, like an animal of prey. A neatly trimmed brush moustache decorated the space between his lip and nose, its carroty color matching his oiled hair, which shimmered like the scales on a goldfish. The rest of his body was equally as thin as his head. He held out a trembling hand. "I'm Joshua Reed, Donna's associate."

Cass shook it. "I'm sorry for your loss, Mr. Reed."

"Call me Joshua. I can't believe she's gone," he said, wiping his nose as he held the gate open. "I've made a pot of tea. Can I get you some?"

She followed him past two offices, stacks of file cabinets, shelves bearing colored folders, and a conference area where a desk lamp burned. The walls were painted dove-gray and sported a variety of charcoal drawings like those in Moore's home. Joshua led Cass to a small kitchen where appliances gleamed and water sloshed quietly in a dishwasher. He poured tea and handed her a mug. The liquid was a pale greenish-amber and a sweet scent wafted on the mist.

He motioned her to the conference area, where he sat and sipped from his own mug. A sandwich sat untouched next to stacks of papers. "Mint. We grow it in the courtyard out back. Donna's big into herbs and I find it soothing to tend to them."

"How long have you worked for Miss Moore?"

"Years. Decades. Let's see." His fingers fluttered over the papers. He found a pen and snapped the cap off, doodling circles as he spoke. "She opened in 1989 and hired me shortly after. I was right out of high school. She sent me to classes for shorthand, word processing, spreadsheets, and even her accounting and tax software. I finished my degree while working here, and just passed the CPA exam."

"Congratulations. You run the office?"

"And do some of the easier accounting work. We run payroll and keep the books for some of the businesses in town. And there's tax season, of course."

"Did Miss Moore have any enemies?" Cass asked.

Joshua leaned his head against the back of the chair, exposing the most prominent Adam's apple Cass had ever seen. It bounced in his thin neck as he swallowed. "That's the thing. Donna is the kindest, most generous person I've ever known. I can't think of anyone who had problems with her, here or in her personal life. Well, of the very little personal life she had."

"She worked a lot?"

He wiped his cheek with the back of a hand. "Always in before six and she rarely left before nine at night."

"Weekends?"

"Usually."

Cass remembered the cross pendant from Moore's possessions. "Where did she go to church?"

He shook his head. "Donna hasn't been to church since her mom died. Said she couldn't stand all the hypocrisy."

"Any family?"

"Her father died way back, and her mother passed away a few years ago. Donna never married. I'm not sure she even dated."

"Was she..." Cass hesitated. "Did she have female friends?"

"If you want to know if Donna was a lesbian, the answer is no. She had friends, girls who went to the same high school, but they rarely saw each other."

"Are there any clients who owe her money?"

"We have a few people who pay the bills for their tax work in installments. But nobody's late on their payments." He sat up straighter and cheek-walked to the edge of his chair, where he perched. "Even if they were, I'm the person who calls to remind them to pay. So it's me they would be mad at. Not Donna."

Cass watched as he scrabbled the papers together and slid them into a folder. "Where were you last night, Mr. Reed?"

He winced. "I knew you'd ask that question. They all do on television. And really, it's the right question."

"Sorry?"

His lips trembled. "She left everything to me. All this." He gestured at the office. "The business and the house. Everything. I'm the only one with motive."

Cass watched in surprise as he folded his arms on the table, dropped his head onto them, and wailed.

CHAPTER 46

JOSEPH FELT A PHONE vibrate in his pocket as he stepped from The Golden Gate into the blazing afternoon. He pulled it out and saw the serial number on the back. "Franklin."

Martinez asked if now would be a good time to talk. The coffee in Joseph's stomach turned sour and he recommended that Martinez meet him at The Golden Gate, then went back inside.

"Is it okay if I meet Detective Martinez here?" he asked as Stan jotted down his order.

"Of course. I'll be right back with your food."

Acid burbled in his throat as he waited for Martinez to arrive. This whole impersonation thing was getting serious. Thanks to the letters Moses and his mother had sent to him in prison, Joseph knew enough about Moses' professional life to grasp some of the lingo and have a general feel for what his brother did as an officer day-to-day. Beyond that, Joseph was in the dark. His improv skills were about to be tested.

The café's door opened and a broad man with close-cropped steely hair entered the cool space. Joseph recognized Martinez from games he and Moses had played with the community's teenagers. Martinez was adequate with a basketball, but it was his physical strength that let him muscle his way up and down the court. He spotted Joseph and slid into the booth across from him.

"Listen Mojo," he said, dabbing sweat from his forehead. "I should have said on the phone that I'm really sorry about your mom and Joseph. I know this is a hard time, but I need to ask you a few questions."

"It's okay," Joseph told him, leaning out of the way as Stan approached with a tray.

"Turkey and hummus on wheat." Stan asked. "Fruit salad and a Dr. Pepper. Carlos?"

"Just a soda for me."

"Done." Stan strode back to the kitchen and returned moments later with another drink. "I'll check back in a minute."

"Healthy stuff," Martinez said, motioning to the plate. He frowned at the computer box on the seat next to Joseph. "A laptop? Man, you hate those things. What's up?"

Joseph swallowed, his brain working furiously. The fact that Moses hated computers, was in fact a dedicated two-finger man when it came to a keyboard, were details that everyone knew. *Why would Moses have a laptop, and more importantly, be using it right after his mother and brother were murdered?* He decided to try honesty. "Joseph made me buy it and learn how to use it." He cleared his throat. "I just thought I could have him with me a little longer if I kept the laptop around." He looked down at his plate. "Stupid, huh?"

"No, man. It's not stupid at all." Martinez scratched his nose. "Maybe you could teach me to use one."

"I'm a total beginner. You'd be better off asking one of those kids of yours to teach you."

"They don't have the patience. You'd think they were born with a laptop in one hand and a cell phone in the other. All this stuff is second nature to them."

Joseph's mind latched on an article he'd seen in last week's Forney Cater, and he realized he had a solution to the gun problem. "We could work a deal if you'd show me how to improve my scores at the range."

Martinez cocked an eyebrow. "Mojo, no amount of practice or training can improve your aim."

"Come on. County sharpshooter? It's a piece of cake for you."

"Fine, we'll trade. But no promises on the scores." He motioned again at the plate. "Eat."

"How's the investigation coming?" Joseph asked, and then took a bite of sandwich.

"Slowly. Cass picked up a pair of running shoes from the foyer at your mom's house. Are they yours or Joseph's?"

"Joseph's. Cass is back?"

"At least until Hoffner gets home. Do you know where Joseph was yesterday?"

He thought quickly about his day and whether anyone could figure out his morph into Moses based on his activities. The interviews he'd attended were over by two o'clock. He'd gone to a donut shop in Shreveport to drown his sorrows from yet another disappointing day of job-hunting and returned home at around five-thirty. He'd driven Moses' car to the interviews, leaving Moses with their mom's Buick, so it was possible that the neighbors would think it was Joseph that had taken his mother out. "Momma had a doctor's appointment around four. Joseph drove her there and to the quilting club. I don't know whether he stayed at the doctor's office or at the meeting."

"If he left her, where would he have gone?"

Joseph shrugged. "I don't know."

"Okay, I'll see what I can find out from the doc and the quilting club. We need to look at your mom and Joseph's paperwork to see if anything pops out. Is it okay if we bring the stuff in your mom's desk back to the station?"

Joseph felt a bit surreal as he continued to speak about himself in the third person. "I'm not sure Joseph's even opened a bank account. When he was arrested, me and mom went to New York and emptied his apartment. Everything we didn't sell is in the attic. You can take all that, too."

Martinez poked his tongue in his cheek. "We'll, uh, need to look at your financial records, Mojo. Sorry, but we have to do it."

"It's okay," Joseph answered, thankful he had taken the time to open his brother's desk this morning. "I know you've got to go through everything."

"Did Joseph have any enemies?"

"You know what he was doing when he got arrested, right?"

Martinez hesitated. "No, not really."

"He was hacking into computers and selling the information."

"Wow. What was he stealing?"

"Names, addresses, social security numbers, credit card data, that kind of thing."

"Who did he sell to?"

"No idea."

"If he was in New York, was he selling the stuff to the mafia?"

Joseph's smile was small. "We didn't even know he was unemployed until he got arrested. He told us he was a contract programmer."

"Go back to the beginning. Tell me everything you remember about what happened with your brother."

"You really think this is about Joseph?"

"It's possible. It could also be about you. We'll get to that later. Tell me about Joseph."

So he did, being as vague as a brother should be when discussing his absent twin's life. And in truth, Joseph and Moses hadn't been close while Joseph was in New York. For no reason other than time got the best of them; each was busy with his own career, his own life. Speaking as Moses, he told Martinez about Joseph's call to their mother to let her know about the arrest for computer crimes. As he talked, Joseph watched Martinez to ensure the older man believed he was Moses.

Martinez took notes for several minutes and Joseph finished his sandwich. He reached for his fork and started on the fruit salad.

"I didn't know you were ambidextrous," Martinez said.

Joseph forced himself to continue chewing, clocking the fact that he held the fork in his left hand. Moses was a righty. *One of those details.* "Sometimes."

"Cool, man. Hey, maybe you should try shooting with your left hand. It couldn't hurt your scores any." He flashed a grin, his white teeth stark in his brown face. "If you don't know who Joseph was selling the credit card information to, maybe the prosecutor in the case did."

"Do you think they'd help us?"

"It's hard to predict what city people will do, but we can try. Let's talk about you. Can you think of any recent cases you've worked that got ugly? I mean, you weren't involved in the whole Church of the True Believer stuff back in the spring, were you?"

Joseph made an educated guess. "Only on the periphery. I don't think they'd come after me."

Martinez eyed Joseph. "Mitch Stone is back at work and going through your files, but you're the only one who will remember details. When you're ready, I need you to go through your cases. Maybe something will stand out."

"No problem."

"Those Mexican drug dealers are still inside, but Rob Conroy is out."

Joseph smiled faintly at the memory of Moses' joy when both arrests went down. "Do you think Conroy did this?"

"Honestly, it's doubtful, but Cass is looking into his alibi. Watch out for him, okay? You caused him a lot of grief."

"Will do."

"One other thing. How does your family know Donna Moore?"

"Who?"

"Donna Moore. She has an accounting office off the square."

Joseph mentally walked the streets branching from Arcadia's downtown. "Green and white awning?"

Martinez nodded.

"I haven't met her. Why?"

"She was murdered last night." He hesitated. "By the same person who killed your mom and Joseph."

Joseph folded his hands and sat back in the booth. His mind was racing. If the same shooter came after both families, then perhaps this was about Moses, and not about him. "There's a link between us and Moore?"

"It is possible that both shootings were random. But she was killed at her house, which is nowhere near where you live."

Joseph shook his head. "I've never heard Momma or Joseph mention her name, and don't remember seeing anything from her in the house."

"I'll get a picture of her to see if that triggers your memory."

Joseph pushed his plate away. "Let's do it now. I can look at case files afterward. The distraction would be good."

CHAPTER 47

IT TOOK NEARLY HALF an hour for Joshua Reed to calm down. Cass's initial reaction to his hysteria was humor. Unless the man had something to gain from murdering the Franklins, it was unlikely he was involved in Donna Moore's killing. Once Joshua's tears abated, she asked, "Did you kill Miss Moore?"

"Of course not. But nobody else benefits from her death."

"If you didn't kill her, and if you're the only beneficiary to her estate, then someone else had a different motive."

He considered this. "Do I need to prove I didn't kill her?"

"That's a good placed to start. Tell me about last night."

"I locked the doors at five and set the alarm, as usual." He squirmed in his chair and looked at her from the corner of his eye. "And then went to a meeting."

"What kind of meeting?"

Joshua chewed his lower lip. "Alcoholics Anonymous."

Cass understood his reticence. From her father's experiences with alcohol, she knew that AA was a dichotomy. On the one hand, the group discreetly publicized its meetings and welcomed anyone with a drinking problem, regardless of how many times they'd backslid. But the AA community was fairly tight-knit. Members limited the information they shared with non-alcoholics about the group's activities. "How long have you been on the wagon?"

He reached into his trouser pocket and extracted a small coin-shaped object, brass-colored on one side, the other a deep red with 'XV' embossed in the middle of a pyramid. Cass recognized it as an anniversary chip. A dish on her father's dresser held quite a collection of the discs, an impressive testament to his many failures at sobriety. "Fifteen years. Almost sixteen."

"Meetings are an hour?"

"Last night was longer. We didn't wrap up until almost seven."

"What did you do then?"

"I had dinner with a friend."

"Which friend, and where?"

Joshua started doodling again. Interlocking squares. Hesitantly, he outlined the rest of his evening: meeting a friend, having dinner at a Greek place in Shreveport, and finishing the night off at a club called The Rainbow Room. It wasn't until he reached this part of the story that Cass understood his reluctance. The Rainbow Room was a gay hangout in Shreveport, notorious for its wild parties. "You went clubbing on a Wednesday?" she asked.

He licked his lips. "It was our anniversary."

"How late were you there?"

"Until about three."

She would check his alibi, but Cass couldn't imagine Joshua Reed having the gumption to kill his employer, or anyone else. She changed the subject. "Had Miss Moore been acting unusual lately?"

"Unusual how?"

"Changes in her emotions, her state of mind. Was she more tired than usual? More energetic?"

He tilted his head. "There were days when she seemed happier. To the extent that I wondered if she was seeing someone."

"Did you ask her about it?"

"Once. She said that it was flattering to have two men in your life, which shocked me. I guess it showed, because she blushed and said she was talking about me and the guy who mows her lawn."

Cass nodded slowly. "Okay, Joshua. I need to make a call. Can I use an office?"

He pointed her to the room on the right, and as she entered she realized that it was Moore's. The woman's diplomas and CPA certificate were displayed on the walls, along with more charcoal sketches. Cass dialed dispatch and got the number for the Greek restaurant and The Rainbow Room and called while looking closer at the artwork. Again, they were all originals and almost surreal in their execution. One revealed the pointy peaks of pine trees. Another what looked like a masked eye. Each was signed by Moore.

It took only moments for the manager of the Greek restaurant to confirm that Joshua had reservations for two at seven last night, and that he was a little late arriving. When Cass described Joshua, The Rainbow Room's bartender confirmed that he was at the club until the wee hours of the morning. Given his bright orange hair, bushy mustache, and whip-thin body, Joshua Reed made a memorable guest.

Cass searched Moore's desk and found a calendar. She turned to the previous day's entries. Moore had been busy: appointments in the morning, lunch around noon, and time for admin work in the afternoon. The time slots for three-thirty onward were marked through. She opened the office door and asked for Joshua's help. "What did Miss Moore have planned late yesterday afternoon?"

"She had an outside appointment. I didn't tell you that?"

"Who with?"

"She didn't say. I assumed it was a doctor's appointment."

Cass flipped back through the calendar and noted several other dates in the weeks leading up to her death when Moore had left early. "You said she always works late."

He pursed his lips, the orange bristles of his mustache poking straight out at Cass, and studied the ceiling. "There have been a few times when she's left early."

"For what?"

Joshua shrugged. "I figured it was female maintenance."

Cass lifted an eyebrow and he blushed.

"Like maybe she schedules all that woman stuff at the same time." He chewed his lower lip. "Maybe not. Let me check her old calendars. We keep them in a storage room."

Cass followed him into a narrow space lined with handmade shelves crammed with folders. Joshua lifted a cardboard box and rifled the contents. He flipped through several calendars, smoothing them open at specific dates.

"Here," he said, pointing to a series of dates more than a year ago. He looked back several pages, indicating other dates. "She left early on these days, but didn't say where she was going. I didn't think anything about it, because Donna didn't talk about personal stuff. But," he turned to the original date, "she took three days off in March."

"Was that vacation time?"

"Donna didn't take vacation."

"But these three days look like vacation."

Joshua breathed out a long sigh. "She didn't call it vacation. The night before she left, Donna said she had business to tend to and would be back in a few days. And she was. I mean, vacation or not, taking a few days off isn't a crime."

"No, it's not. But it was unusual for her. Does Miss Moore keep her personal records here? I didn't find any at her house."

He pulled out another box. "Donna's stuff for this year is in here." A phone rang and he carried the box to the kitchen table before dashing to his desk.

Cass found the expected utility bills, property tax statements, and insurance premium notices. Moore had a hefty bank account, three jumbo certificates of deposit, and two investment accounts. No mortgages. The woman was flush. Joshua Reed would indeed benefit from the woman's death. Cass wondered if anyone else would, as well.

"Joshua?" she called.

He poked his head into the kitchen. "Yes?"

"Where can I find a copy of Miss Moore's will?"

"It's probably in her safe at home."

"Where is it?"

"There's a picture in her office. One of her charcoals. It looks like a mountain from a science fiction movie. The safe is behind it." He wrote a series of numbers on a sticky note and handed it to Cass.

"She did all of the art work here in the office?"

He nodded. "And in her home. Watercolors, oils, charcoals. She called it her life's work." Joshua glanced at a dark image, perhaps a portion of a bird's claw, hanging in the kitchen. "Donna didn't start painting and sketching until a few years ago. Some are kind of bleak, but I think they're very good."

"Me, too. What does she keep in her safe other than her will?"

Joshua shrugged. "I've never opened it. She gave me the combination for emergencies."

"Are you sure you're her only beneficiary?"

He considered her question. "No. Donna told me I was in her will, but I've never seen it. Since she doesn't have any living family, I assumed I was the only one."

She motioned to the open box. "I need to take her personal records with me, and I'll probably have questions about some of your clients."

"You'll need to send somebody with a strong back. We've got years of stuff."

"We'll start with the first five, and go back from there." She glanced up at a corner, at a motion detector. "There's a lot of security here and at her home. Why?"

"I asked her that once, when she upgraded the office system to add motion detectors upstairs."

"Upstairs?"

"Second floor of this building. More storage. She added it to the system about five years ago. We had a problem with squirrels." The phone rang again and he inched toward the kitchen door. "Clients are getting the news about Donna's death. I need to take this."

"What did she say when she added the security?"

"It was strange. Donna said that you never knew who would grab you in the night, and it was better to be safe than sorry."

CHAPTER 48

"OOFH," TRUMAN BREATHED, TILTING his head away from the blossom of acrid odors that rose from a bucket as he peeled its lid off.

"Disgusting," Kado echoed. "Which one is that?"

"First one from the patio," Truman gasped, his fair skin paling.

"Close it. We'll do that one together, later."

Truman opened another bucket and tipped the sludge into a stainless steel pan. He smoothed down the rubber apron covering his uniform. "What now?"

Kado grimaced as he examined the goo. "Strain it. Pick through the solids, looking for anything out of place. Most of this stuff is food." He plucked a bright red lump from the pan and placed it in a glass jar. "That's probably tomato. Or maybe strawberry. Put food solids in a jar to thin this stuff out. You're looking for hair, fibers, any material that doesn't belong. Take a spoonful at a time. Okay?"

Truman nodded. "Any hits on the fingerprints?"

"One on a palm print from the gas pump."

"Really? Is it one of our guys?"

"Unfortunately, no. Calvin Whitehead didn't keep his pumps as clean as the inside of his store." He turned the computer screen so Truman could see the ugly man scowling from a booking photo. "Bobby White."

"Wow. He's been in the penitentiary for how long?"

"It says he transferred from county about six months ago."

"That's a shame," the young officer commented, extracting a curved piece of jar containing a Smucker's label. "He's the one who set his grandma's house on fire to get her insurance money."

Kado balked. "Property insurance?"

"And life. She was inside when he lit the match. Bobby White has enough mean in him to barbeque Whitehead. Anybody else?"

"There were quite a few prints on the countertop near the cash register, but none of them hit. I've got more cards from behind the counter to scan."

The door to the evidence room bumped open and Munk backed inside, carrying boxes of files. He looked over his shoulder at Kado. "From the Franklin house. Where do you want them?"

"How many?"

"Seventeen."

"What is it with people and paper? Did you label them?"

Munk glared.

"Okay, yeah, sorry," Kado said. "Put them in the conference room, away from Calvin Whitehead's boxes so we don't mix them up."

Munk grunted and stepped back through the door.

Kado glanced at the clock and snapped the gloves from his hands. "It's already one o'clock. Thank God nobody else has died. The paperwork alone would drown us. I'll get the fingerprints started and go get coffee. Maybe I can soothe Munk's hurt feelings with cream and sugar. You want some?"

"Sure. And get donuts. Munk'll forgive anything for a dozen glazed."

CHAPTER 49

"CAN WE HURRY UP?" asked the officer who had accompanied Cass through the house. "These paintings are creeping me out."

Cass examined the charcoal sketch that covered Donna Moore's safe. Joshua Reed had described it as a science fiction type of mountain, and Cass could see what he meant. The background was dark and the white mountain stood out in stark relief, almost glowing against it. But there was something odd about the way the top of the mountain peaked and then seemed to lay over on itself, almost as if it were wrapped in a blanket of snow. Cass ran her fingers around the frame and pressed a latch under one side. A click sounded and she swung the painting back to reveal a safe, its keypad flush with the door.

"You'd never know the safe was there."

"Nope," Cass agreed, "you wouldn't. Got gloves on?"

She tapped in the combination and pulled the door.

"Whoa," the officer said. "That's some serious bread."

Cass extracted one strap of cash and fanned it. "Hundreds. This must be ten thousand."

The two emptied the safe, inventorying the contents and placing them in a document box as they went. There were twelve straps of one hundred dollar bills. They found no will, but Cass discovered a pay-as-you-go cell phone and turned it on. The most recent call had arrived at three thirty-five the previous afternoon, around the time Moore left the office for her appointment. She had dialed a different number shortly after receiving the call. Cass turned the phone off and added it to the box.

"I want to check these other paintings. Then we'll go by her office and get her personal records," Cass said as she taped the box and had the officer sign it and the chain of custody paperwork with her.

She walked through the house, thinking the officer was right that the artwork was a little creepy. She tested the paintings and sketches to ensure no other hidden safes existed and wondered where the woman had kept her will. As she examined the artwork, she realized that some of the pieces had a consistent theme. Of clothing.

One charcoal drawing could be interpreted as ragged trunks from two trees, or a pair of scruffy trouser legs. If they were trouser legs, which was just possible if Cass tilted her head and squinted, they would fit into the pair of worn work boots she had spotted at Moore's office earlier in the day. One sketch was smudgy around the edges, but revealed the detail of a warped, dirty belt buckle.

On impulse, Cass lifted the camera and worked her way back through the house, taking photos of each piece of art, wondering if there was a message lurking in Moore's rendering of the world.

CHAPTER 50

OFFICER HUGO PETCHARD STOPPED inside The Golden Gate Café's door and mopped the sweat from his face. He spotted Junie taking an order from a pair of oil field workers and his heart lurched as she laughed and touched one of the men on the shoulder. Flashing a small wave at her, Petchard slid into a booth and waited, fighting the green-eyed monster that was itching to yank his gun from its holster and shoot the workers. Junie brought him a glass of iced tea and sat across from him.

"How's your day been, lover?" she asked.

He glowered. "Okay."

"What's wrong?"

Petchard's glance shot to the two men. Junie reached across the table and took his hand. "It's good policy to be nice to the customers, to laugh at their jokes. I get better tips." She waggled her brows and at last he relaxed. "Good. Let's start again. How's your day been, Hugo?"

He sighed. "A little trying, to tell the truth."

"What happened?"

Petchard's face darkened. "Cass Elliot talked the medical examiner, John Grey, into hiring her as a temp last night, and she came to the Franklin house this morning. She's such a bitch."

"Language," Junie admonished.

"I'm sorry. She's so self-righteous. Like she knows best. Sheriff Hoffner's got no confidence in her, or he would've signed her back on by now."

"I met her this morning," Junie said, releasing his hand and sitting back in the booth. "She seemed quite emotional at first, and then very intense when she was talking with her fellow officers. I only heard bits of their conversation, but she sounded pretty smart to me."

"She might be smart," Petchard groused, "but she's a real pain to work with."

"What happened?"

"Cass reamed me out because I didn't inventory all the stuff Mojo took from his house." Petchard crossed his arms over his chest with a huff. "I mean, I couldn't do that. The man was suffering. I found him bawling his eyes out in his bedroom, like a little kid. And it was his stuff, anyway."

Junie studied him. "Should you have taken an inventory?"

The tips of his ears turned red.

"Lover, were you mean to Cass?"

Petchard's lower lip poked out. "Maybe. A little. But she deserved it."

"I have to get back to work, but we can have dinner. Pick me up at six?"

His eyes brightened. "From home?"

"From the café. I told Sally I'd stay a little longer today." She tapped his iced tea. "Stay hydrated. Tonight, we'll talk more about Cass and the Franklin investigation, okay?"

CHAPTER 51

THE AIR IN THE squad room carried the same pungent odor of sweat and burned coffee that always made her want to suck on a mint, but Cass smiled as she pushed the door open to see Mitch frowning at a computer terminal. She helped an officer unload boxes from Moore's safe and office from a hand cart.

"I need you to go back and take photos of the pictures at Donna's office."

The officer looked doubtful.

"Hey, if you'd rather be back out on patrol..."

"Nope. It's boiling out there. I'll go take pictures of the pictures."

"All of them, please."

"No problem."

Cass joined Mitch at his desk. "What's up?" she asked.

"It's possessed again," Mitch answered, jabbing at the keyboard.

"What are you looking at?"

"Anything Mojo's worked on in the last two years."

"What else have you got open?"

"Um, the time tracking program, the internet, and the word processor."

"That's too much," Cass said, grabbing the handles on his wheelchair and pushing him out of the way. "The case system eats memory and the computer locks if you have more than one other program running with it. That concussion must've been pretty deep. You know this."

"Oh yeah," he answered, reaching for the straightened length of wire coat hanger on his desk. He adjusted one end, slipped it slowly between his brace and leg, and released a long sigh as he scratched. "Heaven."

"What do you want left open?"

"Case system and the internet."

Cass used the task manager to close the remaining programs, and pulled Mitch's wheelchair back.

"Thanks," he said. "What's in the box?"

"Stuff from Donna's safe."

"Like?"

"Cash." She held up two straps of bills and moved the cash to a new box.

Mitch whistled. "What else?"

Cass signed the chain of custody paperwork on the cash and had Mitch witness it. She extracted the rest of the box's contents. "Property deeds, car titles, paid-in-full mortgages. But no will."

"Does she have a safe deposit box?" Mitch asked.

Cass picked up the box of money. "I'll find out."

She walked down the narrow hall to the evidence room, enjoying the familiar thunk of her boots on the linoleum tiles, knocked once, and entered only to gasp as a complicated aroma assaulted her. "What is that?"

Truman's hazel eyes twinkled over the top of his face mask. "Eau de remnants of Calvin Whitehead's storeroom with undertones of sludge from his patio."

Kado looked up from his computer and lifted a mug. "And a hint of coffee."

"It'll never sell," Cass gasped. "You need an extractor fan." She stopped short and looked at all the equipment dotting the counters. "Did you raid the evidence locker and start selling the cocaine?"

Kado laughed. "No, but it took my entire budget for the year."

"How did you afford it?"

"I got it through Craig's List, eBay, and from calls to forensic guys who were updating their labs. It's used, but in good shape. This is Hazel," Kado said, patting the GCMS's housing.

Cass glanced at the gooey concoction in front of Truman. "Buy that extractor fan next, would you?"

"Just for your nose, I'll put it on the list," Kado said. "What have you got?"

"Cash from Donna's safe at home."

"How much?"

"One hundred and twenty thousand."

"Cool," Truman said, leaning over to look in the box. "I've never seen that much cash in one place."

"Y'all need to count it, and would you check it for cocaine?"

"You think she was into drugs?" Kado asked.

Cass shrugged. "I found a pay-as-you-go phone in her safe, too. Seems a strange combination."

Kado and Truman counted the money and signed the paperwork. "Anything else?"

"I need the stuff we brought from Donna's house this morning. I want to see if she has a safe deposit box key."

Kado pointed to a box on a far counter.

"I'll take it with me," Cass said, pulling open the door with her free hand. "The smell is incredible."

Cass entered the squad room to see Mitch squinting at his computer screen. Her cell phone rang and she slid the box onto her desk. She finished the call and sighed. "That was Frannie. She checked with Rob Conroy's neighbors. They said he threw a party last night."

"What time?" Mitch asked.

"They noticed the music and people hanging out on the balcony at around eight, Conroy included. They went to complain at ten-thirty. Things got quiet around eleven, so either everyone passed out, or they left. Frannie tossed his apartment but found no drugs, alcohol, or weapons. There was a trash bag on Conroy's stoop when we were there this morning, but she said it was gone."

"Did she check the dumpster?"

Cass nodded. "Trash collection had already run."

Mitch wrinkled his nose. "If he was at home at eight last night, he's not a candidate for the Franklin murders."

"No, and that makes sense, given that we've got the same shooter killing Donna."

"I guess Conroy would've been too easy. Any luck with a safe deposit box for Donna?"

She opened the box and found two brass keys on a ring: one with USPS engraved on it, the other with a four-digit number. There were fewer than ten banks in Forney County, so unless Moore had opened a box elsewhere, it would be short order to figure out which bank housed the woman's safe deposit box.

"I'll start on a warrant in a minute." Cass turned to the box containing items from Moore's safe. "She also has a prepaid cell phone," she said, tossing the device to Mitch. "I saw one incoming phone number and one outgoing. See if you can find them in the system."

"Why would Donna have a burner?" Mitch asked, pushing the power button.

"I've got no idea, but combined with the cash, it makes her look a little shady. Kado's checking the bills for cocaine. Anything on the phone?"

"I can't see Donna involved in drugs," Mitch said, checking the call register. He looked warily at his computer. "Think I should try a reverse lookup?"

"Go low tech. Call them."

Mitch reached for his desk phone and dialed both numbers. "No answer. And no voice message."

She poured the contents of a padded envelope onto her desk. "I'll bet the call came from another throw away, and the call she made went to one, but see if you can find either number online."

He tapped gingerly at the keyboard. "Nope."

"Any other calls?"

Mitch checked the phone again. "That's weird. All incoming calls are from that one number. All outgoing calls are to the other number.

"Dates?"

"Two last week. Three the week before. Then nothing since earlier in the year. And they follow the same pattern. The first number calls Donna, and a few minutes later, she calls the other number."

"Seems strange if it's her supplier." Cass checked the wall clock. "I doubt her tox results are back. We can check with Grey in the morning."

Mitch's phone rang and he turned to answer it. "Detective Stone."

A surge of elation filled Cass at the sound of his voice uttering those words. In less than twenty-four hours, she was back at work with her partner, feeling as natural as if the past six weeks had never happened. She sorted through the rest of the paperwork from Moore's safe, looking up when Mitch said, "Thanks Jerome, we'll be there as quick as we can."

He cradled the handset and started wrenching the wheels on his chair. "That was Jerome from out at Pecan Grove, that fancy retirement place."

"Blackie Cochran's cousin, Jerome?"

Mitch gave up on maneuvering the wheelchair and reached for his crutches. "He said one of the nurses, Emmet Hedder, didn't show up today and didn't call in sick."

"So?"

"He never misses work. All the old people love him, including the old lady Jerome works for. She sent him over to Emmet's house to make sure he was okay." Mitch grunted and levered himself to a standing position. He wavered, found his balance, and released a deep breath. "Vertical feels good."

"Where does he live?" Cass prodded.

"Behind the golf course."

"Emmet wasn't at home?"

"No, and," he continued, weaving through the desks on his crutches, "one of the windows has been shot through and Jerome thinks he sees blood."

Cass's eyes widened. "You think it's the same person?"

"Who else has been shooting through windows lately?" He wobbled as he reached the coffee bar, and leaned against the counter to catch his breath.

"Stay here. I'll go check it out," Cass said, reaching for her truck keys as the door to the conference room banged opened.

SHERIFF BILL HOFFNER CHARGED in and Cass deflated, all the joy rushing from her body in a woof of breath, no different than if he had gut-punched her. His white shirt and dark brown trousers were still crisp, even after hours of travel. The boots he wore looked freshly polished and every stiff white hair on his head was in its place. His skin was more tanned than usual, and she wondered what kind of leadership-building activities required access to the outdoors. A whiff of soap wafted into the room behind him, and Cass realized that he must've stopped to take a shower and change clothes. And then she understood: *the press, of course.*

"Elliot, get your ass home," Sheriff Hoffner barked, glaring at her. "John Grey had no authority to hire you."

Cass felt blood rush to her face and opened her mouth to reply. Mitch cut her off.

"You might want to rethink that decision, Sheriff," he said.

"So nice to see that everybody's willing to come to work while I'm gone and tell me what to do when I get back." He took in the hip to ankle brace on Mitch's leg. "You got a doctor's release?"

Mitch dug in his pocket and handed over a crumpled sheet of paper. "It's only my leg, Sheriff. My brain is still intact."

Hoffner inspected the note, folded it, and placed it in his shirt pocket. "Where do you think you're going?"

"We've got a possible shooting near the golf course. No body, but blood on an interior wall."

"The note says desk duty, Stone. Sit down. Martinez can go." Hoffner finally looked around the empty squad room. "Where is everybody?"

The squad room door opened and Munk walked in with three coffee mugs clutched in one hand and a handful of papers in the other. Although he must have changed out of his shorts and into his uniform only recently, it already bore evidence of his coffee consumption. His eyes never left the document he was scanning as he pushed past the taller man, fumbled the dishwasher open, and blindly slipped two of the mugs inside. He put the other mug on the counter, turned to a new page, and waited for the coffee to finish brewing.

Hoffner's face softened and Cass was surprised at the flash of humanity the movement revealed. "Officer Munk, I'm sorry you got dragged home for this. Whoever called you was out of line."

Munk seemed startled to find himself in the squad room. "Hey, Sheriff. Nobody dragged me back. I cut my vacation short when I heard about Mojo. And with the Whitehead and Moore murders, I figure the force can use all hands on deck."

Hoffner turned his piercing blue gaze back to Cass where she still sat, hands balled into fists, at her desk. "Elliot, until I tell you otherwise, you're on leave. Pass off whatever evidence you've got to Mitch or Munk and go home."

Fury slapped Cass so hard her vision blackened. She drew breath to speak but heard Mitch's voice over the blood crashing in her ears.

"Bad call, Sheriff." Hoffner's eyes were icy, but Mitch didn't flinch. "There were four murders in Forney County last night. One involving a cop's family. And that officer might still be in danger. We've just received a report of a shooting at another resident's home. Danny is still out with back problems, I'm at less than full capacity, and you want to debilitate your force further by sending a detective home?" Mitch's voice became a snarl. "That's mismanagement, Sheriff. Worse, it's dereliction of duty. Grey did the right thing. Go sign the release and get Cass back to work. You're slowing us down."

Two points of color rose on Hoffner's cheeks as Mitch spoke, and even from across the room Cass could see the purple vein bulging at his temple.

"He's right." Munk stuck his chin out. "The Firearm Discharge Board cleared the shooting weeks ago and everybody's wondering why you've kept her off work for so long. You even ignored the petition that Officer Truman pulled together. You may think you're losing face by signing her paperwork now, but the sooner you bring her back, the sooner you start rebuilding your credibility."

Cass drew a sharp breath. She'd never heard anyone stand up to Sheriff Hoffner the way Mitch and Munk had just done. Unconsciously, she leaned back in her chair and waited for him to blow. Hoffner stood motionless for several seconds, breathing evenly until the color in his cheeks lessened. He sucked air through his teeth, nodded curtly at Mitch and Munk, and spoke to the door as he pivoted to leave the squad room. "Elliot, pick up your keys, badge, and gun from Elaine."

Mitch lowered himself into a nearby chair and nodded at the sputtering coffee pot. "Pour me some of that, would you, Munk?"

Cass joined them. "Do you two have any idea what could have just happened?"

"He could have fired us," Munk said flatly. "Me and Gabriel always come back from Houston reminded that life is far too short. I get home and vow not to tolerate his attitude and even do all right for a while, but over the next year he wears me down. With everything we've got going on now," he shook his head, "there's no excuse for not bringing you back. Besides, I figure I'm doing my job by giving him a reality check."

"He needed a kick in the ass," Mitch agreed. "The man's been off his rocker since the whole Church of the True Believer thing started. Maybe even before that."

Munk handed Cass a mug of coffee and she stirred in cream and sugar. "You took a big risk for me," she said to both of them.

"You're my partner," Mitch stated. "Besides, when I haven't been drugged up over these past weeks, I've had plenty of time to think." Mitch looked at her, his blue eyes piercing. "He's the reason I got hurt."

"It wasn't Hoffner –," she began, but Mitch cut her off.

"He refused to bring in backup, remember?"

Cass and Munk nodded.

"That was the wrong decision. Maybe I should've called the whole thing off, but we were so close. If Hoffner had been doing his job instead of playing politics and trying to impress that blonde reporter from Dallas, his head would've been clear and we would've had the backup we needed. He put both of us in danger." Mitch sipped his coffee. "I won't tolerate that kind of incompetence again. It's too dangerous."

"Me either," Munk added, picking up his coffee mug. "I'm starting on the paperwork from Mojo's house."

"Well, thanks," Cass said. "To both of you. I was ready to explode."

Mitch waved her gratitude away with a crutch before hoisting himself from the chair. "Go get your gun. You're practically naked without it and it's making me nervous. And then bring your truck around back. We're going to Emmet Hedder's place."

"You're on desk duty, Mitch."

He grinned. "We'll pretend the truck is a big ol' desk on wheels."

CHAPTER 52

HOFFNER FOUGHT MIGHTILY NOT to slam his office door, won the battle with his temper, and instead eased the door closed. Leaning against its cool surface, he gave the waves of rage their head, hearing again Mitch and Munk's words, seeing the disdain on their faces. Through the red haze, his brain latched on to the methods for calming himself his leadership coach had taught him. It had worked in the squad room, and he decided to try again. Deep breaths in and out, visualizing the gentle tracks his skis left as he slalomed his way down a pristine mountain slope. Slowly, his fists unclenched and his heart slowed its furious pounding.

He opened his eyes, a feeling of satisfaction settling in his gut. He'd mastered his emotions twice in the last five minutes – resisting both the urge to fire three of his staff and to rip his office door from its hinges. Maybe there was something to this leadership crap after all.

Hoffner dug his fingers into his eye sockets. This had been a long, long day and he was feeling its effects. The last thing he wanted when he arrived at the courthouse was to find Cass Elliot in his squad room. But there she was, and after the hiding Mitch and Munk had given him, there she would remain. He was shocked at their insubordination, but a very small part of him recognized that they were right: he was man enough to admit that he'd waited too long to bring her back.

She looked different from when he'd seen her at the Firearm Discharge Board review, and he hated the fact that he noticed. Her face was thinner now, or maybe harder. The leanness made her look even more like her mother. A fact that still made Hoffner desperately uncomfortable around Cass. He was grateful that she'd been far enough away that her perfume, the same scent her mother always wore, hadn't drifted to him.

The sound of feet hurrying past his office door startled him, and his posture slumped as he took in his office; he'd been gone less than a week and already the paperwork had piled up. He hoped written updates on each of the murder investigations were waiting somewhere in that landslide on his desk. Pushing away from the door, he crossed to his file cabinet and unlocked it to extract Cass's personnel folder. He stopped and adjusted a frame on the wall. It held a photo of him as a young cadet, when his hair was still a deep auburn and his blue eyes burned with passion for the job. Hoffner looked wearily at that young image of himself and wondered where all the passion had gone.

He squinted at his desk and his heart dropped. Every item, from the phone to his desk blotter, even the business card and doo-dad holders, was slightly askew. Irritation flared. Either someone had used his office, or –. He stopped and looked more closely. From the way each object had been moved, someone had deliberately changed the alignment of his things. *Childish*, he thought, taking the high road as he realigned each item with the desk's edge and the object next to it.

Satisfied, he shuffled the tumbling mail into a pile and placed it squarely in his inbox, rummaged through the case folders and ordered them according to urgency, and then placed Cass's file in the center of his blotter. Flipping its cover open, he ignored the photo stapled to the left-hand flap and placed his signature on the top page. He slapped the folder closed and slipped it back into his file cabinet.

Finally, he turned to the stack of case folders. Thank God the press was still occupied with that explosion down in Watuga County. At least three people were dead and word was out that the plant's night-shift manager was a drunk whose failures had led directly to this tragedy. Elaine was on notice that at first sight of a reporter, she was to lock the courthouse doors and notify him. He had to get up to speed on these murders; the last thing he needed was to be caught out by a reporter.

The folder at the top of the pile belonged to Calvin Whitehead, and although he knew it was only his imagination, he could swear the smell of burning flesh wafted from the papers. Hoffner braced himself and started to read.

CHAPTER 53

A GUST OF OVEN-HOT wind blew the truck door into Cass's shoulder as she helped Mitch lift his leg into the county-issue pickup. "Ow," she breathed, sliding the crutches between his legs before pulling the seat belt out so Mitch could grab it. "This might not be such a good idea."

"It'll be fine," Mitch answered, squirming to find a comfortable position. "Just don't have a wreck. Getting out in a hurry might be a problem."

Cass shut the door and turned, surprised to find a black-headed woman with porcelain skin and clear jade eyes standing behind her, purse clutched across her chest as she shifted from foot to foot. She was about Cass's height. Her clothes were a gorgeous raw silk with a full cut, but as the wind blew them against her, her hipbones and collarbones jutted against the fabric.

"Cass? Cass Elliot?" she asked in a breathy voice.

"Yes, ma'am. Can I help you?"

A fleeting smile crossed the woman's face and Cass felt a tug of familiarity. "You don't remember me." She brushed a strand of hair from her face. "I'm Max." At Cass's blank look she continued. "Maxine Leverman. Used to be Wright."

Joy flooded Cass and she yanked the other woman into a hug. "My God, Max, you look so different. I didn't recognize you. How long has it been?"

"Six years. Can you believe it?" Maxine answered. "I heard you were back at work."

"Speaking of," Cass said, "I need to go. Can we catch up later?"

"Um, sure." She bit her lower lip. "Can we talk after you're done with," she flicked a wave at Mitch where he waited in the truck, "whatever?"

"Things are kind of busy right now," Cass hedged. "What if I call you?"

Maxine dug in her purse and pulled out a business card containing only a phone number. A man walked past in the parking lot and Maxine watched until he was out of sight, her green eyes narrowed. She brushed another strand of hair from her face, her expression hesitant. "I need your help, Cass. Call soon, okay? As soon as you can."

She hurried away, head pivoting to take in the area as she made her way across the crowded parking lot.

"Who was that?" Mitch asked as she started the truck.

"Maxine Wright Leverman. Remember her?"

"Really?" Mitch twisted in his seat to watch Maxine as Cass entered the street. "Of course I remember her; you two were joined at the hip from preschool. But she doesn't look anything like Maxine. Max was fat."

"She was not fat, Mitch," Cass protested. "She was a little heavy, and she grew out of it when we were in high school."

"Well she's not fat now." He settled into the passenger seat. "Actually, she looks pretty good."

"She looked kind of thin to me."

"You're one to talk."

"Shut up," Cass responded, hitting the siren and blowing through a yellow light before turning onto the highway. "She looked worried."

"Yeah, she did. That lip of hers was kind of busted up."

"She's been chewing it. That's what Max always did when she was upset."

"What did she want?"

Cass shrugged and passed him Maxine's business card. "She said she needs help and wants me to call her."

His eyebrows went up. "The only people who print just a number on their cards are either very rich," he handed it back, "or very scared."

CHAPTER 54

THE STATION WAS BLESSEDLY quiet when Joseph slipped through the back door behind Martinez. Shift change started in an hour, and he knew his opportunity to think through his next steps was limited. He followed Martinez to the squad room and spotted a photograph of Moses surrounded by a group of grinning kids pinned to a corkboard beside a desk.

Joseph settled into the chair and suppressed a surge of rage at the thought that his brother would never sit here again. The intensity of the emotion startled him. This was not good. To pretend to be Moses and find the man who murdered his family, Joseph needed every ounce of cool logic available to him. Emotion only blurred his thinking. With effort, he cleared his head and examined his brother's work space.

Joseph had visited the squad room with Moses several times, but long ago, when Moses had first joined the force. Little had changed in the past twenty-six years. The walls were a scuffed pale blue, the industrial carpet wearing thin between the long rows of desks. A series of cabinets ran along an interior wall, stretching from the coffee bar to the far windows. He wondered if they held paperwork, or if everything was stored electronically. From the look of the clunker of a computer squatting on Moses' desk, Joseph placed a bet on the file cabinets.

The desk drawers opened smoothly and he fingered through the office supplies, outdated memos, and stale packs of chewing gum. Joseph found folders containing blank forms, but no arrest reports or cell phone bills. Martinez was working at a cluster of desks across the room. Joseph turned Moses' computer on and said a prayer to the gods of technology that the thing would fire up as it clicked, whirred, and stuttered to life. A sign-on screen finally presented itself. Moses must have been the last officer to use the machine, because his name was in the userID box.

The chair squeaked as Joseph rocked and tried to guess his brother's password. What password would a man who hated computers choose? It had to be short and meaningful so that someone like Moses could remember it. Joseph scanned the desk. He took a chance and picked the tethered keyboard up and flipped it over. There it was. A list of user details for a variety of systems for the officers who used this desk, taped to the bottom. Amazingly stupid, but incredibly convenient. He tapped in Moses' password and hit enter. A surprisingly modern home screen opened up.

Joseph found the case management system and used Moses' logon credentials to gain access, then figured out how to sort records by userID. The list of cases Moses had worked on was impressive. Joseph opened the last document saved by Moses. He read quickly and snorted a quiet laugh. In the file, Moses recorded the explanation he gave to an inebriated gentleman about why it was improper to use the tall war memorial on the courthouse lawn as his personal urinal. When the man proclaimed that it was his civil right to pee where he pleased, Moses deftly provided the gentleman a place to rest overnight, at the county's expense. Granted, the wording was pure official-ease, but Joseph could imagine the tongue-in-check thoughts rolling through Moses' head as he two-finger typed the report.

A throat cleared behind him and Joseph jerked back from the desk. A tall man, with hair a snowy white and nose so hooked it looked like a beak, was standing behind his chair. Joseph recognized him as Sheriff Bill Hoffner, and he stood slowly, wondering how Moses would act around the county's top law officer. "Sheriff."

"I got back as fast as I could, Moses. I'm so sorry about your mom and Joseph."

"Thank you, sir."

"You're entitled to leave, Mojo." When Joseph didn't respond, Hoffner nodded at the computer. "You sure you're ready to be here?"

"Yes, sir. Detective Martinez thought that if the shooting is about me, I might be able to find something in my files that would give us a hint about who's involved."

Hoffner glanced across the room. "Detective Martinez, eh?"

"Yes, sir."

"And have you found anything?"

"Not yet."

"I understand you've brushed off your protection detail. I don't think that's wise until we know more about motive for the shooting."

"Yes, sir. But I think I'm fine during the day. I'll be in the station most of the time. I'm staying with Porky Rivers for now and," he glanced down at his civilian clothes, "I'll have my weapon with me tonight."

Hoffner examined him, then nodded and squeezed Joseph's shoulder. "We'll keep the protection on at Porky's during the night, then. But don't hesitate to ask if you change your mind. And if you need to take some time off, to make arrangements or attend to personal business, let the sergeant know."

"Thank you, sir. I appreciate it, and I'll take the time if I need it."

Hoffner released Joseph's shoulder and headed back across the squad room.

Joseph sank into Moses' chair and breathed evenly, trying to bring his furiously beating heart under control. Sheriff Hoffner probably didn't know Moses very well, given how far apart they were in the departmental food chain. But for some reason, lying to the man wearing the biggest badge in the county was unnerving.

Maneuvering to the case system's main screen, a name and number combination caught his attention. Joseph opened the file related to his mother and brother's murder. Only the shell of the investigation had been loaded, probably because the detectives worked so late into the night and were sidetracked by the Whitehead and Moore murders. He closed the file and clicked quickly through several others, realizing the magnitude of the work he needed to do. He thought for a moment and then crossed the squad room. "Carlos?"

"You okay?" the older detective asked.

"I'm not sure how far back I should search. Got any ideas?"

"Let's start with your family and Donna Moore." Martinez ran his hands over his silvery crew cut, his eyes thoughtful. "How do we find that link?" He turned to his computer, opened the case file system and ran a simple search.

A phone vibrated in his pocket and Joseph pulled it out. Moses' personal phone. He checked the screen. Same number as the last call. He silenced the ringer and turned back to Martinez' search. Three hits popped up, all related to DUIs earned by a man from another county. Martinez opened the driver's license database and found Moore's photograph. Pale face, delicate features, mounds of dark hair. "Recognize her?"

Joseph's breath froze in his chest and he fought to keep his jaw from dropping. This was the woman in the photograph with Moses. The white woman who was gazing at his brother with a look akin to love. Something between the two of them had gotten them both killed, and Joseph hated her on sight. He managed to shake his head. "She looks familiar. I might have seen her around town, but I don't think I know her."

"Okay. Work from her home and work addresses outward, and see what crimes have been reported around both."

Joseph squinted at the screen. "Moore's address is out in the middle of nowhere, isn't it?"

"It is, but that's just where meth cookers and drug suppliers like to work."

"Good point. I'll get on it."

Joseph returned to his desk, grateful that he could continue to use the computer instead of plowing through paper files. He worked for fifteen minutes, remembering to peck away at the keyboard as Moses would have done. There were only a few traffic violations on the isolated roads near Moore's home, but several cases of breaking and entering around her office near the square. As he read deeper, Joseph discovered how Moses met Moore. Five years ago, Moses had responded to a tripped burglar alarm at her office in the middle of the night. His notes stated that there was no sign of forced entry. When the business owner arrived, he searched the building's interior and found two squirrels in the kitchen. Apparently they'd discovered a section of siding stripped from one end of the building and built a cozy nest on the little-used second floor, coming and going as they pleased. The door that closed the stairs off from the kitchen was opened earlier that day and did not latch completely, permitting the squirrels full run of The Moore Agency and allowing them to trip the motion sensors.

Joseph leaned back in Moses' chair, now almost deaf to its squeak. Moses had met Moore five years ago and Joseph didn't recognize her photo or name. This meant that Moses had kept his relationship with her a secret. And Moses sucked at keeping secrets, so staying quiet about Moore must have been important to him. Maybe their liaison made someone crazy enough to murder them both. A spurned lover? A redneck who had problems with mixed-race couples? A tiny flicker of hope bloomed in his brain. If these murders were about Moses and Moore, Joseph would find their killer. He still hated her, but neither Moses nor this woman deserved to die because they were in love. Joseph nodded; this was a place to start.

CHAPTER 55

CASS PULLED INTO EMMET Hedder's drive and watched as Jerome, a large man in pale blue scrubs, executed a delicate dance with a well-dressed woman who was trying to get past him to the front porch. The house was a neat one-story brick with a two vehicle carport to the side. Mitch was twisted sideways with the passenger seat pushed as far back as it would go to allow his brace encased leg and crutches to fit in the truck's cab. "Can you get out by yourself?" she asked.

"I'll manage," he huffed, reaching for the door handle but hitting the button to lower the window instead. "Give me a minute."

Cass stepped from the cab and adjusted her belt, enjoying its weight against her hip bones. The sun's heat baked from the driveway and sweat prickled her underarms and between her shoulder blades. "Jerome?" she called. "Ma'am?"

The woman spun at the sound of Cass's voice. She took in the Sheriff's department logo on the side of the pickup, slung a massive purse over her shoulder and marched across the lawn to meet Cass, tucking her dark blue blouse into a pair of dirty beige slacks. Her black hair was loosely styled around a face the color of creamed coffee. "Thank God you're here. Jerome's gone mad. He said the cops were coming but won't let me go in the house or tell me why he called you."

"I'm Cass Elliot, ma'am, with the sheriff's office. And you are?"

"Celia Hedder. This is my house. What is going on?"

Mitch hobbled to join them. "Detective Mitch Stone, ma'am. Are you Mrs. Emmet Hedder?"

"I am."

"Would you mind if we had a word with Jerome?"

"Yes," she stated, placing one hand on her hip. "I would. He can say whatever he has to say to me."

Jerome stood quietly near the porch, waiting. He was a big man, an ex-con who'd spent time in the penitentiary for auto theft and armed robbery and bore a host of prison tattoos as evidence of his time inside. Unlike many of his fellow convicts, Jerome refused to slide back into the dangerous waters of criminal life, and through a quirk of fate found a job working for a rich widow in an exclusive retirement community. He watched them through dark chocolate eyes, his nutmeg-hued skin a bit paler than the last time Cass had seen him.

"Mrs. Hedder might be able to help, Mitch." Cass waved Jerome over and asked Celia, "Do you know where your husband is?"

"That sorry man's not at work? If he's not there, he's probably gone off on one of his little trips."

"I don't think so, Celia," Jerome said. "The old people worry, so he always calls when he's gonna miss work."

"Ma'am, where have you been today?" Cass asked.

"I teach preschool for half a day." Cass figured that explained the green goo mashed into the knees of Celia's beige slacks. "I had a late lunch with my mother, and just got to the house."

"What time did Emmet leave home today?"

Some of the anger left Celia's face. She gave Jerome a rueful look. "I wasn't here."

"Where were you?" Cass asked.

She closed her eyes. "At my mother's house. I've been living there for a while now."

"You're separated?" Mitch asked.

"Not legally, but yes, we're living apart."

"Why?"

Her eyes snapped open and she glared at Jerome. "He's been acting strange for a while now, hasn't he?"

The big man held up both hands. "Emmet's had a hard time, Celia. I don't know why, but something's upset him. I thought maybe it was trouble with y'all's marriage."

"Don't you lay this on me, Jerome. Emmet's the one who's been sneaking off and won't say where he's been."

"When was the last time you were here?" Mitch asked.

"Saturday. I came to check on my plants. Emmet never remembers to water them." Celia looked down at herself. "I came today to get clothes."

Cass exchanged a glance with Mitch. "Ma'am, may I have your permission to look around your yard and the outside of the house?"

"What for?"

"Your husband seems to be missing, and we want to make sure nothing's wrong."

Her lips flattened into a thin line. "Fine. Maybe you can figure out where he's gone this time."

Cass followed Jerome across the front lawn and under the carport where a green Camry ticked as it cooled. Jerome stopped her and glanced at the concrete floor. "I don't know if it means anything, but there's muddy footprints up the drive, through here, and in the backyard."

She squatted. A faint trail of smeared orange-gray footprints ran under the Camry toward the backyard and a similar set, more difficult to see, came back across the open section of the carport. Cass's senses prickled. This was the second time today she'd come across this type of muddy footprint at a crime scene. "The Hedders have two cars?"

"Yes, ma'am," Jerome answered. "Emmet drives a little black pickup."

Cass stood and headed for the large backyard. She estimated that the Hedders owned about two acres, as did each of their neighbors. There were no fences, and Cass had a clear view across the adjoining yards and down the street. A stream gurgled at the bottom of the properties, and across it a narrow strip of woods separated the residential section from the golf course.

"The bedroom window is past the porch." He pointed at the ground. "There's the footprints in the grass. I tried not to step on them."

She squatted again. They were very faint and only visible because the lush St. Augustine was crushed. Cass wondered if the average citizen would have been sharp enough to recognize that the footprints could be evidence, or if it took an ex-con to be so alert. Picking her way across the well-maintained lawn, she used the impressions from Jerome's shoes to avoid leaving another trail. His steps stopped outside a large, paned window. The curtains were tied back and Cass had a clear view into a bedroom housing functional furniture straight from an Ikea showroom. The pale green bedclothes were mussed and a dark substance was smeared on a pillow and streaked across the wall. A section of the headboard was splintered.

Cass pulled her vision back to the house's exterior. She found a single hole through one pane in the middle of the window. Her eyes caught a glint higher up and she spotted a second bullet hole. She wondered why the neighbors hadn't reported hearing shots as she pulled the cell phone from her pocket and dialed Kado.

"Where are you?" Cass asked through the static scratching from her phone.

"Bank vault. Truman finished the warrant for Donna Moore's safe deposit box and Judge Shackleford signed it. What's up?"

"We've got another shooting." Cass gave him the address and snapped the phone closed. She checked the rest of the house, looking for jimmied windows and ensuring the doors were locked, and spotted no signs of disturbance. Jerome had waited by the carport and she joined him there, stopping to check the side door and spotting a dark drop on the carport's concrete near the step into the house. She squatted. Its directionality indicated that the bleeder had been moving from inside the house across the carport. No other drops were visible.

Jerome paused beside her. "Is that blood? Do you think Emmet got away?"

"It's possible, but I need to get inside." She crossed the front yard to where Celia Hedder was grousing at Mitch and interrupted the woman. "Mrs. Hedder, would you unlock the house, please?"

Her eyes narrowed. "What for?"

"Someone fired a gun through the bedroom window."

She gasped, dropped her purse, and stooped to search through it. "Is it Emmet? Is he hurt? What happened? Who would shoot Emmet?" She dumped the contents of her bag on the ground and pawed through the lipsticks, sunglasses, cash, and crayons. Jerome knelt beside her, plucked a set of keys from the tangle of female paraphernalia, and handed them to Cass. Celia swayed and Jerome caught her. She leaned into him and started to cry.

"The house isn't clear, Cass," Mitch said, struggling on his crutches to keep up as she hurried across the lawn and unlocked the front door.

"The shooter's long gone, Mitch. And," she added, lowering her voice, "it looks like Emmet shot back and might have made it out of the house. There's a drop of blood in the carport and Jerome says Emmet's car is missing."

He started to speak but Cass stopped him.

"If I thought there was a chance that someone was inside, I'd call for backup. But there's not. I want to make sure Emmet's not still here and injured, okay?"

Mitch followed her into the cool, silent house, waiting in the tiled foyer. She moved quietly from room to room, stopping in the master bedroom to examine the splintered headboard and blood on the bedclothes and wall, and to spot a bloody handprint on the carpet near the bed. Another dark smudge marred the hall wall. Four narrow strips of dried blood streaked the wall beneath a key holder near the kitchen door.

She returned to the foyer and Mitch. "He's gone."

"He can't be at a hospital. They'd report a gunshot wound."

"Given the height of the blood smear in the hall, the injury is probably to his shoulder or upper arm. It's not bleeding much and he might be able to pass it off as a cut. We'll call the hospitals, but I think he's running."

"From who?"

"Whoever killed the Franklins and Donna. For whatever reason, they want Emmet Hedder, too."

"That's a big leap, Cass."

"I'll bet you breakfast from The Golden Gate for a week that the mud from the footprints in the backyard matches that from Donna's yard, and the slug in Emmet Hedder's wall is a .308."

CHAPTER 56

THE DRY SMELL OF old paper greeted Munk as he untied the black ribbon snugged around the last of the Franklin files. He'd been through all of Martha's and Moses' paperwork, and everything of Joseph's from the attic. There was nothing unusual in any of the bank statements, tax returns, or other bills he'd examined. He'd found no link to Donna Moore. Not even a business card or notation on a piece of paper. His frustration was building. Munk was methodical, particularly in the examination of paperwork. But all of his effort this afternoon seemed to have been for naught.

Munk stretched his pudgy arms over his head before checking his watch. Four o'clock. Gabrielle and her family would still be on the beach, handing out flyers and asking, "Have you seen this girl? Her name is Angel."

Hand.

No hand.

For a moment, the urge to pull on his shorts and t-shirt, jump in the car, and make the long drive to Galveston overwhelmed him. He had washed the clothes in the station's machines, and just in case, repacked them in the car this afternoon. The tank was full of gas and he was ready to go. But the Franklin's autopsy photos were still spread across the conference room table. Neither Joseph nor Martha had had a chance against a gunman perched in a tree in Deadwood Hollow. He convinced himself that Gabrielle and her army of *familia* would be fine on their own. Munk was more use here.

Settling into the plastic chair, he scanned the documents in the top folder. Two marriage certificates for Martha Franklin. One to a Charles Franklin from Magnolia County, Alabama. The second to a

Homer Radcliffe from right here in Forney County, Texas. And two death certificates, one each for Charles and Homer. An oddity was Martha's petition to the court after Homer Radcliffe's death, requesting that her name be legally restored to Franklin. Munk was a young patrol officer when Homer Radcliffe died, and he remembered the gossip that erupted when Martha changed her name back to Franklin. Such things rarely happened in small towns like Arcadia.

There were Alabama birth certificates for Moses and Joseph, and for Martha and their father, Charles. His death certificate, dated May 11, 1967, was also included. Cause of death was listed as 'asphyxia due to obstructed airway'. He put the certificates aside and smoothed open a copy of Martha Franklin's will. In it, she left everything in equal proportion to her sons, which was little surprise. The last papers in the file were held together with a paper clip. Munk gently pulled it off and separated the papers – a blank page protected each side of a thick, creamy document. He smiled, shaking his head. Martha Franklin had earned a degree in education from Judson College. Munk knew Moses' mother from her time as a school lunch lady, when he called her Mrs. Radcliffe and she called him Ernest. With an education like this, her employment in a school cafeteria was a waste. He wondered if she had ever taught school and why she hadn't started in Arcadia.

In a second file, Munk found paperwork related to several car loans, all of them repaid. The folder also contained the original mortgage for the Franklin house, which was in Homer Radcliffe's name alone. That document was marked paid-in-full back in 1988. A second mortgage was dated 2008, and Munk remembered Moses' frustration that Martha took out the loan after Joseph was arrested in New York. Moses also moved back to his mother's home not long after Joseph's arrest, and from the look of Moses' bank statements, he was helping his mother repay the mortgage. Joseph was looking for a job, but with a record, it would take time to find one. His ability to contribute to the household expenses, much less repay his mother and Moses, was limited.

A nasty little thought landed in Munk's brain: *What if Moses was tired of cleaning up after Joseph?* Munk balanced his elbows on the conference room table and rested his head in his hands. Sometimes, he hated this job and the wicked things that went on in his brain, but he let the idea play out.

From riding patrol with Moses on a few occasions, Munk knew that he was ashamed of his brother's arrest, and was anxious when the time grew near for Joseph's release. Could Moses be embarrassed or angry enough to murder his own brother and mother? But if he killed Joseph and Martha, Moses was also Moore's murderer. Munk had heard that Moses spent last night at Porky River's apartment, but Stella was away, and Porky went into the ME's office to help with the Franklin murders and Calvin Whitehead. Moses had the opportunity to kill Moore.

But did he have means? Munk wasn't sure, but he didn't think that Moses owned a gun other than his service issue weapon and a 12-gauge shotgun for killing the armadillos that occasionally ravaged his mother's yard. He'd never heard Moses talk about owning, or even firing, a rifle. Kado said that the Franklin shooter was in a tree roughly one hundred yards from Martha Franklin's house. Moses was a dreadful shot, and there was simply no way he could have hit the side of a barn at that distance, much less one human being. The chances that he could've hit two people were nonexistent. Apparently the killer was standing close to Moore's bedroom window when he fired the single shot that ended her life. Was it possible that Moses could have killed her? Physically, he might have been able to make that shot. He also could have hired someone to do the killing, but from the look of his bank account, Moses had little money to pay for such a service.

Motive. Munk could just about understand how a brother could be driven to kill his twin over embarrassment and financial strain. But what motive did Moses have to kill Moore? None, from the looks of his family's paperwork. There was simply no connection between the two in these files. The chances that Moses had murdered, or paid someone to murder, his family and Moore were slim to none.

With relief, Munk pushed the nasty thoughts away and picked up the last file from Martha Franklin's desk. Several yellowed newspaper clippings fell out. The first was half of an advertisement from a furniture store Munk had never heard of. It had been neatly snipped and no date or paper name was visible. He turned the slip over and his breath caught in his throat.

"Men Found Hanging in Grove", the headline read. A brief story followed, providing scant details of how Charles Franklin, Robert Hedder, and Ben Silverman were hanged and burned to death the night of May 11 in a town called Thayerville. No year was provided; probably because the full date was included at the top of the page. A single photograph accompanied the story. A flash-lit scene showed charred bodies hanging from the branches of three trees. Five men clad in white sheets and hoods stood between the corpses. Two of the men cradled shotguns while the others held flaming torches.

"Good Lord," Munk breathed. He reached for Charles Franklin's death certificate; cause of death was listed as asphyxia. But 'lynching' was Charles' true cause of death. Most of the officers on the force knew that Moses and Joseph's father had died when they were young. But no one thought to question *how* the man had died. Moses rarely spoke of his natural father, and Munk wondered if he and Joseph knew about this horrific event.

The rest of the file contained four short articles about the lynching, two of which expounded on the 'crimes' for which the three men were punished: leering at a white woman and illegal gathering. One reporter speculated briefly on which Klavern the five robed men belonged to. The last piece of newsprint was only a paragraph, apparently clipped from a longer article and glued to an index card: "The Sheriff said, 'The death of these men was a tragedy, and we've done all we can to apprehend the perpetrators of this crime. This file will remain open until new evidence comes to light.'"

Munk sat back in the plastic chair and absently rubbed a coffee stain on his uniform. He understood a bit better now why Martha Franklin brought her sons to Texas all those years ago, and why she wanted to take her first husband's name back. Although Charles

Franklin was ripped from her life in the most hideous of ways, Munk envied her. At least she had closure, something he wasn't sure that he and Gabrielle would ever find.

CHAPTER 57

JOSEPH OFFERED A SILENT prayer of gratitude as a phone vibrated in his pocket. He thanked the officers offering sympathy and worked his way to the hall before checking the incoming call. It was from the same number that had called earlier.

"Yeah," he answered.

"Where the hell are you?" a male voice hissed.

"Beg your pardon?"

Silence, followed by a long sigh. "Sorry, man. I mean, I'm really sorry about your mom and Joseph. I can't imagine what you're dealing with, but I need to see you. Tonight."

Joseph weighed his options. This man had a connection with Moses. Was he a snitch? A criminal Moses had arrested? Someone who objected to Moses' relationship with Moore to the point he was willing to murder them both? Whoever it was, this was the only number Moses called on this phone. Whether benefactor or foe, this man held a unique place in Moses' life and was someone Joseph needed to meet. "Where?"

"I'm in that motel as you cross the county line into Watuga."

Joseph knew the place. It was a filthy little dive he thought had gone out of business years ago. "Room number?"

"Twenty-nine."

"What time?"

"After dark. Bring the medical kit from your car and get extra bandages, tape, and gauze. Pick up clothes, enough for two or three days. Think you can get all that?"

"What do you want —" Joseph began. A group of officers walked past him on their way to evening shift roll call, muttering their condolences. He turned the phone into his neck and thanked them.

"Where are you?" the voice whispered when he raised the phone to his ear again.

"At the station. Why?"

"Are you stupid?"

"What?"

Joseph heard a rustling in the background. "Somebody's at the door. And Moses?"

"Yeah?"

"Bring food. I haven't had anything to eat since last night."

CHAPTER 58

MITCH COMPLETED THE LIFT and shift from his wheelchair to his desk chair with a grunt. Cass looked him over and pulled out her cell phone. A business card tumbled from her pocket and Mitch snatched it from the air.

"Who are you calling?" he asked.

"Darla. It's time for you to go home."

"I've got work to do. Give me that thing." He reached for the phone but Cass moved away.

She took in the dark smudges under his eyes and his sallow skin. "Mitch, you look ready for the morgue."

"Said like a true friend," he muttered, poking the mouse to wake his computer.

"You need to go home and, if you're up to it, come back tomorrow. Otherwise, you won't be any use to anybody at all." She spoke into the phone. "Darla? It's Cass... Yeah, he's done for today... He's so tired, sexy cardinals are the last thing on his mind. Do you want me to bring him home?... Yes, thanks, I'd love to."

Mitch heaved a great sigh as Cass snapped the phone shut. "I guess that's it, then."

She lifted her chin at his computer. "Turn that thing off. It might cheer you up to know that Darla's frying chicken, mashing potatoes, and making cream gravy. Just for you."

He maneuvered out of the system and reversed the movement from his desk chair to the wheelchair. He held the business card up between two fingers as Cass grabbed the handles and shoved him forward. "Maxine's card. You gonna call her?"

"Get your crutches," Cass said, tucking the card in the breast pocket of her blouse. "After supper."

"You're eating at our house?"

"I'm not turning down Darla's fried chicken. And Bruce is bound to be pissy since I left him working on the kitchen by himself. It'll be cold cereal for supper at our house."

CASS BACKED OUT OF the Stone's driveway and waved at Darla. Her stomach was as full as she could remember, and Cass was still savoring the taste of Darla's blackberry cobbler. Her body ached after her first full day back at work, and her mind was spinning with details of the four open cases they were working. She wanted nothing more than to go home and crawl into bed.

Instead, she turned the volume down on the Beatles' "Get Back" and pulled the little white card from her shirt pocket. The first ring had barely sounded when Cass heard a whispered, "Hello?"

"Max?"

"Cass?"

"I know it's short notice, but are you free now? I can come by and we can talk."

"No, no," Maxine said in a breathy voice. "I mean, yes, now is a good time, but we can't talk here."

"Where is here?"

"I have an apartment in that new development off the Loop. Do you know it?"

Stone Briar was a massive complex, expensively designed and executed. Cass's brother Harry and his wife Carly had done work as subcontractors on the project, designing and decorating the club house. "I do. We can't talk there?"

"We need somewhere private. Where are you now?"

"I'm just coming into town. How about Live Oak Park? The one near downtown."

"Okay. It'll take me about an hour to get there."

Cass started. "You're ten minutes away, why so long?"

"I'll ride my bike through the trails."

"Why?"

"So he can't follow me. Bring some of Stan's coffee, would you? Extra large."

Cass pulled up to a stop light on Arcadia's square and looked down at the now silent phone. *Who was following Maxine?*

CHAPTER 59

JUNIE NIBBLED ON THE tip of a breadstick. Officer Hugo Petchard shivered as she closed her lips and then bared her teeth to take a bite. He looked down at his plate of spaghetti and adjusted the napkin in his lap. Junie fought a satisfied smile and ate more of her lasagna. Forney County's only Italian restaurant served good food, and she asked Petchard to bring her here often. The breadsticks provided solid entertainment, too.

"You don't know who murdered the Franklin family?"

The single candle flickered as Petchard leaned into the table. "No, but we do know that the same unsub killed Donna Moore last night. She's one of the top accountants in Arcadia."

"Unsub?"

"Sorry, sweetheart. Police jargon. Means 'unknown subject'."

"I love it when you talk shop. So, no leads?"

"Not yet, but we'll catch the bastard who did this. You mark my words."

"Language, Hugo. It's crass."

He reached across the checkered tablecloth and took her hand. "I'm just a lump of clay, Junie. You'll have to keep working to get me into any kind of shape."

"You're perfect, Hugo, you have a few rough edges to smooth off. We all do." Junie ran her thumb across his knuckles and freed her hand. "It must be difficult to work on so many investigations at one time. You have the Franklins, and the accountant, and that poor man at the gas station. What happened to him? Was it as awful as people say?"

Petchard looked up from his plate. "What are they saying?"

"That he burned to death."

"It's worse than that." He glanced around the restaurant and leaned in again. "He was hanged and set on fire."

"How horrible. Do you have any leads?"

A handsome young waiter approached with a basket of warm breadsticks. Junie smiled at him and caught Petchard scowling as the man turned to another table. She reached out to stroke his cheek. "There's no need for that, lover."

"I don't like the way he was looking at you, Junie. You're so attractive, men can't help themselves. One day –"

"Shhh," she said. "You're the one I want, Hugo. That's why I'm here with you, and not with someone else." His face eased and she picked up her fork. "Now, you were telling me about leads related to that poor man."

"It's frustrating. We don't have anything solid yet, but we're working through the evidence. We'll catch this guy, too."

"I know you will, Hugo. You always get your man." She watched him from beneath her lashes. "Did you take time to think about what happened with Detective Elliot this morning?"

He shifted in the chair and grimaced. "You were right. I let my softer side take over with Mojo when I should've stuck to procedure. Which means that technically, Cass was right."

"That's one of the things I admire about you."

"What's that?"

"Your willingness to look at your actions impartially, and make changes." She touched her lip with the tip of her tongue. "You have such a beautiful soul."

Petchard beamed.

"And you know what comes next, right?"

His face went blank. "A movie?"

She laughed and squeezed his hand. "I meant that you should apologize to Detective Elliot."

"I should do what?"

"Apologize. Show her what a strong man you are. A man who can admit his mistakes." She took a sip of iced tea. "She'll respect you for it."

Petchard concentrated on twirling spaghetti around his fork. He scratched behind his ear and looked up, his lips pursed. "You might be right."

A soft ding sounded and Junie pressed a button on her cell phone. The screen was a harsh glow in the dark restaurant. "I'm so sorry, lover, but I have to get home and call my mother."

"Is everything all right?"

"It's nothing that a phone call won't solve. I just hate that we can't talk about your work any longer. It's fascinating."

"I'll come by the café first thing in the morning and fill you in." He motioned to her plate. "Let's get your lasagna packed up to go. I can't have people saying that I don't take care of my woman."

CHAPTER 60

THE COUNTY LINE MOTEL was about as skanky as they came. A low-slung building sloughing off paint, it hunkered forlornly between a battered liquor store and The Dolphin's X strip club, whose sagging marquee announced that 'Roxanne West with the Million Dollar Chest' was performing for one week only. One light provided stuttering illumination to the empty parking lot and gravel pinged the side of Moses' car as Joseph skirted the gaping pot holes. He drove behind the one-story building, past a small dark pickup, and parked away from number twenty-nine. Cutting the engine, he listened to its quiet ticking and watched for movement along the building and in the barren expanse butting against the parking lot.

After five minutes, he got out and gathered the medical kit, shopping bags, pizza box, and a six-pack of soda from the back seat. The lights were off in room twenty-nine but several dark spots marred the step and a bloody handprint was smeared across the door frame. Joseph tapped lightly and spun at the sound of feet hurrying across loose gravel. A hooded figure, shorter and a bit broader than Joseph, had emerged from behind the dented dumpster and stepped over the basketball-sized stones ringing the parking lot. Joseph touched Moses' gun where it rested against his left hip, and a flash of desperate wonder streaked across his mind: did this thing have a safety, or was it a point and shoot model?

As the man came closer, he reached up and pulled the hood back, revealing a head shaved as bald as Joseph's and a set of ultra-white teeth gleaming in the faint moonlight. Joseph started as a face bearing caramel-colored skin and a sprinkling of freckles across the nose materialized from the night. This was a face he had known all his life. Emmet Hedder and the Franklin boys had grown up together, attending the same school, playing basketball, chasing girls, and sneaking their first tastes of alcohol together. Joseph couldn't believe he hadn't recognized Emmet's voice on the phone earlier.

"Move," Emmet demanded, shouldering past Joseph to the door. He kept a close watch on the space behind the motel as he unlocked the door, seemingly oblivious to the blood on the step and door frame. He slipped inside, unaware of the larger man's surprise. Joseph followed and waited as Emmet closed the door and checked the curtained windows before flipping on a low-hanging overhead light. Emmet unzipped the hoodie and peeled it slowly from his body, exposing a deep gash across the meat of his upper right arm. He disappeared into the bathroom and returned with a towel.

"What happened?" Joseph asked as he dropped the bags on the grimy bedspread.

"The same guy that killed your mom, Joseph, and Donna came after me." He dug in the medical kit and dry swallowed four painkillers and two antibiotic tablets. He held a bottle of alcohol out to Joseph, then positioned the towel under his injured arm. "I woke up just before he fired. He nicked me. I got one shot off and he ran."

Emmet winced as the liquid hit his wound, a string of curses streaming from between his lips.

"Sorry, man," Joseph said. "Celia was at her mom's?"

"Yeah."

"Have you talked to her?"

"Why?"

"To let her know you're okay."

"Like she cares," Emmet answered, flashing a confused look.

Joseph focused on pouring the alcohol. "Enough?"

Emmet motioned to his own medical kit on the room's only chair. "Wash your hands, really good, and stitch me up."

"You're kidding, right?"

"No, I'm not."

"But you're the nurse."

"Hell Moses, I can't stitch it with my left hand."

"No anesthetic?"

"Just do it, man."

Joseph raised an eyebrow and wondered, as he lathered his hands and then tore open a suture packet, how he could manage to do this without throwing up. Emmet sat on the edge of the bed and Joseph stood over him, needle poised. "What do I do?"

"It's like fixing ripped jeans. Pinch the sides together and use a continuous stitch."

Joseph used his right hand to squeeze the wound closed and felt faint as blood oozed from the gash. He drew a deep breath and plunged the needle into Emmet's arm.

"Holy mother," Emmet growled, freckles stark against his paling skin. When Joseph hesitated, he barked, "Finish it."

Joseph pulled the needle through, brought the thread over the wound and made another stitch. "What about the blood on the door?"

Emmet frowned through the pain. "What door?"

"There's blood outside the motel room door and on the frame. Is that from you?"

"Naw, man," he grunted. "Somebody banged on the door when we were talking. It was a drunk, looking for a free bed. He got nasty and I smacked him in the nose." Emmet looked at his arm. "Three more stitches, then tie the thread off."

Emmet collapsed back onto the bed after Joseph snipped the thread but let Joseph spread a thin layer of antibiotic ointment over the stitches and cover them with gauze. Joseph ran cool water over a wash cloth and gave it to Emmet, who wiped the sweat from his face. He lay quietly for a moment, studying Joseph. "Thanks."

"No problem." Joseph grabbed the pizza box and sodas, sat on the edge of the bed, and took a slice. "You probably need food. I do."

Struggling upright again, Emmet braced himself against the headboard. His hand hovered over the open box before dropping to his lap. His voice was quiet. "What do you think you're doing?"

"What do you mean?"

"You'll have to do a hell of a lot better than this if you want to pass for Moses."

JOSEPH CHEWED, HIS EYES flat.

Emmet snorted at the stony silence. "You two have always looked just alike, moved the same, and even sounded alike, but I never really struggled to tell you apart. I know we haven't seen much of each other since you left to go hit the Big Apple. We probably haven't seen each other more than twice since you've been home." Emmet smiled in reluctant amusement. "Even after all these years, you can't fool me, Joseph. You sewed me up with your left hand, didn't barf while doing it, your wallet is in the wrong pocket, and you got mushrooms on the pizza. Moses wouldn't touch a mushroom to save his life." He pulled a slice from the box. "But your biggest problem is the gun."

Joseph looked down at his waist. He had slipped Moses' holster onto his belt after leaving the pizza place. It was positioned on his left hip, ready for a left-handed draw. Looking closer, Joseph realized that the holster was ambidextrous, with belt slots positioned so the gun could be worn on the right- or left-hand side. He looked up.

Emmet shrugged with his good shoulder. "Moses is a righty."

Joseph lowered his head into his hands and rubbed his temples.

"This is not smart, man. Being Moses will get you killed. With this shooter, being Moses' *twin* is enough to get you killed. Joseph. What were you thinking?"

"I've been trying to figure out who would be after Moses or me. Working with the cops gives me access to their systems."

"After *you?*"

Joseph snapped his head up and glared at Emmet. "I've been through Moses' files at the station. There's only one guy who even hinted that he wanted to kill Moses – some tweaker. But the Detectives have pretty much cleared him." He drew a deep breath. "There's one job I got a down payment on, but didn't finish. Maybe someone with links to that customer has come after me, and killed Momma and Moses by mistake."

"Why wouldn't that customer come after you himself?"

"He's in prison in New York."

Emmet was silent for a moment. "Have they figured out whether the same gun killed your family and Donna?"

Joseph nodded.

"Then what's the link between your dissatisfied customer and Donna?"

"I don't know. But I think she was laundering money."

"No way, man." Emmet waved him off and grabbed another slice of pizza. "Donna's the straightest arrow to fly the friendly skies."

"She had a safe full of cash at home. A hundred and twenty thousand. That ain't rainy day money."

"Nope, it's not. Donna is, or was, terrified of being caught without. She thought the financial system might collapse and wanted to make sure she had enough negotiables to get through. They'll find more cash and some gold bars in her safe deposit box." He leaned into the headboard. "This isn't about you."

"Then maybe it's about this." Joseph yanked Moses' wallet from his hip pocket and pulled the pack of business cards out, shuffling through them until he found the photograph of Moses and Donna.

Emmet took the picture. His smile was soft, almost tender. He looked up at Joseph. "What about it?"

"You knew about this?"

"That Donna and Moses knew each other? Yeah. So what?"

Joseph's jaw dropped. "Moses was messing with a white woman, Emmet. Could that be what got them killed?"

"Come full circle, man. If Moses and Donna had a thing, why would the same person try to kill me, too?"

Joseph tucked his chin in. "Were you with her?"

Emmet actually chuckled. "No, and neither was Moses."

"Then what's that picture about?"

"They were friends. We were all friends."

"Then why didn't Moses ever mention her? I'd never heard the woman's name until today."

Emmet's reply was slow in coming. "We weren't the kind of friends that talk about each other."

Joseph opened his mouth to reply, then jumped to his feet and paced the narrow length of the motel room, unconsciously ducking beneath the hanging light fixture. "Who would have a reason to kill all y'all? What could the three of you have done to get you murdered by the same person?"

Emmet ate a bite of pizza and chewed. "I can't do it," he said softly, almost to himself.

"Can't do what?"

"Tell you."

Joseph stopped mid-stride. "Why not?"

"Moses wanted to keep you out of it."

"Out of what?"

The sound of tires crunching on gravel came from the parking lot. Emmet's eyes widened. He eased from the bed and swayed for a moment, then moved to the window and pulled the curtain back a fraction.

"What?" Joseph asked.

"That's twice the same pickup has come by. Get my stuff."

"Who is it?"

"I don't know, but that's the only car that's come this way twice today. I don't know how he followed me, I was watching. Get my stuff," he said again.

"What stuff?"

"Everything. Clothes, medical supplies, dirty towels. Pack it up. We're getting out of here."

Joseph hurried to the bathroom. "Everything?"

"If it has my blood on it, yes."

Joseph scooped up soiled towels, gauze, and tissues and stuffed them in the trash can liner. A pop sounded from outside and Emmet ducked. Joseph stared at him, open-mouthed. "What is wrong with you?"

"Get down! That's a gun, man."

Joseph strode to the window and nudged the curtain aside. "There's nobody out there. It was just a backfire."

"That was a shot from a weapon, Joseph. Mark my words." Emmet crawled up onto the bed and paused, breathing deeply.

His duffel bag was open beside him and Joseph tossed the full trash can liner inside it, stopping short at the sight of a gun and several loaded magazines. "Looks like you're ready for a war."

"Damn right. I'm ready to kill whoever murdered your family and Donna, and who wants to kill me." Emmet glared at Joseph. "You better make a decision, man. If you want to know the truth, then you're in this to help me find him. I'll kill him, you don't have to do that. But if you don't want in, tell them who you really are and get some protection."

Joseph took a step back at Emmet's tone, then tossed the unused medical supplies into the kit and closed it. Emmet grabbed it from him. Joseph heard the rip of a zipper and stared in amazement at the wad of cash Emmet withdrew from the depths of the bag. He tossed the cash into the duffel and struggled to close the kit, then put the top down on the pizza box and grabbed the sodas.

"Where'd that come from?" Joseph asked, his face incredulous. "That must be a few thousand dollars."

"Five thousand," Emmet said. "Donna made sure we kept a stash, in case something like this happened. Moses should have cash in an old shoe box in the top of his closet, in case you need any." He opened the door a crack and peeked outside. Emmet's truck was listing to starboard. "What'd I tell you?"

Joseph knelt to examine the flat tire, and then looked up. "I'm in."

"You sure about that?" Joseph nodded and Emmet checked both ends of the parking lot, and then released a long breath toward the starlit sky. "You'll have to change it."

When the spare was on, Joseph stood and brushed the grime from his clothes. "We're not done with this," he told Emmet.

"Not tonight. I've got to change hotels."

"When Emmet? I have to know what's going on."

His friend, freckles receding to their normal degree of prominence against his caramel-colored skin, spoke evenly. "If you're gonna be Moses, I suppose you do. But brace yourself. I'll tell you things about your family you might not want to hear." Joseph started to speak but Emmet stopped him. "Get all the information from the police that you can about the murders. It'll help. I'll call you. Until then, keep your ass low, Joseph. Very low. And learn to use the gun. Or you will get killed."

CHAPTER 61

CASS SAT ON A park bench sheltered beneath the sprawling arms of a live oak tree, sipping coffee from The Golden Gate Café and sweating in the evening heat. Although her body was still, her mind was busy filtering through the last twenty-four hours. Kado had called as she was on her way to Live Oak Park to confirm that the slug in Hedder's bedroom wall was a .308. His voice was rough with a mix of exhaustion and frustration, and Cass stayed silent in spite of wanting to ask him to meet her after she and Maxine were done. He told her he was going home to bed, but would be in first thing Friday morning to try and match the slug to those taken from the Franklin and Moore homes. Even without the comparison, Cass was confident of the outcome. The same shooter was after Hedder. She struggled to find angles that could feasibly connect the shootings, but the possible links between a retired school lunch lady, a cop, an accountant, and a registered nurse were limited.

And then there was Calvin Whitehead. The person or people who had murdered him had simply disappeared, leaving no trace. Crime scene photos showed a crucifix hanging on the wall behind Whitehead's register, and she wondered if it was worth talking to his priest. The details of a confession were sacred, Cass knew, even after a person died. But the priest might be inclined to talk if he understood the horrific manner of Whitehead's death.

Her mind continued its journey through the anomalies of the day and landed on Maxine Wright Leverman. Mitch was right; she and Maxine had been inseparable through their school years. They shared secrets, dreams, crushes, and a commitment at graduation never to drift apart. And they hadn't. Not until Cass was raped. Her friendship with Maxine was one of the many victims of Cass's withdrawal after the attack. Maxine wasn't the problem with the relationship; the issue was Cass. Specifically, her inability to talk to anyone about the violence, the *violation* she experienced.

Cass caught movement from the corner of her eye, drawing her back from the painful past to her spot on the bench. Sipping the coffee, she watched as Maxine's form glided in and out of the glowing fish bowls created by the street lights. Her head swiveled to take in the area around Cass as she pedaled up. Her bike was one of the fancy trail models and she wore a pair of baggy shorts and a billowing white linen top. The woman's arms and legs were as thin as any runway model's. Only her breasts were out of place. Those were a new addition since Cass had last seen Maxine, and they definitely didn't belong to a woman this skinny. Cass wondered if Maxine was anorexic or bulimic. If neither, she was starving herself to death.

Maxine leaned the bike against a tree and sat next to Cass, pulling the top from her extra large coffee and adding five cartons of cream and five packages of sugar. She stirred vigorously, balanced her elbows on her knees, and started to sip. Cass watched her, noticing the fine lines around Maxine's eyes and those stretching from her nose to the corners of her mouth. Her hair, once long and the blue-black of a raven's wing, was now short and swept back from her face in a headband, absent the silkiness she prized as a teenager. Maxine was no older than Cass, only in her mid-twenties, but she looked more like a woman approaching forty. Traces of the old Maxine were still evident in the tilt of her head, the lift of her chin, and the way she wrapped her hands around the coffee cup as if she couldn't pull enough warmth into her body.

"So. I've got my tongue –" Cass said, offering the beginnings of a line from their favorite comedian in high school, Andrew Dice Clay.

Maxine giggled and bumped Cass with her shoulder. "I've kept up with you, you know."

"Really?"

"Yeah. The cult. That whole shooting mess. How did it feel?"

And there they were, right back to the same old Maxine and Cass. Ask any question and expect an honest answer. "Not good," Cass admitted. "I didn't want to shoot, and I hope I don't have to again. But, I would if I had to."

"I'm glad you can do it," Maxine said. "You know. Kill somebody."

Cass snorted. "Is your brother stealing your panties and selling them to the football team again?"

"If he was back to his panty tricks, I'd kill him myself." Maxine looked around Live Oak Park, turning to check the shadows at their backs, seeming to take little comfort from the tree's protective embrace and the absence of people. "No," she said, her voice low. "I want you to find the man who raped me. I want you to find him, and kill him."

CHAPTER 62

THE SHOOTER PULLED INTO a grocery store parking lot and studied the GPS tracking program on his cell phone. The vehicles had left the motel and were headed in opposite directions. Moses Franklin was going home to Arcadia; Emmet Hedder was driving south, deeper into Watuga County. He'd fired that single shot at Hedder's tire on impulse, and was glad he had. A little terror went a long way and led to mistakes. All to the good.

The shooter closed his cell phone and adjusted the rearview mirror. Grimacing, he scrubbed a finger across his mouth to remove the last traces of Junie's lipstick. Women were high maintenance, but she was worth the effort thanks to the intelligence she collected from that buffoon of a police officer. He checked his reflection again and, satisfied, pushed open the pickup's door and headed to the grocery store to pick up milk.

CHAPTER 63

THE HANDGUN'S RETORT WAS muted by the ear mufflers. Joseph lifted them from his head and watched as the man-shaped target whizzed nearer. Martinez unclipped the paper and whistled. "Not bad, *amigo*. I must be an amazing shooting instructor."

As directed, Joseph had emptied a fifteen round clip into the target as fast as he could, aiming first at the head, then the chest, and finally at the figure's midsection. He swiped at the sweat streaming down his neck. "This is better?"

Martinez nodded. "It's certainly better than usual, particularly the cluster in the head. What are you doing different tonight?"

Joseph yawned. He'd never even held a gun, much less shot one. And he'd never seen Moses fire his weapon. "Just following your instructions. Maybe I'm so tired I'm not over-thinking it."

"After what you've been through in the last twenty-four hours, I'm surprised you're still standing." Martinez checked his watch. "It's nine o'clock. Three more clips, then I have to get back. And we need to schedule my computer lesson. But keep it quiet, okay? I don't want my kids to know."

"Why not?" Joseph asked, thumbing rounds into the magazine. He'd picked up the procedure after watching Martinez load his own weapon.

"They think I'm too old to learn." He nodded. "But a tablet computer can't be all that different from a stone tablet, right?"

Joseph managed a tired smile. "Thanks for this. I know it's not convenient, what with the kids' homework to get done."

"Don't worry about it. This'll force the older kids to help the younger ones. And you're doing so well, I'm glad we came." He clipped a new target to the wire and ran it out, then settled the muffs over his ears. "Again, Mojo, let's see what you can do."

Joseph slipped on his ear muffs and adjusted his protective glasses, then held the handgun up and sighted. Movement caught his attention, and he turned to see Martinez grinning widely. They pulled their head gear off and Martinez said, "That's it."

"What?"

"Hold your weapon up, sight on the target."

Joseph did.

"Man, you should've asked for a left-handed weapon. Or one with an ambi safety and mag release." He studied Joseph's grip. "Go through the motions for me. Don't fire, just show me how you release the safety and the magazine." The sweat on his temples ran cold, but Joseph did as instructed. "*Muy bueno*. You sure you're not naturally left handed?"

"Nope. I don't know why this works better for me."

"Well, you're better off shooting left handed. Put those ear muffs on and let's finish with this target. I'll update your personnel file with these results in the morning. You should've switched years ago."

Joseph felt an odd stab of pride as he slipped the ear protectors back on. He was doing exactly what Emmet had told him to do, better than even Moses could do it. He hoped he'd have a chance to show the former Marine that he was fully committed to their mission. But for now, he pictured the hazy image of their killer and pulled the trigger.

CHAPTER 64

CASS FROZE AT THE words, staring out through the branches curving gracefully to the ground. Swallowing, she tried to add a light tone to her words. "I should arrest you for soliciting a murder."

"I'm not kidding, Cass." Maxine's voice was steady. "Well, maybe a little, about the killing part. But I'm not joking at all about finding the guy who attacked me."

A squirrel scampered between two pools of amber light and a tree limb swayed as it landed. The breeze was picking up and Cass found herself shivering in spite of the evening's heat. She cradled the coffee cup between her hands and steadied her voice. "Tell me what happened. Start from the beginning."

"It was after I got divorced. I lived in Ft. Worth and decided to go out one weekend. My friends were married, and most have small kids. So I went to Dallas by myself on Saturday night, to dance and maybe meet a few people."

Cass glanced at the woman who had been her closest friend all those years ago. Maxine always loved sex, and as a teenager, hadn't been discreet about where she'd found it. Cass wondered if the same were true now.

As if reading her mind, Maxine looked up and met Cass's eyes. Her tongue poked out and touched the bruised place on her lip. "No, Cass. I lost my slutty ways not long after I met my husband. They didn't come back after we divorced." Her lips twitched. "Well, a girl's got to have a little fun."

"Which club did you go to?"

Maxine focused on the squirrel as it hopped from branch to branch. "A place on Greenville. It's not there anymore."

"What happened?"

"I danced a little, had a couple of margaritas."

"On the rocks, extra salt?"

Maxine nodded. "They were watered down, though. Not very good. The dancing, now, that was wild. It was kind of a free for all. Nobody dancing with anybody, everybody dancing with everybody. Know what kind of place I mean?"

Cass nodded. It sounded disturbingly familiar to the place where her rapist had picked her up.

"About an hour into the night I sat down at the bar and ordered another drink. And then like an idiot, I turned around to watch the dance floor. A guy sat down next to me, ordered a margarita like mine, and we started talking and watching the dancers." Her hands twisted in her lap. "He roofied me. He got me on the first drink I had with him, and damn it, I knew better than to let that glass out of my sight. I guess the bartender plunked it down when I turned around and my new friend slipped the Rohypnol, or whatever, right in." She looked at Cass. "I never had a clue what was happening until the next morning."

"Where were you?"

"In my hotel room."

"You rented a room in Dallas?"

Maxine nodded. "I checked in to the Westin and took a cab to the club. I planned to drink and dance, take a cab back to the hotel, find some great eggs Benedict on Sunday morning, and stagger to Ft. Worth in the afternoon. Easy peasy, mac and cheesy." Her smile was small. "I was trying to be good."

Cass poked her. "That's not the Max I know."

"She grew up somewhere along the way."

"How did he know where you were staying?"

"I'm not sure. The hotel receipt was in my jeans pocket, along with my room key. He might've picked my pocket out on the dance floor and realized I was in the Westin. Or maybe he followed me from the hotel to the club."

"Did you call the police?"

She shook her head, refusing to look at Cass.

"Why not?"

Maxine stood and turned to face Cass, gaze focused on the ground. Her hands shook as she unbuttoned the top of her billowing blouse. She dipped the left side down and Cass caught her breath. A circling, loping scar started at Maxine's protruding collar bone and disappeared beneath the lacy edge of her bra. A searing heat ran the length of Cass's scar, which was eerily similar to Maxine's, and her heart galloped against her ribs. It could be a coincidence that Maxine was raped by a man who left a physical reminder in the form of a scar. *Or*, and the thought nearly paralyzed Cass, *maybe the same man had raped them both*. She opened her mouth to speak but was struck dumb by a rising wave of panic.

"It's okay. It doesn't hurt anymore." Maxine pulled the shirt together and buttoned it, then stiffened as a biker rode past, his face obscured by a helmet and the indigo shadows. After he passed, she pulled a plastic baggie from her pocket. With trembling hands, Cass smoothed it flat to display a note. It was written in black ink on a piece of paper from a Westin notepad:

Talk and I'll cut them off. I'm watching.

Cass fought a shudder. "Do you have any other evidence from him?"

"What do you mean?"

"If you'd gone to the police or a hospital, they would've collected semen, combed for his pubic hairs, swabbed for DNA, that kind of thing." Cass patted the bench, soothed by the routine questions. "Did you collect anything like that the next morning?"

Maxine sat and shook her head.

"Did he wear a condom?"

"I'm pretty sure he didn't."

"Have you been tested for HIV?"

"I'm clean. For other diseases, too."

"What do you remember about him?"

"Not much. He was white. I think his hair was dark. He looked like a million other frat boys."

Cass rested her chin in her hand, thoughts whirling as she tried to match Maxine's details to her own. "What made you think he was part of a fraternity? His hair, build, did he wear a certain type of clothes, or have a fraternity symbol on his clothes or jewelry?"

"So much of it is a blur." Maxine clasped her hands in her lap and her fingers scrambled over one another. Her face was fierce. "I have a memory of short, neat hair and dark clothes. And one of those chiseled faces."

"That's a start. Anything else?"

She took her lower lip beneath her teeth and chewed lightly before speaking. "The rest is kind of garbled, I guess from the drugs."

"Give it a try. What do you remember?"

The park's trail lights snapped on, creating golden cones in the growing gloom. A lone man leaned against one of the light poles while a portly Dachshund explored the bushes nearby. Maxine stiffened. "I need to go."

"No, Max. Not yet. He's just walking his dog. I ought to give him a ticket for letting the thing off its leash."

Maxine looked over her shoulder at the man, who had turned and was walking in their direction. "What if it's him? He can't see me with you, Cass, with the cops."

"We're hidden, tucked under the tree. Protected. And I'll duck my head," Cass soothed. "Tell me what you remember, and once he's out of sight, you can leave, okay? That way, if it is the guy who raped you, he won't know where you went."

She nodded then, uncertain. Her voice was barely a whisper. "I have nightmares. And I know they're mixed up, but I dream about the rape. I feel this heavy pressure on my chest and a burning along my scar. I'm scared to death and can't move and he's hovering over me." Her breathing quickened and Cass reached out to hold Maxine's hand, trying to control her own breathing. "I'm looking up at him and his face is all saggy, like it's melting."

"Can you identify any of his features?"

Maxine pressed her lips together and stood her bicycle upright. "It must be the drugs, but his face was messed up, like he was wearing a mask."

Cass's pulse accelerated. "What kind of mask?"

"You'll think I'm stupid."

"No, Maxine, I promise I won't. Sometimes your brain gathers useful information even when it's under stress." Cass looked at her friend. "What kind of mask did he wear?"

Maxine closed her eyes and Cass fought not to vomit as her friend spoke. "It's totally creepy. But I swear that in my nightmares I'm being raped by that president from the seventies who was impeached, Richard Nixon."

CHAPTER 65

HITCH GLANCED DOWN AT the cell phone when it rang, surprised that the old man was calling so soon. He'd been away from Arcadia for six weeks now, and had expected the phone to stay silent for many weeks to come. He lifted it to his ear. "Evening, sir."

"How are you, son?"

"Just fine. And you?"

"How soon can you get home to Arcadia?"

Home. Hitch rolled the word around in his mind while he looked across the bunkhouse. It buzzed with chatter from a Mexican radio station and reeked of stale pinto beans, cigarettes, and farts. Two men played checkers at a small table, and at another, four men were deep into a game of poker. Home was a word Hitch had never understood, but the little cabin secluded deep on the old man's property was a lot closer to whatever home was than this dump. He checked his watch. "Tomorrow morning, sir, if I hitch. It'll take about five hours if I drive away."

"Will there be any trouble with the vehicle?"

Hitch glanced out the window at the selection of battered pickups. His gaze landed on a rusted Ford with no registration. He could swap the plates and doubted the ranch's owners would even realize the heap was missing until Sunday, when they delivered supplies. "No, sir."

"Good. Go straight to the cabin. I'll get some food out there and come by late tomorrow morning."

"Yes, sir." Hitch closed the phone and silently stuffed his few belongings into his backpack. Without a backward glance, he took the Ford's keys from a peg near the door and vanished into the night, his thoughts already on the future and the beautiful detective with fire in her hair.

CHAPTER 66

"AND THEY ALL LIVED happily ever after," Cass said, smoothing the sheets around her niece and kissing the little girl's forehead. The fresh scent of strawberry shampoo and baby powder brought a smile to Cass's lips. Phoebe had suffered a bout of Daddy-homesick-itis this afternoon and Harry quickly scooped his youngest daughter up from daycare and brought her back to the Elliot home. Seeing that he was still up to his elbows designs, Cass volunteered to give Phoebe her bath and put her to bed. There was something pure and almost soothing about watching a child's eyelids droop as they drifted into dreamland, and Cass's mind was tranquil now after the shock of Maxine's revelations. She stood and switched off the bedside lamp, turning as Phoebe called from the bed, voice thick with sleep.

"Auntie Cass?"

"Yes, Feebs?"

"Did they really live happily ever after?"

"Yes, they did."

"Did the princess keep her crown?"

"Of course she did."

"Good," Phoebe sighed, rolling over and tugging the covers with her.

Cass left the door open a crack and flipped on the hall light. Across the hall, the door to Bobby and Mack's old room was ajar, and Cass frowned at the sound of snoring. Farther along, her father's bedroom door was open. Cass knocked and waited for his reply. As with the rest of the house, little had changed since her mother's death over twenty years ago. Her father was sitting in the rocking chair that her mother had used to quiet all seven of their children. A paperback, illuminated by a puddle of white light from a bedside lamp, lay open in his lap. From its size and shape, Cass recognized it as *The Big Book* from Alcoholics Anonymous.

"Hey," she said.

Abe Elliot smiled at his only daughter. "Hey yourself."

She hooked a thumb at the hallway. "Is that Goober?"

"Harry said he turned up asking to spend the night again, and he didn't have the heart to turn Goober away. But it worked fine, because Goober played Go Fish with Phoebe for hours. She won every game, and I think Goober really wanted to win." He glanced at his open door. "Is Phoebe asleep?"

"Finally," Cass said. "I had to tell her the princess story three times before she'd had enough."

Abe cocked his head, a thoughtful expression on his face. "You never went through a princess phase."

"I wonder why?"

"You probably didn't have a chance. With six older brothers, you played cowboys and Indians, cops and robbers, and built forts out in the woods. But you had plenty of green Army men to play with."

Cass grinned. "They were everywhere, and always mutilated. Bobby used to bite their heads off."

"He did, didn't he? I wonder if he ever passed them, or if they're still stuck in his colon?"

"Daddy," she protested, sitting on the bed, "that's disgusting."

Abe frowned. "Come to think of it, I don't remember that you even had a Barbie doll."

"I didn't, but Big Momma made a dress for G.I. Joe, do you remember?"

Abe laughed out loud, then covered his mouth. "Out of an old red-checkered tablecloth. Was it Lloyd who got so upset about that?"

"It was Mack. He was still young enough to love all those G.I. Joes and be offended that I'd tried to turn one of them into a girl."

Abe was giggling so hard tears were in his eyes. "Mack stripped that doll naked and chased you around the house with it, trying to explain the difference between boys and girls."

Cass grinned. "I think that was the first time I realized I wasn't a boy."

Abe's expression sobered and he fingered the book in his lap. "After your mother died, I worried that I couldn't raise a girl. I'd had so much experience with six boys, I wasn't sure I could teach you to do girl things."

"You did all right," Cass said. "Between you and Big Momma, I ended up okay. At least I'm not a cross-dresser."

"No, you turned out pretty wonderful, if I do say so myself."

Cass's heart swelled. Her father's love was something she never questioned, but his praise was rare. "Thanks, Daddy."

"Was there something you wanted?"

She glanced at the book in his lap. "I know you're not supposed to talk about who goes to meetings, right?"

He nodded slowly.

"I need to clear someone. He isn't really a suspect in one of the murders, but it would be good if I could confirm that he was at an AA meeting." Her voice was soft when she continued. "Did you go Wednesday?"

"I got back in time for the six o'clock meeting."

"There's a guy named Joshua who says he was there. He has red hair, a bushy mustache, and his head is," she motioned with her hands, "narrow."

Abe suppressed a smile. "He's kind of unforgettable."

"Was he there?"

"He told you he was?"

She nodded.

Abe ran a hand along his cheek, rough with the day's growth of white beard. Cass loved that whispery sound. "Then I guess I'm not violating a confidence if I confirm that, am I?"

"Thanks, Daddy."

Cass pecked him on the cheek and left him to his reading.

———————

AFTER A QUICK SHOWER, she slipped into a t-shirt and shorts, surprised at how tender the scar on her chest felt, almost as if it were newly carved. Cass checked her email for new notifications, found none, and turned the laptop off. She slid under the covers and leaned against the headboard, finally allowing herself to delve into the emotions stirring since Maxine's confession about the rape.

The circumstances of Maxine's pickup and doping were similar to Cass's own, but that type of thing was far too common to mark Maxine's attacker as the man who had raped Cass. The carving on the chest, however, was unique. As he had done with Cass, the rapist used a very sharp knife on Maxine, slicing barely deep enough to draw blood, but deep enough to leave a scar. Cass tried to remember the section of scar Maxine had shown her. It was still pinkish, which meant that it was relatively new, probably less than a year old. It followed the same meandering path as Cass's did and was similar enough to be drawn by the same hand. And then there was the mask. If the cuts weren't evidence enough that the same man committed these crimes, the Richard Nixon mask was.

It had been six years since Cass's rape. She doubted that he'd been inactive for that long and only started raping again when he spotted Maxine. But it was strange, perhaps more than coincidence that he picked two women from Arcadia. If he kept to the same pattern of spotting women at a club, doping them, then raping and cutting them, it was unusual that no reports of his crimes had appeared in the news. In Dallas, or elsewhere. His little notes must be working.

The evidence she'd collected the morning after her rape was in her bathroom cabinet. At the time, she hadn't really known what she was doing. But she used moistened toilet tissue to swab the glazed and cracking traces of semen from her thighs, combed her pubic hair for traces of his, and used clear tape to lift fingerprints from any possible surface in the hotel room. Every bit of it was stuffed in a tampon box she kept beneath her sink. Given that she was clueless about forensic procedures at the time, she hadn't done a bad job. Any DNA on the pubic hairs would still be good. The semen would be hit or miss. And the fingerprints? Given the number of people in and out of a hotel room, it was hard to say what kind of hits might come back.

Cass wondered why she hadn't told Maxine that she'd been raped, almost certainly by the same man. Why hadn't she confided in her best friend? Given herself the relief of solidarity? Perhaps she had been silent for too long. Maybe it was time to start talking. Not without caution, but talking to people she trusted. Cass thought about Maxine's gaunt face, the huge eyes, that too-skinny body, and decided that she would start feeling Mitch and Kado out about how to process evidence that wasn't collected from a crime scene. Tomorrow, she'd even take the tampon box and stick it in her locker, just in case she worked up the courage to talk to them. If he'd raped Cass and Maxine, there were certainly other women out there whose lives had been damaged, if not outright destroyed by this man.

He was worth hunting.

And just maybe, she thought as she reached out to switch off the lamp, *he was worth killing.*

CHAPTER 67

Friday

IT WAS EARLY, BARELY six o'clock, and conversations in The Golden Gate Café were muted when Goober and Cass pushed inside to hear Dolly Parton's sweet voice coming from the jukebox. Cass yawned widely. She was weary from a night of bizarre dreams, where Richard Nixon sliced open Donna Moore's paintings and sketches, interpreting their meaning.

Wilbur and Wallace Pettigrew lifted a chin in greeting, as did the lawyers in the corner. She waved the folded paper, and then followed their glances to a booth in the corner. Her lip curled as she spotted Officer Hugo Petchard holding hands with Stan's new waitress, Junie. Cass hurried to her customary booth, Goober trailing in her wake, and she sat with her back to the happy couple while Goober slid into the seat opposite.

She'd found him in the dusty kitchen this morning, face confused as he contemplated the handle duct-taped to the refrigerator. His dark, thinning hair was neatly combed and he smelled of soap and toothpaste. She grinned at his lost expression. "Guess you'd better come with me to The Golden Gate, Goob."

"What about my mower?"

"I'll call Bruce and get him to hook up the trailer and bring her to town when he comes. He's got an early class today, so he'll probably get her to The Gate before you finish your pancakes."

Satisfied, Goober had followed Cass from the house, stopping to slip his key into the little machine's ignition. The roads into Arcadia were quiet this early in the morning, and she was pretty sure that Goober had drifted back to sleep against the passenger door, rousing when she parked at the courthouse and cut the engine.

Cass's hair was still damp from the shower she'd taken after her run, and she loosened the French twist at her neck and combed the wine-colored strands into place with her fingers before retwisting the knot. Glancing up to speak to Goober, she was startled to see Officer Mojo Franklin sitting in a booth by the front door, and even more surprised to see a laptop open on the table next to his breakfast. She had never known him to willingly work with a computer. He was in uniform, indicating that he planned to be at work on an official basis this morning. He met her eyes and flashed a wan smile.

Stan Overheart arrived with two steaming mugs of coffee and a fresh pitcher of cream as the jukebox switched to Queen's "I Want to Break Free". "Hey, Cass. Hey, Goober. What can I get for you?"

"Twenty breakfast burritos to go. You can fit five coffees in each of those carrier things, right?"

He nodded.

"Okay, ten coffees. Lots of cream and picante sauce on the side."

"Done. Goober, the works?"

He nodded. "And double bacon?"

"You've got it."

Cass stopped Stan before he turned away. "What's up with Junie and Petchard?"

Stan rolled his eyes. "Hugo moved in on her the first week she was here. Poor girl must've had some real bummers of boyfriends in the past, because she latched onto him, big time. Says she likes the uniform."

"She's a little old for him, isn't she?"

Stan watched them. "She's in her forties, and Hugo's what, in his thirties?"

"I think that's right."

"Maybe he's got a thing for older women."

"She must have a thing for idiots. Good luck to her. Are they always like this?"

"Lovey?"

"I think it's gross," Goober offered, stretching to look past Cass into the far booth.

"He's here every chance he gets, and yes, they're pretty affectionate. So far, it hasn't put the customers off their food, but I'm keeping an eye on them."

Cass chuckled and opened the Dallas newspaper. She passed the funny pages to Goober and started searching the headlines. A feature article described a rape victim's journey to recovery, and Cass scoffed at the woman's simpering descriptions of visits to psychologists, palm readers, and group recovery sessions. She stopped reading after the fifth paragraph and looked for the crime reports. Goober's guffaws at the cartoons made her smile, in spite of the grim reading. A domestic shooting, a knife fight, two arrested for drunk driving – a light night for crime in Dallas – but no mention of rapes. She started at movement next to the table and looked up to see Petchard standing next to her, his eyes focused on the slight gape in the neck of her blouse. "Officer Petchard. What can I do for you?"

He raised his eyes to meet hers and shifted from one foot to another. "You were right."

Cass was silent while she tried to figure his angle. "About what?"

He lowered his voice. "About me letting Mojo take stuff from his house. I talked to Junie about it, and she agreed with you and thought I was rude to you."

Her look was blank.

"So," he continued, "I'm apologizing. I should have checked the stuff Mojo took with him and logged it out of the house. You were right."

"You're talking to a civilian about an open investigation?"

Petchard's mouth hung open. "Are you serious? I'm trying to apologize."

"Apology accepted. Are you discussing an open murder investigation with a civilian?"

"Sheesh," he huffed. "I can't do anything right, can I?"

"I don't know, Hugo. Can you?"

He snorted a reply under his breath, hitched up his uniform's trousers, and headed for the door, banging it closed behind him.

Goober had listened to the exchange and watched Petchard's exit from the café with wide eyes. "He's cranky."

Stan appeared at the table with a bulging sack and two coffee carriers.

"Lover's tiff?" he asked.

"No," Cass said with a smile. "He's mad at me again."

Stan chuckled and took her payment. She said good-bye to Goober, reassuring him that Bruce was on his way to town. She balanced one coffee carrier on top of the other, tucked the top one under her chin to balance it, grabbed the sack of burritos and blinked goodbye to the Pettigrew brothers. At the door, Mojo caught up with her and asked if he could carry something.

She handed over the sack and breathed a sigh of relief as she shifted the coffee carriers so that one was in each hand. "Thanks, Mojo. How are you?"

They walked down the street to the square, squinting into the rising sun, and threaded their way through the early morning traffic circling the courthouse.

"I'm okay. The visitation is tonight and the funerals are tomorrow."

"I heard. I think most of the force will be there."

"I sure appreciate it, but I'm ready for it to be over."

"I imagine so." Cass looked up at him. "When did you learn to use a computer?"

Mojo grinned. "Strange, isn't it?"

"What happened?"

"Joseph *made* me buy it. I really didn't want a computer, but he thought we ought to do all our banking online, so we could take care of momma's stuff as she got older."

"I didn't realize your mom needed help with all that."

"She doesn't. Or didn't," he corrected himself, face darkening for a moment. "But Joseph was planning ahead. And I guess he was right. It does make sense."

"Were you doing your banking on the Wi-Fi at The Golden Gate? An open connection like that, it's not safe."

"Joseph warned me about it." Mojo cut a glance at her. "I was researching Joseph's crime."

"Is there much about it online?"

"Not really. But in a weird way, studying all this hacking stuff makes me feel closer to him. Like I understand him a little better."

Cass thought about her oldest brother Jack, in the state penitentiary for twenty-one years now for rape and murder. She had sought for years to understand what those words meant and to reconcile the actions to the brother she loved. In spite of the horror of his actions, she thought she understood him a little better, too. "I think I get it."

Mojo held the courthouse door open for her. "Thanks. Listen, are y'all having some kind of murder meeting?"

Cass nodded and lifted her hip to wave the card key in her back pocket at the reader. The door clicked and Mojo grabbed it. "Why?"

"Would it be all right if I sat in?"

"What for?"

He hesitated. "Maybe there's something I can offer. And I guess it would make me feel useful."

Cass pushed open the conference room door. Common sense and some vague notion that it was against policy for a family member to participate in the murder investigation of his kin were telling her to decline Mojo's offer. She looked up to see Mitch already positioned along one side of the table, scratching furiously beneath his brace with the hanger. "You okay?" she asked.

Mitch rolled his eyes and nodded. "This is better than sex. But don't tell Darla."

She put the coffee carriers down rubbed her wrists, looking at Mojo. "Are you sure you want to work with somebody like Mitch?"

The big black man placed the bulging bag on the table and peeked inside. "Do I get a burrito?"

"You just ate breakfast," Cass protested.

"Mental energy requires nourishment."

"That's my kind of logic. What are you talking about?" Mitch asked.

"Mojo wants to sit in on our meeting this morning, to see if he can add anything."

"Normally," Mitch said, "I'd say no way. But since Emmet Hedder's missing, too, we need all the help we can get. Do you know him?"

Mojo nodded. "What happened?"

"Looks like somebody shot at him night before last."

"The same night somebody killed Momma, Joseph, and Moore?"

The conference room door opened and Kado stepped in, followed by Truman. It was Mitch's turn to nod.

"Did the same person shoot Emmet?" Mojo asked.

"Definitely," Kado answered. "I compared his slug to the other three. They match."

CHAPTER 68

THE THREE-INCH PILE OF mail loomed ominously, and Sheriff Hoffner took a long sip of coffee before reaching for the stack. After arriving at the office Thursday, he'd been too distracted to go through it all, and Elaine had added yesterday's delivery to the top of the pile. As punishment for yesterday's procrastination, dealing with the mess was his first task of the morning.

He worked methodically. The contents went in one of four stacks: act now, act later, read later, or toss. Almost everything went into the 'toss' pile for shredding. The work was mindless and for that reason, soothing. He reached the midway point and stopped to stretch. His office was small but adequate. Photographs of himself at various points in his career and posing with other dignitaries covered the walls, interspersed with the various awards and certificates he had received over the years. He reached out to adjust his most prized possession: a framed announcement of his appointment as sheriff after the previous sheriff's heroic and untimely death. Noticing dust on the frames, he gently wiped the top and bottom edges of each picture, taking the opportunity to swap the positions of a couple of certificates.

Satisfied, he settled back into his chair and picked up an envelope, only to drop it and reach for the next item. The address was handwritten and Hoffner's ears filled with the rushing sound of his thudding heart. He fumbled with the key to his file cabinet and yanked open the bottom drawer to pull out the baggies holding the previous four letters. He laid the envelopes side by side and compared them to the newest delivery: the handwriting was the same.

Hoffner's fingers trembled as he tugged on a pair of latex gloves. He slit the top of the envelope. The letter crinkled as he slipped it out and he caught the faint scent of Elmer's glue. The letters, again clipped from magazines and newspapers, read:

What did I tell you?

He scanned the other letters in order of their receipt:

How well do you know Moses Franklin?
Where is Moses Franklin?
Why do you trust Moses Franklin?
Moses Franklin is not a nice man.

This latest letter was simply confirming that Moses was not a nice man. Based on what? The fact that someone had murdered his mother and brother? Or was the writer indicating that Moses was the intended victim?

Hoffner ripped the gloves from his hands and shoved back from his desk. He strode from the office and locked the door behind him. In a rare acknowledgment of his limitations, he realized that he needed help. Then his brain shifted gears. It wasn't about help. *Effective leaders delegate.* That was a lesson from his aborted training this week. And he knew just who to delegate to.

CHAPTER 69

JOSEPH FRANKLIN LISTENED WITH rapt attention. The group seemed to accept that he was Moses with little thought. To encourage that perception, he kept his mouth shut, which wasn't hard but was risky; Moses was the talker and doer, Joseph the listener and observer.

His biggest problems were with the clothes and police gear. Although it fit well, Moses' uniform felt awkward on Joseph's frame. The material was soft enough, but putting the whole contraption together was confusing. Joseph had spent time Thursday afternoon surreptitiously studying the officers coming and going from the squad room. This morning, he'd stood before the mirror in Porky and Stella's guest bathroom, adjusting his name plate and the gear on his belt until he felt confident that everything was about where it should be. But still, moving around with all this stuff hanging from his body meant that he had to keep his arms slightly out from his body, or leave a hand resting on one of the many items on his belt. Joseph did his best to keep the twitching and touching to a minimum, but even now, he caught himself lifting a hand to adjust Moses' badge where it hung on the shirt's left breast. He scratched his nose instead.

Driving away from the motel where he met Emmet last night, he'd felt distracted and unsettled. Realizing that the sharp retort they'd heard wasn't a backfire but was indeed an attempt to disable Emmet's pickup was disturbing. More so was the acknowledgment that Moses, Emmet, and Donna were involved in something bad. Probably illegal. So illegal that Emmet wanted to keep Joseph out of it, even though he clearly needed help.

He slept well last night, in spite of the grief that still hung heavy around his heart. Porky was dog tired when Joseph got back to his apartment. They shared a big helping of Stella's chocolate cake with glasses of milk and little conversation, then headed off to their separate rooms. His sleep was dreamless, an unexpected blessing given the turmoil in his life, and he felt refreshed today, ready to soak up information to help Emmet track the killer.

The conference room door opened and a very tall, rather pale man ducked under the door frame, a folder clutched in one hand and a paper bag in the other. Joseph recognized him as Porky's boss, the county's medical examiner John Grey. He sat next to the chunky, rumpled officer called Ernie Munk, snagged the bag of burritos and pulled a cup of coffee from one of the carriers. A very neat young officer with exhaustion in his eyes sat next to Munk; they called him Truman. Moses had mentioned him, saying that he was impressed with the younger man and thought he would be promoted to detective before long.

Detective Mitch Stone was at the head of the table, his wheelchair positioned sideways to allow his leg to stick out. Detectives Cass Elliot and Carlos Martinez sat along Joseph's side of the table. The forensics guy, Tom Kado, sat at the end of the table opposite Mitch, sorting through a stack of white cards smudged with fingerprints. Sheriff Hoffner had poked his head into the room earlier, peeking around the door like a turtle sticking its head from its shell. He told Mitch to come see him immediately after they were done.

"Since he doesn't seem to be tied to the others, let's start with Calvin Whitehead. What have we got?" Mitch asked.

"Nothing from a forensics perspective, so far," Kado answered. "Truman's helped me go through everything we gathered from inside the store, and there was nothing useful. We need to work through the sludge from the patio, and," he held up the white cards, "I still have some fingerprints to process."

Mitch looked to Munk. "Anything from his paperwork?"

"Not yet, but Whitehead had tons of it." Munk took a sip of his coffee and stirred in another packet of sugar. "His murder feels personal to me, especially with the swastika carved in his chest."

Joseph fought to keep his expression neutral. It wasn't related to his family's murders, but the mutilation was so strange that he tucked it away in his capacious memory.

Martinez balanced on his chair's back legs. "I want to talk to Father Reeder to see if he knew Calvin Whitehead. Cass, you want to come with me?"

She nodded. "I haven't worked on the Whitehead case, but I'd like to dig into it."

"Is that going to be too much with the Franklin and Moore murders?" Mitch asked.

"Not until we find a link between the two."

"Mojo?" Mitch asked. "How did you know Emmet Hedder?"

"We've been friends since we were kids," Joseph answered, switching to Moses mode.

"What can you tell us about him?"

Joseph shrugged. "Emmet's a good guy. He joined the Marines straight out of high school and spent time in the Middle East or Africa. Libya, maybe? He went to Panama and Iraq the first time around. Retired after twenty years and became a registered nurse. He works out at that fancy retirement place, Pecan Grove."

"Did he have any problems?"

"Nothing of a legal nature. Emmet and his wife have had trouble lately, but it sounds like the kind of thing couples always go through."

"I know Carlos asked you about whether your family knew Donna Moore yesterday. Did anything come to mind over night?"

The photograph of Moses and Donna weighed heavy in his wallet. "None of us did business with her and I don't think Joseph or Momma knew her socially. I sure didn't."

"Do you know why Emmet wouldn't report Wednesday night's shooting to the police?" Cass asked.

Because he wants to kill the man himself, Joseph thought. "No, I don't. Maybe he's in shock from his injury and laying low."

She nodded slowly. "Grey, did you get Donna's tox results back?"

The medical examiner had eaten and listened while everyone spoke, barely stirring. He swallowed and wiped his mouth with a napkin. "She was clean."

"Kado," Cass said, turning to look at the forensics examiner, "what about the cocaine?"

Joseph turned with everyone else to look at the dark-haired man.

"The concentrations on the bills I tested were slightly higher than average, but that's still a very low level of coke. I don't think it indicates the money has been near drugs in any quantity."

"There has to be a link between the three families," Cass stated. "We've put out alerts to area doctors and hospitals, asking them to let us know if someone matching Emmet Hedder's description comes in. Until we find him, there's not much we can do except go through his paperwork and talk to his wife again."

"I'll see if she's calmed down enough to talk," Mitch said. "Anything else?"

Grey opened the folder he'd brought with him. "We confirmed that this is Calvin Whitehead through his dental records. While looking at the body, Bernie found a few other things that might be helpful. Has everybody's food settled?"

Joseph wondered what he meant, but nodded along with the others.

Grey pushed the folder to the middle of the table. "They're kind of hard to make out, but Bernie found several tattoos on Whitehead's body."

Everyone leaned in to get a closer look, and Joseph felt bile rise in his throat at the sight of the man's blackened, peeling skin. No one else seemed affected by it, and Joseph wondered how long, how many dead bodies, it took before someone could develop an immunity to something like this.

Kado spoke. "I don't see anything."

Grey turned to a second photograph and indicated a darker patch. "This is as clear as we can get it with our equipment. There's a circle, and inside it, a cross with uniform length arms."

Kado's face paled. "And a drop of blood in the middle?"

"We couldn't make that out from the photograph. Why?"

"It's a symbol the Klan uses."

"Ah," Grey said. "That makes sense." He turned to another photograph. It showed a charred claw, with one patch of white, unblemished skin. "This is Whitehead's right hand. This section of unburned skin was beneath his ring. When we took it off, we found that tattoo, a cross. It looks hand drawn rather than professionally tattooed."

"Did he spend time in prison?" Kado asked.

"I'll run a check to see if he's listed in the system," Mitch answered. "If he was Ku Klux, there's a chance he was picked up at some point. And Munk will have to see what he can find in Whitehead's files."

"Is there anyone around here you could ask about him?"

"Klan, you mean?"

Kado nodded.

"We haven't had any activity in Forney County for a while. I'll call the other counties and see if they've got any connections or informants."

"Were there more tattoos?" Kado asked.

Grey nodded and pushed the folder to the center of the table. "Let me know if you want us to excise one. You might be able to get a better shot of it with your equipment." He passed the paper bag to Kado. "This is what was left of his clothes and in his pockets. His wallet is there, but it's a melted mess."

Mitch glanced up at the clock on the wall. "If there's nothing else, let's get to work. Daylight is burning, and I need to see what Hoffner wants."

CHAPTER 70

OFFICER HUGO PETCHARD HELD up the red stop sign and tooted his whistle. The crawling traffic stopped and a flurry of tiny people scurried past, wobbling like ducklings beneath their overloaded backpacks. Several children waved at one of the cars, calling, "Mrs. Hedder, Mrs. Hedder!" The tired-looking woman wiggled her fingers in reply.

Petchard studied her to ensure she wasn't a pedophile, then his mind drifted from his small charges to dinner with Junie last night, and breakfast at the café this morning.

She was such a rarity, a true Southern woman. Modest, chaste, full of sunshine, and beautiful, Junie was all the things he imagined in a perfect woman. Even though she was probably smarter than him. But she didn't rub it in. In fact, one of her greatest pleasures was listening to him talk about work, and he'd made a special stop in the station this morning to check on the various investigations, to give her a taste of what his world was like. She'd listened, rapt, her gorgeous lips slightly parted. Even an hour later, the thought of those lips worked their magic and he adjusted his orange vest to hide the slight swell in his trousers.

Petchard jumped at a horn's bleep and realized that the children had cleared the crosswalk. He tweeted twice, lowered the stop sign, and stepped to the sidewalk. A BMW driver flipped him the bird as it rolled past, and Petchard fought the urge to reply in kind. Junie insisted that school crossing patrol was the most important job he did. So, instead of responding with a one finger salute, he forced a thin smile. He felt a tug on his orange vest and looked down to see a little girl gazing up at him, her massive backpack sagging around her knees.

"Cross me, mister," she said.

He lifted the backpack to her shoulders, then puffed out his chest and tweeted his whistle.

CHAPTER 71

MITCH PUT HIS SHOULDER into Sheriff Hoffner's office door and braced it open with a crutch. He hopped inside and pushed the door closed behind him, settling into a chair. Hoffner hung up the phone and gave Mitch a bleak look.

"We've got a problem," he said.

"What's that, sir?" Mitch asked.

Hoffner responded by handing several evidence bags to Mitch who read the letters. "Where did these come from?"

"Here in Arcadia."

"When did you get them?"

"They've come one each for the last four Fridays, except," he said, pointing to the last letter, "that one. It's postmarked yesterday."

"Mail gets delivered the same day?"

"If it's in the box early and courthouse business, yes."

Mitch studied the sheriff. "Is this some kind of harassment?"

"I don't think so."

Mitch read through the letters again. "You think this is the person who shot the Franklins," he stated.

"If so, he killed Donna Moore and tried to shoot Emmet Hedder, as well."

"So maybe this," Mitch waved the letters, "whatever it is, is the link between the families. He must know by now that he didn't kill Moses or Emmet." Mitch rubbed his lower lip. "You need somebody independent to look into Moses' activities."

"I know that," Hoffner growled. "But this is sensitive."

"Of course it is. That's why you need the Texas Rangers, or at least a detective from another county."

293

"I don't think there's anything to this. But, if there's something going on with Moses, Mitch, I want us," he motioned between himself and his detective, "to be the first to know. We can figure out what to do about it if you find something."

Mitch sucked his teeth, then gave a sharp nod. "What do you want me to do?"

"Look at Moses' case files and the personal records that Munk brought to the station. Bank records, utility bills, whatever. Find out what this guy is talking about. But keep it quiet. I don't want anybody to know that we doubt Moses."

Mitch lifted the letters. "We have to fingerprint these. So Kado has to know. And I've got to tell Cass."

"Absolutely not."

"Sheriff, I don't know what your problem is with the woman, but she's my partner, and," he held up a hand to quiet Hoffner's protests, then pointed at his brace, "she'll have to do any leg work."

Hoffner dropped his head into his hands and rubbed his temples. "Fine."

"Give me a frank assessment. Do you think this is valid?"

"Somebody's trying to kill the man, Mitch. At this point, we can't afford to think anything else."

CHAPTER 72

CASS GLANCED OVER TO see Martinez hunched over his desk, taking notes. He caught her look and waved. From the tone of his voice, she could tell he was on the phone with a family member. She tapped her watch and he gave her a sheepish grin. She wondered whether it was his wife giving him a list for the grocery store, or one of his kids talking to him before school. If there was one thing Martinez valued above all else, it was his family. Cass simply rolled her eyes, returning his smile.

She opened the squad room's copy of the Forney Cater and skimmed the articles. More details of the Franklin and Whitehead murders, along with information about Donna Moore's shooting. All three by-lines read 'Wally Pugh', and Cass wondered where he got his information. It was accurate. He'd written the articles in a factual, non-inflammatory tone, and Cass was grateful. She wasn't sure that the other area papers would be so kind in their coverage of Arcadia's problems. Especially if they could take the focus off the Watuga gas plant explosion. She folded the paper and checked Martinez again. He was still on the phone, brows drawn together in a stern expression.

Moore's case file was on her desk, and she turned to the photographs of the artwork from the woman's office and home. From the flavor of her dreams last night, something was nagging at her about the way the drawings seemed to fit together, as if they were part of some larger canvas Moore wanted to create. A puzzle of sorts.

Her life's work, Joshua Reed said Moore had called it.

She spread the photos across her desk and started moving them around, first placing the section of what appeared to be a trouser leg above the boot, and the enlarged, distorted belt buckle above this.

There were five charcoal sketches of white science fiction-type mountains, each slightly different, and these she put to one side.

A figure appeared beside her desk and Cass looked up to see Bernie Winterbottom attempting to brush the wrinkles from his safari outfit. "Good morning, Cass. How are you?"

"Good, Bernie. How did you get into the station?"

He held up a white plastic rectangle. "Elaine gave me one. I hope that's okay."

"Of course it is." She used a booted foot to hook a nearby chair and slide it over for him. "You smell like charred meat. What's up?"

"Apologies. The dead are aromatic, particularly those who have cooked." He sat and his pale lids closed over his extraordinary green eyes.

"Are you okay, Bernie?"

He nodded. "We all long for an easy death. But some are so graphic that they are difficult to erase from the mind."

"Calvin Whitehead?"

"And the gentlemen from the gas plant explosion in your neighboring county."

"It was bad?"

His English accent grew thicker. "Two of them died from internal injuries suffered as a result of the concussion from the explosion. Not the easiest of deaths, but bearable because they died very, very quickly. The third man died as a result of his burns, which were significant. It was a truly nightmarish way to die."

"I can't imagine," Cass said. "Will you be all right?"

Bernie's lids slid back up, revealing those penetrating eyes. "Thank you, my dear, yes. I'll go back to my dusty archaeological site and in time, the horrifically dead will recede." He studied the photographs on Cass's desk and seemed to gather himself. "I found what appears to be a bullet hole through Mr. Whitehead's leg. Through the meat of his left calf, to be exact. I suspect a small caliber weapon."

"No slug?"

"I'm afraid not. Kado didn't find one?"

"He's still processing all the sludge from The Whitehead Store. I'll tell him to be on the lookout. What do you think it means?"

"Perhaps they needed to subdue him. Or, if this is Ku Klux Klan related, it might play some role in their murder process." Bernie smoothed a hand over his unruly golden hair and moved two photographs together, and then apart. "Unusual. Are they evidence?"

"They were hanging in Donna's house and office. She did them all."

"Really?" Bernie pulled one of the science fiction mountains closer. "She was talented. Why did you photograph them?"

"I'm not sure. It's almost as if she was trying to speak through them. Her assistant said that Donna called them her life's work."

Munk pushed into the squad room, speaking softly into his cell phone before snapping it shut. He stopped at her desk and exhaled, running both hands over his pocked face and the growth of new hair sprouting on his head. It seemed he'd stopped shaving it.

"Everything okay?" Cass asked.

"That was Gaby. They had a near miss this morning."

"With Angel? What happened?"

"Someone at an orphanage outside of Galveston thought they had her. Gabrielle got all excited, said she knew this was Angel. The photograph the woman brought looked exactly like her. But it wasn't."

"How do they know for sure?"

"Blood type. Hers can't work with ours." He dug his fingers into his weary eyes. "I hate it when this happens. Gaby just breaks down afterward."

"Do you need to go back to Galveston?"

"No. They're coming home tonight. Gabrielle wants to be at Joseph and Martha's viewing for Moses."

"I'm so sorry."

Bernie reached up to pat Munk on the shoulder. "It must be excruciating."

He smiled, his expression bleak. "It is." Looking down at her desk, he motioned to the photographs. "What's this?"

"They're Donna's. She did them all."

"Oh, yeah. I remember the first time I saw them in her office. I thought they were a little weird." Munk reached forward with a pudgy finger and pulled a charcoal sketch of a pair of clasped hands toward him.

"She did your taxes?" Cass asked.

He nodded. "Donna started doing this artsy stuff out of the blue. Kind of went wild and painted a bunch of them at once. One year there were normal pictures on the walls, the next, these."

"I think that one's good," Cass said, nodding at the clasped hands. She looked closer. "But the view is from the back."

"What?"

"Those are the pinkies facing out toward the viewer. If you look, you can see a thumb poking past that knuckle, right there."

Bernie and Munk leaned in and nodded. "Very strange," Bernie said.

"Did you talk to her about why she started painting and sketching?" Cass asked.

"I did, the first year these were up. She said they helped her purge old demons." Munk looked at his watch. "I need to get back to the paperwork. Give me a shout if you need anything."

Bernie stood and motioned to the photographs. "Would you mind if I took these with me? I'd like to study them more carefully."

"Do you see a pattern?" Cass asked.

"As you said, there's something about them, it's almost familiar. If it wouldn't be any trouble…"

"Of course not. I'll print another set."

"Cheers." Bernie gathered the photos together and turned to leave.

The squad room door banged open and Elaine darted in, swerving past Munk and then Bernie, her wild curls swinging. "Hand delivery, honey," she said, placing an envelope on Cass's desk and stopping to peck Bernie on the cheek. He blushed and hurried out.

"Who from?" Cass called.

"Some skinny gal in big shades and a floppy hat," Elaine said, following Bernie.

Cass's name was written on the outside of the envelope in a wide, curvy script. She slipped a letter opener under the flap and pulled a clipping from a Ft. Worth newspaper, dated today. A sticky note was attached:

"*I'll bet donuts from The Palace that it wasn't suicide and the note said: 'Talk and I'll cut them off. I'm watching.' M.*"

The small headline read "Rape Victim Death Questioned" and the story was brief. A twenty-three year old Ft. Worth native, Sarah Hill, was found dead in her apartment Thursday morning, hanging from a second-floor banister. The woman was known to police because she was found by a maid unconscious and bloodied in a downtown hotel one Sunday morning, several weeks previously. Police discovered a handwritten note at the scene, threatening the woman if she contacted the police. The article said that police had not ruled out either murder or suicide, and the investigation into the woman's death was ongoing.

Cass's blood ran cold as she decided she wouldn't take Maxine's bet. The article didn't describe Sarah Hill's injuries, but Cass would bet those donuts from The Palace that her assailant had left a long, loping cut from her collar bone to her breast. Cass realized that she was clutching the neck of her blouse, holding it closed. She folded the article and slipped it into the pocket of her tan Dockers, then wrapped her fingers together to still their trembling.

So, he *was* watching.

Somehow he knew that Sarah Hill's rape had been reported to the police. Either he watched the room after he left, or he had some way of following what was going on in the police department. His knowledge could come from something as simple as a police scanner. It could also come from something as diabolical as employment within the Ft. Worth department.

Or, Cass realized, he might've seen an article in the newspaper.

She ran a search on the internet for news about rapes in Ft. Worth, but found only two articles concerning sexual assaults in the last eight weeks. One occurred in a park, the other in an alley. Today's notice of Sarah Hill's death also popped up, but no story about the original rape appeared.

Which brought her right back to acknowledging that the rapist was watching his victims, at least in the Dallas / Ft. Worth area. Maxine was right to be worried; this guy meant business. Cass considered her predicament. Technically, she could contact the Ft. Worth detectives working Sarah Hill's case to get the details on her rape. But by doing so, she could place Maxine, or even herself, at risk if the rapist found out Cass was checking on similar crimes. Now that he had a taste of death, would killing come easily to him?

Blood pounded at her temples as she realized that this was the time to use Maxine's note and the evidence she had collected after her own rape.

She shoved back from her desk and headed for the squad room door.

"Hey," Mitch called. "Where're you going in such a hurry?"

"To see Kado," she answered.

CHAPTER 73

KADO DUG HIS FINGERS into his shoulder muscles. Bleary eyed, he watched the IAFIS screen for a moment, hoping that the normal ten to fifteen minute wait for responses would hold this morning. These were the last of the fingerprints from The Whitehead Store and nearly the last potential lead they had in Calvin Whitehead's murder. The evidence room door clicked open and Kado swiveled to find Cass standing inside ashen-faced, her back to the wall. "You okay?"

One hand held a plastic shopping bag. The other held the neck of her blue blouse closed. Cass looked at him for a long moment. "Do you have a minute?"

"Yeah," he answered, pushing the print button as the first IAFIS response popped up on his screen. He snagged the piece of paper and rolled around the table, stopping next to her. His dark eyes probed hers. "*Are* you okay?"

"I don't, I mean, yes. I am. I'm fine." She drew a ragged breath and put the bag on the backlit evidence table. "But I need to tell you something."

He nodded for her to continue. Cass opened her mouth but no words came out. Kado felt a fist slam into his stomach. His wife had worn the same expression when her oncologist told them that her cancer was no longer in remission and was in fact, terminal. To this day, Kado associated that look with fear of the unknown; specifically, fear about how another person would react to the message, and how it might change their perception of you. That day, he had reached for his wife's hand when in reality, she had probably needed to be held. He'd never seen Cass look so uncertain. Kado stood abruptly, sending his chair spinning. In a swift movement, he pulled her into his arms. She looked up, surprise in her violet eyes, and he kissed her. Electricity shot through him and Kado tightened his grip, one hand at the small of her back, the fingers of the other feeling the silk of her hair while he cradled her head. Footsteps clattered by in the hall and Kado released her, sure that his expression was as startled as Cass's. He swallowed hard.

"I need water, you want some?" he asked.

Without waiting for an answer, he fled through the evidence room door and down the hall to the squad room. Uniformed officers finishing the night shift or preparing for the day moved out of his way, frowning in his wake. Once at the coffee bar, he pulled two bottles of water from the refrigerator and leaned against the counter, forcing himself to breath and willing the emotions ricocheting through his body to still. He opened his eyes to see Mitch crossing the room in his wheelchair.

"You okay?"

Kado attempted a smile at the irony of Mitch asking the same question Kado had asked Cass moments earlier. "I'm fine."

"You don't look fine."

"Made a decision. Probably a bad one."

"Cass said she was coming to see you. Is she okay?"

"She's probably furious with me, but yes, she's fine."

Mitch studied Kado's face, and then looked down at the piece of paper the forensic man held. "You got anything I can help with?"

Kado started and looked at the paper. It was the crumpled response from IAFIS, requesting that a representative from the originating agency contact a specific sheriff's office. "There's a hit on one of the prints from Calvin Whitehead's store. Would you follow up?"

Mitch snagged the page and maneuvered his wheelchair in a jagged u-turn. "Phone work is my specialty these days."

Kado made his way back to the evidence room through the crowd of officers waiting for roll call. Cass was standing over his computer, examining the hit on the IAFIS screen.

"There's no name here," she said, taking a bottle of water from him.

He studied her profile and realized that she was in control again. Her color was almost back to its normal peaches and cream and from what he could see of her eyes, they were clear. He studied the screen with her. "And no crime is listed," he said.

"Is that unusual?"

Kado shrugged. "It happens sometimes with classified cases or prints loaded for elimination purposes. Mitch is calling the sheriff's office that submitted it. We'll see what he finds out." He reached for her arm and turned her away from the screen, stunned again by an overwhelming urge to kiss her. Instead, he bit the inside of his lip and nudged Cass toward the chair at the evidence table where the plastic shopping bag waited. "I'm sorry. For what I did. Before."

One corner of her mouth lifted.

Kado blushed. "I mean I'm not sorry, but I'm sorry that I kind of jumped you."

"It's okay. I mean, most gals get kissed after a little dinner and maybe a movie, but this was unique."

"Maybe we can try the dinner and a movie thing."

Cass drew a deep breath. "Maybe we can talk about it another time. I need to get back to work."

"Okay. What did you want to tell me?"

She snagged the bag and headed for the door. "Nothing. Sorry I interrupted you."

"It seemed important. Was it something to do with one of the cases?"

"Um, actually, yeah." She moved the bag behind her back. "Bernie found a bullet hole in Calvin Whitehead's body. Through his left calf. Keep an eye out for the slug when you're going through the sludge, okay?" Cass lifted the bottle in a salute. "Thanks for the water."

The door snicked closed and Kado stood, head tilted to one side. Through the warm buzzing in his head, he wondered why women and their secrets were so hard to comprehend.

CHAPTER 74

CASS SLIPPED THE TAMPON box in its plastic shopping bag in her locker and shut the door, then put a finger to her mouth. It had been years since the feel of a man's lips against hers had caused such a reaction, and her senses were overwhelmed with exhilaration and terror. She stood for a moment with her eyes closed. She wasn't sure that Kado was ready for a relationship, but by the same token, she didn't know if she was, either. Cass patted the locker's door: at least her secret was safe. Her fellow officers were plenty brave when faced with an armed criminal, but there wasn't a man on the force who would open a box of tampons. Not even on a bet.

In the squad room, Martinez was still on the phone and she fiddled with the coffee pot, buying time as she waited for it to finish brewing. The warm feeling from Kado's kiss was dying away, and with it, the rush of terror. Calmer now, she realized that hearing Maxine reveal that she had been raped, and then reading the note and newspaper clipping, had shaken her. Worse than she thought possible. Her dreams were still hazy, blistering replays of the rape, but in her waking hours, Cass thought that her emotions were under control. Apparently not.

She knew that she needed help to find this man, and sooner rather than later. Something stopped her just now, when Kado was available and she could have unloaded the evidence. But that would mean talking about the rape. In essence, trusting Kado and Mitch with the biggest horror of her life. She'd never told another soul what had happened, and apparently she wasn't ready to talk, even now. But she had to come to terms with spilling her deepest secret, and find a way to trust them with it. Just not today.

The coffee pot burped, bringing Cass back to the squad room. She reached for two mugs, turning to search the room for Mitch. He was leaning back in his chair, the phone cord stretched as far as it would go, with a clipboard spewing paperwork balanced on his brace. A blue-capped pen whipped back and forth in his hand, tapping a furious rhythm against the notepad. Cass caught his attention and waggled a mug. He nodded.

By the time Cass placed the coffee on his desk, Mitch had the hanger out and was scratching deep under his brace. "God, I hate this thing."

"Why don't you take it off while you're sitting here?"

"Too many pins sticking out of me, too much Velcro on it. It's easier to slide the hanger under and do some strategic maneuvering."

"When does it come off?"

"Maybe next week. Depends how sadistic the doc is feeling when I go back to see her."

"A lady doctor? Hope you're on your best behavior."

"I try, but it's hard." He extracted the coat hanger and lifted the mug to his lips, blowing lightly. Mitch's face was pale, and Cass realized that he must be exhausted. For his first day back, yesterday had been a long one. "Kado's fingerprint lead didn't work out," he said.

"What's the story?"

He lifted and shifted to the wheelchair, and then snagged the coffee and clipboard. "Think you can get me to the evidence room?"

Cass handed him her mug and maneuvered his wheelchair through the alley of desks the other officers had created to ease his passage in and out of the room. They made it down the hall and turned the sharp corner into the evidence room by working his wheelchair back and forth by degrees. Kado watched their entrance with an amused smile. "What's up?"

Mitch waved the clipboard. "Got a fingerprint corruption problem."

Kado groaned. "What is it?"

"Dude's dead."

"Huh?" Cass and Kado said in unison.

"The guy who left the fingerprint is dead. So, the print must be smudged or something."

"Is that the one from Alabama?" Kado asked, rummaging in the landslide of fingerprint cards on his desk.

"Yup."

"It's clear as a bell, see for yourself," Kado said, skimming the card across the evidence table.

Mitch caught it and clicked his tongue. "Well, that's troublesome."

"The problem is in Alabama. They must've cross-loaded the print with somebody else's information. Were they helpful?"

"The gal who answered the phone was pretty insistent that we screwed up. 'Texas twits', I think she called us."

Kado sighed. "Twits?"

"When I told Miss Congeniality that the fingerprint was good," Mitch glanced at Kado, "'cause I knew it would be, she said to have my forensics guy call her forensics guy." Mitch ripped a section of paper from the clipboard and zipped it, along with the fingerprint card, across the table to Kado. "You, my friend, have the honor."

"Okay," Kado said. "I'll call."

"Before you do," Mitch said, glancing over his shoulder at the closed door and pulling a short stack of evidence baggies from the depths of his clipboard, "there's something both of you need to know."

CHAPTER 75

"DO YOU HAVE A photo of this," Kado said into the phone while looking down at his notes, "Calvin Whitman?"

He glanced up as Truman backed through the evidence room door, a cup of Golden Gate coffee in each hand and a bag between his teeth. "Uh huh... Sure, I understand. Let me check something else and get back to you... Yeah, thanks for your time."

Reaching with one hand for the cup Truman held out, he cradled the phone's handset and then dug the fingers of the other hand into his gray eyes. He looked up at the young officer in his crisp brown uniform. Truman's hazel eyes were bloodshot, his face puffy, and even his blond crew cut was wilting. "You look as bad as I feel," Kado said.

"Didn't sleep much last night."

"The cases?"

Truman yawned. "One of my sisters is home with her daughter. She's still at that crying and eating all the time stage."

"She's not sleeping through the night?"

"Nobody's sleeping through the night." He pulled a ham biscuit from the bag, unwrapped it, and squeezed jam over the top.

Kado stared. "Didn't you eat breakfast in the conference room?"

Truman nudged the bag across Kado's desk. "I got some for you, too," he said, taking a bite.

"You're still hungry?"

Truman nodded.

"Oh, to be young again."

Truman swallowed. "Are we starting on the stinky container this morning?"

"I need you to do something else first. Are you okay out at The Whitehead Store by yourself?"

"Yes," Truman said, taking another bite.

"I'm having fingerprint problems."

"How so?"

Kado reached for a fingerprint card and held it up for Truman to see. "I've got one very clear fingerprint lifted from behind the counter at Whitehead's store."

Truman nodded again.

"It's a match to a print on file with some podunk county in Alabama. They insist that the guy the print belongs to died in the late seventies. His name was Calvin Whitman."

Truman unwrapped another biscuit. "Similar to Whitehead."

"It's probably a mix-up. But, I have to prove that the print we lifted is good."

"That means we need another one."

"Exactly. Go out to the store and dust those areas only Calvin Whitehead would have touched."

"Like?"

"You'll find several, since only Calvin worked there. Lift the cash drawer from the register and dust it inside and out. There's a credit card machine behind the counter, an older model that doesn't have a signature screen. Dust it all over, including the bottom. Pay attention to that clear piece of plastic that you rip receipts from. Open the gas pumps and dust the areas near the receipt paper and inside the cover."

"How about the stockroom?"

Kado shook his head. "Someone making deliveries might have left fingerprints back there. Stick to the front of the shop for now. When you're done at the store, go to his house and lift prints from the kitchen and bathroom." Kado studied him. "Do you remember how to dust for prints, which powder to use, all that?"

"You want me to go alone?"

"If you're okay with that. I've got tons to do here."

Truman beamed. "Absolutely." He stood and brushed non-existent crumbs from his uniform as he headed for the door.

"Scott?" When the young officer turned, Kado pointed to a toolbox resting on the countertop. "Unless you plan to blow powder out of your ass and grow bristles on your fingertips, you'll need a forensics kit."

KADO'S SMILE DISAPPEARED AS Truman's steps faded down the hall. He wondered if the tingle in his gut came from the kiss or the guilt. Never had he grabbed a woman and laid one on her, and Kado feared he might've just committed assault. The only saving grace was that Cass hadn't punched him. And although she looked surprised, she hadn't pulled away. His offer of a date was still open, too, so Kado decided to leave the tingle alone.

Forcing his attention back to work, he locked the forensics room door, plugged in an iron, and slid five trays onto the table. When Mitch brought the Mojo letters to him, Kado placed each between two pieces of bond paper impregnated with a solution of ninhydrin and left them to absorb the chemical. Now, he smoothed the hot iron over each sandwich and peeled the covering sheets back to look at the pages: no prints.

Kado checked his watch and chewed his lower lip, debating. With a resigned sigh, he positioned each envelope between two pieces of bond, placed each in a tray, and slipped them inside a cabinet. It would create a ton of work, but if it got them one step closer to their murderer, it was worth it.

CHAPTER 76

THE CHURCH'S INTERIOR WAS dim after the morning's bright glare when Cass stepped inside behind Martinez, and it took her eyes a moment to adjust. When they did, she was surprised at the simplicity of the decor. Her images of the Catholic Church were based on pictures of the Vatican and ornately decorated buildings in big cities. In contrast, Arcadia's only Catholic Church was beautiful in its simplicity.

She followed Martinez into the sanctuary and watched as he dipped his fingers in a basin and made the sign of the cross. "Carlos?"

"Yeah?"

"Where are all the paintings and gold trim?" she whispered.

He chuckled. "We're what you'd call a poor parish, *chica*. We manage to keep the lights on and the roof from leaking." He cocked his steely head at her. "You okay?"

"Yeah, why?"

"You seem a little, I don't know, off. Flustered, maybe."

"Just tired, I guess." *Yeah*, she thought. *Exhausted from being kissed by the forensics guy and figuring out that the man who raped me also raped my best friend and probably killed a woman.*

Martinez pursed his lips. "You've never been in a Catholic Church before?"

She tucked a loose strand of dark red hair into her French twist and shook her head.

He pointed over his shoulder. "That's called the narthex."

"The foyer?"

Martinez nodded and turned to the area she knew as the sanctuary. "This is the nave. It kind of means 'ship', like we're in Noah's ark. We can sit three hundred in here, and Father Donald packs it full for four masses on Sunday."

The nave's walls were pure white, the floor slabs of gleaming oak planks. The pews and kneeling benches were also of oak and bare of cushions. Cass and Martinez carried on deeper into the church, stopping in a small crossing.

"This," he said, motioning to open rooms on either side of the nave, "is called the transept, and is the part of the church that makes it look like a cross from above."

Cass gasped as she looked to each side. The spaces were decorated as simply as the rest of the nave, with one exception. Each side of the transept housed a floor-to-ceiling stained glass window. Rays of colored light fell across the simple white walls and oak pews. The window to the left reflected the birth of Christ; the one to the right, his death. "Wow," Cass said.

"Carlos, I trust you're telling our guest about the history of those windows," called a voice from the back of the nave. Cass turned. A short, bald, bespectacled man walked up the center aisle. He was dressed head to toe in black, save the white collar at his neck. "I'm Father Donald Reeder."

"Hello Father," she said, shaking his warm, dry hand. "I'm Cass Elliot."

"Detective Elliot, of course. I've seen your photograph in the newspapers. A difficult situation, I imagine."

"It's certainly lasted longer than I would've liked."

Father Reeder smiled. "I'm sure Carlos is glad you're back at work. Now, did he tell you about the windows?"

Cass looked at the burly detective, surprised to see a flush creeping across his cheeks. "No," she said, "he didn't."

"Well do so, Carlos, while I tend to things on the altar. I don't imagine you're here for a social visit, so give me a minute and I'll join you."

The priest crossed himself and took the single step up onto a platform.

"That's the sanctuary," Martinez said. "See the high altar?"

Cass leaned sideways to see a table that looked as if it were carved from granite. A simple wood box rested on top of the altar, and an overhead light in the shape of a lantern hung from a long chain. The sanctuary's back wall was home to a large crucifix bearing a thorn-crowned, bleeding Jesus. She shivered. "What's in the box?"

Martinez grinned again. "That's the Tabernacle. It houses the Blessed Sacrament."

"The what?"

"The body and blood of Christ."

"Like crackers and juice for communion?"

"*Amiga*, you crack me up."

Cass's smile was hesitant. "Um, the windows?"

"Huh?"

"Father Reeder said you should tell me about the windows."

"Well, we raised the money for them several years ago. It took a long time, because they were expensive."

The priest motioned them to the front pews. "Carlos not only spearheaded the fundraising for this substantial project, he drew the design."

"Really?" Cass asked, turning to look at both windows more closely before sitting down. "They're beautiful, Carlos. I didn't know you were so artistic."

Martinez slid into the pew behind Father Reeder and Cass, the blush returning to his cheeks.

Father Reeder chuckled. "Humility is one of Carlos' gifts, which makes it difficult for us to celebrate all that he does for the church. He's raising money now for a cloister garden."

Martinez cleared his throat. "Father, we have some questions that might be a bit delicate."

"What did I tell you?" the priest asked Cass. He turned to Martinez. "You know I'll help if I can."

"You've heard about Calvin Whitehead's murder?"

The priest nodded.

"Did you know him?"

"I did. He converted to Catholicism when he moved to Arcadia." Father Reeder paused. "That must have been more than thirty years ago."

"I've never seen him at mass," Martinez said, and Father Reeder smiled.

"Calvin wasn't what you would call a practicing Catholic. He had moments when he needed the church, and he came to us then."

"For confession?"

Father Reeder hesitated, then nodded.

Martinez rubbed his strong hands across his face and his silvery crew cut. "Father, we're at a loss as to who killed Calvin. He lived in a remote area with few neighbors. He has no family as far as we can tell. Is there anything you can tell us about him?" Martinez held up a hand when the priest protested. "I know that confession is sacred, but can you think of anything Calvin might have said that would be helpful? He lived in Arcadia for more than thirty years but barely left an impression. Did something significant happen in his past? Was he fearful? Did he even tell you where he came from?"

Father Reeder bowed his head as if in prayer. Cass flashed a glance at Martinez, who sat stone still. After several moments, the priest raised his head and crossed himself. "Calvin was a troubled soul. More so than most. He came to the church seeking absolution, but was a reluctant convert." He smiled softly. "Although he didn't possess faith enough that God could grant him direct forgiveness for his sins, he seemed to accept that a priest would be an effective intermediary for confessing his transgressions and providing suitable penance."

Martinez squirmed in the pew. "Father, I know all sin is equal, but are we talking venial or mortal?"

"Mortal," the priest whispered. "I've never heard another confession like Calvin Whitehead's. He was deeply disturbed by his actions, and yet he still believed that he'd done the right thing. In the early days he only hinted at his past. I kept telling him that he could not be cleansed entirely of his sin until he brought it all before God. It is only recently that he has laid bare his full confession to me."

"If he'd been reluctant to tell you what happened for so long, Father, what brought it out of him now?"

It was Father Reeder's turn to squirm. "Calvin's colleagues were…," he began. "No, that's not right. There were several people involved in Calvin's sin. And they were dying. Calvin himself was aging. He wanted to make a full confession before he died."

Martinez spoke quietly. "There's more to it, isn't there, Father?"

The tip of Father Reeder's tongue touched his top lip. "Yes. His friends, these other people, were not dying of natural causes. Instead, they died in accidents. The type of accidents that happen every day. But Calvin seemed convinced that they were being murdered."

"Why?"

"He believed that the people he had wronged were seeking vengeance."

"And he was afraid that he was next."

Father Reeder nodded. "But I don't think he was in his right mind."

"Why?"

"Because the people he had wronged weren't capable of seeking vengeance."

Martinez nodded. "Because those people, the people he sinned against, were dead. By Calvin's hands and those of his friends."

The priest met Martinez' eyes for the briefest of moments before he lifted the rosary to his lips and began to pray.

CHAPTER 77

MITCH WAITED FOR HIS computer to warm up, absently moving the coat hanger beneath the brace. Morning roll call was long over, officers spilled from the room in a rush of testosterone and off-color jokes, and Mitch breathed in the motionless air with relief.

He had been utterly exhausted when he got home last night, and not much better this morning. But the last twenty-four hours had brought him more exhilaration and satisfaction than he'd felt in weeks, so when the alarm sounded this morning, he levered himself from the bed, peg-legged it to the bathroom, and then faced a stand-off with his petite wife over breakfast.

A true Southern woman, Darla had a genteel nature wrapped around a spine of steel. She flat out refused to drive him to the office. He threatened to phone a cab. She called his bluff. He hopped to the kitchen counter and scanned the Yellow Pages. Victory within his grasp, he announced that the nearest dispatch office was over fifty miles away, and the round-trip fare would likely be as much as a car payment. The steel bent. But only so slightly and only after he promised to call if the pain in his leg didn't subside by noon.

The last thing Mitch had done before heading home the previous night was run a search through the national crimes database to identify murders with characteristics similar to Calvin Whitehead's. The computer clicked through the last of its starting routine and the envelope-shaped icon blinked. He opened the email program and groaned; sixty-four cases waited in his inbox.

He leaned back in his chair and pulled the hanger from beneath his brace, then clicked on the first email and started to read.

Chapter 78

TRUMAN BURST INTO THE evidence room with a wide grin on his face. He slid the forensics kit onto a counter and presented a fistful of fingerprint cards to Kado, then gagged. "You started on the stinky bucket without me?"

"Smear some Vick's under your nose and take over. Do the same as with the gunk from the storeroom. Spread it over the strainer and look for unusual stuff."

"Have you found anything?"

"Nothing relevant. Just twigs, leaves, some skin and burned clothes. Keep your eyes open for a slug, or fragments." Kado flipped through the cards and explained about Bernie's discovery of a bullet track through Calvin Whitehead's left calf. "Some of these are good."

"Thanks. I dusted everywhere you told me to."

Kado jiggled the mouse to wake his computer and maneuvered to IAFIS, scanned three of the prints and started a search.

"Why not compare it to the other print?" Truman asked.

"It's the same," Kado assured him, "but this way, there's no question about a match. Let's get some coffee."

In the squad room, they found Mitch hunched over a pad of paper, desk phone wedged between his ear and shoulder, scribbling notes and muttering into the handset.

The coffee was gone, so they prepared a fresh pot and were waiting for it to finish brewing when Cass and Martinez came into the room, smiles on their faces.

"What's up?" Kado asked.

"Calvin Whitehead murdered somebody, or somebodies," Martinez announced as Mitch rolled up in his wheelchair. "We just don't know who. Or when. Or where."

"The priest told you this?" Mitch asked.

"Not exactly," Martinez answered, flashing a glance at Cass, "but he let us read between the lines."

"I'm pretty sure Calvin Whitehead is from some little town in Alabama, so maybe he murdered someone there," Kado announced. "We had one clean print from behind the counter in Whitehead's Store that matched a file out there, but their forensics guy disputes it."

"What a surprise," Martinez muttered under his breath.

Kado bristled, but Truman spoke before he could answer. "It's a perfect print, Carlos. The Alabama people are being difficult."

"But to be thorough," Kado added, "Truman picked up more prints that are almost definitely Calvin's. I'm running them through IAFIS right now. When we get a match to that same file in Alabama, I'll call and find out what the deal is."

"How long will this take?" Martinez asked.

"I'll check," Kado said, taking a cup of coffee and heading for the squad room door.

Martinez scratched his steely crew cut. "What can we do now?"

Mitch accepted a cup of coffee from Truman. "You can talk to Emmet Hedder's wife, Celia, about how Emmet is connected to the Franklins and Donna."

Martinez looked at Cass. "Can you come with me?"

"Sure. She teaches school."

"That should make her easy to find." He looked at Mitch. "What are you up to?"

"Looking for crimes similar to Calvin Whitehead's. I went back three years and got sixty-four matches. It's slow going, but I'm working my way through them."

"Any luck?"

"Not yet, but I'm only on number ten."

"Why don't you," Truman began, lowering his voice, "ask Mojo to help. He looks a little lost."

Mitch turned to see the officer running both hands over his bald head while staring at his computer screen. "Mojo?" he called.

Mojo shifted his gaze. "Sir?"

"You got time to help me make some calls?"

"Yes, sir," Mojo answered. "About what?"

Mitch worked his wheelchair into a u-turn. "Meet me at my desk and I'll explain."

Truman followed Cass and Martinez and ducked inside the forensics room, stopping to scoop a glob of Vick's from the jar and smear some under his nose. He listened as Kado spoke into his phone.

"Would you have him call me as soon as he gets in, please?... Yeah, that's the number. Thanks."

Truman slipped a rubber apron over his uniform and pulled on latex gloves, then popped the lid from the bucket on the evidence table, drawing back as the odor hit him. He caught his breath and looked inside. Thankfully, Kado had nearly completed processing it. The sludge was a smoky stale mixture of gray and black lumps and water. He scraped a ladle-full, pulling up a hunk of the semi-solid mass, then moved it to the strainer and poured. He poked at it and found a soggy piece of material. Truman used tweezers to spread it over the strainer, picking a few twigs and bits of lead from wrinkles in the cloth. Kado hung up the phone and joined Truman at the evidence table. "Bullet fragments?"

"I think so," Truman said.

Kado examined one under the magnifying glass. "I'd guess a .22, but there's not much to work with." He looked at Truman. "Do you think this is how they subdued him?"

Truman plucked at the cloth. "The fragments were twisted inside this fabric with other debris from the patio. That tells me that the lead was on the ground and got washed away from the body along with all the other stuff. If the lead was already fragmented, that means they probably shot him before they hung him, while he was on the ground."

"More torture."

"Maybe."

"Jesus." Kado took a long breath and pointed at the cloth. "What is that?"

"T-shirt?"

Kado took the tweezers and examined a partially burned tag. "It's a sheet. See that? Something about thread count."

"But why would he have a sheet at the store? He didn't sell that kind of stuff."

"Grey brought his clothes over this morning. If there's more sheet, maybe they used it to immobilize him."

Truman placed the fragment on a clean piece of paper and teased it out. Kado settled on the other side of the table and slipped the still damp clothes from a bag. He peeled a blackened chunk away from a strip of dark leather. "Calvin's belt, I think. Carlos said most of his work trousers were black polyester blends. This must be part of his pants."

Truman helped Kado separate a twisted clump of sooty fabric into three distinct pieces: one was ribbed, perhaps from an undershirt; a second was smooth and thin, similar to the fabric from a dress shirt; the third was also smooth but slightly thicker. Kado laid this piece of fabric and the fragment of sheet side-by-side. "They're probably from the same sheet, or maybe a pillowcase. And it was on his body. But why?"

"Maybe," Truman offered, "because that's what the Klan wears."

"You think the Ku Klux killed him?"

"We didn't see any evidence of his involvement in the store, and Detective Martinez didn't find anything unusual in his house. But Whitehead had the tattoos." Truman shrugged. "Maybe he wanted out, and the Klan didn't want to let him go."

CHAPTER 79

THE CABIN WAS A small building, ancient but still solid, with a tin roof and sweet water from a deep well. Once home to some great-great-uncle or another, the old man had used it decades ago to house his occasional mistresses, and now as shelter for the men he hired as crew boss. The old man found Hitch sitting on the front porch, sipping coffee, and felt relief slide deep into his bones. As he pulled the heavy pickup to a stop, the old man thought that with his weathered Marlboro-man appearance, Hitch and the cabin belonged together. "Morning, son. Have any trouble on the way back?"

"No, sir. I left the vehicle near Texarkana and hitched the rest of the way. Would you like some coffee?"

The old man eased into a rocker. "With a little cream."

Hitch retreated into the gloomy interior and returned with two full cups. He handed one to the old man and sat on the porch's top step, back against the rail.

"You hear about the murders?" the old man asked.

"I picked up a Forney Cater on the way in. Which one is bothering you?"

"Calvin Whitehead, the man killed at his gas station."

"The article was brief. What happened?"

The old man told him about the hanging and burning. "Whitehead and I were colleagues of a sort. There's a possibility that his death might be the first move against myself and my associates." The old man watched Hitch absorb this information. He'd never known how much Hitch had gathered about the old man's activities and The Church of the True Believer when he'd done the old man's bidding in the past. If Hitch thought the old man's interest in Whitehead's death was unusual, he hid it well.

Hitch drained his cup. "What can I do for you?"

"For now, I need you back crew bossing. There's some heifers need sorting and branding on the west property. Pick up a crew and get started. I'll let you know if something else comes up."

Hitch brushed off his jeans and stood, collecting the old man's empty cup. "We'll get it done."

"I know you will, son," the old man said. "And I'm glad you're back home."

CHAPTER 80

THE COLLECTION OF TINY blanket-draped mounds remained motionless as Celia Hedder closed the classroom door behind her.

"Any news?" she asked, gently touching the swollen area beneath her eyelids. Her lipstick was smudged and her skin had the sallow look of someone who hadn't gotten enough sleep the night before. Worry had bled all the anger from her features. Yesterday, she was furious and on the verge of divorce. Today, she was a frightened wife who wanted her husband back.

"Yes, ma'am," Cass said, handing her a cup of coffee from The Golden Gate Café. "We know that the same person who murdered the Franklins and Donna Moore tried to kill Emmet."

"But you don't know who?"

"Not yet."

Celia drew a deep breath. "What can I do to help?"

"Tell us about Emmet's relationship with the Franklin family."

"They were inseparable as kids. All three of them." Her face softened. "When we got married, Emmet couldn't decide which of the Franklin twins would be his best man, so he asked them both. After Joseph left to go up north, Moses and Emmet stayed close. They spent hours out there playing basketball with that program for at-risk kids. I guess Joseph did too, once he moved back, but I don't think Emmet ever really reconnected with Joseph."

"Did y'all do business with Miss Moore?"

"No."

"Emmet wouldn't know her socially?"

Celia gave a startled laugh. "I can't imagine that we move in the same circles. Unless…" Her expression turned thoughtful. "Maybe she has a relative at the retirement home and Emmet met her that way."

Cass shook her head. "She doesn't have any living family. At least not in Arcadia." She watched as the other woman rubbed her eyes. "Celia, where would Emmet go to hide?"

"I don't know. I guess they could hide him out at Pecan Grove. Have you checked with Jerome?"

"We've asked him to contact us if he hears from Emmet. Does he have any family in the area?"

"No. He has a brother in Colorado and a sister in Atlanta."

"Do you think he would run to them?"

She took a sip of coffee and then shook her head. "They fell out a few years ago. I haven't been allowed to call and talk to them, or send birthday cards or Christmas presents to their kids."

Martinez stood nearby, massive arms crossed over his chest, face set in a frown. "What happened?" he asked.

"Emmet didn't tell me, but I heard him yelling at one of them over the phone. Something about chickenshit cowards. He hung up so hard he pulled the kitchen phone off the wall." A light dawned in her eyes. "That's about when he started to change."

Cass nodded. "You mentioned that yesterday. And that he was sneaking off without saying where he was going." She hesitated. "Was he having an affair?"

"If so, he's found women all over the South."

"Ma'am?"

She released a long sigh. "When Emmet started acting funny, I wondered if he was cheating. He'd call from work and tell me he was taking a short trip but wouldn't tell me where he was going. Then he'd be home in a day or two. Once, I think he was gone for three days. I asked, but he never told me where he had been. He just clammed up. And for Emmet, that's saying something. That man never shuts up; he even talks in his sleep."

"You thought he was seeing someone in different locations? The same person?" Cass prompted.

She fingered the coffee cup's lid. "An affair was the only thing that made sense. I checked the phone bill for strange numbers – nothing. I checked the internet history for porn sites, dating services, chat rooms – nothing. I even checked his clothes when he came home. No lipstick, no perfume. He must've rented a car for every trip because the mileage on his truck never went up more than a hundred miles. There was nothing unusual on the credit cards like hotels or restaurants, but he did take money out of the bank every time. When I got the statement, I knew where he'd gone, or at least that he'd been in that spot to withdraw money. Make sense?"

Cass nodded. "Which spots?"

"Little nowhere places. One in Tennessee, another in Louisiana. Maybe one in Alabama."

"How many trips did he make?"

Celia tipped her head back. "Ten? Twelve? He seemed to go to the same place a few times, then move on to somewhere new."

Movement in the classroom caught Cass's eye and she saw a tiny pony-tailed figure sit up. "I think nap time is over," she said.

Celia glanced through the window. "I'd better get back inside."

"Celia, it would help if we could see your financial records."

"What for?"

"Those places that Emmet visited," Cass explained, "they may have something to do with why someone tried to kill him."

Her eyes widened. "You think one of those women is after him?"

Cass shrugged. "She had to have a reason to kill Miss Moore and the Franklins, too. It's a remote possibility. But we'll take any lead we can get."

CHAPTER 81

THE PLASTIC CONFERENCE ROOM chair squealed when Munk rocked back on two legs to stretch. He pulled the rubber caps from his thumbs, wiped the sweat on his uniform's shirt, and reached for his cold coffee.

He sipped, studying the stack of Calvin Whitehead's boxes in the 'remaining to be scavenged through' pile. Munk had made amazing time this morning; only six were left of the original seventy-six, but his hopes were falling that he would find anything of use. He'd figured out Whitehead's filing system and worked backwards from current to oldest. Whitehead made a modest living from the gas station and paid his personal and business related bills on time. There was no sign of a loan, only the usual lines of credit associated with a gas station and small shop. Absolutely nothing was out of place. No unusual deposits or withdrawals, no unexpected payments. No notes, no address or phone book, not even a doodle, coffee cup ring, or grease smear on any of the papers. Just dust. Years of dust.

The conference room coffee pot was empty. Munk stood, preparing to make another pot. A sealed water bottle on the counter caught his eye. One of Gabrielle's fondest wishes was that Munk would drink more water. So, in deference to his wife and his kidneys, he cracked the seal and gulped down half the contents, surprised at the water's silky freshness. It wasn't coffee. Or a soda or shake. But it wasn't bad. He slipped the rubber caps on his thumbs and went back to work.

When it came to paperwork, Munk was a machine. For some reason, he had the ability to comprehend data quickly, understand patterns, and spot anomalies. Perhaps working with silent rows of numbers provided a sort of meditation that allowed him, for a short time, to block the recurring horror of his living nightmare.

Hand.

No hand.

He blinked the memory away and began his routine. Remove the lid and scan the neatly labeled folders for anything unusual. Extract the files one at a time and thumb through the contents, again scanning the details for variations from the norm. Only a small stack of papers rested on the coffee counter, each bearing a colored sticky note and Munk's tightly scripted comments. This fact in itself allowed Munk to draw a conclusion about Whitehead: anyone who kept this much business related documentation without so much as a reference to his personal life was hiding something.

Munk lifted the top on the last box and rubbed his hands together, a smile cracking his pudgy, pock-marked face. The box was labeled '1979', and Munk guessed this was the year Calvin Whitehead moved to Arcadia and opened his business. These documents were bound to be interesting.

Following his routine, he scanned the folder labels and then extracted the files, one at a time. The deeper he worked into the folders, the slower his pace became and the higher the stack of potentially interesting documents grew. The last folder was chunkier than the rest. He lifted it from the box and opened the flap, drawing a quick breath. This was it. The treasure trove.

The top documents related to Whitehead's purchase of the house and gas station in 1979. He'd paid $155,000 in cash, which was quite a tidy sum back in the day. The opening statement from a local bank showed an initial deposit of $25,000, also in cash. The rest of the papers were charges for improvements to the house and shop. The file's final invoice was brief, citing only that Whitehead had purchased two safes from a firm in Stanton. The bill was pricey, but provided no indication of what type or sizes of safes were purchased, or where they were installed.

Munk leaned back in the squealing chair, rubbing his protruding belly. The bank statements showed little activity in the first eighteen months that Calvin Whitehead lived in Arcadia, and then reflected the normal debits and credits involved in running a business. Everything, all of the improvements, were paid for in cash. Unusual. As was the purchase of two safes. The use of one in a convenience store was expected. But two? Perhaps Whitehead expected to do a roaring trade.

Munk reached for the crime scene photos and flipped through them, spotting a small safe tucked beneath the counter, out of the customer's view. No other safe was visible in the photos from the store or Whitehead's home.

Pushing back from the conference room table, he picked up that last invoice and walked to the coffee bar. He punched the safe company's number into the phone and waited as it rang. Munk reasoned that the second safe must be in Whitehead's house. And a man only needed a safe at home to protect his guns, his valuables, or his former life.

CHAPTER 82

"DETECTIVE ELLIOT? DETECTIVE?"

CASS was lost in the memory of Kado's lips touching hers as she walked up the courthouse sidewalk. She looked over her shoulder to see Wally Pugh darting between slow moving vehicles. He drew a notebook from his trouser pocket and wiped the sheen of sweat from his face. "Good morning, Detective. I hear you're back on duty now."

"Hey, Wally. Sheriff Hoffner signed the paperwork yesterday."

"From what I heard, it took John Grey's hiring you as a temp to get the sheriff's attention." Wally extracted a pen from the protector in his shirt pocket.

Cass shrugged. "What's up?"

"I wanted to ask about –" His beady black eyes darted from Cass to a spot over her shoulder. A small camera hung around his neck and he pressed the button to turn it on. "Is that Rob Conroy?"

With a stab of apprehension, Cass turned to find the ex-con leering from his perch on a bench about twenty yards away. Thankfully, this time he was fully dressed, if in filthy jeans and blue shirt. His dark brown hair was combed straight back from his face and glistened with gel. A flock of pigeons fought with three chickens over the bread scraps at his feet, and the plump ginger cat twined between Conroy's legs, watching the birds. Cass turned back to the reporter who was sighting in on the ex-con. She stepped out of the way. "I believe it is."

"Fat Frannie said he was out. Why is he living in that dump of an apartment? I heard his parents had *beaucoup* life insurance. And the house was insured. So, even though his fine was," Wally tilted his head back and thought, "about ten thousand and he had to pay a lawyer, he should still have plenty of cash."

Cass lifted an eyebrow. "That was way before your time."

"I'm an investigative reporter. I investigate."

"I have no clue about Conroy's cash situation. My only concern is that he stays on the right side of the law."

"Do you think he's dealing again?"

"I've seen nothing to suggest that he is. Maybe you should talk to him about life after prison. I'm sure he'd have some interesting stories to tell."

Wally's nose twitched. "I've thought about it, but I'm not sure Sheriff Hoffner would want to hear what he has to say."

"What do you mean?"

"Through the grapevine, I've heard Conroy might want some payback."

Cass glanced over her shoulder. Conroy lifted a cup from The Coffee Shop in a mock salute. "For what? The bust was clean."

"But it was Mojo, the worst shot on the force, who found him. And Hoffner's made jokes about what an idiot Conroy was for shaking and baking behind a police officer's house."

"What else?"

Wally waggled the notebook. "You scratch my back…"

"I'm not getting near your back, Wally."

"A little information exchange, Detective. That's all I'm asking."

"What kind of information?"

He stepped closer. "The Franklins. Donna Moore. I hear they're linked. I also hear that Emmet Hedder's missing and there might be a link with him, too."

Cass pushed her sunglasses up on her nose. "Wally, you know I can't comment on –"

"– an open investigation. Blah, blah, blah. Off the record, Detective. I just want an angle I can investigate. For example, is it true that the slugs match in all three cases?"

His source was good. Cass nodded once.

"Any leads?"

"Not yet. We're looking at their business and private lives to see if we can find a connection."

Wally scribbled. "Good. I won't use your name."

"Your turn. Hoffner and Conroy."

"Conroy was an up and comer in the drug underworld before Franklin busted him."

"So I've heard."

"Apparently Hoffner's mockery followed him to prison, and he had a hard time living it down. Mojo and Hoffner knocked his street cred back. Word is, he wants his old life back and has plans for payback."

"Word from who? What kind of plans?"

"That's the best I can do. I'll keep an eye on him, though. I think there's a story just dying to get out."

"Watch yourself. Forney County's not much of a drug hotspot but things can turn nasty fast."

Wally slipped the pen into his protected pocket. "Be seeing you."

Cass watched him ease across the street, and then she headed for the courthouse. Rob Conroy's face was tilted back to bake in the late morning sun. He whistled as she drew near.

"Is there something I can help you with?" she asked.

"Nope. Just enjoying the weather on this beautiful summer morning." He waved with The Coffee Shop cup. "How's your day going?"

"Fine, thanks. Be sure to throw that cup away."

"Yes, ma'am. Have a nice day, now."

Cass walked up the courthouse steps and barely noticed the podium at the top; her skin was crawling as his gaze lingered on her body. Pushing through the front doors, she stopped and took a deep breath.

"You okay, honey?" Elaine asked from her alcove.

Cass nodded at the young couple holding hands on one of the wooden benches, then crossed the foyer to Elaine's alcove. "Rob Conroy is sitting out front. Have you ever known him to do that?"

Elaine stifled a snort. "The only time he's come near the courthouse it's been kicking and screaming in the back of a patrol car. What does he want?"

"I've heard he's not happy with Mojo or Sheriff Hoffner."

Elaine's eyebrows shot up. "You think he's looking for trouble?"

"I don't know. I just think it's weird that he's out there. Keep an eye on him and let one of us know if he moves, okay?"

She nodded, curls bouncing with the motion. "No problem."

CHAPTER 83

THE PHONE SLIPPED AS he wrote, and Kado hunched his shoulder to bring the handset up against his ear. "Would you repeat that?"

The forensics man from Thayerville, Alabama, sighed. "Calvin Whitman. Born September 13, 1935. Died December 27, 1978. White male. Six feet two inches tall, two hundred and ten pounds. I still think something's wrong with those fingerprints."

"I can fax copies to you. I'll even overnight an original to Alabama," Kado said, finishing his notes. "But I'm absolutely certain that your dead Calvin Whitman has been living in Arcadia for over thirty years."

"It doesn't seem possible."

"Why?"

"I'm looking at his file. His house burned the night of December 27. The fire started from faulty Christmas tree lights. The house went up fast. His bedroom was on the second floor but they found Whitman in the remains of his bed in the living room. Looks like the middle of the house collapsed and most of the second story dropped to the first floor."

"How did they confirm that it was Calvin Whitman?"

"Let's see." Kado heard a sneeze. "Sorry, I had to dig this file out of storage. You're lucky we still have it. This was part of a group scheduled to be shredded last year. I don't know why they missed it." The sound of shuffling paper came through the phone. "Here we go. Seems they found a ring that belonged to Whitman on the right hand, and some of the hair was still on his head. From the photo in the file, he had very thick black hair."

"Was an autopsy performed?"

"Yes. Cause of death was smoke inhalation."

"Dental comparison?"

"Umm," more paper shuffling, "no."

"Isn't that odd?"

"Maybe. No fingerprints, either, probably due to the fire damage to the body. A deputy confirmed that it was Whitman. Nobody questioned his identification. Say, Tom?"

"Yeah?"

"Do you have a photo of this Calvin Whitehead? He must have been an old man, right?"

It was Kado's turn to shuffle through paperwork. He located the crime scene photos and found only one photograph of Calvin Whitman. It was hanging on the wall behind the cash register and Kado needed a magnifying glass to see it clearly in the crime scene photo. In the picture, Whitman was frowning at the camera as he held a pair of scissors, ready to snip a ribbon stretched across the little store's doors. Half a dozen locals looked on, smiling broadly. "There must be a driver's license photo on file, and that'll be within seven years. We've got one early photo of him in a newspaper. Do you want a copy?"

"Of both, please."

"Do you have one for me?"

"Yeah, I'll send it when we're done." He sighed heavily again. "If you're right, you know what this means for us?"

"Yup, you've got an open case."

"A very old, very cold murder case."

"And the very dead Calvin Whitman or Whitehead is your prime suspect."

"Man, I'm gonna land in a white-hot shit storm."

"Sorry about that," Kado said, with genuine feeling. "When you send Whitman's photograph, would you include his arrest record?"

"What arrest record?"

"Well, why is he in your system?"

"For exclusion purposes, of course."

Kado felt dread tighten his gut. "What do you mean?"

"I didn't mention it earlier?"

"Mention what?" Kado asked as the dread uncoiled along his spine.

"Calvin Whitman was Thayerville's sheriff when he died. Had been, for close to twenty years. Everybody loved him. This, his still being alive, means that he's a criminal. *That's* why I'm gonna land in a shit storm."

CHAPTER 84

THE COURTHOUSE DOORS CLOSED with a wheeze behind Sheriff Bill Hoffner, and he waited before the podium on the shady portico as Mayor David Rusted took up his position at Hoffner's shoulder. Flashbacks to his last encounter with the press seared the sheriff's brain, and he shoved his trembling hands into his pockets. He hardly needed a podium, given that only a few stations were represented, along with a couple of newspaper reporters and that weasel of a man who reported for the Forney Cater and KOIL. But the physical barrier provided a sort of comfort. Talking to the press was an awkward do-si-do; they tried to pry information from him, while he attempted to figure out how much they already knew and limit the additional facts he provided.

Leadership lessons from the past few days fluttered through Hoffner's mind: listen with intent; walk in the other guy's shoes; make eye contact; a little gratitude, of the genuine variety, goes a long way; say you're sorry and mean it. *Kindergarten stuff*, he thought, and then shrugged mentally. Maybe the leadership crap would've gotten interesting later in the week.

"Afternoon, gentleman," he said, angling his cream colored cowboy hat lower over his face. "I'm sorry it's taken me so long to get to you, and I appreciate your patience. I'm the sheriff of Forney County, Bill Hoffner. This gentleman," he motioned to the large figure standing beside him, "is Arcadia's mayor, David Rusted."

One of the reporters, a narrow man wearing a shirt bearing an Alma newspaper logo raised a notebook. "Jim Long, Sheriff, from the Alma News. I understand that you've had four suspicious deaths in the county in the last forty-eight hours, is that correct?"

"Yes, Jim," Hoffner said. "The Forney Cater has carried the stories for the past two mornings. Three residents were killed in their homes, and a fourth at his place of business."

"That fourth man, is that Calvin Whitehead?"

"It is."

"He was lynched, correct?"

Hoffner felt Mayor Rusted stiffen beside him, and he fought hard not to step back from the podium. A greasy layer of sweat formed on his forehead. Although it should have been crystal clear that the mechanics of Whitehead's death were commonly used in lynchings, no one on the force had yet used the word. "We haven't categorized his murder as a lynching at this time, Jim."

Another reporter, a hefty man with a dab of beard on his chin and sweat rings under the arms of his blue shirt, raised his hand and Hoffner pointed to him. "Yes?"

"Is it accurate that Calvin Whitehead was hanged, then set on fire?"

"I'm afraid that's the case."

"Sounds like a lynching to me. Why don't y'all call it what it is?"

A rush of anger colored Hoffner's cheeks. He watched as the fat reporter's cameraman moved forward and adjusted his lens. "I didn't catch your name."

"Darrell Tooley, from Channel Nine in Stanton."

"Well, Darrell, the term lynching implies that some form of vigilante justice was enacted upon the victim. We're still gathering facts about Mr. Whitehead's death and can't say for certain whether vigilantes were involved." The hefty reporter opened his mouth again, but Hoffner leaned closer to the three microphones attached to the podium and carried on. "I would ask anyone who visited The Whitehead Store on Wednesday afternoon to contact the sheriff's office. We'd be interested in your observations about Calvin Whitehead on that day, and to know whether you noticed any suspicious activity."

Hoffner pointed to the weaselly local reporter and noticed a new figure making its way up the sidewalk.

"Wally Pugh, Sheriff, reporting for the Forney Cater and KOIL. Is it true that one of your officers was targeted by a killer on Wednesday night, and that the shooter got the wrong people?"

"From our investigation so far, we don't believe that Officer Moses Franklin was Wednesday night's target."

"Then it was his mother or brother they were after?"

The figure reached the cluster of reporters and stood staring at the sheriff, a slight smile on his lips. Hoffner drew his attention back to the question. "We're still investigating, Wally. Joseph Franklin, Officer Franklin's brother, was recently released from prison in New York. He served time for computer related crimes. We are considering the possibility that one of his former associates is the killer."

"If that's the case, Sheriff," Wally asked, "why would the same person target Donna Moore, one of the accountants here in Arcadia, and the nurse, Emmet Hedder?"

The reporters exchanged glances and jotted notes.

Damn it, Hoffner thought. *There's a leak.* "That's something we're investigating."

Wally Pugh looked down at his notepad and then up at the sheriff. His pointed features twitched. "How are Joseph Franklin, Donna Moore, and Emmet Hedder connected?"

"At this point, we're not aware of any connection between all three families. Neither the Franklin family nor the Hedders did business with Miss Moore. She attended a private school; the Franklin boys and Hedder went to public school here in Arcadia. Again, we'd ask the public to help with this matter by sharing information about their relationships, if any."

The big reporter spoke up. "If there's no connection between Franklin and Moore, does that mean the murders were random?"

Start a panic, why don't you, fat boy? Hoffner thought, sweat rolling between his shoulder blades. "If this killer is targeting people randomly, and I don't believe that he is, then he's putting himself to quite a bit of trouble. The Franklins and Miss Moore live in opposite parts of the county. Once we find a connection between the victims, we'll find the person who killed them."

The reporters were silent and Hoffner was preparing to draw the press conference to a close when the fat reporter adjusted his glasses. His lips were pursed in a prissy moue, and Hoffner fought the urge to sneer. "Sheriff, is it possible that another of your officers is dirty?"

Hoffner's blood ran cold. "What did you say?"

"Dirty cops happen. Even in a place as lovely as Arcadia. Two of your own officers were linked to that cult a few weeks ago. Is it possible that Officer Franklin is dirty and that the killer shot his mother and brother in error? I mean, I've heard he wasn't such a nice guy."

Hoffner stared at the fat reporter, wondering if whoever was sending letters to him was also sending them to the press. Mayor Rusted cleared his throat, and Hoffner spoke in a low voice, his tone razor sharp. "Moses Franklin is a highly respected officer on the Forney County force. He's been with us for twenty-six years, and has served in a courageous and professional capacity during that time. Whatever you've heard, from whatever source, is wrong."

"I'm just saying, Sheriff," the fat reporter continued. "If there's no connection between the Franklins and Moore, and there's nothing in Joseph Franklin's background that makes him a target, Moses had to be up to something. Are you investigating him?"

Hoffner's bowels contracted and he flushed a deep red. The man hovering at the edge of the small crowd stepped fully into view. Hoffner's eyes narrowed as he struggled to place the face. The man pointed a finger at him and mimicked firing a shot from an imaginary gun. With a wink, he turned and sauntered away. It happened in a matter of seconds and Hoffner watched him go while leaning into the microphone. "Be careful what you report, Mr. Tooley. Officer Franklin could have a suit for defamation on his hands. This press conference is over. Thank you for your time, gentlemen."

Turning, Hoffner bumped into Mayor Rusted, and the rotund man shuffled out of his way.

"Wait, Sheriff," Jim Long called.

Hoffner stopped and looked over his shoulder.

"When will you hold another press conference?"

"It won't be today, boys," Hoffner answered. "Visitation for Officer Franklin's family is tonight. And to be clear, the press is not invited."

———————————

THE LOBBY WAS COOL and quiet when Sheriff Hoffner and Mayor Rusted stepped inside. The mayor's eyes, dark indentations in his pudgy face, were curious as he spoke. "Who was that, Bill?"

Hoffner swept the hat from his head and tried to smooth his hair into place. "Rob Conroy. Remember him?"

"He's out?"

"My detectives have talked to him about the Franklin shooting, but his alibi is solid."

"Are you anticipating trouble? He threatened you, remember?"

Hoffner smirked. "No, I'm not worried about Conroy. It won't be long until he's cooking again and sampling his own product. We'll send him back to Huntsville." He headed for the entrance to the police station. A leadership lesson hit him, *gratitude*, and he turned back to Mayor Rusted. "Thank you, David Wayne, for joining me out there. Talking to the press in a situation like this is never easy."

Rusted stepped closer and lowered his voice. "Is it true, Bill? About Whitehead? Was he lynched?"

"Frankly, I hadn't made the connection between the way Whitehead died and lynching." He seemed to choose his words carefully. "I don't see how one person could've killed Calvin Whitehead. His injuries, David Wayne, were severe."

"He was beaten?"

Hoffner's voice was almost a whisper. "No. But he was shot through the leg, had a swastika carved in his chest, and his killers made certain that he was alive when they hung him."

"So that he would strangle to death?"

"So that he would feel the pain of being burned alive."

The mayor took a small step back. "That's horrible."

"That's some kind of anger. I think that reporter's right. Lynching describes perfectly what was done to Calvin Whitehead."

CHAPTER 85

MUNK MET KADO AS he stepped into the department's main hall. "There's something hinky about Calvin Whitehead," Munk said, motioning for Kado to follow him to the conference room.

"You're not kidding," Kado said. "It's after two o'clock. I've got to have lunch. Aren't you hungry?"

Munk stopped in his tracks. "Now that's a first."

"What is?"

"I've never been so absorbed in anything before that I didn't notice I was hungry."

Kado grinned. "That must be some serious hinky. I sent Truman to get food. Let's see who's in the squad room."

They found Mitch still on the phone, Cass working through Moore's paperwork, and Martinez making notes on the interview with Celia Hedder. Truman poked his head around the door. "Catfish is in the conference room. I was going to get barbeque, but I'm not ready for that. Munk, I moved your stuff to the counter."

They congregated around the scuffed table, passing cartons of cole slaw, beans, fries, hush puppies, and fried catfish between them.

"Carlos," Cass said. "What did you find out from the quilting club?"

"They only served desserts at the meeting Tuesday night," Martinez said, looking over at Kado, "so that's not where the tomato stuff on Joseph's shoes came from."

"What about the gasoline on his clothes?" Mitch asked. "Find a receipt in his or Mrs. Franklin's things?"

"Nope," Munk answered. "No receipts dated Wednesday."

Kado shrugged. "Maybe it's nothing, like Carlos says. If they paid cash, they might not've taken a receipt."

"Where is Mojo?" Cass asked.

"He went home to get ready for visitation at the funeral home." Mitch answered. "It starts at six."

"He's been so stoic," Martinez said. "Almost like he's half a Mojo."

"He was like this after his divorce, remember?"

Martinez nodded as he chewed. "Yeah. He kind of withdrew. The worse she behaved, the quieter he got."

"I think he's still in shock. Who wouldn't be?" Mitch said. "But he's focused. The work he did following up on crimes similar to Whitehead's murder was useful."

"What did you find?"

"Out of the sixty-four hits, we've got seven that are reasonable matches."

"In Texas?" Kado asked.

"All over the South within the last three years. The law office in each jurisdiction is faxing the files to us."

"Will you ask Mojo to help you go through the files?" Cass asked.

"Maybe," Mitch answered. "Having something to do seemed to help him today."

"Getting them buried will be good for him," Munk said. "He can move on. Will everybody be at the visitation tonight?"

"I think so. Even the officers on duty are planning to stop by."

Kado took a long drink of iced tea and looked at Munk. "Calvin Whitehead. What's hinky?"

"Who searched the house and store?" Munk asked.

Martinez swallowed. "Me. Truman, too. Why?"

"How many safes did you find?"

"One. It was beneath the cash register," Truman answered.

"There's another one under the floor, somewhere in his shop or house," Munk said, wiping a smear of tartar sauce from his shirt.

"His house is pier and beam," Martinez said. "It would be easy enough to hide a safe beneath the floor there. I think his shop is on a slab. What do you think we'll find, Munk?"

"Cash, possibly some links to his life before Arcadia," he answered, reaching for the container of beans and plopping a heavy spoonful onto his plate. He wiped a brown streak from his uniform's shirt.

"Whitehead's life before Arcadia?" Kado offered before Munk could continue. "You're not going to believe this. His name was originally Calvin Whitman."

He filled them in on his conversation with the forensics examiner from Alabama, about Whitman's alleged death in 1978, and his role as the sheriff of Thayerville for almost twenty years.

Munk choked as Kado stopped talking. "Where?"

"Thayerville, Alabama. Why?"

"Unbelievable," Munk muttered, shoving back from the table and squatting on popping knees in front of a towering column of boxes. "Where did I put that thing?"

The others watched in bemused silence as he found the box he wanted and bumped Truman from his spot at the end of table, sat the box down, and extracted a file. Munk wiped his hands on his shirt, opened a folder, and flipped through the aged papers inside. He selected a piece of yellowed newspaper and placed it on the table. "There has to be a link between the Franklins and Calvin Whitehead."

They passed the article from person to person, faces somber as they read about the lynching of Charles Franklin, Robert Hedder, and Ben Silverman. Kado looked at Munk as he passed the paper to Detective Martinez. "Charles Franklin was Moses and Joseph's father?"

"Yes. I found a marriage certificate for Martha and a Charles Franklin, and a death certificate for Charles dated May 9, 1967, same as that first article," Munk said, turning several more pages. He handed Kado the small slip of newspaper glued to an index card. "This must be a paragraph clipped from a later article. It quotes a sheriff. I assume that it's the sheriff of Thayerville and the article refers to the men who committed the lynching."

"Cause of death?" Kado asked.

"'Asphyxia due to obstructed airway'," Munk quoted.

"That's an understatement," Truman whispered.

"You think Calvin Whitman was Thayerville's sheriff when Charles Franklin was lynched?" Kado asked.

Munk nodded. "If he was sheriff for twenty years and disappeared in late 1978, then he was in charge in 1967."

"How in the world did the Franklins and Whitehead end up here? In the same town?" Kado asked.

"Not just the Franklins," Cass said quietly. "Emmet Hedder's family, too."

Mitch scanned the articles again. "Mojo said they were childhood friends with Emmet. But he didn't mention that both families came from Alabama, or that this," he motioned to the clippings, "had happened."

Martinez stirred. "He may not know. Some families never discuss the terrible parts of their past."

"Seriously?" Truman asked.

A bleak smile crossed Martinez' face. "There are some things about my ancestors that my parents didn't want us to know. More to protect us than anything."

"What about the Silverman family?" Cass asked. "Who are they?"

Nobody answered.

"Okay, what bearing does any of this have on our murders? Whitehead's or the Franklins' and Moore's? And does it have anything to do with Emmet's disappearance?"

"The fact that most of these people came from the same location could be coincidence. The Whitehead Store is in the middle of nowhere. The Hedders and Franklins probably didn't know it was there," Mitch said. "And since he changed his name from, what was it, Kado?"

"Whitman."

"Whitman to Whitehead, the Franklins and Hedders probably had no idea the sheriff of Thayerville was here in Arcadia. And if Whitehead might've been Klan at one point, he probably wouldn't have been in the same places the black folks were. I talked to our neighboring counties about Klan activity. Where they've had any, Whitehead's name hasn't come up. That doesn't mean he hasn't been active here, but we have no indication that he has been. So let's go back to Thayerville." Mitch leaned back in his chair, hands laced behind his head. "Calvin Whitman needed to disappear. Why?"

"Maybe somebody he arrested got out of jail and came after him," Truman offered.

"Possible," Mitch conceded. "But why not re-arrest them? Why run away?"

The conference room door popped open and Elaine's heart-shaped face appeared. "Mitch, I've got paper coming through the fax machine non-stop. I'll get it to you when everything's out. Carlos?"

"Hey, Elaine. What's up?"

"I know you're busy and I'm sorry to do this to you, but another senior citizen has gone missing. One of the neighbors asked for you since you worked the Iris Glenthorne case. Bring me some catfish when you come through."

He groaned but pushed away from the table. Munk filled a plate for Elaine and handed the detective two glasses of iced tea. Martinez turned at the open conference room door. "Once these murders are solved, I'm proposing a catch and release program to put GPS tags in everybody over sixty-five. Anybody else game?"

CHAPTER 86

MAYOR RUSTED PULLED HIS office blinds closed and sat rigid in the cool, silent room. He fished the cell phone from a pocket with trembling hands, and pressed a speed dial button.

"News, Mayor?" the old man asked.

"I don't believe that Calvin was randomly targeted." The mayor heard the old man puffing on his pipe, and pictured a flame dipping into the bowl and then gobbling at the matchstick. An image of Whitehead's burning body flashed across his brain, and he shuddered.

"Go on," the old man said.

"Someone shot him in the leg and carved a swastika in his chest. Hoffner said they took care not to kill him before they hung him, so he'd be sure to know that he was being lynched."

"Lynched?"

"Hoffner held a press conference a few minutes ago."

The pipe clacked against the old man's teeth. "Damn it, David Wayne. Why didn't you call?"

The mayor waited until the clacking stopped. "He came by my office on his way outside, and I had no opportunity."

"You said 'they' took care while they were lynching him. More than one person killed him?"

"Hoffner said he didn't think one person could murder Calvin like this. It would've taken more than one to subdue, torture, hang, and burn him. What do you think it means?"

The old man was quiet for a time. "If Hoffner's right and multiple people came after Calvin, then I believe that reduces the odds that they are targeting members of The Church. This sounds more like a

Klan killing than anything, but Calvin wasn't involved with the Klan. Not since he's been in Arcadia, anyway."

The mayor's body relaxed into the wide desk chair, and it groaned beneath his bulk.

"But you need to keep an eye on this investigation, Mayor. I've been wrong before, and whoever committed a murder this brutal deserves our watchfulness and respect."

CHAPTER 87

"HOFFNER WOULD KNOW WHAT would make a man run from his responsibilities," Cass said as the conference room door slammed open before it could fully close behind Martinez.

"Watch your mouth, Elliot," Hoffner barked, barging into the room. His face was flushed and a drop of sweat trickled down his cheek. "You think I'm a coward?"

Cass looked up at him. "No, sir. We just need your perspective."

Hoffner yanked his fingers through the hat humps in his hair and edged around Mitch's extended leg to the coffee counter. He snapped a paper towel from the holder and wiped his face, seeming to struggle with pursuing Cass's comment. "About what?" He held a hand up. "Wait, where's Franklin?"

"Gone home to get ready for the viewing tonight," Munk offered. "Why?"

"Is there a chance," Hoffner said, exchanging a glance with Mitch and then checking and leaning against the counter, "that Moses Franklin is dirty?"

Munk shifted and his chair squeaked. "Why would you ask that, Sheriff?"

"The press asked."

Mitch grimaced. "You held a press conference?"

"Of course I did." He looked at Cass. "That's one of my responsibilities."

"Sheriff, you really should check with us before you go talk to the press. Just to make sure we're all on the same page." Mitch rubbed his eyes. "I've had a look at his case files and there's nothing unusual. Anybody else?"

Munk ran a hand over his pink, peeling head and shrugged. "There wasn't anything unusual in Mojo's or his mom's financial records. I've ridden with Mojo off and on, and there's never been a hint that he was into something bad."

"Me, too," Truman added.

Hoffner released a long breath. "That's what I thought."

"What did the reporter say?" Cass asked.

"That he'd heard Moses wasn't such a nice guy."

Mitch, Cass, and Kado exchanged glances. "Tell Munk and Truman about the letters, Sheriff," Mitch said.

And so the sheriff did. Munk and Truman shook their heads when he finished speaking. "There's nothing off about Mojo, sir," Truman stated. "He's as clean as they come."

The room was silent for a moment. "Why would the press target Mojo?" Kado asked. "Did this reporter have a copy of the letters?"

"I don't think so," Hoffner replied. "He only made the one comment, and that could've been an anonymous tip. And we have a leak in the department. Wally Pugh from over at the Forney Cater knew that the slugs matched between the Franklins, Moore, and Hedder."

Cass mentally cringed, but then reminded herself that Wally had the information before she confirmed it for him. Hoffner couldn't nail her as the leak.

The sheriff continued. "This reporter thought that if there's no link between the Franklins and Moore, or Hedder and Moore, there must be a link between Mojo and Moore."

"That makes sense," Mitch said. "But if there is a link, we haven't found it. Yet. But before you talk to the press again, make sure you've caught up with us. We're picking up speed and you need to stay in the loop."

Hoffner nodded, his blue eyes hooded. "What did you want my perspective on, Elliot?"

"Kado discovered that Calvin Whitehead is really Calvin Whitman from some place in Alabama."

"Thayerville," Kado supplied.

Hoffner sucked his teeth. "You sure about that?"

Kado's ruddy complexion darkened. "I am. We've confirmed it through multiple fingerprints. Their forensics guy sent a photograph through email." He passed a black and white picture to the sheriff. "Cass says it's him, and he looks like a younger version of the man in the newspaper article in the store. I've faxed a copy of that article and his driver's license photo to Thayerville."

Hoffner studied the paper.

"Kado also learned," Mitch continued, "that Whitman allegedly died in a house fire in 1978. They recovered a body from the scene and identified it as Whitman's."

"He faked his own death?"

"Apparently so. When he was sheriff of Thayerville."

Hoffner's hoary eyebrows shot up. "Why?"

"That's what we were trying to figure out. Cass thought you might have an idea of what would make a sheriff fake his death and give up that post."

His icy blue gaze snapped to hers and her jaw tightened. "You've been sheriff here for over thirty years," Cass said evenly. "You're the only one of us who knows what kind of pressure a man in the top job faces. Is there anything that would make you leave in the middle of the night, run away?"

"The obvious answer is a criminal who came after him. One he didn't think he could fight off. But there are other things that could've gone wrong." He blinked. "Corruption. Blackmail."

"Good." Mitch nodded. "What kind of corruption or blackmail would a sheriff face?"

Hoffner checked the chair next to Truman, and sat. He pulled a snowy handkerchief from his pocket and absently wiped the table in front of him. "Shake-downs, maybe, of motorists passing through his town or county. Businesses that got tired of paying protection money to the force." He shrugged. "Maybe he was rigging some of the cases so defendants were found guilty. Or innocent."

"He might've taken money?" Munk asked.

Hoffner looked down the table at the plump officer, scowling at the stains on Munk's shirt. "Perhaps."

"That would explain some things."

"Like what?" Mitch asked.

Munk leaned forward and placed his forearms on the table. "Calvin Whitehead materialized in Arcadia in 1979. Nothing in his paperwork references his life before that time. But he paid cash for his house and store, and for all the improvements. Several hundred thousand dollars in total."

Hoffner whistled.

"It's a hefty chunk of change, especially for that time," Munk agreed. "And I think he has a safe in his house or the store that might have some of his old life in it. He bought two safes. I talked to the business that sold them and the owner remembered the order. One of the safes is behind Whitehead's counter, under the register. The owner didn't know where Whitehead put the other safe. His boys delivered it but didn't install it."

"What kind was it?" Hoffner asked.

"A floor safe. The owner remembered because they only sold one that year. It was two feet long, two deep, and two wide."

"You can get a lot of stuff in something that big," Kado commented.

Munk nodded. "But it would be easy to hide. I'll look for it this afternoon."

"Truman, would you go with him?" Kado asked. "You can take a picture of that newspaper article behind the counter."

The young officer nodded. "No problem."

Mitch shifted in his wheelchair. "We need to talk to Thayerville's current sheriff, to find out what he knows about Whitman's time as sheriff." He turned to Hoffner. "Will you do that, or do you want me to?"

"I'll do it," Hoffner growled. "One thing I can't stand is a dirty cop."

"Before you call, let Munk fill you in on the lynching. It took place during Whitman's tenure as Sheriff."

Hoffner started. "One of the reporters asked why we weren't calling Calvin Whitehead's death a lynching."

"Interesting," Mitch said. "I always think of a lynching as a mob thing."

"He was strung up," Truman said. "The technicalities of his death make it look like a lynching."

"If he was dirty, Whitman's time as sheriff might have caught up with him." Munk scratched absently at a crusty spot on his uniform shirt. "And whatever he was into must've been bad. 'Cause this is some hellacious payback."

CHAPTER 88

HOFFNER WIPED THE PHONE'S handset with his handkerchief, then dialed, and asked to speak with the head man. He'd been over the information his team had gathered this morning, and found the whole affair stunning. That a sheriff from another jurisdiction chose to obtain a false identity and start a new life in his own county was unbelievable.

"Yes, Sheriff Hoffner, was it?"

"That's right."

"I'm Sheriff Studebaker. My forensics man has talked to yours and shown me your evidence that my Calvin Whitman was your Calvin Whitehead."

"You concur?"

"I suppose I must."

"Why the hesitation, Sheriff?" Hoffner heard a chair squeak through the phone, followed by the sound of a door closing.

Studebaker's voice was muted when he spoke. "I was the deputy. It was me who identified Whitman after the house fire."

The silence on the line grew uncomfortable. Hoffner drew Kado's file nearer and scanned the neatly written notes. "From what I understand, you didn't have much to go on."

"No, I didn't. The corpse wore a ring of Sheriff Whitman's."

"Which could easily be moved from one man's hand to another man's."

"Yes, and it was damaged in the fire. Then there was the hair."

"How did any of the man's hair survive a fire that rendered his face and body unidentifiable?"

"I don't know. But Whitman had a fine head of hair. It was thick, very black, and he kept it slicked back. The body in the fire had similar hair. Despite the smoke and the smell of seared flesh, it even retained the scent of Whitman's pomade."

"Why didn't you request a dental comparison?" Hoffner asked.

"I was certain the dead body belonged to Sheriff Whitman. We all were. Our coroner agreed."

"Were there any men reported missing who were the same build as Sheriff Whitman, with the same type of hair?"

Studebaker's answer was slow in coming. "We did receive a missing person's report on a man with physical characteristics similar to Whitman's. But that was almost six weeks after Whitman's death. He was dead and buried by that time. The rubble from the house cleared."

"It didn't cross your mind that Whitman might have scampered and left this man in his place?"

"One of my men did suggest it, Sheriff Hoffner."

"And?"

"It was simply a joke. There was nothing unusual in the fire."

"Nothing at all unusual, even around the time of the fire?"

The line was silent as papers turned in the background. "I'd forgotten this. We had two reports of an unfamiliar pickup in the vicinity the night of Whitman's blaze. Once the fire was ruled accidental, the report was inconsequential. No crimes were committed in the area, so the matter of the pickup simply fell away."

"You had no suspicions that Whitman might've faked his death and used that unfamiliar pickup to leave Thayerville?"

"None." Studebaker breathed into the phone and then blurted, "Frankly, I was glad to see him go."

Hoffner leaned back in his chair. *Now we're getting somewhere*, he thought. "Why is that, Sheriff Studebaker?"

A snort came through the phone line. "No, I didn't want the sheriff's job that badly. Now that I've been in it for nearly thirty years, I would much have preferred to remain a deputy. You've been on the job for a long time, too, haven't you? You'll know the kind of hassles it brings."

Hoffner agreed that there were times when sheriffing was challenging, but he couldn't imagine not wanting, absolutely having to have, the top job. "You misunderstand me, Sheriff Studebaker. I simply wondered what it was about Whitman that made you glad to see him go."

"He was, well, let's just say that he was difficult to work for."

"Whitman was on the take, and you weren't comfortable with that, were you?"

"What makes you think that?"

"He came to Arcadia with several hundred thousand dollars in cash."

Studebaker burst out laughing. "Several *hundred* thousand?"

"Or more. My men are out at his house now, trying to find a concealed safe. I think we'll find cash inside, and perhaps information about his time as sheriff of Thayerville."

Studebaker sighed, a contented sound. The acknowledgment that his former boss was crooked seemed to relax him. "It was a dark time for the department. Sheriff Whitman was on the take. You name it, he was into it. We were a dry county back then, but for the right price, you could serve any type of liquor you wanted. Officers would go and pick it up for you. We even provided prostitution, in discreet locations, of course."

"Surely the premiums for booze and whores weren't that high, were they?"

"No. He owned the judges as well. If you wanted a particular verdict in your trial, or the trial of a friend or neighbor, it was yours for the right price. That's where the real money was."

"Hundreds of thousands worth?" Hoffner asked, his mind reeling.

"Over Whitman's twenty years as sheriff, and considering his take coming up through the ranks, I suppose so."

Hoffner made a few notes as he considered this. "How did you manage to steer clear of it all?"

"I didn't need the cash."

"Pardon?"

"My family comes from old money, Sheriff Hoffner. And my father was in the state legislature. Whitman wanted me on the force, seemed to think the Studebaker name lent credibility to the department."

"You took Whitman's place after his death?"

"I was appointed by the county commissioners to finish out Whitman's term, and have been voted in ever since."

Hoffner sucked his teeth. "It's come to my attention that there was a lynching in Thayerville."

"Which one are you referring to?"

"I beg your pardon?"

"We've had several lynchings in Thayerville over the years. I assume you're referring to one of those that took place during Sheriff Whitman's tenure, correct?"

Hoffner cleared his throat. "How many were there?"

"Five during his term, most of them early on. Can you identify anything about the lynching that you're interested in?"

"It occurred in 1967. Three men were murdered —"

Studebaker cut him off with a slow recitation. "Charlie Franklin, Bob Hedder, and Ben Silverman. I remember it well."

"Sheriff Whitman was in charge then?"

"Yes, he was."

"Were you on the force at that time?"

"Fresh from college and at the bottom of the totem pole, assigned to traffic duty." His voice was reflective. "Back in the days when people liked to see an officer directing traffic. I worked the major intersection in town, Main and First, and knew those men."

"What triggered the lynching?" Hoffner asked.

"I never knew. Not the real reason. None of the men was a problem. Or their families. The rumor that went through the station house and made the paper was that the three had leered at a white woman, frightening her. And there was something about an illegal gathering. Although how three men could constitute an illegal gathering is still beyond me."

"The newspaper article I saw had a photograph of five men in white sheets."

"Yes, the Klan was responsible."

"Was anyone ever arrested for these deaths?"

Studebaker breathed heavily. "No, Sheriff Hoffner, I regret to tell you that no one was held accountable for murdering those three men."

"Do you know who was involved?"

"Yes. Very clearly. A lynching always drew a crowd. I know the article you're referring to. Although the photograph only shows those five Klansmen, many of our good citizens stood around and watched those men be beaten, hanged, and burned to death. It happened in early May. The temperature was in the mid-seventies that day, and it was cooling down when the men were killed. But lynching is hot work and the five Klansmen took their hoods off after the bodies were up and burning. They put the hoods back on to pose for the photographer."

"People saw them?"

"Yes, they did."

"But no one was arrested."

"That's correct."

Hoffner straightened the papers on his desk as a vision of that night in 1967 materialized in his mind. The faces of four of the men responsible for murdering Franklin, Silverman, and Hedder were blurred, but the face of the fifth man, that was very clear. "Sheriff Calvin Whitman was among them, correct?"

"Yes, he was."

"That's why no one was arrested when the lynching occurred."

"It is."

"Why don't you do something about it now?"

"Arrest the remaining four? Don't imagine that I haven't thought about it over the years, Sheriff. But I'm not sure how to go about it anymore."

"Why is that?"

"I know where two of those five men are. Whitman is probably in a cooler in your morgue, and one of the men died in Thayerville. But the other three? They left long ago. I wouldn't know where to begin to find them."

Hoffner grunted. It was time to come to Cass's question. "Why did Calvin Whitman fake his death in 1979?"

"I have no idea."

"Was he in danger of losing his office?"

"Not at all. His elections weren't even contested."

"It couldn't have been money problems. Why die? Did he have family?"

"A son. Whitman's wife died in childbirth."

"The boy wasn't in the house when it burned?"

"We were scared to death we'd find his body. Turns out he was spending the night with a friend."

"That was clever of Whitman."

"In hindsight, it was."

"Where's the boy now?"

"I don't know."

"Well, what happened to him after his father died?"

"He was taken in by one of Whitman's friends."

"Not a relative?"

"There were no relatives. Whitman and his wife had no siblings and the boy's grandparents were long dead."

Hoffner chewed on this. "So the son had no idea that his father was alive?"

"I have no reason to think that he did."

"Who received Whitman's insurance benefits, Sheriff Studebaker? Life, home, pension, that kind of thing."

"The woman who tended to the boy after his mother died received a little money. A few hundred dollars, I think. The rest was put in a trust for the boy's benefit, with some money available for his care every year, and the balance available to him on his sixteenth birthday."

"And you have no idea what could have caused Whitman to leave Thayerville in such a dramatic fashion?"

"Until today, Sheriff Hoffner, I didn't realize Whitman had left Thayerville at all. I'll think back over those years and see what some of the other old-timers can remember. If anything comes to mind, I'll let you know." Studebaker paused. "How did my Whitman, your Whitehead, die? I assume it wasn't a natural death or you wouldn't have bothered running his prints."

"Now that's truly ironic. He was hanged and burned to death."

It was Studebaker's turn to grunt. "A lynching. Poetic justice, it seems. Who did it?"

"We have no leads. That's one of the reasons I wanted to talk to you. It takes some determination and planning for a man to walk away from his life, especially to leave a child. We wondered if whatever he was running from when he left Thayerville finally caught up with him here in Arcadia."

CHAPTER 89

TRUMAN SHONE HIS FLASHLIGHT through the white latticework and shook his head. His face, flushed with mid-afternoon heat only moments ago, had lost its color. "Nope. Write me up, fire me, whatever. I'm not gonna do it."

"Wimp."

"Come on, Munk. Why would he put it down here? We didn't find a way to get to a safe from the house. How could he get to the dang thing while crawling under here? There's no room to move."

Munk's knees protested with several loud pops as he eased to a squat next to Truman. He squinted into the gloom, following the beam of Truman's flashlight. The crawl space beneath Calvin Whitehead's pier and beam house hadn't been entered in years, if not decades. No more than three feet high, the area beneath the house was draped with webs. *Brown recluse spiders and black widows*, Munk thought, suppressing a shudder. "It can't be in the shop or under his metal building. They're both on a slab."

"You're probably right, but let me look. It won't take long."

Munk peered into the shadowy recess one more time. "All right. Let's start with the shop."

Truman offered Munk his hand, but the older man struggled to his feet by himself. "I've got to lose some weight," he panted.

"Try protein shakes," Truman said.

"Nasty."

"You get used to it." Truman led the way to The Whitehead Store, signed the crime scene log, and waited while the officer on duty unlocked the front door.

"How much longer do we have to stay out here, Officer Munk?" the patrolman asked, pushing his mirrored sunglasses up on his nose.

"Has anybody bothered you?" Munk asked.

"I've had a few drive-bys, but nobody stopped."

"Then keeping somebody posted is worthwhile. We'd have looters and people trying to get a look inside if you weren't here."

"Hurry up and get this case closed, would you? This place gives me the creeps." The officer shivered in spite of the day's heat. "And it stinks."

Disturbed dust motes danced a dervish in the golden slabs of sunlight falling through the store's wide front windows. The smell of moldering food was muted, but Munk wondered what kind of nastiness waited in the storeroom. Beyond the sunlight's edge, the shop was a murky haze. Truman found the light switch and fluorescent tubes stuttered to life, releasing a low buzz before bathing the aisles in a cool white light. Munk stood with his hands on his hips, surveying the parallel rows of shelves neatly stacked with goods. Packages of miniature donuts drenched with powdered sugar caught his eye, and he turned resolutely away. "Ideas?"

"I guess we look for anomalies in the floor. A trap door or something. And check beneath the floor mats," Truman answered.

They worked their way along the aisles, probing at the occasional loose linoleum tile and lifting the heavy rubber mats in front of the doors and behind the counter. Nothing. At last they faced the door to the storeroom. Munk extracted a small pot of Vick's from his pocket and smeared a dab beneath his nose. Truman did the same, then tied a red kerchief over his nose and mouth, bandit-style, and reached for the doorknob.

The smell of scorched meat melding with the stench of rotting food made their eyes water. Truman hurried to open the door into the small courtyard, gulping a breath of marginally fresher air before turning to survey the shelves of unopened boxes and the reddish mess still staining the floor.

The stockroom tiles were all in place and still firmly glued down. Truman scooted stacks of boxes aside and attempted to move some of the shelves. Nothing. Munk pulled gingerly at the shelf units fixed to the walls to see if they were mounted on hinges. Again, nothing.

He turned to Truman. "That safe has got to be beneath the house."

"We still need to look at the courtyard."

"It's a slab out there too, isn't it?" Munk followed the young officer outside and studied the small space. Truman had spotted a door secured with a padlock in the courtyard's outer wall. A short, sloping roof disappeared into the yard beyond.

"Tool shed?" Truman asked before darting into the storeroom and returning moments later with Whitehead's keys. Behind the door they found a space roughly four feet square that housed a neatly arrayed selection of tools: hammers, screwdrivers, pliers, and electric and battery powered saws and drills.

Truman's face was bleak as he relocked the shed and examined the courtyard. He pocketed the keys and went to work. Munk studied the cracked concrete, glancing up at the faint scorching that marred the sycamore's branch and quickly pulling his gaze away. Truman was moving equipment and lifting stacks of pallets, working his way around the small space. He tugged on a folded tarp piled high with flattened cardboard boxes stored beneath the shop's overhanging eaves. The young officer turned to look at Munk, a smile shifting the red handkerchief. "Jackpot."

CHAPTER 90

CASS LIFTED THE FINAL box of documents to her desk and rifled its contents. These were the last of Donna Moore's personal and business records for the prior five years. Cass sincerely hoped they wouldn't have to look farther back in the woman's life; Moore kept meticulous notes about her hours at the office, and since she spent the majority of her waking hours there, about her life. It all seemed a bit sad.

She found a calendar and paged through it, marking the dates when Moore was absent from work or had left early. As her assistant Joshua Reed had indicated, the accountant rarely took time off. In fact, prior to the last four years, Moore was away from the office during business hours only two or three times each year. And her absences were explained by doctor or dentist appointments, or training classes. But in the last four years, she'd taken unexplained time off on several occasions. Slots in the calendar were neatly blocked off with no notations as to where she was going or what she had planned. On some dates, business appointments were scratched through as if Moore decided to leave the office on short notice. Cass recorded every anomaly but could see no pattern in the woman's absences.

Mitch was working his way through Emmet and Celia Hedder's bank statements, identifying instances when cash was withdrawn from locations outside the immediate area. He picked up the hanger.

"How's it going?" he asked Cass.

"Donna wrote everything down." She grabbed a calendar and flipped to a page early in the book. "You and Darla had your taxes done on March eighth last year."

"We did?" he asked, inching the hanger beneath the brace.

"According to this you did."

"What else?"

Cass tapped her notepad. "I've got thirty-seven unexplained absences from the office over the last four years."

"How long was she gone?"

"Sometimes, for a couple of hours in the afternoon or early evening. On a few occasions, like in March last year, three days."

Mitch reached for a stack of bank statements, leaving the hanger protruding from his brace. "What days?"

"Just before you went to see her about your taxes," Cass said.

Mitch's face was contemplative. "Emmet Hedder withdrew three hundred dollars from an ATM in Kentucky on one of those days."

"So?"

"Maybe they were together."

"Come on, Mitch. They didn't even know each other."

"As far as we know."

She gaped. "They were involved? Having an affair?"

Mitch started scratching again. "I remember that visit to Donna's office. She was always pretty straight, very professional. But that day, she seemed really happy about something. Darla even said she was glowing."

"You don't really think she was involved with Emmet Hedder, do you?"

Mitch opened a desk drawer, scrounged around, and extracted out a phone book. "There's one way to find out."

"How's that?"

"Talk to the woman who owns that old folks home where Emmet works and see when he's been away from work for the last few years."

———

IT WAS CASS WHO ended up persuading the owner of Pecan Grove Residential Retirement Community and Gardens to share the dates Emmet had been absent from work, because Darla came to collect Mitch for his physical therapy appointment. He left the squad room under duress, whining about spousal abuse and demanding better pain medications.

Cass dialed Pecan Grove and had trouble getting past the secretary to the owner. At first, the woman simply refused to talk to Cass without her lawyer. She seemed determined to keep Pecan Grove out of the press. It took some persuading to convince her that Cass wasn't a reporter and the police department didn't have a problem with Pecan Grove. The problem wasn't even with Emmet Hedder. In the end, the icy owner's fears of press coverage and her anger over Emmet's unexplained absence melted when Cass told the woman they thought that Emmet's life was in danger. She promised to fax his employment records to the police station immediately.

Cass waited in Elaine's alcove, listening as the curly-headed receptionist soothed frustrated courthouse visitors with her honeyed voice. Bernie Winterbottom stood and offered Cass his chair. She waved for him to sit and leaned against the counter housing the fax machine, one ear cocked for its familiar purr.

"Did you have time to look at the photos of Moore's artwork?" she asked.

"Yes, I did. She was an excellent artist."

"Any ideas what they're about?"

"I'm afraid not. Each, however, is drawn or painted from an unusual perspective."

"How do you mean?"

Bernie angled a hand upward. "It's almost as if you are viewing the object from the ground upward. Or from a position beneath the object."

"I don't get it."

"It's as if you were lying on the ground looking up at a tall tree. Imagine the sketch of the trouser legs. They are fuller at the bottom, and grow narrow as they get to the top."

"What does it mean?"

He shrugged. "Until we understand what the artwork represents, we can't decipher why Miss Moore chose to use that upward perspective."

"Well, thanks. I wouldn't have picked up on her perspective." Bernie's smile was shy. "How's the dig?"

He smoothed a hand over his unruly golden hair and straightened his safari vest. "Quite good, thank you. The developer has finally accepted that it is in his best interest to allow us to explore for Caddo burial sites before he begins construction."

"How can it be in his best interest?"

Bernie leaned forward, his green eyes twinkling. "Through a contact in the archaeology world, I've discovered that he's one of three finalists in the running to design a new office park in Houston. I've offered to put in a good word for him with the contractor if we're allowed to proceed with the exploratory excavation. And the work we'd like to perform shouldn't put him back more than a few weeks."

"What kind of influence do you have over this office park development?"

"Didn't I mention it?"

"Mention what?"

"My brother owns the company that is acting as general contractor for the development."

"Is he based in Houston?"

"No, in Dubai."

Cass blinked. "The Dubai in the Middle East?"

"Yes, that one. He does a bit of work for the royal families over there."

Cass studied the Englishman with curiosity. "Have you ever worked for the royal families?"

"Only at home." He smiled up at her. "The Queen Mum was my favorite. A tough old bird, but a gentle soul when it came to antiquities. I have hope for Prince William. He has a bit of his mother's sensitivity about him."

Cass suppressed a smile. It seemed that scruffy Bernie Winterbottom pottered about in elite circles. The fax machine hummed and Cass watched as papers slid into the receiving tray. "Any plans to go home?" she asked.

Bernie's glance shot to Elaine. She was helping an elderly Hispanic woman with her property tax forms. He lowered his voice. "It may be sooner than I wish."

"Why is that?" Cass whispered.

"Mum phoned. Donald, my contractor brother, can't get away from Houston and she needs someone at home."

"Are there just two of you?" Cass asked, collecting the pages from the fax machine. "Two brothers?"

"Not exactly," Bernie answered, flushing. "But we're the two with Mum duty."

"Oh. Okay. Well, I hope your mom gets better soon." Cass headed for the secure door to the police station, only realizing as she swiped her card that Bernie didn't say his mother was sick. "Families are bizarre," she muttered to herself, spreading Emmet Hedder's paperwork across her desk.

It was all straightforward. Emmet Hedder started working at Pecan Grove Residential Retirement Community and Gardens as a nurse five years ago. He worked full-time, five days a week from eight to five. On occasion, he arrived at the facility at around six in the morning, finishing by three in the afternoon. He worked some overtime in the evenings or at the weekends, perhaps when the residents needed additional care. It seemed that Emmet had two weeks of vacation, and he took this in small bites here and there throughout the year.

Cass started working from that first February forward, noting month by month when Emmet worked the six to three shift, and when he took vacation. When she finished, she compared the results to Moore's absences from her office. Unbelievable. Cass leaned back in her desk chair. Mitch was on to something. On many of the days when Emmet worked a shift that ended at three, Moore had blanked out her calendar from three or four onward. When Emmet took vacation, Moore was absent from the office for the same length of time on almost every occasion.

Elaine hurried into the squad room and dropped several sheets of paper on Cass's desk. "These came through after you left." She raised an eyebrow. "They're weird. See you at the funeral home."

Cass glanced at the handwritten note on the top page. "I should've mentioned these when we spoke. I showed them to Emmet but he didn't know who would've sent them. Perhaps they came from the person who tried to kill him." Pecan Grove's owner had signed at the bottom.

She flipped through the remaining four sheets, amazement growing. There was one line on each page, words formed from letters cut from magazines and newspapers:

How well do you know Emmet Hedder?
Where is Emmet Hedder?
Why do you trust Emmet Hedder?
Emmet Hedder is not a nice man.

Cass snatched the phone's handset and dialed, glancing at the clock. It was nearly five. She barely had an hour to get home, change, and get to the funeral home for the Franklins' visitation. She spoke briefly to Pecan Grove's owner, arranging to have an officer collect the originals of the four letters. She punched in the sheriff's extension, jabbing the disconnect button at the last minute. They needed Moses' personnel records to see if he had been absent from work at the same time as Emmet and Donna. But given Hoffner's irritation with her, things would go more smoothly if Mitch asked for them.

She turned off the computer and whispered to the empty room, "That's why you make the big bucks, my friend. Hoffner hazard pay."

Chapter 91

IT TOOK THE LOCKSMITH over an hour to drill through both safes. He stepped away from the hole in the concrete, an expression of respect on his face. "They don't make 'em like this anymore."

Before he poured the slab for his courtyard, Calvin Whitehead had dug and fortified a rectangular space. It was protected by a hardwood trap door on hinges, which was further protected by a tarp. The hole housed the floor safe and a battered metal footlocker. Inside the safe, they found straps of currency worth three hundred thousand dollars wrapped in thick plastic, a woman's wedding ring, a photograph album whose pages were yellowed and brittle, and a package of papers, also wrapped in thick plastic.

Truman cracked the padlock on the footlocker with a crowbar. He cocked his head as Munk lifted the lid, and then took a step back.

"You've never seen this stuff up close?" Munk asked.

"No. It makes me kind of nauseous."

A little stack of booklets was bound with a red ribbon. Munk reached in with a gloved hand and unknotted the bow. "These are rare." He held up one titled *Constitution and Laws of the Knights of the Ku Klux Klan* and gently fanned the pages. "I think this is the pocket edition. This," he held out a slim volume titled *Klansman's Manual,* "contains the instructions on how to initiate a new Klan member. It talks about duties and ceremonies, and even includes a penal code."

Truman reached a finger out, but quickly withdrew it.

"It is kind of nauseating," Munk said.

"How do you know so much about this stuff?" Truman asked as Munk pulled a silky purple costume decorated with colorful patches from the trunk and held it up.

"I did some research after James Byrd Jr. was lynched in Jasper. His death was appalling."

"I remember," Truman said. "I didn't think that kind of thing could happen in America anymore."

"Me, either." He examined the patches. "Whitehead had standing in the KKK organization."

"But not around here, right?"

Munk fingered the material. "I don't think so. This looks old. He must've been involved back in Thayerville."

Munk and Truman prepared a quick inventory and moved the foot locker to Truman's truck. The floor safe was welded to sections of rebar whose ends were buried in the concrete slab. They emptied its contents into a cardboard box, shut the safe's door, the hardwood trap door, and re-covered the area with the tarp and boxes.

The safe inside the store contained what they guessed was Wednesday's take for sales and they took this cash with them.

Back at the courthouse, they locked the contents of the safes and the foot locker in the evidence cage. Truman looked at Munk. "I know it's awful, but I'd rather inventory this stuff than have to go to the Franklins' viewing."

Munk nodded. "Dead folks in the wild are one thing, but it's a whole different matter once that corpse hits a casket. Tonight is for Mojo. Clean up and let's go."

CHAPTER 92

JOSEPH FRANKLIN BENT DOWN to accept condolences from one of his mother's friends. She hugged him tightly with one arm; the other balanced a glazed pound cake on a platter. The tears and powder on her cheek leached into the damp fabric of his suit jacket, blending with those of the other little old ladies who had expressed their grief so openly. This one was a bird-like thing, fragile compared to his mother. He patted her gently on the back and dabbed his eyes with a handkerchief even though he hadn't shed a tear today.

Joseph had spent a good deal of the afternoon wondering how his brother would handle this situation if their roles were reversed. Moses would be inconsolable. He would weep openly and hug fiercely. But Joseph couldn't do it. His grief was silent, wrapped in a tight knot buried deep within his soul, a burning ache that he was sure would never ease.

Perhaps Moses had it right. Let it all out. Feel the pain and let the cleansing tears flow. But Joseph wasn't built that way. His best bet was to let the world think Moses was overwhelmed with grief, to the point that tears were barely possible.

Joseph eased away from the white-haired woman, who gave him a watery smile and started toward the kitchen. Visitation at the funeral home had ended at seven, and although Joseph couldn't remember a time when he had been so tired, physically or emotionally, he joined the throng at his mother's home and did his best to receive and thank a seemingly endless stream of mourners. There were so many faces. Most he didn't know. Students, now grown and with their own children, remembered "Mrs. Radcliffe" from her days in the school cafeteria and told him how sad they were at the loss of his mother.

Each offered remembrances of their favorite food and how she would sneak extras to them without their having to ask twice. If it was possible to love a woman you saw for no more than five minutes each day, the students she fed loved his mother.

A bevy of women from the quilting club and church had come to the house earlier to prepare for the wake this evening. Their presence was possible only because a crime scene clean-up team had pushed his case to the top of its list. Members of the police force had pitched in to replace the shattered backsplash tiles and paint the walls, and a glazier had managed to replace the pierced kitchen window. When Joseph stopped by earlier to change clothes, he was stunned to see the kitchen in clean and orderly condition, as if his mother and brother hadn't lay dying in its confines only two days previously. The house was again peaceful, the echoes of death stilled, a semblance of life returning. Someone had mowed and edged the lawn. The beds were freshly made and quilts for pallets aired for the arrival of his mother's family from Alabama. Tonight, the kitchen and dining room tables groaned under the weight of sliced ham, chicken, vegetables, pitchers of tea, and desserts of astonishing variety. It seemed that people cooked in times of trouble. The blue-haired casserole brigade would stuff the freezer with homemade meals, and Joseph could survive for weeks, if not months, with a visit to the grocery store for only milk and fresh produce.

Porky's girlfriend, Stella, had made it back from her aunt's surgery in time to help, and she led him to an open spot in the corner. He numbly accepted a plate piled high with food, surprised to feel his stomach growl. "How are you holding up, Moses?"

He stared down at the plate. "I'm okay. I'll be glad when tomorrow is over."

"I know you will. You're welcome to stay with us as long as you like. There's no rush for you to come back here."

"I appreciate it, Stella. But I need to be home now. This is where I belong."

"Keep it in mind. You're welcome any time."

Stella moved away and Joseph found himself face to face with Officer Hugo Petchard and the woman from The Golden Gate Café. Joseph searched his memory and retrieved her name: Junie. Petchard was dressed in civvies and extended a hand. Joseph shook it, face expressionless

"I'm really sorry for your loss, Mojo."

"Thanks, Petchard."

"Me, too, Officer Franklin," Junie said. She was dressed in a high-necked black top and calf-length black skirt. Her dark hair was brushed straight back from her expertly made-up face. Joseph realized that she wasn't so much attractive as she was striking. Tall, somewhat slender, with a broad forehead, defined cheekbones, angular jaw, and full lips. Runway model material. Her eyes never left his. "It's such a tragedy."

"Thanks. Junie, was it?"

She nodded, a slight smile on her lips.

"Did you have a chance to eat?" He motioned to the dining room table. "There's a ton of food here."

Junie held up a wadded napkin. "Death always brings out the best in a cook. Whoever cleaned and repaired your kitchen did a wonderful job. And fast, too. The backsplash behind the stove is perfect. They even found a new head for the rooster."

Petchard slipped an arm around her waist and pulled her close. "We'll get out of your hair, Mojo. But we'll see you at the funeral tomorrow."

"Sure," Joseph said. "I'll see you tomorrow."

———————

MITCH WATCHED AS PETCHARD led a tall woman from the Franklin's living room. A steady stream of mourners was coming and going, spilling from the small house onto the front and back lawns. He lowered his voice. "Who are these people? I don't recognize half of them."

"They're Mojo's family from out East," Cass answered.

Mitch ate a bite of fruit salad and motioned with his fork. "Who's with Petchard?"

Cass glanced between Mitch and his wife Darla. The three of them stood in one corner of the crowded living room. "Her name is Junie. She works for Stan and Sally at The Golden Gate."

"She's kinda funny looking."

Darla poked her husband in the ribs before collecting their plates and glasses. "She's quite attractive. A bit Angelina Jolie."

He looked at her again as Darla headed for the kitchen. "What's she doing with Petchard?"

"Stan said he made a beeline for her when she first came to town," Cass said. "And for whatever reason, she seems to like him."

"Well, there's something wrong with her."

"What do you mean?"

"Any chick who's interested in Petchard must have some kind of psychological problem," Mitch said, watching until the front door closed behind them. "I just wonder what hers is."

"Guess what?" Cass said, lowering her voice. "I got Emmet's employment records from Pecan Grove. Emmet and Donna were away from work at the same time."

"Maybe they were having an affair."

"There's more. Emmet's boss got letters about him like those the sheriff got about Moses."

"With the letters cut out of magazines?"

"Yes. Implying that Emmet was up to something bad."

"Somehow, the three are linked, aren't they?"

She nodded. "We need to see Moses' time sheets."

"Did you ask Hoffner for them?"

"You think he'd give me anything I asked for? That's your job."

A buzzing sounded and they looked down to see a phone skittering across a small table. Mitch adjusted his crutches, grabbed it, and flipped it open. "Hello? Anybody there?" He closed the phone and reopened it, checking the number. "Wonder whose this is?"

He checked the phone's recent call history and its information.

Mojo strode up. "Did I miss a call?"

"Yeah," Mitch said, closing the device. "Sorry, man. I should've known this was yours. Whoever it was didn't speak and," he looked down at the little device, "didn't leave a message."

"If it was important, they'll call back." Mojo pocketed the phone and turned as someone tugged on his arm. He drifted away and Cass glanced up to see Mitch watching Mojo with a confused expression on his face.

"What is it?" she asked.

"There's something about the number that was calling him. I've seen it before, but I don't know where."

"Is it important?"

"If it is, it'll come to me." He grinned. "Probably in the middle of the night. Hey, are you gonna eat that brownie?"

CHAPTER 93

MITCH AND DARLA TOOK their leave and Cass wove through the crowd to the kitchen. Martinez accepted an overflowing plate from an elderly woman, who shooed him away and turned to help someone else.

"How's it going with the old man?" Cass asked.

"I suspect," Martinez answered, moving to stand near the kitchen windows, "that he wandered off. The house was unlocked, his car is in the drive, and his wallet is in the house."

"Alzheimer's?"

"Not officially. But the neighbors said he was forgetful. I've called Watuga County to see if we can get the tracker dogs."

"Any luck?"

"They're in Stanton, working on a missing kid. They can't get here until tomorrow morning at the earliest."

"Why not?"

"The dogs have to rest their noses between victims or something like that." He swiped a cookie from Cass's plate and headed for the door. "We're sweeping the neighborhood again, just in case. See you later."

She returned to the living room to see Maxine talking to Mojo. Her mind whirled back to their conversation in the park last night and the newspaper article Maxine had left at the station this morning. Cass settled in the corner and wasn't surprised when Maxine hugged Mojo and then joined her, picking at the plate of food Cass held. "Hey," Cass protested. "Get your own."

Maxine raised a finely plucked eyebrow. "This is your second, isn't it?"

"So what?"

"So, I'm being a friend by sharing calories."

The two nibbled companionably, watching as Sheriff Hoffner made his way across the small living room and shook Moses' hand. They talked for a moment, heads together, then Hoffner clapped Moses on the shoulder. Mojo pulled a cell phone from his pocket and turned into the wall to talk, covering one ear with his hand.

"Poor Mojo," Maxine said. "It's such a shame."

"How do you know the Franklins?"

"Moses helped me one night when I had a flat."

Cass giggled.

"Shut up. I know I'm not mechanically inclined. Thankfully, Moses drove past. He must've seen me struggling with the jack."

"How do you know what a jack looks like?"

Maxine cut her eyes at Cass. "You showed me back in high school, remember?"

"That was a bad night. You let me change the flat on your dad's car all by myself."

"I helped. I popped the trunk. And it wasn't that bad."

"Not for you. I was filthy when we got to that club, what was it called?"

"Nexus. It was over in Stanton, in that skanky ol' warehouse."

"That's it. I smelled like rubber and road grime, and you looked fabulous. I didn't get asked to dance all night."

"Not my fault. We could've waited for someone to come along and help us."

"Oh, Max," Cass sighed. "You and your knights in shining armor."

"They always turn up right when you need them."

"For you, they do. It was Moses this time?"

She nodded. "He was off duty, but stopped anyway. I sent him one of those cookie bouquets to say thank you, and we texted for a while. Moses is a really good guy, but he's so messed up right now, he hardly seems like himself."

"What do you mean?"

"He's so withdrawn. He didn't even recognize me." Maxine shrugged. "But once I reminded him who I was, he hugged me and said he was glad I came." She sidled closer to Cass, watching the crowd. "Can we talk some more? About… it?"

Cass stopped herself from shivering by sipping her coffee. She steeled herself and turned to Maxine, who still picked at the food. "I have to tell you something."

"What?"

"He raped me, too."

Maxine took a step back, her gaze dropping to Cass's shoulder. "You have a scar?"

Cass nodded. "It was six years ago."

"In Dallas?"

"Yes."

Maxine turned and stared at the room, but Cass could sense her mind spinning. "Did you report it?" Max asked.

"No."

"He left a note?"

"No." Cass drew a deep breath. "I was running, Max. The guy I was dating in College Station dumped me for some blonde with pneumatic boobs." She glanced apologetically at her friend, who waved her concern away. "I ran. To Dallas. And started drinking."

Max smiled at an elderly black woman who settled on the couch, then glanced back at Cass. "It must've been bad if you were drinking."

"It was. But that doesn't excuse what I did."

"What are you talking about?"

"I put myself in that situation, I gave him the opportunity. Giving in to the rage at my boyfriend, the pain. The embarrassment. Getting drunk. Good Lord, with my father? I knew better."

"You were nineteen, Cass."

She drew a breath. "I collected some evidence. Semen, pubic hairs, fingerprints."

Maxine's eyes widened. And then she frowned. "The mask?"

"Richard Nixon. He must have a ritual, a pattern."

"The bastard."

A palpable relief slid through Cass at Maxine's words, a weight physically disappeared from her shoulders. *She believes me.* "You're the first person I've told about this. Ever."

"That makes us even."

"I need to ask some questions."

"Want me to come to the station, officer?" Maxine asked with a smile.

Cass reached for the food. "If he raped you in Dallas, what makes you think he's watching you in Arcadia?"

Her clear green eyes cut over at Cass. "'It is illogical, Captain'," she quipped, and then nodded. "Good question. Maybe I've taken the warning in his note too seriously. Maybe not, given what happened to that poor girl in Ft. Worth. But there was something about him. Something almost familiar, but not quite. Do you know what I mean?"

This was a possibility Cass hadn't considered. "You think he might be from Arcadia? He might know you?"

"Or maybe from Ft. Worth. Anything is possible, Cass. And I don't want to take the chance that he might see me talking to the cops."

"You're talking to one now."

"In a very natural setting."

"So, you don't want me to put any of this on file, is that right?" Maxine nodded.

Cass felt the irony of what she was about to say, considering that she hadn't filed a police report at the time of her rape. "Then there's not much I can do to help you."

"You can check that piece of paper I gave you for prints, for starters. That's why I kept the thing."

Cass lowered her voice. "It's not that easy, Max. To identify prints on paper you need a special chemical and —"

Maxine flicked her fingers. "Whatever. Just do it."

"I can't just do it. There's special forensics equipment involved."

"Isn't the forensics guy that hunky dark-haired man? The one near the fireplace?"

In spite of her frustration, Cass snorted a laugh. She should've known Maxine would have pegged all attractive males in the area. "Tom Kado. You haven't bedded him yet?"

"No, but I've seen his picture in the Forney Cater. Besides, he's into you, not me."

Cass flushed. "There's all sorts of protocol. He has to have a case number –"

"You're as stupid about men now as you were in high school," Maxine said, cutting her off. "Honey, bat those violet eyes of yours at him and ask for a favor." She pulled back. "You're gorgeous. There's no way he would turn you down."

Cass glanced up and caught Kado watching. She flashed a quick smile. "Speaking of gorgeous, you look great, but you're a little skinny, Max. What's up?"

"I guess that's one good thing to come out of all this. I've dropped every ounce of fat I had in high school."

"You were never fat –," Cass began.

"Maxie Maxine, Mondo Max, hefty, chunky, blubber box, whatever. I was a lot fatter than I am now. I might be too skinny, but I don't want to put much weight back on."

"You look anorexic, Max."

"Pish," she answered, waving a hand in a movement reminiscent of her mother. "I haven't had much of an appetite lately. It'll come back."

"When did you get the boobs?" Cass whispered.

"They were a wedding gift from the ex-husband. That should have been my first sign that things weren't going to work out. Although I haven't had many complaints from male companions since the divorce."

Kado walked across the room and stopped in front of the two women. He blushed. "I'm heading out, but wanted to say good night."

Maxine poked Cass with an elbow. "Introduce me?"

Cass cut a warning glance at Maxine and cleared her throat. "Kado, I'd like for you to meet a very good friend. This is Maxine Leverman. Maxine, meet Tom Kado, our forensics examiner."

Maxine held out her hand, palm down. "Aren't you a gorgeous creature? Charmed, I'm sure."

Kado took her hand, gray eyes wide. "It's nice to meet you."

"Don't worry sweetie, I don't bite. Well, I don't bite Cass's boyfriends. Usually."

Cass grimaced. "It's a genetic thing, Kado. She sees a handsome man and can't help herself. Have a good night."

"Handsome, huh?" he said, grinning as he turned and walked away.

Maxine giggled. "He is a hot little number. You'd better not keep the boy dangling, some other girl might come along and snatch him right out from under you. So to speak."

"Dear God, Maxine," Cass said. "I work with the man."

"And a detective outranks a forensic examiner, right? So you really are on top."

Cass chuckled as a thought occurred to her. "Have you had sex since the rape?"

"Well, of course. Why?"

"What do you tell them about the scar?"

"*If* they ask, I tell them it's body art."

"What?"

"Like a tattoo. Only it's a scar."

"Something you did willingly? On purpose?"

Maxine nodded.

"And they believe you?"

"You are such an innocent, Cass. A horny man will believe anything a naked woman tells him. He's putty in her hands." She sighed and leaned into the wall, snagging a bite of ham. "Stop changing the subject. Will you help me?"

Cass's phone buzzed and she pulled it from her pocket. Petchard's name flashed at her. She pushed the button to silence the call. "What if I don't?"

"I'll get a private investigator's license and a gun and kill him myself. Then I'll hide the body out in the woods for the hogs to eat. Nobody'll be the wiser."

Cass chuckled. Maxine would do it, no doubt. Her mind worked furiously. Four murders and a missing, injured man targeted by the same killer. Whispers of corruption about the man whose family they were mourning, and about the missing man. Cass's professional life was full to overflowing, and until they caught this shooter and whoever had burned Calvin Whitehead to death, her time to work surreptitiously on Maxine's behalf — and her own, if she was truthful – was limited. But the investigative wheels were already in motion, in her mind at least. And the thought of Maxine with a PI's license and gun permit was too much to contemplate. "Fine. I'll do what I can. But," she cautioned in the face of Maxine's restrained dance of triumph, "you'll have to be patient. Things are crazy right now, and this stuff takes time."

Cass's phone rang again. "What do you want, Petchard?"

Her expression turned hard as granite. After a very short conversation, Cass shut the phone and snapped it open again.

"I'm sorry, Max. I have to go," she said, taking a step toward the front door. "I'll call you later."

"What happened?" Maxine asked, reaching for her friend.

Cass's violet eyes flashed. "Daddy."

CHAPTER 94

CASS ARRIVED AT SHADY Grove Cemetery as Bruce and Harry were sliding a prone Abe Elliot onto the back seat of Bruce's pickup. Little Phoebe peered over the front seat, mouth a perfect 'o'. A few rubberneckers had slowed to watch and Cass flashed her headlights to move them on. Bruce wore filthy coveralls and his dark hair was speckled with dust. Harry was still dressed for the office in a starched white shirt with the sleeves rolled back, khaki slacks, and a walnut colored tie that brought out the golden brown of his eyes. Petchard perched on the short rock wall that enclosed the cemetery, watching.

"Drunk?" she asked her brothers.

"As a skunk," Harry confirmed, wrapping a seat belt around his daughter and closing the truck's door.

"An Elliot never does anything half-assed." Bruce wiped his forehead. "He's practically catatonic."

"What kicked him off?"

Harry and Bruce exchanged a look. "It's May," Harry said.

"Of course it is," she breathed.

"I haven't been watching him," said Bruce.

"Me either," Harry added. "We'll get him home and start rinsing him out."

"You're not going to let him sleep?" Cass asked.

"Nope," Bruce answered. "We'll make him wish he'd made it one more day." He opened the toolbox in his pickup's bed and tore a trash bag off a nearly empty roll. "Clean up the grave, would you?"

Cass watched them leave and wondered if she could stay somewhere else tonight. Nobody would get much sleep. She acknowledged Petchard with a lift of her chin and her feet followed the path to her mother's grave of their own accord. Crushed beer cans and two empty bottles of her father's favorite poison of late, tequila, marked the spot where his wife was buried. What a shame to ruin such a beautiful place with rubbish like this.

Shady Grove Cemetery was one of the oldest in Forney County. The massive oak and pine trees blocked the last of the twilight, creating cavities of shadow where mismatched headstones jutted like a fairy tale giant's jagged teeth. Despite its painful associations for her family and the eeriness that evening brought, Cass had always found Shady Grove a restful place. She started picking the trash up, turning at the sound of footsteps.

Petchard leaned against a tall headstone carved in the form of a fierce angel. "I could've arrested him for public intoxication."

"Thanks for calling me instead."

"And for assaulting an officer. He took a swing at me."

"You're lucky. His aim is usually pretty good." She hesitated. "How did you find him?"

"This is on my way home. He was staggering around the headstones when I drove past, but was already back to your mom's grave by the time I got out of the car. He collapsed after he swung at me." Petchard moved from the shadows and stood with her, facing the gravestone. "Why'd he do it? Your mother didn't die today."

Cass read the simple inscription.

Nell Elliot
Beloved wife, mother, and daughter
June 7, 1953 – May 21, 1990

"May is always a problem." She faced Petchard. "This is the month, twenty-two years ago, when Hoffner stormed into our house and arrested Jack for rape and murder. My mom died a year later."

Petchard's eyebrows shot up. "I heard about your brother not long after I joined the force, but I didn't know Hoffner arrested him."

"He did."

"And he hired you anyway?"

"I didn't rape or murder anybody." She looked again at the headstone. "I'm not sure Jack did, either."

Petchard drew a sharp breath. "You think Hoffner arrested the wrong man?"

"I know that Jack's arrest made his career." She shrugged. "But every family probably thinks their loved one didn't do the crime. And we'll never know. The case file is gone. The old forensics guy, Hank Comfry, lost it somewhere along the way." She bent to gather more cans. "Where's your girlfriend?"

"We went to the viewing in separate cars. She had stuff to do tonight."

"Well, thanks for calling me instead of a squad car."

"No problem. Just remember, you owe me." He smirked as he pivoted to strut away. "And I'll collect, Elliot. I'll definitely collect."

CHAPTER 95

JOSEPH FRANKLIN STEPPED FROM his brother's car and took in the parking lot. Emmet Hedder had picked a seedy motel near downtown Arcadia where rooms were available by the hour. When Joseph had challenged his reasoning for sticking himself right in the middle of things, Emmet said that the shooter would expect him to run farther away, not closer. He chose to hide in plain sight.

Satisfied that he was alone, Joseph took the bags from the trunk and trotted around the pink motel. Emmet's instructions had been explicit: park at the southern end of the building with the car facing the road. He was adamant, but refused to explain.

Light trickled around the threadbare curtains as Joseph tapped on the door. He heard a bolt slide back and slipped inside when the door opened. Emmet closed it behind them, throwing the bolt and sliding a chain into place.

"Kind of wimpy, isn't it?" Joseph asked, nodding at the slim protective measures.

"Wait until you see the window latches," Emmet said. He motioned for the medical kit and pulled his t-shirt off.

Joseph helped Emmet place a new pad of gauze over the injury. The skin was cool to the touch and its color normal. "I did a pretty good job with those stitches, if I do say so myself."

Emmet chuckled. "Thank you, Dr. Frankenstein. But at least it's healing."

Joseph dug through the sacks he'd left on the table near the door. "I have a ton of food from the visitation."

Emmet took a sandwich and ate a huge bite. "Thanks."

Joseph pulled a beer from another bag and waggled it at Emmet.

"No thanks," he said. "You shouldn't either. Got a soda?"

"Yeah. Dr. Pepper?"

Emmet nodded.

"Why no beer?" Joseph asked.

"You've got a freak hunting you, man. A dude who wants you so dead he's willing to shoot people before making sure they're his target. You need your wits about you. Every one of them."

"Good point."

Emmet ate another bite of sandwich and chased it with the Dr. Pepper. "How did the viewing go?"

Joseph sat on a straight-backed chair and leaned against the wall. "'Bout like viewings always go. Too many tears, too much food." He popped the top on a soda.

"Funeral is tomorrow morning?"

"At ten."

"Wish I could be there. Did anybody come in from Alabama?"

"A bunch of people I don't really know."

"Who called them?"

"Momma's preacher, I think." Joseph chugged his Dr. Pepper and burped. "Tell me who this guy is and why he's trying to kill you."

Emmet scooted up on the bed, propping himself on two wafer-thin pillows. "There's a chance, maybe one percent, that these shootings aren't related to what I'm going tell you. But I can't think of any other reason why someone would come gunning for the three of us." He tilted his head against the headboard. "All I can figure is that we got caught."

"Caught doing what?"

Emmet closed his eyes. "Seeking vengeance, man."

"Vengeance for what? From who?"

"From the men who murdered our fathers, Joseph. That's who."

CHAPTER 96

CASS STEPPED INSIDE AND prepared for battle with her father, then stopped short. The kitchen was quiet and nearly devoid of motion. All the cabinets were gone and only jagged bits of sheetrock clung to the wall's ribcage of studs. To her amazement, Abe Elliot sat perfectly still at the scuffed table, a look of repentance on his face. His white hair was dripping and he wore only a t-shirt and a pair of worn cut-offs. A tattered slipper graced one foot. Goober sat next to him, spooning something into Abe's mouth. Harry and Bruce stood uneasily in one corner of the demolished kitchen, their clothes damp. Cass read from their body language and the strawberry blossoming on Bruce's cheek that their father had woken from his stupor in a violent state of mind.

She sidled across the linoleum floor, grateful to see that today's construction mess was gone. Harry turned to face her, shifting a bag of frozen corn against the back of his head. "Oh no," she whispered.

"It's fine. He swung, I slipped and hit my head on refrigerator." Harry scowled at the offending appliance where it sat hiccupping near the middle of the room. A dark smear marred its avocado surface. "It's usually up against a wall."

Re-enacting a scene played too often during their childhood, she motioned to Harry to lower his head from its six feet three inches height so she could examine the split in his scalp, then turned Bruce's face to the light to see his bruise more clearly. "Harry, that cut might need stitches. Do you want to go to the emergency room?"

He touched the back of his head and examined his bloody fingers. "Bleeding's slowing down. You can put butterfly bandages on it tonight. I'll go see Dr. Rambo tomorrow if it still looks bad." He leaned into the wall. "It was good of that guy to call you. He's an officer, isn't he?"

"Yeah, Hugo Petchard. And that call wasn't a freebie. He wants something in return."

Bruce frowned. "What do you mean?"

"For most officers, something like that would be a courtesy. But Petchard thinks he kept Daddy out of trouble." At Harry's sidelong glance, she said, "And I guess he did. But he thinks he's going to use the fact that he didn't arrest Daddy to get something from me."

"What does he want?"

"Doesn't matter," Cass answered. "If I get to Sheriff Hoffner before he does, I'll shut him down." She leaned forward to listen to Goober's soft words, then pulled back. "Where did he come from?"

"Goober was mucking out the kitchen when we got home," Bruce said, stretching his jaw. "We tore out of here so fast after we got your call, we must've left the house unlocked. Harry put Phoebe to bed and then helped me get Daddy into the shower and cleaned up. We brought him down to start forcing water and coffee into him, and Goober was cooking. I think there must be some Elliot in his family tree."

"Why?"

"We eat when times are bad, so we must think that food helps. Goober seems to have the same attitude. Those are scrambled eggs."

"Really?" Cass asked. "Daddy hates eggs."

"Goober said it's something he learned from the old lady who adopted him. Apparently she liked a little tipple now and then, and he used eggs, toast, and Sprite to settle her stomach and sober her up."

Cass watched them, her heart breaking a little more for the life Goober had led. "Why is Daddy so still?"

Harry shrugged. "He's never hit you before, and apparently he doesn't hit non-family members."

She leaned forward again to listen to Goober. His voice was still soft, but the words he spoke were brutal. "Goober is... well, he's fussing at Daddy for getting drunk. He wouldn't stand for that from one of us."

"It's either because this is the first time he's been drunk in front of Goober," Harry said, lowering his voice to a whisper, "or because he knows Goober's retarded. It's got to be embarrassing to be scolded by somebody with Goober's IQ."

The squeal of tires broke the quiet and Harry grimaced. A car door slammed and a pale flash streaked past the kitchen window. The door opened with a bang and Hurricane Carly blew in, her eyes wild and her bleached hair disheveled. At the sight of Abe and Goober, a snarl escaped her and Bruce stepped aside as she stalked toward Harry. "Where is she?" she growled. "Where is my baby?"

"Phoebe's upstairs asleep, Carly. Leave her be." Harry moved the frozen corn from the back of his head and her jaw dropped at the sight of blood.

"I can't believe you'd want our child exposed to this –," she glanced around the bare kitchen and when her gaze landed on Goober and Abe, she sneered, "– this filth."

Harry rocked as if punched and Cass stepped between them, facing Carly. "Get out," she ordered in a low voice. "Phoebe is sound asleep. She's in no danger here. Harry will take her to school in the morning and the two of you can negotiate who will pick her up. You're not waking that child to prove a point."

Carly's chin flew up and she jabbed a finger at Harry. "Mother told me you Elliots were white trash. I was too stupid to see it. But mark my words, Harry, no judge will give you even partial custody while you're living with a drunk, a retard, a woman who shoots her fellow officers, and," she looked Bruce up and down, "the county queer. I'll make sure of it."

Tears sprang to Bruce's eyes and he covered his mouth with his fist, smothering a laugh.

She spun and stormed across the kitchen, slamming the door so hard it shook in its frame. Cass eyed Harry. "I hope the crown was worth it."

"Except for my daughters, I'm not sure it was. Guess I'd better get serious about divorce proceedings. I'm sorry about that."

Bruce held up his mobile phone. "Carly's always been a drama queen. And now we've got it on video."

Goober had turned when Carly entered the kitchen and watched with fascination as the quiet scene unfolded. Now, he scraped the last of the eggs from the plate and told Abe to open up. He did. Goober slid the food into his mouth and waited until Abe's lips closed, then pulled the spoon out. Abe chewed and swallowed, and Goober held up a pink sippy cup shaped like a ballerina and tapped Abe's lips with the straw. Her father sipped and swallowed. Next, Goober slathered butter on a piece of toast, cut it into small bites, and fed them to Abe. When all the food was gone, Goober patted Abe's arm and turned to the entranced group.

"He can go to bed now," Goober said.

"Thanks, Goob," Bruce said, approaching Abe with a degree of caution.

"It's okay," Goober said. "He won't hit you."

"You sure?" Harry asked.

"Yes. Leave a bottle of water next to the bed."

He picked up the dishes after Harry and Bruce had maneuvered Abe through the kitchen door. Cass intercepted him on his way to the make-shift sink. "How did you do that, Goober?"

He shrugged and rubbed his hands on his overalls. "I told him how mean it was to put his kids through something like this. That he ought to be more respectful to y'all."

"Well, it seemed to work," Cass said, washing the dishes. "It sure would be nice if he stayed off the bottle for good this time."

"There's too much sadness for him to bear. That's all it is. Otherwise, your dad is pretty nice."

She tilted her head and regarded the man so many people discounted. "That's about the smartest thing anybody's ever said about my dad's situation, Goober. How did you figure that out?"

He picked up a dish cloth. "Mrs. Keller told me. She had a lot of sadness, too."

"You've had a fair amount, Goober," Cass said softly. "So have I. But we don't drink."

"We're different, Cass. You and me, we're made different from other people."

She thought about that. "I guess you're right, Goober." Cass locked the kitchen door and flipped off the overhead light. "I'd better go take care of Harry's cut and get to bed. You should, too. We've had enough drama for one night."

CHAPTER 97

THE AIR IN THE motel room had grown warm and Joseph turned on the air conditioner beneath the window. The unit groaned to life and the curtains undulated to the musty stream of air. "What are you talking about?" Joseph asked.

Emmet sighed. "What do you know about how your dad died?"

"A brain aneurysm."

"Not Homer Radcliffe. Your *dad*. Charles Franklin."

"He died when we were about three." Joseph shrugged. "A heart attack, maybe? Momma never talked about it."

"You were barely two years old, Joseph, and he was lynched by five white men. They strung our daddies up and roasted them. They shot Donna's daddy in the leg first, because he kept trying to get away. But he got cooked, too."

Joseph's smile was small. One of Emmet's gifts was his ability to weave stories that could either entrance or horrify. Sometimes both. Joseph and Moses had encouraged him to take up writing when they were younger, but Emmet was a pragmatist. He pursued a nursing degree after leaving the military, stating that personally, he liked to eat and he'd never met a fat writer. "Come on, man. If my real daddy was lynched, don't you think Momma would have told us at some point? How do you keep that a secret?"

"People react differently to something as horrific as murder. One thing I know about your momma, Joseph, is that she loved peace above all else. The woman couldn't even kill a spider. If one got in the house, she'd scoop it onto a piece of paper and dance and squeal until she tossed it out the door."

"She could flatten a cockroach."

"Too true. But her heart was gentle. Maybe because of the way your daddy died, or maybe that was just her nature. She wanted nothing more than for you and Moses to have peaceful, productive lives. It's very easy to see why she wouldn't have told you what happened to your daddy."

Joseph's bottom lip poked out. "If Moses knew, he would've told me."

"He couldn't tell you."

"Why not?"

"You two grew apart when you were up North. He didn't know how you'd take it. We did tons of research to find these men, and it took a long time to finally act on the decision to kill them. We didn't murder the first man until after you were arrested."

"Me and Moses didn't grow that far apart. If he found out something like this, Moses would've told me, New York or not, and regardless of whether I was in prison."

Emmet sighed. "How would he do that? He couldn't write it in a letter. Or call you. Moses thought it would be cruel to drop something like that in your lap."

"I've been home for weeks. He hasn't said a word."

"By the time you got out, it was too late."

Joseph leaned forward, his face fierce. "Too late to tell me how our father died? Why?"

"You're on parole, man. It was too risky for you to be involved."

"There is no way Moses would kill a man. Unless he had to for his job. And what does any of this have to do with Donna Moore? She's white."

"Her real daddy's name was Silverman. He was a Jew."

The tone in Emmet's voice told Joseph that he was deadly serious. Joseph dropped his head into his hands and looked down at the floor, rubbing the toe of his shoe on a bare spot in the carpet. "Who told you?"

"Granny. Y'all never went back to Alabama, did you?"

"No. I don't even remember Alabama."

"All three families left not long after the lynching. We went back almost every year. But I didn't know until 2006. Granny told me before she died." His face wrinkled in thought. "Are you carrying Moses' wallet?"

Joseph nodded.

"Take it out."

Joseph pulled it from his hip pocket.

"There's a little zipper, inside where the cash goes."

Joseph found the zipper and pulled it open. A piece of paper was inside. Joseph extracted and unfolded it, eyes widening as he read.

"Believe me now?" Emmet asked.

"Where did he get this?"

"I got a copy from the newspaper in Thayerville after Granny told me what happened."

"You didn't believe her?"

Emmet lifted the gauze bandage and ran his fingers lightly along the stitches in his upper arm. "I wanted to know what the public record said."

"This is all?" Joseph asked, holding up the paper. "This is the only article they printed about a lynching of three men?"

"There were a few more. All bullshit. The last article said that they were out of clues and the case would remain open until they had new evidence."

"Which never came."

"Which never came," Emmet agreed.

"Strange fruit," Joseph whispered, running a finger over the image of their fathers' charred bodies dangling from branches. "Like Billie Holiday sang."

"What?"

"Never mind." Joseph thought for a moment. "Donna didn't have a problem with roasting these men alive?"

Emmet snorted. "She was the one who wanted to torture them before they died."

"I guess I can understand wanting that kind of vengeance. At a distance. But this was face to face. Why was she so brutal?"

"Maybe it's an Old Testament thing. Donna called us avengers of blood. Said we deserved a life for a life." Emmet tilted his head to one side. "Donna was a few years older than us. So she remembered her daddy better than we remember ours. She had actual memories of him. I think my memories of my father come from photographs." He shrugged. "Maybe she had even more to be mad about, because Moore diddled her."

"He what?"

"Messed with her. Abused her."

"Her stepfather?"

"Yeah. She was pretty screwed up when you look at everything. I mean, she was smart and very good with money. But once we told her what happened to our daddies, she was the one who wanted to go after the men."

It was Joseph's turn to snort. "Come on, Emmet. It's easy to say that now that she's dead."

"I'm serious. Once we told her what had happened, all these memories came back to her. Somehow, she watched what happened."

"She was there?"

Emmet nodded. "And saw it all."

"Did they know she was there?"

"It's possible. She must've been about five years old. Granny said everybody knew Donna because she would slip out of the house and go looking for her daddy."

"By herself?"

"Thayerville was a small town. Granny said kids ran around all the time, so nobody thought anything about a little girl that they recognized wandering around, if they even bothered to notice."

"And she found her daddy at a lynching," Joseph whispered.

"She suppressed the memories. That happens sometimes with severe trauma. Once we told her, she tried working her memories out through art, by painting pictures and drawing sketches of what she saw. They're hanging in her office and her house."

"Didn't that scare the customers off? Paintings of a lynching?"

Emmet smiled. "They're kind of abstract. Donna was a good artist. She painted the actual burning in bright colors. Then sketched the aftermath in charcoal."

"But that wasn't enough for her?"

"Donna blamed them for what happened to her. She said that if her daddy had still been alive, her mother never would have left Thayerville and married the first man she came across, and Donna wouldn't have been abused."

Joseph pondered this. "I guess there's some logic in that."

"There's a hell of a lot of logic in it."

"Why did you go along with her?"

Emmet looked down at his hands, motionless in his lap. "I did it for my momma. She never stopped grieving for our daddy."

"And Moses? Why did he do it?"

"At first, Moses wanted to track them down and let the law handle it. But the more we talked, the more we realized that if justice hadn't happened in over forty years, it wasn't gonna happen."

Joseph stood and paced the small room. "I can't see Moses as a killer."

"In fairness, Joseph, Moses changed a lot after we found this out. And that's one of the reasons his wife left him." He looked down at his hands. "That's why Celia's gone. I've changed and can't go back to who I was."

"Changed how?"

"We were both more cynical. Moses was always kind of upbeat and happy-go-lucky, you know? Like whatever was wrong with the world would get sorted out eventually." When Joseph nodded, Emmet continued. "He lost that when he found out how his daddy died. Not entirely, but his view of things changed."

"Changed enough that he was willing to kill these men?"

"Not only kill them, but find them and plot their deaths. Planning and executing a murder is not something you can share with your spouse. The secrets eat at you. They get bigger and a wall grows up between you."

Joseph digested this. "Why did everyone leave Thayerville? Back in the day?"

"Granny said Mrs. Silverman was stirring up trouble. She hated that woman. Granny always believed she lost her family because Mrs. Silverman couldn't keep her mouth shut," Emmet said. "I guess she thought that being white entitled her to some sort of justice for her husband."

"What do you mean?"

"She wouldn't let it lie. She kept calling the sheriff, wanting to know how the investigation was going, and then contacting the press when the police stonewalled her."

"But why did they leave?"

"In the end, the families didn't have a choice. They burned the Silvermans out."

"What?"

"They set the house on fire with Mrs. Silverman and the children in it."

Joseph gaped. "Children?"

"There was a boy. Older than Donna. She was sleeping with her momma that night and they both got out. He died in the fire."

"Dear God."

"After that, all three families packed up and moved."

"Who set the fire?"

"Probably the same people who did the lynching."

Joseph sat and ran both hands over his slick, bald head. "How many have you killed?"

"All of them. All five." He seemed to reconsider. "Well, one was dead before we got to him. His trailer house burned to the ground. We killed the last one this week. He was living right here in Arcadia, big as life. Can you believe it?"

Horror filled Joseph's face. "Calvin Whitehead? I saw those pictures. You hung him and burned him to death?"

"Damn straight we did. He was Klan. All of them were. They were evil, Joseph. These weren't the first men they lynched. Or the last."

Joseph swallowed. "The swastika? Who did that?"

"Me."

"He was shot through the leg. Was that Donna?"

Emmet nodded.

"If those men are all dead, then who killed Momma, Donna, and Moses? Who's trying to kill you?"

Emmet flashed a weary smile. "That's the question, isn't it?"

"You mean all this vigilante shit is what got Momma killed? The man who killed my mother was avenging the death of somebody that he loved?"

"That's the only scenario that makes sense."

Joseph shook his head. "This has to stop, Emmet. Enough people have died. You almost died. We need to take this to the police."

"Don't be stupid, Joseph."

"Seriously. You need protection. Maybe I do, too."

"What do we tell them?" Emmet asked, grimacing as he pushed himself higher against the headboard. "That me, Donna, and you – 'cause you're Moses now – have been plugging white men all over the South for the last three years? And that somebody figured out who was doing the killing, and has come to kill us?"

Joseph stared at him.

"See what I'm getting at? Maybe they'll find this guy and put him in jail for killing your mom, Moses, and Donna. But they're gonna put *us* in jail for killing those white men."

"What do we do?" Joseph whispered.

"We turn the tables. We find him, and we kill him."

"How?"

"You have to keep track of what they know. When they get close to the shooter and figure out who he is, we take him."

Joseph dropped his head into his hands again and rubbed his temples. "Good Lord. Where does it end?"

Emmet touched his wounded arm. "This is serious, man. It doesn't get more illegal than this. I don't know what will come afterward, but I intend to be the last man standing. Are you gonna stand with me?"

Joseph opened his mouth to answer as a bullet smashed through the window and thunked into the wall over the headboard. Emmet slid off the bed and yanked the lamp's cord from the wall. Joseph sat frozen in his chair until Emmet kicked him.

"Give me your gun," Emmet yelled as the window crashed open and a rock bounced off the bed.

Joseph struggled to pull the gun from its holster and Emmet snatched it from him. He fired three times at the window and the men heard a high pitched yip and the sound of scraping across gravel, and then running.

Emmet lowered the weapon, plucked the brass casings from the carpet, and then motioned Joseph to his feet and held out a hand for help up. He lifted the curtain and peeked out. "Get everything in the bags. Everything. We gotta get out of here. Now."

Joseph shoved medical supplies into the kit and food wrappers and cans into the plastic bags. Emmet grabbed his duffel bag and disappeared into the bathroom. Joseph heard the squeal of hinges and saw Emmet dropping the bags through a window. Joseph realized that a small alley ran between the two motel buildings. Emmet wanted Joseph to park on the building's south side to provide an escape route.

"Come on," Emmet said. "I think he's gone, but we'll go around the back way to check. Once we're clear, get out of here as fast as you can and meet me at that strip center on the Loop. Park near the trees."

Joseph scrambled through the window behind Emmet. "That's too public, somebody'll see you."

"We'll just look like two black men with car trouble."

"What do you mean?"

"I should've known after he found me last night," Emmet answered. "That's devious. He put some sort of tracking device on my truck, and maybe your car. We've got to find them and get them off."

CHAPTER 98

KADO LET THE MEMORY of Cass's upturned face fill his mind for a moment and reveled in the sound of her voice speaking the word 'handsome'. Then he opened his weary eyes and surveyed the nasty motel room. Martinez stepped out of the bathroom and shook his head. "Everything's gone. All the linens. Even the liner from the trash can."

Kado studied the bullet hole in the wall. "You know who was in this room, right?"

"That's a .308 slug?"

"I'd bet breakfast from The Golden Gate that it is."

"Emmet Hedder was here? Why here?"

"And how did the shooter find him?"

"One thing at a time," Martinez said. "Get that piece of lead out of the wall and see if it matches the others."

Kado lifted an eyebrow. "What? Don't go with my gut? Use science to confirm my hunch?"

Martinez widened his stance.

"I'm not complaining," Kado said. "You and I might find common ground after all."

An Asian man and a slip of a girl struggled to lift a piece of plywood into place over the empty window frame. Kado motioned to Martinez and the two took over, securing the board with a hammer and nails.

"Sir," Martinez said. "Is this your motel?"

The Asian man shook his head, his stringy hair flying. "My parents own the place. I'm Sam. I cover the night shift."

"Who's registered in this room?"

"Eddie Vedder."

Martinez began jotting a note and Kado stopped him. "As in the Eddie Vedder from Pearl Jam?"

Sam nodded. "We get a lot of that. Not Vedders in particular, but false names."

"You don't check ID?" Martinez asked.

"Not if they're paying cash."

"Can you describe him?"

"Light colored black man. Shaved head. In his thirties, maybe forties." Sam shrugged. "It's hard to tell with black people."

"Anyone with him?"

"Not that I saw."

"Do you remember his eye color or any unusual characteristics? Scars? Tattoos?"

Sam pursed his lips. "His eyes were kind of funny, a light brown with yellow specks in them. And he had freckles. That should help. You don't find many black men with freckles."

"Anything else?"

"He seemed to favor his right arm."

"How so?"

"It moved slow when he lifted it to sign the register."

"Thank you," Martinez said, flipping his notebook closed. "We'll be in the room for a while, dusting for prints."

"Whoa," Kado said. "Let's try something else first." He jogged from the room and came back a moment later with a photograph. "Is this Eddie Vedder?"

Sam nodded. "Yeah. You know who he is?"

"We do now."

"So we can clean the room?" Sam asked.

"Not quite. I have to get that slug out of the wall."

"What does that mean?"

"I'll have to cut away the sheetrock and dig it out."

"Great," Sam sighed. "Eddie Vedder stays at our motel and I'm filing on insurance for damages. That's so rock 'n' roll."

CHAPTER 99

THE SHOOTER LEANED CLOSER to the mirror and bit back a whimper as he wrapped the small round bandage over his ear. He'd heard that there were few nerve endings in cartilage. Given the pain that was radiating through his neck and scalp, he could firmly denounce that notion. One more scrub with a damp paper towel to remove the last of the blood and he stood back and adjusted his hair. Instead of pushing it back, he ruffled it and let it fall over his ears and forehead. The bandage disappeared. His fingers still trembled from the adrenaline rush. That shot was too close. Millimeters to the right, and it would've been his brain. Hedder or Franklin. It didn't matter who had pulled the trigger. The time for playing was over. Both would suffer when he caught up with them. And he would catch up. Sooner rather than later.

Someone banged on the bathroom door and he opened it, shouldering his way through the crowded Dairy Queen to pick up his order of fries and a strawberry shake. He took a seat near the window and powered up his laptop. Thanks to the fast food restaurants, free internet access abounded nowadays, even in a place as backward as Arcadia.

"Hey, darling. I thought you hung out at The Golden Gate."

He looked up to see one of the staff hovering next to his table, a red tray piled high with discarded food wrappers and plastic baskets balanced on one hand. She was a curvy brunette and in a different lifetime, he would have enjoyed getting to know her better.

"Had to have a fix tonight. Stan and Sally don't do milkshakes."

With her free hand, she reached out and touched his bangs where they tumbled across his forehead. "Love the new look. It's kind of scruffy. But it works on you." She checked her watch. "Three more hours. Then it's home to wash the grease out of my hair, soak these feet, and sleep for ten hours."

"I hear you," he answered with a grin.

"Let me know if you want a refill on that shake. It's on me." She winked and sauntered away.

The shooter tilted the laptop's screen inward and fired up the GPS tracking program. Comparing it to his cell phone, he stifled a chuckle. The tracking devices on Hedder's and Franklin's vehicles were motionless near a shopping center on the Loop. He wondered if he'd caught one of them with the single shot from his rifle. No matter. The batteries on the devices were almost gone and he was ready to draw this little game to a close. He sucked the last of the milkshake down and ate the remaining fries, ready to go home and crash. His plans for the weekend were picking up speed.

CHAPTER 100

Saturday

DARLA STONE WATCHED HER husband flail beneath the sheets. She leaned over to check the clock on the nightstand: three fifty-five, right on time. Mitch's nightmares were much more physical since the accident, and she supposed he was reliving his frustration at abandoning Cass in a dangerous situation. Their bond was strong, Darla knew, not from any physical attraction, but from the years that Mitch spent as a virtual member of the Elliot household as Jack Elliot's childhood friend. She waited, letting the dream play out, recognizing that he wasn't far from waking himself up.

He sat bolt upright and clawed at his immobilized leg. Mitch's eyes were wild and a muted scream struggled to escape his throat. Darla touched his shoulder. His gaze flew to hers and he crumpled then, slumping toward her. She stroked the blond hair from his sweaty forehead. "Same dream?"

He nodded against her breasts and stomach.

"I only ask because it could've been a dog dream. You looked like you were chasing a car. Or maybe a postal employee on a bike."

She felt a slow grin move across his face. "Sorry I woke you."

"Not just me. You better apologize to the boy over there."

As if on cue, a lanky greyhound jumped onto the bed, his hind legs scrambling for purchase against the comforter. He laid his bony head on Mitch's thigh and his delicate brows twitched over soulful gray eyes. Mitch rubbed the dog's silky ears. "Hey, Zeus. You'll have to teach me how to catch that guy on the bike. It's hard work."

Zeus rolled over, presenting his skinny belly. Mitch scratched. "It was the same dream, but different this time," he said, looking over at his wife.

She switched on the lamp. "How?"

"I see the flickering light from the campfire and I have to get to that clearing. Like always, my leg won't move and it drives me crazy. This time, I can hear a phone vibrating. I look down, and there it is in my hand, but I can't get the damn thing open. It just keeps buzzing and buzzing."

"Why are you dreaming about a buzzing phone? Yours rings, doesn't it?"

He nodded. "I don't know. Maybe I –"

Mitch stopped, his mouth hanging open, and Darla nudged him. "Maybe you what?"

"Oh, God." He yanked on the sheets, trying to untangle himself. "I was tired, I didn't make the connection. I need to get to the courthouse, Darla."

"Mitch! It's four o'clock Saturday morning. It can wait. It probably should wait until Monday."

"No, no, this really can't wait." He swung his good leg off the bed and then struggled upright.

"Are you nuts?" she asked, sliding out of bed and watching him limp to the bathroom. He stopped and turned, his eyes desperate. She shivered. He'd worn the same look when he woke in the hospital that horrifying night, terrified that something bad had happened to Cass. When he spoke, his voice was dead serious.

"Darla, I hope I'm wrong, but if I'm not, things are about to get very nasty for a fellow officer."

Chapter 101

ACROSS THE COUNTY, JOSEPH opened his eyes and stared at the ceiling of Moses' room, letting his brain work through whatever problem had woken him. He'd developed the ability to emerge from sleep fully alert while in prison. It was a useful skill because it allowed him to retain the remnants of his dreams. Tonight, they revolved around the woman from The Golden Gate Café.

Whoever cleaned and repaired your kitchen did a wonderful job. And fast, too. The backsplash behind the stove is perfect. They even found a new head for the rooster.

Those words had bothered him when she spoke them, but he still didn't know why. He got out of bed and padded down the hall to the kitchen, switching on the soft lighting beneath the cabinets to avoid waking the relatives sleeping on the sofa and living and dining room floors. He filled the carafe and spooned grounds into the filter, then waited as the coffee brewed, studying the backsplash. The woman, Junie, was right. The work was very good, and completed quickly. He leaned closer to the stove. The damage to the tile was completely gone, vanished. Repaired so perfectly that, with the exception of the two bodies at the funeral home, the shooting might not have happened. The whole the kitchen sparkled.

What was it that bothered him about what Junie had said?

Joseph walked slowly around the compact area, trying to see it through her eyes. Last night, she probably came in through the hall door, picked up food, then left through the door that led to the combination dining and living room. She had a chance to see every aspect of the kitchen. As had everyone else who visited yesterday.

What was wrong with what Junie said?

The coffee pot spat a final few drops into the carafe. Joseph poured a mug and started at the sound of slippered feet on the linoleum. Turning, he spotted a tiny body in footed pajamas dragging a teddy bear across the kitchen. The little girl stopped and craned her neck to look up at him, breaking into a sleepy grin. "Coffee-milk?" she asked, and Joseph smiled back.

"I can't remember your name," he whispered, picking her up and sitting her on the counter.

"I'm Amelia. This is Froggy," she whispered back, hoisting the bear for him to see. "And you're Cousin Moses."

"I am. Why do you call your teddy bear Froggy?"

"Because I like frogs the best. So far. But I like that chicken, too." She pointed to the tile rooster. "She has a pretty face. I might change Froggy's name to Birdie."

"I see," Joseph answered, her answer tugging at him. He filled a mug half full with coffee, topped it off with milk, and stirred in sugar. She sipped from the spoon he held to her lips and nodded approval.

Joseph shifted Amelia from the counter to a chair at the kitchen table and spilled a little coffee-milk in her saucer, then watched as she puffed her cheeks out and blew. She gave Froggy a chance to blow, then lifted the saucer and sipped. A ripple of sound came from her chair and she looked over her shoulder at her bottom, then frowned down at Froggy.

"What was that?" Joseph whispered.

Amelia giggled. "Froggy farted."

Joseph stifled a laugh. He poured a second mug and sat next to the child, looking at his reflection in the repaired kitchen window. He stared through the ghost of himself and tried to bore through the woods to the tree in Deadwood Hollow. To the bough that had supported the man who destroyed his family.

And then he knew.

Joseph watched as Amelia finished the last of her coffee-milk and held her mug out for more.

"Go back to bed, baby. It's too early for Froggy to be up. And Cousin Moses has business to tend to."

Amelia placed the mug in its saucer, presented her cheek for a kiss, and shuffled into the living room dragging Froggy the bear behind her. Joseph stared out the window again, excitement sparking through his synapses.

He was certain the papers hadn't printed details about where in their home the Franklins had died. And while Officer Hugo Petchard would have access to the case files, Joseph hadn't seen his initials on any of the entries related to the murders. Petchard had barely come inside the house; the man couldn't stand the smell. He had no knowledge of the details of the crime. There was no way Junie could know that the backsplash had been damaged by a bullet, that the tile bearing the rooster's head was shattered.

Unless she had seen it through the scope of the rifle that killed his mother and brother.

CHAPTER 102

THE HAPPY SOUNDS OF Sister Sledge's "We Are Family" poured through door and Cass gave a startled laugh at the sight of Junie dancing across the empty café. She plucked a coffee pot and mug from the counter and met Cass at her regular table, her grin wide.

Cass smiled in return. "You're full of energy this morning."

"Glad to be alive. Some days are like that," Junie replied as she poured. She took in Cass's black suit and maroon blouse. "I wouldn't have thought dark red would work with your hair, but it does. You should wear it down more. It looks good loose."

"Yours, too," Cass said. "I like it brushed forward."

Junie fingered the dark mass. "I thought I'd try something new. Are you going to the funeral today?"

Cass nodded.

"Me, too. Moses is such a nice man. This must be terrible for him." Junie put the coffee pot on a nearby table and pulled an order pad from her black jeans. Her make-up was meticulous and she wore another mock turtle neck, this one a chocolate brown that brought out her dark eyes. "Do you want your order to go? Like that forensics guy?"

"Kado's already been in?"

"He said that he and some other detective came to the courthouse really early. Kado? That's his name?"

"Tom Kado," Cass confirmed.

"Ordered six sausage biscuits and four coffees to go. What can I get for you?"

If he's buying that much food, Mitch must be in, Cass thought. She shook her hands, limbering her wrists to tote the coffee carriers to the courthouse. "Give me ten coffees and ten breakfast burritos."

Junie lifted an eyebrow as she wrote.

"I know," Cass said, "but it sounds like it's going to be a long day for a lot of us."

———

CASS DID A DOUBLE take as she walked past Sheriff Hoffner's office and spotted a slab of light falling beneath the door. A thought slipped into her brain. *Let's see what happens when I take Hugo Petchard's advantage away.*

She passed the forensic room, noticing light and movement behind the door's frosted window, and carried on to the empty squad room. She'd slept surprisingly well last night. Once Harry and Bruce got their father up the stairs to his bedroom, everything had been peaceful. Instead of spending the evening cleaning up the ramshackle mess Abe usually left after a binge, they'd gone quietly to bed. All thanks to Goober.

Sliding the coffee carriers and bag onto the counter, she shook her hands to restore circulation, lifted a coffee cup from the container and added cream and sugar. Hesitating, she snagged another coffee cup and headed back down the hall.

At her knock, Hoffner barked, "Who is it?"

She opened the door a crack. "Cass, sir. May I come in?"

"Why are you here so early, Elliot?"

Hoffner wore a crisp white shirt, open at the neck, a tuft of snowy hair peeking through. A black suit jacket hung from the coat tree in the corner, and Cass caught sight of a dark blue tie folded on his credenza. "I thought I'd better come in and get started before the funerals." She held out a cup of coffee.

Hoffner's nostrils flared as he took in her thick, dark red hair, hanging loose around her shoulders, then he nodded.

"It's black, sir. I wasn't sure what you put in it."

"Thank you, Elliot. Is that all?"

"I wanted to tell you what Officer Petchard did last night."

His eyes hardened beneath his hoary brows. "Go on."

"Officer Petchard called me when he was on his way home from Mojo's house. He'd spotted my dad in Shady Grove Cemetery." Cass cleared her throat. "My dad was drunk, and ended up passing out on my mom's grave. Instead of arresting him for public intoxication, Officer Petchard gave me and my brothers the opportunity to deal with my father privately. That was a kind thing to do, and I thought you should know."

Hoffner removed the lid and wiped the coffee cup's rim with a napkin. "Was Abe driving?"

"From the look of things, he didn't start drinking until he got to my mom's grave. Bruce and Harry took him home, and I cleaned up the mess in the cemetery." She waited patiently while he studied her, wondering if Hoffner would remember how meaningful the month of May was to her family.

Finally, he nodded. "That was kind of him. I'm glad you and Officer Petchard are finding common ground. He's got potential, Elliot. And connections. You could do worse than to have him as an ally."

Not in his fondest dreams, Cass thought, but she managed to keep a straight face. "Yes, sir."

"Is there anything else?"

"No, sir."

At his curt nod, she left and pulled the door closed behind her, wondering how two people could have such different views of the world and the people in it.

CHAPTER 103

THE GOLDEN GATE CAFÉ smelled of Costa Rican coffee, and Joseph gratefully accepted a mug from Stan as he switched on Moses' laptop.

"How are you holding up?" Stan asked.

"I'm all right. Thanks for coming to the house last night. And for bringing sandwiches."

"We were glad to do it. Sally wants us to close and come to the funeral, and I think we will."

"I'd appreciate having you there."

"Good," Stan said, pulling an order pad from his pocket. "Breakfast?"

"Please. But not too much food."

"Half a ham and cheese omelet with whole grain toast?"

"And some hash browns."

"Good choice. I'll get it started."

"Stan," Joseph said as the older man started to turn away. "What is Junie's last name?"

"Archer. Why?"

"I just wondered. She's been very nice about my mom and brother. Where's she from?"

Stan leaned in and spoke softly. "Her license says Tennessee. She's been kind of quiet about her life. Makes me think she's been through some hard times, you know?"

"Yeah. Has she been with you long?"

"Six weeks. Maybe a little longer. I'll get your order in."

Joseph pulled the laptop toward him and prepared to complete several searches. Last night, Emmet had told him that Donna Moore called the little killing trio 'avengers of blood'. When Joseph returned home after seeing Emmet, he found his mother's worn Bible. He licked a finger and gingerly turned the onionskin pages, scanning for references to avengers of blood. He used the concordance to locate references in Numbers and Deuteronomy, but got lost in the spidery notes crawling in the margins of almost every page. Time slipped by as he squinted to read his mother's handwriting. Finally, the tiny print was too much for his tired eyes and he gave up, deciding to use a more modern means of understanding the phrase. Now, he sipped Stan's coffee and decided to try the most direct route. He typed in 'avengers of blood'.

The seat's vinyl protested with a squeal as someone slid into the booth. His new companion was tapping a coffee cup in a meaningless rhythm. Joseph slowly lifted his gaze from the computer screen and the tapping stopped. A skinny white man with a jailhouse complexion sat across from him. The rank odor of an unwashed body wafted across the table. Joseph squinted. The man looked vaguely familiar. *Moses*, he thought. *I am Moses.* "Can I help you?"

The man's tongue darted lizard-like from between his lips. "You don't remember me? Grief does strange things to people, but I've never heard of it causing amnesia." He took a sip of coffee. "Sure was sorry to hear about your momma and brother. Me? I just knew it was you who got killed. Wouldn't be surprising that someone comes after a cop, would it?"

Joseph stayed silent, scrolling through the vast database in his head, trying to match the man's voice and face to someone he'd known before.

"Your brother, Joseph. He was a hacker, wasn't he? A good one, from what I've heard. But in all my time in the can, I never heard of anybody doing violence to a computer criminal. I wonder why somebody would start with your brother?" The tapping began again.

An image from a booking photograph snapped into Joseph's mind: sunken cheeks, sallow complexion, scabby skin, scraggly hair, wild eyes. "What do you want, Conroy?"

A reptilian smile crept across the other man's face and he swiped at his nose. "That veil of grief is lifting, is it? Good." He leaned forward. "I don't know who took those shots at your house, but I do believe that you were the target. I'm not saying that you should have died instead of Joseph. That would be illegal, wouldn't it? Wishing a Do Right Boy dead? But as a reformed citizen of Forney County, it's my duty to recommend that you watch your back. And pass that message along to Detective Stone and ol' Hoff, would you? Gotta take care of those who serve and protect, don't we?"

Joseph's eyes flattened. "That's mighty kind of you, Conroy. I'll make sure we keep an eye on you, too. Wouldn't want an ex-convict being targeted by an angry public, would we?"

Conroy slipped from the booth. "See you around, Officer Franklin."

"I expect you will."

Joseph watched as the thin man hitched his jeans up and left the café. Stan appeared with more coffee. "Who was that?"

"An ex-con named Rob Conroy."

Stan flicked his ponytail over his shoulder and stood, head cocked to one side, gaze thoughtful. "Name rings a bell. What'd he do?"

"He was a meth cooker."

"I remember. It was in the news when we moved here. He's out already?"

Joseph nodded.

"Is he causing problems?"

"I don't think so, Stan, but keep an eye out."

"I'll let you know if I hear any grumblings about him."

"Thanks, man. I appreciate it."

Stan moved to another table to take an order, leaving Joseph to his laptop. His search led him to several websites that discussed Jewish and Christian interpretations of the Bible. The phrase 'avengers of blood' translated from the Hebrew term "go'el ha'dam", which meant blood-avenger. This was the next of kin responsible for enacting the privilege of seeking revenge for a slain family member. Under the Old Testament, vengeance was only permitted in cases of premeditated killing or willful murder. In cases of accidental homicide, the killer could flee to one of six cities of refuge and live without fear of retribution until the high priest died. At that time, the killer was free to return to the land of his inheritance. However, if the killer was found outside the city of refuge before the high priest died, the avenger of blood had the right to kill him.

Joseph leaned into the booth's cushioned seat and sipped his coffee. Technically, Moore's interpretation of the Old Testament was correct and she, Moses, and Emmet were entitled to kill the men who had willfully murdered their fathers. However, modern interpretations of a 'life for a life' meant that it was the state that had an obligation to prosecute a murderer. Since the state failed to even attempt justice in the case of this lynching, Joseph understood why the unlikely trio had started out on their path of retribution. And in spite of his brother's status as an enforcer of the law, Joseph thought Moses would've been able to justify this type of killing.

The question was, could Joseph?

His mother and brother had been taken from him in a violent act. Joseph believed that the detectives were doing their best to find the killer. But Joseph had a strong hunch that he knew the killer's identity. If he could confirm that hunch, would he share the information with the police, or with Emmet? As he finished his coffee and waved to Junie for a refill, he knew he wasn't sure. Not yet.

"Hey, Moses," she said softly, watching him even as she poured. "Are you ready for today?"

"I am," he said. "And I'm also getting close to the person who killed them."

Behind perfect mascara and eyeliner, her dark eyes twinkled. "I'm not surprised. Hugo tells me how good the Forney County force is at what they do."

He leaned forward and lowered his voice. "Not the police, Junie. Me. I'm getting close."

She pulled back, her eyes more serious. "You'd take the law into your own hands?"

"Once I find the man who killed my family, yes, I will. Wouldn't you?"

Junie studied him, chewing the bright red lipstick from her lower lip and tapping a short, unpolished fingernail against the coffee pot. "No. I wouldn't kill someone because they murdered my family."

Joseph cocked his head. "You wouldn't?"

"Nope. But I would kill the people who murdered my family before I had the chance." She tapped the pot three times, and then flashed a smile. "I'll go check on your food, Moses. Be back in a tick."

CHAPTER 104

"YOU WERE RIGHT."

CASS heard Kado's voice as she opened the door and a swarm of butterflies fluttered to life in her stomach. She fought back a smile and did a double take at the straps of cash and stack of yellow-ish bricks on the evidence table. "Is that gold?"

Kado nodded, grinning. Cass caught his glance as he took in her hair, hanging loose around her shoulders. "Want to hold one?"

She slid the coffee and burritos onto the counter next to a stack of sausage biscuits, and gasped as she hefted one of the bars. "It's heavy."

"Twenty-seven and a half pounds."

"Where did all this come from?" she asked, waving her elbow at the cash and gold.

"Donna's safe deposit box."

Cass thought for a moment. "Did you test the currency for drugs?"

Kado nodded. "It's clean."

"So she wasn't laundering money."

"At least not for a drug runner."

In a quiet voice, Mitch asked, "How's Abe?"

She flushed and returned the bar to the stack. "I didn't see him this morning, but he was okay last night, considering."

"Casualties?"

"He got Bruce with a punch to the cheek, and Harry slipped and split his scalp."

Mitch winced. Kado watched the exchange with a look of curiosity.

He might as well know now, she thought. "My dad's a drunk. He's in AA, but can't seem to stay on the wagon. He's almost always violent unless he passes out before one of us finds him." She looked to Mitch. "Goober actually helped sober Daddy up."

"What was he doing at your house?"

"He's been staying with us since he found Calvin Whitehead. It freaked him out." She drew a deep breath and released a sigh that spoke volumes about her dysfunctional family. "Did you find anything else interesting in Donna's safe deposit box?"

"Before we get to that, there was a shooting at that dive of a motel near downtown," Mitch said.

"That pink stucco place?"

"Yeah. Emmet Hedder was there." Kado provided the details.

"I wonder why he won't come to us for help?"

"We think he wants to settle things himself." At Cass's raised eyebrow, Kado nodded at Mitch. "You tell her."

"Let's start with the worst of it." Mitch reached for his hanger and poked it beneath his brace. "Moses Franklin is involved in all this."

"In all what?"

"In whatever caused somebody to want to kill the Franklins, Donna, and Emmet."

Cass swiveled a chair around and sat. "What are you talking about?"

Mitch released the hanger and dug his fingers into his eye sockets. When he dropped his hands, Cass realized how exhausted he looked. She glanced at Kado and saw the same worn expression on his face. His gray eyes were bloodshot and dark stubble shadowed his jaw. Both made him even sexier.

"Do you remember," Mitch said, "when that cell phone vibrated at Mojo's house last night?"

Cass absently rubbed a finger across one of the gold bars. "Kind of. Mojo came and got it, didn't he?"

"But I answered it, and nobody was there. Nobody spoke, anyway."

"So what?"

"The number that flashed on the screen from the incoming caller? It was from the same phone that called Donna's cell. The one you found in the safe at her house."

Cass rocked back in her chair, all thoughts of romance gone. "Are you sure?"

"It gets worse." He looked at Kado and then reached for a cup of coffee. "You tell her, my head is spinning."

Kado sighed. "In the brief time that he had the phone, Mitch looked at Mojo's call history and the phone's information to try and figure out who the phone belongs to. It isn't used often. Most people make several calls each day, right?"

She nodded.

"Until recently, Mojo's phone received calls only from Donna's phone. And it received those calls sporadically."

Cass peeled the wrapper from a breakfast burrito and squeezed picante sauce over the top. "What do you mean?"

"Mitch said there was one call Wednesday afternoon from Donna's phone. She called twice the week before. Three times in April. Then nothing until a few calls in December of last year. That's all Mitch was able to see."

"And Mojo's outgoing calls?" Cass asked.

"Only to one number. The same number that called Mojo's phone when Mitch answered it last night."

"So that same number called Mojo back?"

"Right. But the incoming calls from that number didn't start until after Donna was murdered Wednesday night. And those have come from the number that called Donna's phone." Kado tapped the cell phone on the evidence table. "The *only* number that called Donna's phone."

"What are you saying? That Moses, Donna, and some unknown person had a call circle going?"

"Yes," Mitch answered.

"So Moses really did know Donna, even though he said he didn't."

Mitch nodded slowly.

"Why would he lie?" Cass asked.

Mitch stretched a long arm across the evidence table, shuffled through a pile of paper, and snagged several documents. He passed her one. "Maybe because of this."

Cass skimmed it. "Donna Moore was adopted?"

"By Harry Moore in 1970. She was born Donna Silverman in 1962. Guess where?"

Cass shrugged and took two additional pieces of paper and a silver Star of David on a chain that Mitch held out.

"Thayerville, Alabama," he said as she read the 1962 birth certificate and the announcement in the Calvary Baptist Church bulletin from 1970 about Moore's baptism. "She was Jewish, but converted with her mother when they moved here."

"Thayerville. That's where Martha Franklin came from."

Mitch nodded. "And where Charles Franklin, Ebenezer Silverman, and Robert Hedder were lynched. Their fathers."

"So, there's actually a long history between the Franklin, Hedder, and Silverman, now Moore, families." Cass sipped her coffee, her violet eyes clouded. "You think the person who called Moses last night when you answered the phone, Mitch, is Emmet Hedder?"

"Yes."

"What's so super secret that they need separate phones to talk to each other? Or, really, to pass messages to each other. Because that's what was happening. One called the second, who called the third."

"That's what we're trying to figure out," Kado said. "From Donna's phone, we can match many of the dates and times she received a call from the unknown guy –"

"Emmet, right?" Cass asked.

Kado nodded. "We can match the times of some of those calls to times she was away from the office, or to shortly before she left the office."

"That makes sense given how often they were away from work at the same time." She looked at Mitch. "Did you tell Kado about Emmet's letters?"

Mitch nodded. "The originals were on your desk. They're exactly like the letters Sheriff Hoffner got about Mojo."

"It's almost like somebody's been stalking them. Trying to disrupt their lives before deciding to kill them. I wonder if Moore got the same kind of thing?"

Kado's gaze was thoughtful. "I doubt it. The letters went to Mojo's and Emmet's bosses. Donna was her own boss. She couldn't be threatened in the same way."

"Good point." Cass sipped for a moment. "If Emmet and Donna were meeting, isn't it possible that Moses was meeting them, too?"

"It is." Kado showed her a hand-written matrix. "We've gone back and looked at old shift assignments. Every time that Donna was away from work, Moses was, too."

"How could that be? Shifts are assigned days, sometimes weeks, in advance."

"Yeah," Mitch said, "but anybody can switch a shift. And on some days, he was already off."

"It could be coincidence," Cass said, "that all three were off of work at the same time."

"It could be."

"And that they had some weird call circle going."

"Maybe."

"But you don't think so."

"No," Mitch said. "And neither does Kado."

"So, what were they up to?"

Kado and Mitch exchanged a glance. "We think," Kado said, "they were on a murder spree."

Chapter 105

JOSEPH KNOCKED ON THE sheriff's office door and turned the knob at the muted, "Come."

"Morning, sir," he said. "I'm sorry to bother you, but Rob Conroy had a word with me at The Golden Gate this morning. He said that me, you, and Mitch should watch our backs."

Hoffner's nostrils flared "A threat?"

"Not explicitly. In fact he said that it would be illegal to threaten a 'Do Right Boy' and was speaking as a concerned citizen."

"I wouldn't worry about Conroy. The detectives have ruled him out of involvement in your mother and brother's deaths and it sounds like he's using drugs again. If so, I doubt he'll have the fortitude to come after one of us." Hoffner's eyes narrowed as he took in the younger man. As the silence grew longer, sweat formed on Joseph's brow and he fought the urge to squirm. The sheriff's face seemed to soften. "I expect today will be hard for you, Moses. Are you sure you want to be at the station this morning?"

"Yes, sir. It'll help keep my mind occupied."

"I'll see you at the church then, before ten o'clock."

Joseph tiptoed past the forensics room. Although he wasn't hiding, he wanted to keep a low profile until he knew where the investigations stood and learned more about Junie Archer. He settled in Moses' chair, turned the computer on, and waited for it to run through its start-up routine. He'd come up empty-handed in his search for information on Junie on the internet. It was time to use more powerful channels.

Once the case management system was running, Joseph dug through everything the detectives had collected on the shootings. It didn't take long. For the time being, they had no link between Moses, Emmet, and Donna. Which meant that he and Emmet could operate below the radar for a while longer. After exhausting all the evidence in the shootings, Joseph opened the system file on Calvin Whitehead's murder. If Emmet was telling the truth and the three of them had killed the man, Joseph needed to know where the investigation was headed. He scanned the documents added since his last visit and opened an attachment. Joseph blinked. A photograph of a younger Calvin Whitehead stared at him from the screen. Dark, thick hair, deep brown eyes, and a strong face, just like Junie Archer's. Joseph scrolled down the page and caught his breath.

Calvin Whitehead was really Calvin Whitman, former sheriff of Thayerville, Alabama. The notes indicated that Calvin Whitman had a son, but made no mention of a daughter. Even though their last names differed, the resemblance was too strong for Junie to be anything but a blood relative of Whitman's. A niece, maybe? If Whitman had a son, he was probably the shooter, and Junie was working to gather information through Officer Hugo Petchard and the other cops who came to The Golden Gate. But regardless of whether she pulled the trigger, Junie was part of the puzzle.

Joseph read on. By the time he finished with the case updates, he thought he knew how all the pieces fit together. The detectives had no idea that Calvin Whitehead's murder, the Franklin and Moore killings, and the attempt on Emmet Hedder's life were linked. But that knowledge vacuum wouldn't last long.

He printed and collected several pages, then switched his computer off. Emmet was right. It was time to turn the tables. He pulled a cell phone from his pocket and dialed. "Emmet? I've got it. I know who we're after. Or at least," he clarified, "I know who knows."

CHAPTER 106

CASS'S JAW DROPPED. "A what?"

Kado sighed. "Murder spree might be too strong. But we think they were tracking people down and killing them."

She gathered her hair and twisted it up, then jabbed two pencils into a straggly French twist. "Who?"

"The men who lynched their daddies," Mitch answered. "It's the only thing that makes sense. Tell her about the shoe."

"What shoe?" Cass asked.

Kado reached into a milk crate and pulled out a massive running shoe. "You picked Joseph's shoes up at the Franklin's house, remember?"

She nodded.

"One of the shoes had red stuff caught in the tread. It contains sucrose, tomatoes, garlic, strawberries, and loads of preservatives."

"Yeah, you found that earlier. So what?"

"That's the same stuff that was on the floor in Calvin Whitehead's stockroom."

"You think Joseph Franklin was there and stepped in it? That he *killed* Calvin Whitehead?"

"Well, with that and the gas on his clothes –"

"Hang on a minute, Kado," Mitch said. "Pull up Whitehead's case file. She doesn't know what Hoffner learned last night."

"What are you talking about?" Cass asked, circling the room to Kado's desk.

He swiveled the monitor to face her. She scanned the notes from Sheriff Hoffner's phone call with Thayerville's sheriff. "Good Lord. No wonder they never arrested anybody for the lynching. The sheriff was in on it."

Kado nodded.

"So you think Joseph killed Whitehead in revenge?"

"With help from Emmet and Donna."

She struggled for words. "That's a gigantic leap."

"Maybe," Mitch agreed. "But it's the only thing that makes sense given what we know."

Kado started packing evidence into boxes while Mitch shuffled papers into piles. Cass returned to her chair. "There are two possible problems with your theory," she said.

"Tell us," Mitch said.

"First, has anybody else involved in the 1967 lynching died?"

"Hoffner's contacting that sheriff from Thayerville to find out who was involved and where they are now." Mitch rolled his wheelchair forward, careful not to bang into anything with his extended leg, snagged a stack of file folders, and rolled backwards to his original spot by the evidence table. "These are police reports from the seven murders around the country that are similar to Whitehead's."

"Five men were involved in the lynching, so after Whitehead's death, we only need four."

Mitch nodded. "In these crimes, each victim was burned to death. That's one point of similarity. A second point is that each body had at least one bullet wound somewhere. Head, chest, gut, leg. But only three had the swastika carving in the chest; were wounded in the leg; burned; and hung exactly like Calvin Whitehead. If our theory is right, then it's very possible that these three men were part of that lynching crew in 1967."

"What about the fifth man?"

"Maybe they haven't found him yet."

Cass tapped a finger against her lips. "Did you match the locations where these men were murdered to Emmet Hedder's ATM withdrawals?"

"Most of the men lived remotely. Emmet's withdrawals were at ATMs in the closest big cities. It's not exact, but it links them a little closer."

"Okay, second thing: Joseph's been in jail until a few weeks ago. If Donna, Moses, and Emmet have been hooking up, why would Joseph be involved in killing Calvin Whitehead? Those are his shoes that have food mashed in the tread. And his clothes with the gas on them. Did they bring him into their little scheme when he got out of prison?"

Mitch and Kado exchanged another glance. The forensic man shrugged. "Tell her. It's no more fantastic than anything else we've come up with."

Mitch's eyes were bleak. "We think Joseph's still alive."

CHAPTER 107

THE HOTEL WAS SO new the smell of his coffee was overridden by the fumes from fresh paint, turning Joseph's stomach. Saturday morning cartoons played silently on the flat screen TV, and he wished that ending this would be as easy as ordering a kit from ACME or setting the Coyote up for a dash off the nearest cliff. Emmet placed the last page on the bed and flexed his right arm.

"Still hurting?" Joseph asked.

"Not bad."

Joseph eyed a piece of hotel room stationary bearing Emmet's distinctive scrawl. "What's that?"

"My will. I need you to witness it."

"What?"

"I don't have one. This is as good a time as any to get it all down on paper."

Joseph leaned back in his chair and interlocked his hands on top of his bald head. "You're afraid of this guy?"

"Call it prudence."

"You've never been prudent, Emmet. If you're feeling your mortality, and I guess with this guy," Joseph gestured at the paperwork, "that's reasonable, you'd better make amends with Celia."

"She won't talk to me, man."

"When was the last time you tried?"

"A few weeks ago, when she left for her mother's house."

"How much does she know?"

"How do you tell your wife that you're hunting down and lynching the men who murdered your father?"

"Celia's about the best looking woman I've ever seen." Joseph held his hands up to block Emmet's hairy eyeball. "I don't know why she married your ugly ass, but you're lucky to have her. And as fragile as she looks, she's tough. If you think you might die sometime soon, you'd best get square with her today."

Emmet picked up the paper and a pen. "Just sign it."

Joseph did.

Emmet folded his will and slipped it into his back pocket, then sat on the bed and tapped the printouts. "The files don't mention this Junie woman. Where'd you meet her?"

"She works at The Golden Gate Café. Have you seen her?"

"I go to The Coffee Shop. She's dating a cop?"

"Hugo Petchard."

"That's clever."

"It would be if he knew anything about the investigations."

Emmet stood and refilled their cups from the hotel's coffee pot. "What did she say to you this morning?"

"I asked if she would kill the person who murdered her family, and she said no, but she *would* kill the people who murdered her family before she had the chance."

"Fascinating. You think she's working with Whitman's son?"

"Yes." Joseph flipped through the paperwork and extracted Whitman's photograph. "She's the spitting image of this man, only she wears make-up. Junie has to be a blood relative. A niece, maybe. But there is one problem."

"What's that?"

"She's been in Arcadia for six weeks. That means she's known about y'all since before then."

"So?"

"So how did she and her cousin, or whatever, find out about you? From what she said this morning, she wants revenge because you killed her family before she could. Which means that she knew Calvin Whitehead was here and that you were planning to kill him. Does that make sense?"

"I don't see how she could know," Emmet said. "We identified Whitehead about eighteen months ago."

"Why'd you wait so long to kill him?"

"We figured that killing somebody in Forney County would be riskiest. There was a better chance somebody would recognize us, so we wanted to kill the other men first."

Joseph stared at him for a long moment. "How did you figure out that Whitehead was involved in the lynchings?"

"By accident. I stopped to get gas at The Whitehead Store and recognized his face. I'd seen Calvin Whitman's picture in the courthouse out in Thayerville, from his time when he was sheriff. The man was supposed to be dead. So we figured he ran from Thayerville for some reason."

"You killed a man based on one look at his face?"

"We weren't trigger happy, Joseph. Moses and Donna did their own reconnaissance, and then I went back out and snapped a photograph of him with my phone. It wasn't great, but it was good enough that we could compare it to photos on the internet."

Joseph digested this. "Why did Junie come here in the first place six weeks ago? How did she even know about you?"

"What's her last name?"

"Archer."

Emmet shrugged. "The Archers are prominent people out in Thayerville. If she's some sort of relation to Calvin Whitman, then maybe his family and the Archers inter-married."

Joseph chewed on this. "Did you kill anybody from Tennessee?"

"Why?"

"That's where she came from."

Emmet pursed his lips. "We were in Tennessee last autumn. That's the closest we've been to getting caught."

"What happened?"

"Bad timing. We used separate cars because two black dudes and a white woman driving the back roads in the South still attracts attention. We were turning on the main highway, off the road where our victim lived, and a cop pulled up behind us."

Joseph's eyes widened.

"No lights, no siren, but he came up fast. We always left the scene in different directions, so Donna turned left and we went right. The cop followed us for about three miles. I was driving and Moses watched him in the side mirror. It looked like he was running the plates. He even turned on his lights but sped up and went past us."

"That's it?"

Emmet shrugged. "He got a good look at us as he went past. Why?"

"The cop was a man?"

"Yup."

"Junie's cousin, maybe."

"Maybe, but the guy we killed wasn't called Archer or Whitman or Whitehead."

"Were you in your own cars?"

"No, man. We drove to Shreveport and rented vehicles."

"If the cop was the cousin, that's how he found you. Getting information from the rental company."

"I guess it's possible. It's about the only thing that makes sense." Emmet went silent.

"What are you thinking?" Joseph asked.

"It's time to end this. We use Junie to find him and then take him out."

"And Junie?"

"We can deal with her later, or maybe she'll just disappear after her cousin is dead." Emmet started opening drawers in the desk. "We've got to take the fight to him."

"To do that, we have to find him. What are you looking for?"

"A pen and paper."

"For what?"

"Phone technology has come a long way in the few years you were in prison, man. We're turning the tables on him." Emmet checked his watch. "You'll have to hurry, but you can get to the store and back here, and still make the funeral."

"What are you talking about?"

"You're going shopping, Joseph. After you bury your kin, we're going to find the bastard who killed your people and Donna. And then we're going to kill him."

CHAPTER 108

THE SHOOTER DRESSED IN dark colors for the Franklin funerals. There was no point in standing out when so many cops would be present. In fact, simply attending was a bad idea, but he couldn't resist. Besides, one never knew what kind of gossip one could overhear with so many men in uniform buzzing around. And that luscious detective, Cass Elliot, would put in an appearance. What a gorgeous creature. He wondered if he could capture an image of her with his phone and decided to try. In addition to his memories of the killings, her photo would provide a nice reminder of his visit to this intellectual wasteland they called Arcadia.

His time in Forney County was drawing to a close. He was done toying with Hedder and Franklin; after the injury to his ear last night, slight though it was, all the fun had gone out of the stalking and terrorizing. Although the gaps in his knowledge about the investigations were growing, he was certain that the police had no idea who had committed the Franklin and Moore murders. Officer Hugo Petchard had become a waste of time as a source. He was, however, still a useful tool for gaining access to general goings on in the department. Junie had performed admirably. She was a natural at deception and he enjoyed having her around. In fact, being with her felt like slipping into a second skin, like coming home. Given that he'd be starting a new life after he left Arcadia, he might keep her on full-time.

Taking a look in the mirror, he brushed his hair over his ears and flashed a practice smile. Not too bright, not too sad, a tad teary. It was important to fit in, even to blend in, today. Getting the facial expression right was an immense help. He turned and tried it on the black cat watching from the toilet's tank. "What do you think, Sheba?"

She graced him with a bored glance and then jumped from the tank to twine herself between his legs. He swore and swatted at her, then used the tape brush to remove her hair. Satisfied at last, he smoothed down his lapels and went to collect his rifle.

Show time.

CHAPTER 109

"WHAT ARE YOU TWO smoking?" Cass asked, yanking the pencils from her French twist, shaking her hair loose, raking it into a tight bun, and jabbing the pencils back in. "We're burying Joseph and his mother today."

"Maybe we're burying Moses instead," Mitch said.

"Are you serious?"

He nodded.

Cass leaned forward and put her elbows on the evidence table, looking back and forth from Kado to Mitch. "What makes you think Joseph is masquerading as Moses?"

"Several things that kind of came together," Mitch answered. "Since his mom and brother were killed, Moses has had a total personality switch."

"Understandable."

"Perhaps, but there's barely a glimpse of the old Moses. This Moses is quiet, observant. The old Moses couldn't keep his mouth shut to save his life. And this one can sit still and concentrate for long stretches of time. When he helped me chase down those crimes with similarities to Calvin Whitehead's murder? He sat at his desk for over an hour without moving or looking up. Have you ever known Moses Franklin to do that?"

Cass caught her lower lip between her teeth and tugged. "Never. He hates the computer. He's usually up talking to somebody or finding an excuse to get outside. Maybe he's worn down right now, and needs time to adjust to the new reality."

"Okay, how about this: the new Moses, his reports are flawless. Complete sentences with punctuation, good grammar, and no typos."

Mitch shifted in his wheelchair and reached for another coffee. Cass nudged the carrier toward him. "And, I've caught him typing really fast. Using all his fingers. By the time I get to his desk he's gone back to two fingers. But when nobody else is in the squad room, I can hear him tapping away. If my chair is angled the right way, I can see him typing. It's bizarre."

Cass cracked a smile. "I guess that's one solid piece of evidence that this isn't Moses. He used to bribe me with donuts from The Donut Hole to write his reports. If they were from The Palace, I might've caved. Anything else?"

Kado turned to his desk. "Look at this."

Cass joined him and examined the computer screen. "What is it?"

"Carlos went to the shooting range with Moses on Thursday night. Look how Moses performed."

She leaned in. "He doesn't get scores like this."

"And see what Carlos wrote?" Kado asked, scrolling farther down the page.

"'Moses shows greatly improved marksmanship when using his left hand to aim. Observed him manipulating the safety and releasing / installing a magazine and noted no concerns with his continued use of a right-handed gun'," Cass read out loud. She looked across the room at Mitch. "I've never known him to do anything left-handed. Have you?"

"No. Basketball, softball, writing, eating. All with his right hand."

Cass sat and stared at the forensics table. "He was using a laptop at The Golden Gate Friday morning. Moses always eats at The Coffee Shop. But he said he was using Wi-Fi at The Gate to research Joseph's crime."

"I can't imagine that Moses even knows what Wi-Fi is, can you?" Mitch asked.

"He said Joseph was teaching him, but it seems strange that his brother dies and suddenly he's using hotspots." She studied the ceiling tiles. "If you're right, and Joseph is pretending to be Moses, why? He's a felon impersonating an officer. That's a serious crime. Why take the chance he'll get caught?"

"Revenge," Kado said, rolling his chair from the desk to the forensics table. "He wants to keep up with the investigations so he can find the person responsible."

"And do what?" Cass's expression was incredulous. "I don't know Joseph at all. He was gone to New York by the time I joined the force here. But if twins are opposites, Moses is the one with all the emotion. I could see him tracking somebody down and killing them." She stopped then, realizing what she had said. "Maybe it is possible that he was involved in Whitehead's murder, but we need more than strawberries and tomatoes smashed in his shoe tread and gas on his clothes. Back to Joseph, *if* he's the one who's alive. Do you really think he wants to kill whoever shot his mom and brother?"

"Maybe his job is just to figure out who did the killing," Mitch said, "and let Emmet follow through. Emmet was a Marine, remember?"

The door to the evidence room creaked open and Sheriff Hoffner stepped inside. His cool blue glance slid over Cass as he squeezed past Mitch's leg. He stood silently, a stack of files in one hand and a single piece of paper in the other. Mitch shot Cass a warning glance and then asked, "Find anything, Sheriff?"

"Sheriff Studebaker came through with some history. Whitman's decision to fake his death makes a sort of sense now." He scanned the paper in his hand. "When I asked Studebaker about the lynching in Thayerville, he asked which one I was talking about."

"Good Lord," Kado said, crossing his arms over his chest. "How many were there?"

"Five in Magnolia County during Whitman's tenure as sheriff."

"He was sheriff for twenty years?" Mitch asked. "That's a lynching every four years."

"Most occurred early in his tenure. What's notable about that many lynchings in one place is that no one from outside the county came to investigate. Studebaker said the civil rights people came in and tried to stir things up, but they never lasted long."

"Somebody scared them off?" Mitch asked.

Hoffner nodded. "For some reason, the federal government finally got involved in mid-1978 and started looking into both the lynchings and the level of corruption in Sheriff Whitman's department."

"Whitman got scared and ran," Cass said.

Hoffner flicked a glance in her direction. "And Studebaker came through with names for the four men who were with Whitman at the Franklin, Hedder, and Silverman lynching."

Mitch rifled through the papers on his clipboard and pulled out the list of the seven men who died in a similar manner to Calvin Whitehead. "Who are they?"

"Eric Jackson, Jimmy Holland, Arlin Ross, and Boyd Dudley. Studebaker said that Dudley died in Thayerville. You got a match on the other three?"

Mitch nodded. "They're all here. None of them lived in Alabama when they died."

"Studebaker said they drifted away when he started cleaning up the department and the county. They weren't safe any longer."

"Why did Boyd Dudley stay?" Cass asked. "Why not leave when the others did?"

"Dudley received custody of Whitman's son and apparently the man was too deep in the bottle to make a move away from Thayerville."

"How did Dudley die?" Kado asked.

"House fire."

"When?"

"Five years ago."

"Any sign of foul play?"

Hoffner placed the stack of folders on the evidence table. "Technically, no. It was Dudley's habit to pass out in his recliner while drinking and watching TV. The fire started near his chair. They suspected that he had a cigarette in his hand when he fell asleep."

"Studebaker thought there was something funny about the fire?" Mitch asked.

"Everybody did. But they couldn't prove anything." Hoffner took a cup of Golden Gate coffee from the carrier on the evidence table. He turned and snapped a paper towel from its holder, wiped the lid's rim, and then took a sip. "There was some belief that Dudley abused Whitman's son. The boy cleared out the money his father left him and ran away in 1985, when he was sixteen. He hasn't been seen since. Studebaker's trying to hunt him down. He said he'd check back this afternoon."

Mitch shifted in his wheelchair, a thoughtful expression on his face. "Studebaker thinks Whitman's son came back a few years ago and fried the man who was abusing him?"

"It's a possibility he's considered. Boyd Dudley's body was almost completely destroyed in the fire. His trailer basically burned down around him."

"Nobody spotted the fire?"

Hoffner shook his head. "He lived in a remote area, well off the county road. Sounds like he was a mean cuss. Nobody went down his way without a reason."

Mitch sucked his teeth. "There was no swastika carved into his body? No bullet hole in his leg?"

"The coroner's report is brief," Hoffner said, raising his coffee cup to the files on the forensic table. "It doesn't document any damage to the body other than that from the fire."

"No police investigation?" Cass asked.

"Coroner ruled it an accidental death. No need for one. And according to Studebaker, nobody mourned Dudley."

"This helps," Mitch said, leaning forward and scooting several of his files to one side. "We can focus on the other three: Jackson, Holland, and Ross. Let's see if the local forces turned up any clues about who killed these men."

Hoffner glanced at the clock. "Leave it until later. It's almost time for the funerals." He turned and left the room.

Cass waited until the door closed. "He doesn't know you think it's Joseph who's alive?"

"No," Mitch said. "I don't want him to go off half-cocked until we know for sure."

"What you're suggesting is insane, you know that, don't you?"

Mitch and Kado nodded.

"Who else knows what you're thinking?"

"Nobody, yet," Kado said. "But we want to tell Munk and Truman so they can keep an eye on him."

She released a long sigh. "Since this Boyd Dudley died in a house fire, everyone involved in that lynching is dead now. Whitehead was the last one."

"And if the Franklins hadn't been killed, we never would have looked at Moses as a possible suspect."

"They would've gotten away with it," Cass stated.

"Yes, they would've," Mitch agreed. "And they still might."

CHAPTER 110

CELIA HEDDER TURNED OFF the shower and felt cool air wash over her skin. She whirled and came face-to-face with Emmet. The sound of her wet palm connecting with his cheek echoed in the tiled space. Emmet touched his face with his fingertips, and then reached for his wife.

"Don't you dare, Emmet Hedder. You lost that right when you disappeared." She jabbed at his shoulder and Emmet flinched. Her hand flew to her mouth. "There was blood, Emmet. Are you hurt?"

"It's nothing. Just a few stitches."

Celia's lower lip trembled. Emmet reached for her. She backed away but he pulled her close and cradled her head against his chest, absorbing the shudders that racked her body as she sobbed. He eased her from the shower and wrapped her in a towel, then led her to the bed and dried her tears with his thumb. "I needed to see you, Celia."

"*You* needed to see *me*? I didn't know if you were dead or alive, Emmet. I know you stopped loving me a long time ago, and I'm not sure why you've stayed this long. But surely you could've let me know you were alive."

Emmet tightened his grip. "I've always loved you, Celia. I've never been unfaithful. There were some things that I had to do, and I didn't want you involved."

"Why not?"

"It was too dangerous."

She pulled back and looked at him. "What have you gotten into, Emmet?"

"It's complicated."

"And I'm not smart enough to understand?"

"You're the smartest person I've ever met, Celia. A lot smarter than me."

"Then tell me."

He looked at the clock on the bedside table. "You'll miss the Franklin's funeral."

"But maybe I'll keep my husband. So talk."

CHAPTER 111

A BEAD OF SWEAT formed on Cass's temple and tickled as it rolled down her cheek. She resisted the urge to swipe at it until the pastor finished praying and Mojo tossed handfuls of reddish soil onto the caskets. Cass watched him closely, looking for confirmation that he was Joseph instead of Moses. The big man's countenance was stoic, his eyes masked behind mirrored sunglasses, but the slump of his shoulders betrayed the grief he carried. Cass risked a slight movement of her head and to check on the others. They were arranged in a rough triangle to allow a full view of the cemetery and the attendees.

Mitch and Darla Stone were positioned slightly to her right. Martinez, Munk, and their wives were standing opposite, to keep a view on the area behind Cass and Mitch. Kado and Truman were stationed at the point of the triangle, covering the area behind the other two groups. Munk and Truman wore their formal uniforms while Kado and Martinez were dressed in dark suits with subdued ties. Cass had never seen Kado in a suit and was surprised at how elegant and at ease he appeared. She sighed quietly; he oozed sex appeal even in such somber circumstances. Mitch wore a pair of blue jeans with one leg cut off at the thigh, along with a suit jacket, white shirt, and tie, and looked right at home in spite of the bizarre ensemble. The wives wore simple black dresses and looked stunning, even if Gabrielle Munk's normal sparkle appeared diminished from her time in Galveston.

Cass glanced down at her outfit and grimaced. When she started digging through her closet this morning, she realized to her great chagrin that she didn't even own a skirt. Instead, she wore a black pantsuit with low-heeled black pumps and a maroon silk blouse. She itched to rip her jacket off and let her body cool down.

Moses stepped to the side to speak with the preacher, Hoffner at his shoulder, and Cass watched as people shuffled forward to murmur a quiet prayer at the foot of the graves. The crowd at the cemetery was massive, swelling with stiff officers sweating through their formal summer uniforms. Blacks, whites, Hispanics: everyone was flushed and batting at the air, thick and sticky as honey, with paper fans bearing the funeral home's logo and the hopeful verses from the 23rd Psalm. A marquee was positioned near the gaping graves, rows of chairs peopled with distant Franklin relatives and the eldest attendees. Children fidgeted and scratched at their Sunday clothes.

Bruce and Harry Elliot made their way past the graves to speak quietly with Moses. Harry was in a dark gray suit, his cottony hair hiding the cut on his scalp. Bruce wore dress slacks and a tweed jacket, every inch the professor. He also wore a large pair of sunglasses that did little to conceal the bruise on his cheek. Despite the injuries, she realized that her brothers cleaned up rather nicely. Her father's reluctance to attend the funeral was no reflection of the degree of respect he felt for the Franklin family; rather, he hated funerals and the loss they represented. Cass had never known him to attend one, or to visit a cemetery without a bottle in hand. And in some ways she was grateful he wasn't here. News of his drunken encounter with Officer Hugo Petchard had swept the department and the community, evidenced by the sideways glances Cass and her brothers received during the church service.

Mitch leaned forward and whispered, "See anything?"

She shook her head. "You?"

"Darla spotted Goober." Mitch pointed discreetly past Martinez and Munk. "See him?"

Cass searched the crowd. "He dressed up."

Mitch snorted.

"Well, he did. Those overalls are new, and I've never seen him in a white dress shirt, have you?"

Darla spoke in a low voice. "I saw him at Tascall's yesterday and helped him pick it out. I tried to get him to wear a tie, too, but the thought of a noose around his neck terrified him. He decided to button the shirt to the top."

"Did you tell him it was okay to wear that greasy ol' baseball cap?" Mitch asked.

Darla bit her lip. "We didn't discuss headwear."

"There's Petchard and Junie," Cass said, watching as the couple edged close to the graves, holding hands. Petchard wore his formal uniform and Junie was dressed in black: a jacket and long skirt, low heels, and a simple blouse. The scarf tied around her neck was also black.

Beside Cass, Darla shivered. "Mitch introduced me to her at the church earlier. She's stunning, but she gives me the willies."

Cass turned to take in Darla's profile. "What bothers you?"

Darla studied the other woman and then shrugged. "I don't know. She made me feel... icky. Like she was sizing me up." She grimaced. "Sorry. That's not much help."

Wally Pugh sidled up alongside Mitch, a camera dangling from one hand, the ever present notebook from the other. His beady black eyes shone. "Sad, isn't it? Are you here looking for the Franklin's killer?"

Cass cut her eyes at the reporter. "Wally, this really isn't the time."

"Look, I'm not trying to be crass, but people want to know who killed the Franklins and Moore. They might not be so spooked except for what happened to Calvin Whitehead. That was creepy. Sadistic, even." He shifted and watched Moses Franklin, lifted the camera and then let it drop to his side. "Any leads on Whitehead's murder?"

"We're making progress," Mitch answered. "But there's nothing concrete." He cut a glance at Wally. "Yet."

Wally's tongue flicked out to touch his lips. "You'll let me know first?"

Mitch nodded.

"Fair enough." The reporter turned and studied the crowd. "Who's that with Petchard?"

"Her name's Junie."

"A date?"

Mitch nodded.

"Will wonders never cease?" Wally lifted the camera and discretely took a photo, and then moved away, circling nearby gravestones, his movements sinuous.

CHAPTER 112

JOSEPH ACCEPTED PETCHARD'S MUTTERED condolences and watched in amusement as the man stepped aside to scan the crowd. Petchard's pale complexion was broiling in the late morning sun, but his jaw was set and his eyes narrowed. As the officer's head swiveled to encompass the narrow strip of blacktop running through the cemetery, Joseph realized that Petchard was preening for his woman.

Good luck with this one, Joseph thought, watching as Junie fiddled with her phone before dropping it in a pocket on her jacket. *She's about as cold as they come.*

Junie offered Joseph a hug. "I'm so sorry for your loss, Moses," she whispered, close enough that her breath feathered his ear.

Joseph touched his cheek to hers and lost his balance, falling into her. With the dexterity of a New York pickpocket, he palmed the phone and then steadied himself. "Sorry about that, I must be a little tired."

"Maybe now that the funerals are over you can move on."

"There are a few loose ends I'll need to tie up first. But they'll be taken care of soon enough."

"They will?"

"Keep your eyes open, Junie, and watch what happens."

Her smile was almost impish. "I will, Moses, and you do the same, you hear?"

CHAPTER 113

THE SINGLE PAGE OF his will was on the kitchen table, crumpled into a tight ball. Emmet watched as his wife drained the last of her green tea and put the mug in the sink. Fully dressed now, she was staring through the kitchen window, shoulders hunched nearly to her ears. At last, she turned. "I don't agree with what you've done, Emmet. But I think I understand it."

He waited.

"It's Moses they're burying today?"

"Yes."

She turned back to the window. "I wish he'd never met Donna Moore. That your Granny never told you what happened to your father and theirs. That Donna hadn't egged you on."

"I can't undo it, Celia. And these aren't nice people that we've killed. Their actions, the lynching, started it all."

"What now?"

"I finish it. Or, I suppose that Joseph and I finish it. He won't seem to let me do this alone."

"Is he a liability?"

Emmet considered her question. "In some ways, yes. He doesn't know how to handle a gun."

"Donna didn't either."

"But Moses did. And Donna was a quick learner. She didn't balk at what we had to do. I don't know how Joseph will handle it once it comes time to kill this man."

"What if you didn't?"

"Didn't what?"

"Kill him."

"Then he'd kill me. And Joseph. And probably you, Celia." He eyed her. "And I can't let that happen."

Slowly, she nodded. "What comes after?"

"I come home and go back to work."

"And the police?"

"Have no idea that there's a link between the man we're going to kill and us."

"What will you tell them about why you've been in hiding?"

"Post-traumatic stress."

Celia rolled her eyes.

"It'll work. A decorated soldier flips when somebody shoots at him, goes into hiding, and only comes out when he thinks the coast is clear."

"You never were any good at backing down from a fight." She sat and traced a pattern on the tabletop with her finger. "I don't like it."

Emmet's voice was gentle. "He's clever, Celia. I don't know how he identified us to start with, but he tracked us to Arcadia and used GPS devices to follow us around town. I don't have a choice. I have to finish this. For Moses and Donna. For me. And even for you. I can't risk that he'll hurt you as a way of getting to me."

"And then you'll come back to me?"

"Yes, I will."

Celia licked her dry lips. "How can I help?"

CHAPTER 114

THE CROWD AT THE cemetery was thinning and Joseph spotted Petchard opening the door to a battered Honda. He watched as the skinny man gave Junie a chaste kiss and ushered her into the car. Petchard about-faced and marched to the main road and traffic duty.

Fingering the two cell phones in his pocket, Joseph excused himself from the small group gathered at the graves and trotted toward the Honda. As he drew near, Junie disappeared from view and then popped up again, scowling. Joseph tapped on the passenger's window and the frown morphed into surprise, and then a flirtatious smile. As she leaned across to open the door, Joseph squatted. "Is this yours? I found it on the ground."

She snatched the phone from him and powered it on. As she worked, Joseph eased the second cell phone under the passenger seat. "Thanks for finding it," Junie said, checking the screen. "I hadn't realized I'd lost it until just now. I was about to panic."

Joseph uttered a silent prayer that she hadn't noticed his movements. Via his shopping list this morning, Emmet requested only a prepaid cell phone and a roll of duct tape. Once Joseph returned to the hotel with both items, Emmet powered up Joseph's laptop and activated, and then charged, the phone. Joseph watched as he created an anonymous account at a website offering free real-time GPS tracking and downloaded software to the phone. Once that was done, Emmet showed Joseph an online map with a red dot in the center. "That's the phone," he'd told Joseph. "We'll know exactly where she goes."

"What's the duct tape for?" Joseph asked.

"Ideally, you want to get the phone inside her car. If you can't manage that, tape it beneath the bumper or inside a wheel well. Our biggest risk is that she drives through a puddle or goes through a car wash. But the phone doesn't have to work for long."

"Why not?"

"We'll be done with Junie and her cousin before the weekend is out."

Joseph felt a small wave of triumph and said to Junie, "No problem. They're so small these days, they're hard to keep track of. Are you working this afternoon?"

"Just to help re-open the café."

"And then what?" Joseph asked.

"I'll probably take a nap and get ready for tonight."

"Big plans?"

She smiled. "A little hunting, I think."

"Squirrel and turkey are in season."

"Oh, I don't waste time on small prey. I'll be hunting something bigger. The most dangerous game of all, in fact."

Joseph unfolded his long frame, and then bent over to look her in the eye. "Be careful out there, Junie. With big game, the prey can easily become the predator."

———————

PETCHARD TOOTED HIS WHISTLE and waved the line of mourners through the cemetery gates. He drifted to the left to look for Junie's car and was surprised to see Mojo climbing from the passenger side with a grin on his face. He caught his breath as the tall man bent down to look back into the car

The green eyed monster bared its talons, and Petchard fought hard to stay in place. A horn beeped and Petchard automatically motioned for traffic to resume. Mojo shut the door and tapped the top of the car, then Junie's Honda was easing into the line waiting to exit. Out of pique, Petchard made the mourners wait until all cars had passed. He stepped back into the road and motioned the cars forward, eyes narrowed behind his mirrored shades as Junie inched forward. He raised a hand in greeting but the air whooshed from his lungs as she drove past without a glance in his direction, a wide smile curving her lips.

CHAPTER 115

CASS TURNED IN HER spot next to Mitch and Darla to see Maxine weaving through the thinning crowd. She looked stunning in her funeral outfit: patent leather pumps, a fitted suit whose skirt skimmed her knees, movie star shades, and a wide-brimmed black straw hat.

She stopped next to Cass. "The forensic guy looks good in a suit, Cass. And he was checking you out earlier."

Mitch and Darla's heads swiveled to look at Kado where he stood talking to Truman, and then returned to take in Cass who was blushing furiously. Darla's brown eyes twinkled. Mitch's mouth opened and then shut when his wife jabbed an elbow in his ribs.

"Sorry," Maxine said with a grin. "Thought everybody knew he was hot for you." She leaned in to hug Cass and whispered, "You owe me donuts," then patted Cass's hip.

Cass's fingers brushed paper and she watched as Maxine drifted to another cluster of people. She pulled the note from her pocket. It was a newspaper clipping with a sticky note in Maxine's swirling handwriting:

We have to stop him. A dozen chocolate glazed. M

The article confirmed that Ft. Worth police had labeled Sarah Hill's death a murder and were pursuing her killer. A bolt of electricity shot up Cass's spine. This was it – the race was on to see who would find this rapist first. Cass's mind flew to the tampon box stuffed full of evidence in her locker at the station and she started when Mitch asked, "What's that?"

Crumpling the clipping, she stuffed it in her pocket. "Nothing. Do you think we're done?"

Mitch glanced at Darla, who nodded. "Can I ride with you?" he asked Cass.

"Mitch," his pretty wife warned.

"I've got work to do. Cass can bring me home."

"Oh, no you don't," Darla said. "You were up before dawn and need a nap. You can ride with Cass to the courthouse. I'll pick up lunch and meet you there, then wait for you."

"That's a good deal for you," Cass said. "I'd love it if somebody made me take a nap."

"If Maxine's right, Kado might sign up for that job," Mitch said, and winced as Cass's fist connected with his shoulder. "Ow, woman. I'm still in a delicate state."

"You will be in a delicate state if you don't mind your manners," Darla said. "Rough him up, Cass. He needs a little polishing."

CHAPTER 116

AMELIA WIGGLED FROM HER mother's arms and raced across the lawn, Froggy the bear slapping the ground. Joseph swept her into the air and growled. She howled, planted a kiss on his check, and said, "Come make me coffee milk."

"I will. You take care of Froggy on the ride back to Alabama, okay?"

She nodded and he released her, watching with a sad smile as she toddled back to the car. Joseph waved as the last of his distant relatives pulled out of the driveway and heaved a huge sigh once the front door was shut behind him. His cousins had done him the great favor of cleaning and straightening the house this morning. Someone had even dead-headed the roses. The refrigerator was still bloated with food from the visitation last night. There was literally nothing for Joseph to do but contemplate killing a man, and the fact of his own mortality.

He stood at the mantle over the fireplace, gazing at the last photograph of his family and wondering what his mother and brother would think if they knew that he, their geeky little Joseph, was setting out to avenge their deaths. His mother would be horrified, no doubt, but Moses? Given what Joseph had learned about his twin, he thought that Moses would approve. As long as Joseph didn't get caught.

Following Emmet's lead, Joseph scribbled out a will, leaving everything to his little cousin Amelia, asking that whoever probated the will liquidate his assets and establish a college fund for her. He'd debated whether to write the will as Moses or Joseph, but decided to stick with his cover story and use Moses' name. He was scrawling a signature as his phone chirped.

"Are they gone?" Emmet asked.

"They just left."

"I've been following Junie's car, man. She's staying out in the middle of nowhere. A satellite map shows nothing around them for about a mile. Come get me."

"What for?"

"I'm not going into this blind, Joseph. We're going out there now."

"It's the middle of the afternoon, Emmet. They'll see us."

"She's already gone back to town. We'll drive past the house, park, and walk through the woods around the place. I need to get the lay of the land."

"And then?"

"We'll figure it out as we go, man. Step one, come get me."

CHAPTER 117

MITCH WAITED UNTIL DARLA turned her back. He snagged a tortilla chip, swiped it through the guacamole, and popped it into his mouth. Darla turned then, dark eyes narrowing as she took in the innocent look on her husband's face. She studied his plate, clean of the grilled chicken, black beans, and salad he had eaten in protest while the others had devoured enchiladas, chimichangas, refried beans, and piles of chips, salsa, and guacamole. Cass watched the silent marital exchange with amusement and drank the last of her iced tea.

Martinez' phone rang. He answered, grabbed a taco, and then pushed back from the table and headed for the door. Cass heard him giving directions to the K-9 unit who were ready to search for the missing old man. Grey, Bernie, and Porky sat at the far end of the table, studying autopsy photos from the killings Moses, Donna Moore, and Emmet Hedder might have committed. Kado had filled a plate and taken it back to the forensics room, and young Truman was sitting at the computer in the corner of the conference room, eating with one hand and entering details on the evidence taken from Calvin Whitehead's safe and trunk with the other. Surveying the culinary wreckage scattered across the table, Cass stood and cleared the remnants of the meal.

Munk pushed back from the table and patted his rounded belly, pulling his hand away to check the smear of sour cream sauce across his uniform's shirt. "Thanks, Darla. That hit the spot."

"I'm sorry Gabrielle missed lunch."

"It's always hard after a trip to Galveston." He plucked at the stain. "It takes her a few days to get her energy back."

Darla dipped a napkin in a glass of water and dabbed at the greasy spot. "Mitch said you had a false alarm about Angel?"

"Even after all this time, Gaby's hopes soar when it happens." He rubbed a hand over his balding head. "She has so much faith, Darla. Gaby believes that Angel is out there, waiting for us to find her."

Darla examined her handiwork and released Munk's shirt. "What about you, Ernie? Do you still have faith?"

Mitch flashed her a look, but Darla ignored him, focusing on the tubby officer.

Munk chewed his lip, a decade of worry and weariness etched into his pock-marked face. At last, he nodded. "I do, but it's different from Gaby's. Her faith is visceral, intense. She can *feel* that Angel is alive. My faith is more practical." His eyes were tired when he lifted them to meet Darla's. "I don't know how I would survive without it."

She reached out and held his hand for a moment, then released it as he turned to check on Truman.

Grey scooted the autopsy files to the middle of the table. "It's disturbing."

"What's that?" Mitch asked.

"How similar these three murders are to Calvin Whitehead's killing." He snagged his earlobe with his thumb and forefinger and began to rub. "There is a progression in efficiency from the earliest murder to Whitehead's."

Cass wiped the table and sat next to Mitch and Darla. "How do you mean?"

"The autopsy picked up a fractured skull in the first victim. The second two had deep contusions around the kidneys. Whitehead's body showed none of those types of injuries."

"That tells us," Bernie said, "that the killer or killers learned from their mistakes and gained confidence with each killing. The earlier victims had to be subdued through violence. Whitehead did not."

"That might be what they used the sheet for," Truman said from the corner. "We found scraps of sheet tangled in Whitehead's clothes. Maybe they immobilized him that way, rather than by hitting him."

"Quite possible," Bernie agreed.

Grey pushed back from the table and levered his long body into a standing position. "Sorry to eat and run, but we've got a full house."

Bernie scooted his chair around to sit next to Truman. Porky stopped and sat next to Cass, Darla, and Mitch. "I need to tell y'all something."

"What's up?" Mitch asked.

Porky rubbed at his eyebrow, devoid of the hoops and studs that usually decorated the space. "I'm worried about Moses."

"Why?"

"He hasn't been himself since his momma and Joseph died. And…"

"We've noticed it, too. What's bothering you?" Cass asked.

Porky spoke in a whisper. "His voice. Joseph sang bass and Moses sang tenor." He plucked at his yellow scrubs. "But at the church today, the voice coming from Moses was definitely bass, not tenor."

"You think it's Joseph who's still alive?"

His expression was miserable. "I don't know why he'd lie."

"It's okay," Mitch said, exchanging a glance with Cass. "We do."

CHAPTER 118

JOSEPH REVERSED ONTO THE dirt track and slipped Celia's green Camry into park, its nose facing the road. Although the overhanging trees provided shade, heat built inside the car as soon as he cut the engine. They'd avoided the county road that passed directly in front of Junie's house and were somewhere behind it. Emmet unzipped a duffel bag and pulled out a 9 mm. He popped the magazine, checked it, then slapped it home, chambered a round, and set the safety. He handed the weapon and a spare magazine to Joseph.

"I've got Moses' gun."

"You can't use his department-issue weapon, they can match the slugs."

"You sure we should carry? I thought you said we're here to get the lay of the land."

"We are. But we're not going in naked. Come on." Emmet stored Moses' gun under the seat and scowled when Joseph used the remote to lock the Camry, causing the horn to beep.

"Sorry," Joseph whispered. "Which way?"

Emmet consulted the map on his phone. The GPS tracker indicated that Junie's car was still in Arcadia. He zeroed in on the location she'd visited after the funeral and walked to the gate at the end of the little track. "See those trees?" He pointed across a pasture dotted with red cows. "Her house is through that stand of pine, about half a mile from where we are now."

"But, the cows, man. Those things are big. What if they don't want to share their grass?"

"Then we'll shoot them." Emmet grinned at Joseph's startled expression. "Just kidding. They're either pets and want to be fed, or they'll be kind of wild and stay away from us." He scanned the herd. "See that one?"

Joseph followed his outstretched arm and nodded.

"That's the bull."

"How can you tell?"

"That's not an udder."

"Oh. Yeah."

"Stay away from him and the calves. If a cow comes after you, run. If they still chase you, turn around and get big."

"Big?"

"Yeah, bulk up. Broaden your chest, stand up tall, put your arms out. Growl, but don't shout. We can't afford the attention." At Joseph's look of unease, Emmet added, "As long as you stay out of their way, they'll stay out of yours. Okay?"

Joseph wiped at the sweat beading his forehead. "Are you sure you don't want to go around the road?"

Emmet rolled his eyes and hopped over the gate.

CHAPTER 119

PETCHARD CIRCLED THE SQUARE and paused to peer into the employee parking lot behind The Golden Gate Café. He caught his breath. Junie's battered old Honda was there. Guts churning, he parked his patrol car behind the courthouse and hurried inside, out of the sweltering heat.

The station was cool and blessedly quiet. The locker room was empty and he stripped out of his sweaty dress uniform, showered, and put on a fresh uniform. He was heading to the station's exit when the sheriff's voice stopped him. "Office Petchard."

He about-faced, ice water running through his veins. "Sir?"

The Sheriff took in his sunburned face. "You didn't wear any sun protection?"

"No, sir. I forgot."

"You might want to put some lotion on that. It looks bad enough to blister." He waited for Petchard to nod. "Just back from the cemetery?"

"Yes, sir. It took a while for all the traffic to clear."

Hoffner hesitated. "Thank you for taking on that assignment. It was hot work today and it looks like you're suffering because of it."

Petchard lost the battle to keep his eyebrows from jumping on his forehead. Appreciation of any kind from the sheriff was rare, and over something as simple as traffic duty, was unheard of. But Petchard had never been one to miss an opportunity to brown nose. "Of course, sir. I was happy to do it. For the department and for Mojo."

Hoffner nodded. "Someone called and said there were kids playing behind the elementary school. Not on the playground, but near the administration building. Take a ride over and see what's going on."

Inwardly, Petchard groaned but he turned smartly on his heel before the sheriff could see his pained expression. "Don't worry, sir," he called over his shoulder. "Consider it done."

CHAPTER 120

JUNIE GRIMACED AND LIFTED a hand to her temple.

"You okay?" Stan Overheart asked. He took the tray of salt and pepper shakers and helped her into a chair.

"Headache."

"Looks like a bad one."

She opened one eye. "It's a whopper."

Sally put her bony hand on Junie's forehead. "No fever. It's probably from the heat this morning. Although you've looked a little peaked lately. You might've picked up a bug."

Stan checked his watch. "Go home. Get some rest and come back tomorrow morning if you feel up to it."

"Are you sure?"

"Yeah. Can you drive? We can close up and run you home."

"It's okay. I'll drive slowly."

"Call if you need anything," Sally said.

Junie managed a smile. "Definitely."

Chapter 121

CASS STARED AFTER THE skinny morgue assistant as he left the conference room. "Maybe it is true."

"That Joseph's the one who's alive?" Darla asked. "Are you serious?"

Mitch nodded.

His pretty wife sat back, frowning. "Why?"

"We're not sure yet, but it's a dangerous decision, being Moses."

"Well, I doubt he's doing it for fun, Mitch. There must be a very serious reason for him to pretend to be Moses."

"That's what worries me."

The conference room door opened and Mayor Rusted's round face peered in. "May I join you?"

"Sure," Mitch said. "What can we do for you?"

The mayor pulled his bulk into the room and closed the door. "I understand that you're making progress on the murders."

"Did you talk to the sheriff?"

"At the cemetery." The mayor wiped a sheen of sweat from his face with a handkerchief. "You've learned more about Calvin Whitehead's life? Found an old trunk of his?"

Mitch nodded slowly. "We did."

"Is it true that he was a Klansman?"

"It looks that way, although we've found no indication that he was active in this area."

"I see." Mayor Rusted shuffled toward the table. "You found nothing else unusual?"

"How do you mean?" Mitch asked.

"If he was Klan at one point, he could've belonged to other immoral groups at some time." He leaned closer. "The Church of the True Believer, perhaps?"

Mitch studied the fat man, his gaze inscrutable. "We've found no indication that he had a connection to The Church, Mayor."

"Good, good." Mayor Rusted straightened, rubbing his hands together. "Well, it's good to know they're not active again. That was a nasty business. And the investigations into the Franklin and Moore murders?"

"Coming along."

"Good," he repeated, reaching for the door. "Well, I'll leave you to your work. Thank you, Detectives."

With a soft click, he was gone. Mitch stared after him.

"What's wrong?" Cass asked.

"I've never known him to take an interest in an investigation before."

"He was curious about the whole Church of the True Believer thing, remember?"

"He was."

"It worries you?"

"It's probably nothing."

Cass cleared her throat. "You came to the courthouse to check on something. What was it?"

"I'd hoped that Sheriff Studebaker would have some news about Calvin Whitman's son. And I wanted to go over those files on Jackson, Holland, and Ross to see if there's anything about their murders that links back to our little killing trio."

"Did you check with Hoffner?"

He reached for the stack of files in the middle of the conference room table. "Darla took him a plate of food earlier. He's still waiting for Studebaker to call."

"Do you want help with those files?"

"No, I'd rather do it myself."

Cass touched Maxine's newspaper clipping in her pocket. "I'll go see if Kado needs a hand with anything."

"I'm sure he'll be happy to have your hand helping with anything," Mitch said.

Heat rushed up Cass's neck and cheeks. "What's that supposed to mean?"

Darla smacked her husband's shoulder and he winced. "He watches you, Cass. Maxine noticed and so did I," Darla said, leaning close. "Last night at the Franklin house. Today at the cemetery. And he seems like a nice guy. What's wrong with getting to know him a little better? It's not like you're dating anybody."

Cass looked back and forth between Mitch and Darla, two people who loved her as much as her own family did, and took a big step. "He lost his wife not long ago."

Darla nodded. "Kado told me about it."

"He did?"

"Yes. It was a horrible experience. I think it broke his heart to lose Caroline, but he's healing now."

"I'm not interested in being the rebound girlfriend."

"I don't think he's that kind of guy, Cass. He's not pinballing from woman to woman, trying to mask the pain of losing his wife. Kado's grieved for her, maybe still is grieving, but I think he's someone you can trust."

"And he's got the hots for you," Mitch repeated, dodging Darla's smack. "If he's mean to you, Bruce and Harry will punch him out."

"That did wonders for my dating game in high school." She drew a deep breath. "Okay." She cut her eyes at Mitch. "I'll go ask if he wants that hand. We'll see what happens next."

CHAPTER 122

PETCHARD MADE THE TRIP to the elementary school in record time. He circled the buildings and found a pile of cigarette butts near a back door, but no kids or open windows or doors. He reported in to the dispatcher that all was clear and then hurried back to the square.

Inside The Golden Gate Café, he slipped the mirrored sunglasses onto his forehead. Junie was nowhere in sight. Petchard nodded at an older couple seated in the corner booth and then waved to Sally Overheart in the kitchen. She slid plates of food onto a tray and met him at the counter. "Goodness, that's some sunburn. Have you put any aloe on it? I have a plant in the kitchen."

"That's okay," he said, wondering what kind of freaky new age voodoo aloe was. "I thought Junie was working after the funeral."

"You just missed her," Sally said, filling glasses with iced tea. "She had a headache. Stan told her to take the afternoon off."

"Is she all right?"

"A little dehydrated after the funeral. She'll be fine." Sally handed him a take-away cup and hefted the tray. "She's been gone about twenty minutes. Give her a call; I'm sure she'd love to see you."

Petchard thanked her and sat at a table. He slipped his cell phone out but hesitated before dialing Junie's number. For the first time in their relationship, he was confused about her feelings for him. There was something different about her today. She'd been distant, almost distracted. Which was worrying. Junie always paid close attention to everything Petchard said, hung on his every word, but this morning at the church and at the cemetery, he'd found her gaze locked on Mojo more than once. When he asked if she was all right, she smiled and re-engaged in the conversation, but kept sending surreptitious glances at Mojo. Seeing his fellow officer climbing from Junie's car had been almost too much. Mojo hadn't returned to the station this afternoon. No one would expect him to, of course, but Petchard wondered where he was now.

At that thought, the green-eyed monster woke and raked its claws through Petchard's bowels. He responded by snapping the phone closed, waving good-bye to Sally, and stepping back into the oppressive heat. Sweat popped out on his forehead and between his shoulder blades and Petchard sucked the last of his iced tea while slipping his shades back on. Trotting toward the square, Petchard's mind crawled with images of Mojo sitting in a booth: Junie smiling as he ordered; touching his shoulder; offering a comforting word. A man who had set foot in The Gate perhaps twice in his whole life now practically considered it his home away from home. And combined with Junie's reluctance to spend time with Petchard this week, there was only one conclusion that worked.

Stomach churning, he glanced at his watch. It was against policy for an officer to use his personal vehicle for business purposes, but Petchard reasoned that he wasn't going to see Junie on business. Instead of rounding the courthouse to pick up his cruiser, he made a beeline for his pickup.

CHAPTER 123

A CLOUD OF DUST stirred up by the young herd hung heavy in the mid-afternoon air. The old man studied his pasture with a practiced eye and wondered how long he could afford to feed this crop of calves. His Bermuda grass, normally full and lush by now, was brown and dry enough to burn. If the rains didn't come, and soon, he'd have to sell most of his stock. The cost of rebuilding his herd and his pastures would be enormous if this drought continued.

His phone chirped and the old man put his truck in park. "David Wayne? News?"

"We're clear," Mayor Rusted panted. "They've found nothing to link Calvin Whitehead to The Church."

The old man studied the yearling heifers in their portable corral. Hitch and his crew were sorting the cattle for branding or a trip to the sale barn. The process was running smoothly, with little upset to the young animals. Hitch seemed to have a way with them, and had selected men who were experienced in handling cattle. The old man slipped his pipe between his lips and puffed. "How do you know this, Mayor?"

"I asked."

The old man spat the pipe out. "You did what?"

"I asked Detective Stone if there was any link between Whitehead and The Church. He confirmed that there was not."

He rubbed his eyes with gnarled fingers. "David Wayne...," he began.

"I asked about the Franklin and Moore murders, for cover. They're none the wiser." The man's voice rose in pitch as though sensing the old man's disapproval.

A rambunctious heifer broke away from the cowboy who was holding her. He grabbed a lasso and the rope floated through the air. With help from his partner, he pulled the heifer in, rolled her onto her side, and branded her. She was up and he was pushing her toward a gate before she knew what had happened. The old man lowered his window and the smell of burned hair and hide wafted in on air hot enough to bake bread.

He slipped the pipe back between his teeth. "Let it rest, David Wayne, and let's see what happens next."

"Of course," the mayor answered, relief in his voice. "I wanted you to know that we're safe."

"I appreciate it. We'll have no further contact unless something unexpected happens, agreed?"

"Agreed."

The old man snapped his phone shut and wondered if Mayor David Wayne Rusted had outlived his usefulness, and settled in to watch and wait. Hitch was home, and if the mayor acted rashly in the future, it would be short work to shut him down.

CHAPTER 124

CASS OPENED THE DOOR to the forensics room to see Kado positioning a digital camera over a piece of paper. She waited while he took several photos. "What is that?" she asked when he straightened.

"A long shot."

"What do you mean?"

"These are the envelopes used to deliver the letters about Mojo."

Cass blanched. "Fingerprints?"

Kado nodded and transferred the images to his computer and labeled them.

"Did you fume them?"

"No, this is something new. I soaked some bond paper with a solution of ninhydrin and acetone, let it dry, then sandwiched each envelope between two pieces of the treated paper to let the solution soak in on either side. All you have to do is run a hot iron over the sandwich and the prints show up."

"How many did you get?"

"Maybe two dozen on all five envelopes. If I don't get anything from these, I'll look for prints on Emmet's letters." He loaded the first fingerprint into IAFIS and set the system running. When he turned to her, his face was flushed and the words tumbled from his mouth. "I need to apologize for jumping you like that yesterday." He drew a steadying breath. "I owe you an explanation. You know that my wife died not long ago?"

She nodded.

"I haven't even been interested in women since then. Until I met you, looking at a woman was like looking at a piece of furniture."

Cass waited.

"But you're different. Do you remember the first time we met?"

She smiled. "I do."

"I'd been out at the hot house that burned, the one where somebody was growing marijuana. I'd been up all night, smelled like bad barbeque, and was covered in ash. Old Comfrey left the forensics lab in a mess and I was wondering how I'd ever get it organized and manage all the normal forensic work. In other words, I was totally distracted. But seeing you in the squad room knocked the air out of me." Kado looked at the computer screen and loaded another fingerprint. "It was the first time I'd felt a hint of life since Caroline died. And then I didn't feel anything but guilt. For most of my life, she was the only woman for me. We were perfect for each other. Thinking about you, being attracted to you, it felt like I was betraying her. I thought that if I didn't let you have any space in my head that I could get rid of you, of the way you made me feel."

"Did it work?"

"No." Kado sat in his desk chair and twirled gently from side to side. "Because you started showing up in my dreams. And Caroline started to fade away."

"I'm sorry," Cass said in a low voice.

Kado's face was pale now. "Before she died, Caroline told me that if I loved her, I'd keep breathing so that one day, I could live again. That's the most selfless thing I've ever heard anyone say. And I promised her that I would try."

Cass's heart was pounding and she leaned into a cabinet, careful not to bump the microscope. "Why are you telling me this now?"

His gaze was intense. "All the death this week has made me realize how uncertain life is. I knew it from Caroline's death, but we had time to plan for that. Mrs. Franklin, Joseph, Donna Moore, Calvin Whitehead. They didn't know what was coming for them, had no idea that they would die this week." Kado looked down at his hands and his voice was quiet. "You've let me breathe again. I have to know if we can even try to have a relationship."

She drew a slow breath, allowing her lungs to fill to the point of bursting before slowly releasing the air. Kado was offering her something she hadn't considered possible in years, a chance to have a normal relationship. For the first time since the rape, she reached out instead of closing in, and said, "Yes."

His gray eyes shot up to meet hers, a careful hope in them. "Yes?"

"Yes. We can try." She held up a hand as he started to speak. "I understand that you're still dealing with," she hesitated, "Caroline's death. I get that. But as a disclaimer, you should know that there are things about my life that are screwed up. Things that make me who I am, but that I've never talked about."

"Do you want to talk now?"

"Maybe not ever. But how about we try over dinner tonight?"

A dimple dove deep into his cheek when Kado smiled, and he turned back to the computer. "Dinner's good. Did you come in for something specific, or just to hear me spill my guts?"

"Does that ninhydrin soaked bond trick work on any type of paper?"

"Most types, yes."

Cass pulled the bagged note from her pocket and held it out to him. Kado read it and looked up. "'Talk and I'll cut them off. I'm watching.' What is this?"

"It's one of those things that make me who I am, and that I've never talked about. Can that be enough for now?"

His nod was slow. "What do you want me to do with it?"

"Lift some prints and run them."

Without a word, he gloved up and took the note from its baggie, then slipped it between two pieces of ninhydrin impregnated bond and placed the tray in a cabinet.

Maybe Maxine is smarter about men than I give her credit for, she thought. "How long?"

"A few hours." His computer dinged and he turned. "You idiot," he breathed. "Smart enough to keep your prints off the letters but not off the envelopes."

Cass peered over his shoulder. "I can't believe he has the brains or the balls to write letters like that." She spun on her heel and headed for the door.

"Where are you going?" Kado called.

"To find Rob Conroy," Cass said, "and finish him."

CHAPTER 125

"YOU'RE SURE THIS IS it?" Joseph asked.

Emmet nodded. "Not much to look at, is it?"

"On a waitress's salary, maybe it's all she can afford."

"Don't forget her cousin. If they came to Arcadia to hunt us, he's probably staying here, too. No point in spending extra money on rent." He studied the old house and barn. "It's quiet. I'm going to take a closer look."

"He might be here."

"Or he might not. Cover me while I head for the barn. Ready?"

Joseph nodded when he really wanted to shake his head, and watched, gun ready, as Emmet crouched and ran across the overgrown patch to the back of the weathered barn. Their trip through the pasture and woods had been uneventful, but Joseph's senses prickled with each step, sure that someone was watching. As Emmet peeked inside the filthy windows at the back of the barn, Joseph scanned the trees around the house and spotted a security light on a pole, but no cameras. Emmet waved him forward.

"There's nothing in the barn but tools and an old pickup," Emmet told him. "Let's go check out the house."

Over Joseph's whispered protests, Emmet squatted and peered around the corner to examine the old farmhouse. After a moment he pulled his head back. "All the shades are drawn on this side. There's a small front porch, but I can't see much of it. There's probably a back door, and maybe a cellar. Come on."

He sidled to the barn's corner and took a look. "Cover me," he said, but before he could move Joseph grabbed his arm and dropped low to the ground. "What is it?" Emmet snapped.

"Listen," Joseph whispered.

Emmet's eyes widened as the sound of tires crunching across gravel reached them. The car drew closer and stopped, its engine idling. A chain rattled and protesting doors trundled open, then a car door slammed and the engine revved. They felt vibrations through the aged slats as a vehicle pulled into the old barn. Then the engine died, the doors slid back into place, and the chain rattled again.

They waited, but heard no door open. Emmet lowered himself to the ground, parting a patch of thigh-high Johnsongrass to watch the house. A door finally slammed and he lay prone for several minutes before pulling back and joining Joseph against the barn wall. "It's a chick. Junie," he whispered. "She walked around the house before going inside. I guess she was checking to see if anybody's been here since she left."

"Her cousin's not here?"

"Since she's checking the perimeter, probably not. Let's get inside."

Joseph put a hand on his arm. "What if she's sitting there, waiting for her cousin or watching TV? What then?"

"She's just come in from work and will be distracted getting changed, or whatever chicks do when they get home. No time like the present, man. Let's go."

Emmet checked the house again and with Joseph covering him, darted for its side. Joseph followed, heart pounding. His eyes widened as a mechanical rattling started and settled into a steady hum. A chugging whine followed.

"Air conditioner," Emmet said. "Window unit. And a water well."

Joseph drew a deep breath and released it. "What are we going to do?"

"Find Junie and make her tell us who's trying to shoot our asses. It's that simple." He studied his friend with somber eyes. "It's still not too late to back out, Joseph. I can do this alone. Go back to the car and wait."

"No." A drop of sweat fell from Joseph's nose. "I'm in."

Emmet nodded. "It's gonna get nasty. No two ways about it. Stay behind me and don't pull the trigger unless you absolutely have to. And if you do shoot, try not to hit me." He turned then, and crept toward the back of the house.

CHAPTER 126

WITH ONE HAND PRESSED to her forehead, Junie reached behind the curtain and turned the shower on, then opened the medicine cabinet. The headaches had lost their intensity in the last few years and she could usually manage with over the counter painkillers. The prescription for Imitrex was long out of date; she hated the drug's side effects and avoided taking it unless the migraines grew unmanageable. A flash of pain stabbed behind her right eye. She leaned against the countertop and tried not to vomit, then twisted the child-proof cap and compromised, popping a single pill.

Holding her head as steady as possible, Junie stepped back in the bedroom and turned on the ancient air conditioner perched in the window. She'd snapped on the unit in the living room downstairs when she came in, planning to check the GPS units in the men's cars, but now decided to take a nap and let the drugs work. She stripped and checked the shower. In this old house, the water heater was located next to the kitchen, and it took ages for the hot water to make the climb up the ancient pipes to the second floor. Junie leaned into the mirror to examine her face. Eye liner and lipstick were a hassle to remove, and she couldn't be bothered.

She stepped under the shower and closed her eyes, letting the scalding water wash over her shoulders and back. The drug eased into her system and her bunched muscles relaxed. The last few days were the longest she could remember and the lack of sleep was taking a toll on her physical and mental energy. Although the psychological stalking had been satisfying, it was time to draw the game to a close and blow this saccharine-sweet town. She could rest for a couple of hours and hopefully wake refreshed and without the headache. After tonight, Arcadia would be only so much fluff in her navel.

Junie soaped her slender body and was studying the small patch of pubic hair she'd left during her last waxing when she heard a faint chime. She froze. Water sluiced over her as she strained to listen. The sound was a quiet tone from a box in her bedroom that told her when a connection over a door or window was broken. Her mind raced and she tried to remember throwing the deadbolt, sliding the chain, and turning the lock on the doorknob when she came home, but couldn't. She blinked back the cocoon of pain relief, slipped from the shower and ran a towel over her body, fighting a sharp stab in her head. Alert for sound, she moved into her bedroom, dressed carefully but quickly, and reached under a pillow for her compact Glock 9 mm. She pulled a spare clip from a drawer in the bedside table and shoved it in her back pocket.

A creak sounded and Junie recognized it as coming from the tired linoleum in the kitchen. She took three light steps across the room and eased into the hallway, her back pressed against the wall. The pain in her head ballooned and she stood perfectly still, waiting for it to reach its crescent. When the sharp stab started to subside, she started toward the stairs.

CHAPTER 127

EMMET SWORE UNDER HIS breath when the floor creaked. The pipes groaned as water ran through them, covering the sound of their movements. Emmet motioned for Joseph to take the door on the left side of the kitchen and indicated that he would take the door directly in front. They would clear the first floor and work their way up to and through the second floor.

Holding his breath, Joseph eased forward, testing the boards before he let his full weight come to rest on them. Emmet nodded approval and did the same. Joseph's door swung open without a sound and he found himself in a laundry room. A basket of clean, folded clothes sat on the olive green dryer. A peeling door with a rusty knob was ajar at the far end of the narrow space and Joseph moved toward it. He steeled himself and peeked around the open door to see faint light shining through the filthy glass panels flanking the front door. Another creak sounded and Joseph's heart raced. Emmet's determination to end this today seemed profoundly more insane than heroic. An image of his mother and brother's bodies flashed across his mind and Joseph swallowed hard against the fear rising hot in his throat.

He pressed his cheek to the door and held his gun in a two-handed grip like the cops did on television. The door swung open with a nudge. A staircase sat at the far side of the small foyer and he tiptoed over and leaned around the banister. The stairs were empty, dust motes almost motionless in a pale shaft of sunlight. He wiped a drop of sweat from his eye and took two steps toward a second door leading off the foyer when he sensed movement and felt a cold pressure against his skull.

Joseph froze. The pressure of the weapon eased as a figure leaped lightly over the handrail and landed behind him with barely a thump. The smell of soap followed.

Breath brushed the back of his neck. "Where is he?"

"Who?"

"Emmet."

Joseph swallowed. "I came alone."

The gun bumped the back of his head with enough force to smart. Joseph winced. "Where is he?"

"I don't know."

"In the house?"

Joseph hesitated and the weapon jammed the back of his head again. "Yes."

"Hold the gun by the barrel and lift your hands."

He did so and caught the pale flash of Junie's silhouette as she snatched the weapon from him. "Now or later, I have no problem blowing your brains out, Moses." She nudged him. "Forward."

He complied, turning the knob with one hand while keeping the other at shoulder height. The door swung open with a small squeak of the hinges and Joseph stopped in his tracks.

Emmet swiveled and aimed his weapon at them. "Shit."

"Place the gun on the floor and kick it to me."

With a blazing glare, Emmet did.

"The door to your right. Open it, go inside, and sit on the couch. One bullet to Moses' brain Emmet, and then I'll kill you, so play nicely."

Emmet grew still. "Who are you?"

"We have a lot to talk about, the three of us. Go inside and sit down." Joseph hesitated, watching Emmet for some sign to act. The gun's barrel stabbed his head and he stumbled forward, feeling blood trickle down his scalp.

CHAPTER 128

"I'M CHANGING THE TERMS of his parole," Fran Starkowsky huffed. "First floor apartments only."

Cass waited as Fran eyed the last three stairs to Rob Conroy's landing. Her dark funeral clothes were devoid of sequins and suitably somber, if still capacious. Fran lifted the skirt of her caftan, revealing shapely ankles and black patent stilettos, and marched up the steps. Cass was glad she'd taken the time to change into her usual button-down shirt, Dockers, and boots at the station.

Fran positioned herself to one side of the door and reached into the depths of her garment, extracting an ID wallet and gun. Cass motioned the apartment complex's manager farther along the balcony. At Fran's nod, Cass pounded on the door. "Police, Conroy. Open up."

Slathering barks sounded through the door.

Cass raised her voice. "Come on Rob, open up. We know you're in there."

Still nothing. Fran cooed and the barking changed to an excited whine. Cass reached for the doorknob. It twisted at her touch and she looked up at Fran, whose expression sobered. She nodded and Cass pushed inward, squatting and stepping inside, a surprisingly agile Fran at her back. The large black woman swooped the pit bull up in her arms and shushed the dog.

The apartment's interior was in gloom and it took Cass's eyes a moment to adjust. A hump on the sofa turned out to be a ratty blanket and a stack of cushions. Fran moved lightly to the opposite side of the room, the now placid dog cradled in one massive arm, and lifted a pile of clothes with the tip of a shoe and grimaced. The apartment manager's head popped into view in the open door and Cass waved him back. "Where is he?" she whispered.

"I'll check the kitchen," Fran said. "You take the bedroom and bathroom. Don't think I could stand it in there."

Cass pushed open the only door off the living room to see a naked body sprawled facedown across a bed. A snore sounded and Cass sighed. She checked the closet and bathroom, grimacing at the filth. Holstering her gun, she pulled on a latex glove and lifted a corner of one dirty sheet to cover Conroy's moon-white bottom. She nudged the bed with her knee. "Wake up."

He grunted and flipped over, flailing his arms and legs and giving Cass an unfettered view of his partial erection. "Oh, Lord," she groaned, tossing a pair of sweatpants over the offending appendage. "Conroy!"

One eye fluttered when the fabric landed on his midsection. He knuckled the sleep gumming his eyes and then reached for his ears, extracting a pair of wax darkened plugs. A happy confusion clouded his face. "Now this is the kind of dream I'm talking about."

"Get up and put some clothes on. I'll be in the living room with Frannie."

He blinked. "A three-way? Is it Christmas?"

"Your pecker would explode, Conroy. Get dressed." She retreated and ordered over her shoulder, "Take a shower first. You reek."

CHAPTER 129

DARLA STONE GASPED. SHE was standing behind Scott Truman and Bernie Winterbottom, staring as an image filled the computer screen. "Who is that?"

"Calvin Whitehead," the young officer answered. "In his younger days. Why?"

Darla looked at Mitch. "You didn't mention that Calvin Whitehead had a daughter."

"He doesn't," Mitch answered. "Not according to the sheriff in Thayerville."

She turned back to the computer screen. "Hugo Petchard's girlfriend Junie is a dead ringer for this man."

Munk pulled Mitch's wheelchair to the corner where Truman sat, and they examined the shot of the young Calvin Whitman. "I've only seen her once or twice," Munk said. "But she's got the same dark hair and eyes, and her face is the same shape."

"If Whitehead didn't have a daughter, do you think she's a relative?" Mitch asked.

"Mitch Stone, I swear to you that this girl is Whitehead's daughter." Darla tapped Truman on the shoulder. "She must be in her late thirties or early forties, right?"

The young officer shrugged. "Probably."

"And Calvin Whitman didn't come to Arcadia until 1980 or so?"

"'Seventy-nine," Munk answered.

"Then this is his child from Alabama. Maybe she was born out of wedlock, but she's his." Darla studied the young Calvin Whitman again. "I'd bet a dinner of my fried chicken, mashed potatoes with gravy, butter beans, and a Texas sheet cake on it."

"With pecans in the icing?" Mitch asked.

Darla nodded.

"Bernie, what do you think? Could Junie be Calvin Whitman's daughter?"

The English forensic anthropologist studied the photo of Calvin Whitman. "I don't believe I know the young lady in question. I'd need an image of her to compare to Whitman."

Darla opened her phone. Mitch groaned and she shrugged. "I was discreet, and I wanted to compare her to Angelina Jolie."

Bernie asked Truman to load the photograph onto the computer. He did so, and displayed the images side by side.

"Amazing," Mitch said.

"There's a strong resemblance," Bernie agreed. "They could easily be from the same family. Did Calvin Whitman have any brothers or sisters?"

"According to the sheriff in Thayerville, no. Neither did Whitman's wife."

"So she isn't a niece." Bernie asked Truman to enlarge Junie's picture. "Her features are similar to Whitman's. The jaw, for example, is wide and rather square. See how it drops almost straight down from her ear and then angles to the chin? Just as Whitman's does. And her chin has a flat base that gives it a square appearance. The eyes and nose are very similar to his. I can't tell about her brow given that her hair is brushed forward." He paused. "Actually, that's a bit strange."

"What's strange, Bernie?" Mitch asked.

He cocked his head to one side. "I hesitate to mention this because I can't tell if there's an Adam's apple given that she's wearing a scarf around her neck, but these are very masculine features."

"What are you saying?" Darla asked.

"My observations are inconclusive, my dear," Bernie said. "But there is a distinct possibility that she is actually a he."

CHAPTER 130

ROB CONROY EMERGED FROM his bedroom washed but naked and flexed for the two women. Cass winced. Fran Starkowsky held up a talon-tipped hand. "No sir, Robbie boy. We are not having this conversation with your tiny todger winking at us. Cover that little worm up. And the rest of you."

Conroy 'woofed' and waggled his hips, then pranced back to his bedroom.

"He's cheerful," Cass said, grimacing at the sound of her shoes on the sticky kitchen floor. "You think he's tripping?"

Fran chewed her darkly painted lower lip. "If he's not using already, it won't be long."

He emerged again, this time dressed in saggy sweats and a grimy University of Texas shirt. He squatted to kiss Rosie on the head and the dog licked his chin. "I need coffee."

"Why aren't you at work?" Fran asked.

"They shut down for the funerals." He sauntered into the kitchen and lifted the coffee pot from its machine. Brown sludge filled the bottom third. Conroy made a cursory effort to rinse the pot, then filled it with water and poured the goo back into the coffee maker. He pulled the basket out, dumped new grinds on top of the existing soggy pile and pushed the 'on' button. A box of sugary cereal was on the counter. Conroy stuck a hand in and ate them dry. He ran a forearm under his nose. "So, no sex?"

Cass flashed him a warning glance.

"Can't blame a man for trying. What do you want?"

"You've threatened an officer of the law, Rob," Fran said. "Do you realize what kind of trouble you're in?"

"Threatened who? With what?"

"Moses Franklin, you idiot."

Conroy rolled his eyes. "What a whiner. I said hello to the man at The Golden Gate this morning and told him I was sorry for his loss."

"We know about the letters," Cass said.

"What letters?"

"We've got your prints on a letter sent to Sheriff Hoffner."

Conroy wrinkled his nose. "I don't write letters."

"Your fingerprints say otherwise," Cass said. "If your memory is that bad, we can continue this discussion down at the courthouse."

Conroy sprinkled cereal on the floor for Rosie, then filled his mouth. The coffee pot gurgled and Conroy poured, unstuck the top from a sugar bowl, and dumped a cascade of the white granules in his cup. "I'm not going anywhere. The only stuff I mail is bills."

"How did your fingerprints get on the envelope of a letter about Moses?" Cass asked.

He frowned. "They could've transferred from one of my bills or something."

"Highly unlikely."

"Well, maybe I touched it somewhere."

"Like where?"

He sipped, and then his eyes brightened. "What did it look like?"

"What?"

"The envelope. What color and size? Handwritten address or typed? Stamped or franked? Return address or not?"

"Standard white envelope. Address handwritten. Stamped. No return address. Mailed from Arcadia."

"I swear." He poured the rest of the coffee in a bowl for Rosie. "No good deed goes unpunished."

"What are you talking about?" Cass demanded.

"All I did was pick up a letter for a woman. She dropped it and being the gentleman that I am, I picked it up."

"What woman?"

"That hot chick who works at the café."

"Last time I was in The Golden Gate, only Stan and Sally were there," Fran said. "Who are you talking about?"

"A waitress. She's been there a few weeks," Cass answered absently. She spoke to Conroy. "Junie dropped a letter and you picked it up?"

"I tried to give it back but she asked if I'd put it in the mailbox. So I did."

"When was this?"

Rosie finished her coffee and jumped up on Conroy, nosing him in the groin. He rubbed her ears. "I dunno. Few days ago. Day before yesterday. Yeah, Thursday. Why? Is she threatening ol' Moses? Maybe she's a better shot than the last person who tried to kill him."

"Watch yourself, Robbie," Fran said.

"I'm not threatening Officer Franklin. But somebody's out to get him."

Cass interrupted. "You think she's hot?"

"She reminds me of a skinhead down in Huntsville. Dark hair, strong face, tall drink of water, and sexy as they come. He was a tough one, too. A bit aloof, but I like them that need breaking in." He ground his hips in a provocative move.

"Enough," Cass said. Her mind was reeling. She lifted her chin at Fran. "Can I leave you with him?"

"Oh yes." The massive woman reached into her caftan and extracted a lidded cup. She shook it at Conroy and smiled. "It's time for Tiny Todger to perform, Robbie. Drop 'em and pee."

CHAPTER 131

PETCHARD WAS ENGAGED IN a lively conversation with himself about the likelihood that Junie had the hots for Moses Franklin when he rounded a curve on the little country road and slowed to a stop. A green Camry was backed into a dirt track. He frowned as he recognized the parking sticker in the windshield. The woman who drove it taught at the elementary school where Petchard spent his mornings pulling crossing duty. Did she live out here?

He twisted in the seat, getting his bearings. Petchard had chosen to come the back way to Junie's because she didn't know that he knew where she lived, and he wasn't sure he wanted her to know. From what he remembered, there were only remote farmhouses out this way. He stretched to look past the Camry and saw nothing but pasture and a busy bull mounting a cow. Why would a teacher leave her car out here? Petchard closed his eyes and pictured her face, trying to remember her name. The kids seemed to know and love her. Once when her Camry was first in line as he stopped traffic, a parent had encouraged her daughter to wave and say good morning.

"Say 'hello' to Mrs. Who?" Petchard muttered. "Sounded like wetter. Better. Cheddar. Deader. Edder. Fedder. Gedder. Hedder." His eyes opened. Maybe it wasn't the woman who was out here. Emmet Hedder was still missing. If Junie had a thing for Moses, was it possible she could be into Emmet, too? Petchard gasped as the green-eyed monster exploded in his gut. He clenched the steering wheel and punched the gas pedal, sending his truck fishtailing as he spun out toward the main road and Junie's house.

CHAPTER 132

A LIGHT ON HIS phone glowed and the sheriff snatched up the handset. "Hoffner."

"It's Sheriff Studebaker. I'm glad I caught you."

Hoffner relaxed. "Thank you for getting back to me so quickly."

"I'm not sure you'll want to hear what I've found out."

"Bad news?"

"Strange news. Thanks to some fierce phone work by my staff this morning, we've found Calvin Whitman's son."

Hoffner's mind landed on one of the leadership lessons his instructor had drilled into them: *inclusion.* "Hold on a minute, Sheriff. I'd like for my detectives to hear what you've got to say."

He put the call on hold and studied the buttons on his desk phone. Finally, Hoffner hurried down the hall to the conference room. Everyone was clustered near a computer in the corner. "Is anybody working on county business today?" he demanded.

Munk exchanged an expressionless glance with Mitch. "Bernie's helping us with Whitehead's murder. You need to see this, Sheriff."

"In a minute. Where's Elliot?"

"What do you need?"

Hoffner flushed. "To transfer a call from my phone to the one in here."

Truman spoke up. "I can do it."

Hoffner nodded. Truman wove his way out of the room and was back in a matter of seconds. He moved the phone from the coffee counter to the long table and pointed to a flashing red light. "That line."

Darla Stone reached for Mitch's wheelchair but Munk scooted her out of the way and maneuvered Mitch away from the computer. She spoke quietly. "Sheriff?"

His gaze softened. "Yes?"

"I'm waiting to take Mitch home when he's done, but I can wait outside if you'd like."

"I trust your discretion, Darla." Hoffner jabbed the button and everyone shifted to crowd near the table. "Sheriff Studebaker, are you still there?"

"I am."

"You're on speakerphone with the detectives and officers working Calvin Whitehead's murder. You said you found his son?"

"Yes, Sheriff, we did. Turns out he was working up in Tennessee." His voice crackled over the line and Truman jiggled the cord until the static cleared.

"And you said that's strange?"

"He's gone AWOL. Been missing for about six weeks now."

Mitch motioned for Sheriff Hoffner's attention, but he waved the detective away. "Why is that strange?"

"Because he's a SWAT sharp shooter. A highly valued employee. His boss said Whitman's never been a problem. They've checked his apartment and with his friends. There's no sign of foul play. It's like the man vanished into thin air."

CHAPTER 133

CASS PUSHED OPEN THE door to The Golden Gate. Her unease with what Rob Conroy told them had grown during the drive from his apartment back to downtown. She struggled to imagine the kind of problem Junie could have developed with Moses Franklin in the short time she'd lived in Forney County. She spotted Stan Overheart helping a customer and waited on one of the padded chrome stools at the counter. "Is Junie working today?" she asked once they were alone.

"She had a headache so I sent her home early."

"What do you know about her?"

"Tea?" When Cass nodded he poured them both a glass and sat next to her. "What's up?"

"I'm not sure. Maybe nothing."

Stan sipped his tea and straightened as his wife came to join them. "Cass is asking about Junie."

"Why?" Sally asked.

Cass hesitated. Stan and Sally Overheart had spent most of their adult lives running a music shop in the Haight-Ashbury section of San Francisco. Their retirement to Arcadia more than a decade ago was prompted by Sally, who wanted to run a café in her hometown. They were hippies, tried and true, and although the Overhearts were a respected part of the Forney County community, they remained wary about official intrusion into their lives. "It's probably nothing," Cass said, "but Rob Conroy mentioned something that I want to ask Junie about."

Stan raised an eyebrow. "Conroy the meth king?"

"That's him."

He looked at Sally and she nodded. "What do you want to know?"

"What's Junie's last name?" Cass asked.

"Archer."

"She's from Tennessee?"

"That's what her license said."

"Why did she come to Arcadia?"

Sally swiped at the counter with a damp rag. "She showed up one day and asked if we needed any wait staff. It was right after Mitch got hurt and you were suspended. The press was still here and it was crazy." She smiled at Stan. "We hadn't even thought that we needed help until she showed up, but she's been a blessing. Junie's a hard worker and doesn't complain, no matter what we ask her to do."

"But she's very private," Stan added. "When I've asked about her family, or where she grew up, she changes the subject. You get the feeling that she doesn't want to talk about her past."

"Have you noticed anything unusual about her?"

"Unusual how?"

"Has she done or said anything that makes you think she's not who she says she is?"

Stan played with the end of his ponytail and looked at Sally. "Tell her."

"I don't think it's any of our business." Sally crossed her arms over her skinny chest. "Much less that of law enforcement."

Gazes locked, Sally and Stan entered into a silent battle of marital wills that Cass observed with interest. Stan finally spoke. "Cass asked about unusual, and what she did is unusual."

"I'm sure there's a perfectly plausible explanation for it."

"Do you trust Cass?"

His wife nodded.

"Then tell her what you saw."

Sally scrubbed a non-existent spot on the counter before meeting Cass's eyes. "If I tell you this and it has no bearing on whatever you need to know, will you forget it?"

"Yes."

"This one afternoon, not long after Junie started working for us, I went to the ladies room and Junie came out of the men's room."

Cass looked back and forth between Stan and Sally. "Maybe she used the men's because the ladies was occupied."

"It was empty," Sally said.

Cass raised an eyebrow. "Maybe she was cleaning."

"Nope. Stan had already done that. And I wouldn't even have noticed," Sally said. "But the flush was wrong."

"There's a problem with one of the handles," Stan explained. "It sticks and you get a double flush. Even if you jiggle it. The plumber says it's a defect in the manufacturing."

"I still don't get it," Cass said. "Why does it matter that the toilet double flushes?"

"It's not the toilet handle that sticks," Stan said. "It's the handle to the urinal."

CHAPTER 134

PETCHARD SLID TO A stop in Junie's gravel drive and cut the truck's engine. Vision narrowed to a green-tinged tunnel, he stormed to the porch and jabbed at the doorbell. The chime sounded clearly, and although he heard no movement over the air conditioner's wheezing, he sensed the house growing still. He peered through the sheer curtains protecting the dirty window in the door, but the interior was dim. Stepping back, he took the time to turn and look around the yard. Petchard spotted the barn with its doors chained shut. He crossed the small yard and went up on his tiptoes to peek through a grimy window. Junie's battered Honda was inside. She was home. And ignoring him. Or…

His gut clenched and Petchard whirled to face the house again. If Emmet Hedder was here, maybe Junie was trapped. In danger. Perhaps she hadn't answered the doorbell because she *couldn't* answer the doorbell. He dropped to a crouch and crept back to the farmhouse, easing around its perimeter. Curtains were tightly drawn over each window. A well pump clicked and whined in the backyard. As quietly as he could, he mounted the steps to the front porch again and reached for the doorknob. It refused to turn. He tiptoed back down, circled to the back of the house, and tried the kitchen door. The knob turned.

Petchard swallowed and pulled his gun from its holster, then slowly pushed inward.

Chapter 135

"SHERIFF STUDEBAKER? THIS IS Detective Mitch Stone. Can I ask you a question?"

Hoffner glared.

"Of course," Studebaker answered.

Mitch leaned closer to the phone. "How certain are you that Calvin Whitman never had a female child?"

"While he lived here, he only had the one child, a son. But he may have had another child after he left Thayerville."

"You told Sheriff Hoffner that Calvin Whitman Jr. was abused. What evidence do you have of that abuse?"

"Mostly rumors. But we had suspicions that Boyd Dudley, the man Whitman chose to care for his son, abused the boy. There was speculation that he let others abuse him, as well."

"Sexually?" Kado almost whispered the word.

"Pardon?" Sheriff Studebaker asked.

Kado straightened. "This is Tom Kado, sir, forensic examiner. Was the abuse physical or sexual?"

"Probably both. It was one of those secrets that everybody knew but nobody talked about. There was speculation that Dudley sold the boy as a prostitute. Child services took him away from Dudley once, when he turned up at the emergency room with a cigarette burn on his neck."

Darla's eyes flashed and Mitch put his hand over hers. "They didn't keep him?" he asked.

"Dudley told child services that the kid was prone to play with his matches and cigarettes, and burned himself."

"They believed him?"

"They gave the kid back to him. Before he left Thayerville when he was sixteen, the boy had withdrawn from his friends and his teachers. He was a bright kid and did very well in school until his father died. Then his grades started to slip and his behavioral problems started."

"What kind of problems?" Sheriff Hoffner asked.

"Fist fights, skipping school, drinking at an early age." Sheriff Studebaker said. "The boy even wore make-up and dressed as a girl for a while. Apparently it was a fad with some of the musicians back then. I was relieved to find out he'd turned his life around and became a law officer. You seem focused on Whitman's son. Do you think he's involved in his father's murder?"

"We have absolutely no evidence of that," Sheriff Hoffner said.

"But we do have a woman who's new in town. She bears a striking resemblance to the photograph of a young Sheriff Calvin Whitman that your department sent across," Mitch added. "We're trying to figure out who she could be."

"What's her name?" Sheriff Studebaker asked.

"Junie Archer."

Static crackled on the line and Truman wiggled the cord.

"Sheriff?" Mitch asked.

"I'll be damned," Studebaker said slowly. "Calvin Whitman's wife was an Archer. She died while giving birth to his son. Whitman named the child after himself. We called the boy Junior, or sometimes Junie or June. That's a mighty big coincidence, but I suppose it's possible that there are women named Junie Archer who have no relation to the Whitman family."

"I doubt there are many who resemble Calvin Whitman so closely," Mitch said. "Is it possible that Calvin Whitman, Jr. is a cross dresser?"

"A man who wears women's clothes? I think he'd outgrown that stage by the time he left Thayerville, but I have no idea. The men on the Tennessee force had nothing but praise for him, so if he is dressing up, he's doing it very quietly."

Hoffman's hoary eyebrows rose on his forehead. "What do you make of all this, Sheriff Studebaker?"

"It's curious that a Junie Archer has turned up in the same town where Calvin Whitman was living. The Calvin Whitman Jr. on the Tennessee force was definitely a man." He was silent for a moment. "I'd like to see a photograph of Junie Archer if you have one. But if you think she looks that much like Calvin Whitman, maybe the cross-dressing thing holds water. In your shoes, I'd want to talk to her. She could very well be the perp who murdered Calvin Whitman in your jurisdiction."

"I don't think so, Sheriff," Mitch said slowly. "We believe it was the children of the men lynched in 1967 who killed him, and Whitman's son who killed them."

"How would Calvin Whitman Jr. even know those people? And why would he want to avenge the death of the man who abandoned him?"

"Maybe they deprived him of what he desperately wanted," Mitch said. "The chance to kill the man who left him with that monster Boyd Dudley."

CHAPTER 136

EMMET HEDDER WATCHED AS Junie turned up the fan on the rattling window unit and pressed the hand holding the gun against her temple. Beads of sweat dotted her upper lip and her face was pale, but her gaze never left them. With her free hand, she adjusted the heavy curtains, releasing an army of motes to dance in a golden strip of sunlight. The blond cop sitting on the couch sneezed. Junie pointed the Glock at them and took a short-barrel 12-gauge shotgun from behind an armchair. It trembled slightly and Emmet's mind clicked into nursing mode. He'd never seen the woman before today, but her movements were on the sluggish side and he was willing to bet that she was either in pain or doped up. Maybe both. He shifted on the sofa and her glance flew to him. Her chocolate brown eyes were clouded. *Pain*, Emmet thought. *A migraine.*

She raised an eyebrow. In spite of her slow movements, her voice was clear. "I hadn't counted on tying up my loose ends so easily. This will be downright fun."

"Who are you?" Emmet asked. This was the first time he'd had an opportunity to speak since the cop tiptoed into the living room, right into Junie's grasp.

She smiled, but stayed silent.

"What's going on?" the cop asked. As Junie had herded Emmet and Joseph into this dusty little room, they'd heard the grumble of an engine and tires sliding across gravel. Continuing to hold the gun on them, Junie deftly parted the curtains and released a groan. She'd put a finger to her lips and waited patiently as the officer snuck inside after pounding on the front door. A muted chime sounded from a small box on the mantle as he opened the kitchen door. They'd listened as he worked his way through the house, eventually easing the living room door open and stepping over the threshold, leading with his gun. It took Junie only a moment to disarm him and steer him to the same couch where Emmet and Joseph sat. Now he was perched on its edge, hands clasped between his knees. He was badly sunburned, even the scalp peeking between his thinning crew cut was glowing a furious red. Still, he sat quietly, green eyes darting between Junie and the two men, his expression alternating between confusion and anger. The black name tag pinned to his shirt read 'Petchard'.

"Junie, what did they do to you?"

"What did they do to me?" Her lips curved in a small smile. "That's sweet, lover. What are you doing here?"

His Adam's apple bobbed as he swallowed. "I, um, went by The Golden Gate and Sally said you didn't feel well. I wanted to check on you."

She studied his uniform. "Are you still on the clock?"

"Technically, yes."

"Who knows you're here?"

"Nobody."

"Are you sure, lover?"

He nodded.

"And how do you know where I live? I'm sure I've never mentioned my address."

"I followed you home once." Her face darkened and he hurried on. "You were so secretive about where you lived, Junie. I just wanted to know in case you ever needed anything. So I could get here in a hurry."

"You're sneakier than I thought," Junie said. "I wish I'd known. You could've been much more useful."

Petchard licked his lips. "Junie, what are they doing here?" He glanced at the guns in her hands. "If they've hurt you in some way, I'll arrest them and that'll be that."

"That's sweet, Hugo, but I don't think they'll cause trouble for anyone after today." Her attention shifted back to Emmet and Joseph. "We'll wrap our business up very quickly, in fact."

In spite of the air conditioner chugging in the window, a bead of sweat ran down Emmet's cheek. He fought the urge to swipe at it. "Who are you working with, Junie, and where is he?"

She pouted. "So, I'm unimportant?"

"As long as you have that shotgun pointed in my direction, you're very important."

"Wise. Who do you think I'm working with?"

"Calvin Whitman's son."

Junie looked at Joseph, a respectful smile on her face. "You weren't kidding this morning when you said you were getting close, Moses, were you?"

He stayed silent.

"Where is he?" Emmet asked.

"Not as far away as you might think."

"And what relation are you? Cousin?"

Junie changed then. It was nothing more than a relaxing of facial muscles, a drop of the shoulders, and the release of her diaphragm. "This is the one useful thing I learned from that deviant, Boyd Dudley," she answered in a huskier voice. "How to become someone else."

From the corner of his eye, Emmet caught the startled expression on Officer Petchard's face. Joseph gasped. In spite of the make-up, Junie's face had clearly become that of a man.

"You make a pretty good looking chick, Calvin. Can I call you Calvin, or do you prefer Junie?" Emmet asked.

She shifted again, her features becoming more feminine, her voice softer. "Let's go with Junie, since she's been so helpful here in Arcadia. When we're done, maybe I'll make it a permanent change."

Recognition dawned in Emmet's eyes. "That was you in the police car in Tennessee, wasn't it?"

She smiled and winced slightly.

"How did you trace us back to Arcadia?" And then he nodded. "If you're one of the state cops, you would've had access to all sorts of records."

"And people. I knew the woman at the car rental place. She was happy to let me have a look at the records for those two cars in exchange for a night out and a roll in the sack."

Movement caught Emmet's eye and he turned as Petchard gagged. The officer had paled beneath his sunburn and he was shaking. "You're a man?" he croaked.

She looked at him with tenderness. "I'm sorry I lied to you, Hugo, but I needed you to help me find them."

"But," he pointed at her chest, "you've got tits."

Junie laughed then, a sound of genuine pleasure. "And I thought you were so courteous. You've been a big help. And you're such an idiot that it's almost like killing a dumb, friendly dog." She shifted the Glock and steadied her aim. "But it's better for everyone if we take your genes out of the pool."

CHAPTER 137

CASS SQUEEZED INTO THE narrow drive beside Petchard's personal truck and turned down Aerosmith's "Dude Looks Like a Lady". Although Stan didn't have Junie's address, he had driven her home when a migraine put her out of commission. His directions were excellent, right down to the red mailbox by the road and the raggedy tire swing hanging from the tree in the front yard. Cass squinted into the sun streaming through the windshield, sweat prickling her scalp as soon as she cut the engine. A little farmhouse sat alone in a yard that was already dying in the scorching heat. A weathered barn was off to one side, two wide doors pulled together and secured with a shiny padlock. She rolled down a window. The stillness of the heavy afternoon was broken by a sputtering mechanical hum. She listened harder and realized that she was hearing a window air conditioning unit. Her phone rang.

"Where are you?" Mitch asked.

"Following a lead. Why?"

"What lead?"

"Kado found Rob Conroy's prints on one of the envelopes Moses' letters came in. Conroy denied he wrote them, but said he picked up a letter Junie dropped and she asked him to put it in the mail box."

"Of course she wrote the letters," he said in a matter of fact tone. "That actually makes sense." She strained to hear him as he muffled the phone to speak to someone else. "Where are you?"

"Junie's house."

"Inside?"

"Not yet."

"Good. Get away from there and wait for backup."

"What are you talking about? What's going on?"

"For once, would you do what I say and ask questions later?"

Cass cranked the engine and raised the window, relishing the cool air as it washed across her face. "Fine, O Exalted One. But why?"

"It's complicated. We think Junie Archer is Calvin Whitman's son."

She stopped, hand poised to slip the gear shift into reverse. "Say again?"

"Whitman's son was sexually abused by his guardian, Boyd Dudley, and probably others. They dressed him as a girl and Dudley might've sold the boy as a prostitute. The son disappeared from Thayerville when he was sixteen, and nobody knew where he was until today. Truman emailed a photo of Junie to the Sheriff over there. He confirmed that the girl looks like Calvin Whitman and his son, Junior, whose nickname was Junie. Archer was his mother's maiden name."

She squinted into the sun.

"Cass, are you there?" Mitch asked.

"He's a cross dresser? A transvestite?"

"I don't know the right word, but he's a dude that dresses like a chick."

"It's weird, but it fits with something Stan said about Junie using a urinal at The Golden Gate." She raised her sunglasses and studied the farmhouse. No movement. "Where did they find the son, Mitch? What was he doing?"

"He was in Tennessee working for the state troopers as a sharp shooter."

"A sniper? Do you think he killed the Franklins and Donna?"

"It's not clear yet, but maybe."

"His motive?"

"I don't know. But the men who were involved in the lynching, the men we think Emmet, Moses, and Donna killed, were probably tied up with Boyd Dudley."

"And might've abused him?"

"It's possible."

She pondered this. "Why did he come to Arcadia as a woman, Mitch? Why not come as himself?"

"Maybe he thought people would be nicer to him if he was a woman. Maybe he wants to have a sex-change operation. I don't know. Does it matter?"

"Whether he thinks of himself as a woman or a man, it might play into his mindset."

"I guess we'll figure that out later. For now, stand down until backup arrives."

"I can't, Mitch, I —"

"Cass," he said, groaning. "Would you please —"

Scratching sounds came through the phone and then Cass heard Sheriff Hoffner's voice. "Elliot?"

"Sir?"

"I am ordering you to move away from the Archer woman's house and wait until backup units arrive. Once we have the area secured, we'll decide how best to approach her. Do you understand me?"

"Sir, I just —"

She heard a sharp intake of breath. "Elliot, this is a direct order."

Cass hesitated, her gaze sliding to Petchard's pickup. She'd been back on duty for not quite three days, and already she was bucking the system. "Yes, sir."

"Good," Hoffner barked, then disconnected the call.

Cass cut the engine. "I *will* wait for backup. After I have a look around."

———————

PETCHARD'S FACE FLUSHED AND he tensed. Emmet's military experience let him visualize each move before Petchard made it, and he mentally prepared for the man's death. Time slowed. The officer's jaw clenched and he pushed to his feet, preparing to charge. Junie swung her arm in a blinding arc and pointed the Glock at the window, fired a single shot, and turned the gun back on Petchard, who froze mid-step. Joseph had flinched but was now perfectly still, leaning forward on the couch, hands hanging near his ankles. His eyes flicked to meet Emmet's and then returned to staring at the floor.

"Now look what you made me do," Junie complained. A cone of sunlight fell through a hole in the curtain and dust motes danced a dervish in the golden rod. She twitched the gun's barrel at Petchard, urging him back to the couch. He complied, crumpling into the worn cushions and hiding his face in his hands. Emmet could barely hear her soft woman's voice through the ringing in his ears. "Sit still while the grown-ups finish their conversation, Hugo. You're still important to me, lover. But not for long."

CASS FLATTENED ON THE seat as the shot rang out. Heart thrumming against her ribs, she peeked over the dash. Nothing moved, not even the leaves on the trees. She opened the truck's door, pushing it almost closed behind her. In a crouch, she backed between her truck and Petchard's and slipped behind the barn.

The late afternoon was once again quiet, the air conditioner's gurgling and hiccupping the only sounds. Cass eased her head up to look through the barn's grimy window. The interior was neatly organized, if dusty. Two vehicles were parked inside, a black truck and a rust-bucket of a Honda. Junie and Petchard were both still here.

She rubbed dirt from the window and studied the pickup. It was black from front to back; even the bumpers and hubcaps were painted. Cass lowered her head and swallowed hard, thinking back to the night she'd nearly been hit by a black pickup racing away from Deadwood Hollow. When the Grove boys' little orange Vega was smashed by someone fleeing the Hollow. The night Martha and Joseph Franklin and Donna Moore were killed. She peeked into the barn again and entered the truck's license plate number as a note on her phone. If this was the same vehicle, they should find orange paint on one of the bumpers, and that could tie Junie a little tighter to the murders.

Sliding down the barn's wall, she wiped sweat from her brow and refocused on the current situation. Petchard. That idiot. Leave it to Hugo to get involved with a murderous cross-dresser. She took a deep breath and continued to the far side of the barn where she dropped to the ground and peered around the corner. A patch of Johnson grass provided cover and she inched forward, gaze sweeping the small area. Still no movement. Cass flipped open her phone and pushed a button. "One shot fired from inside Junie's house, Mitch," she whispered. "How far out is backup?"

"Fifteen minutes, at least."

"Tell them to come in silent, no sirens. Park down the road and approach on foot. From what I've seen so far, all the curtains are drawn. There's a noisy air conditioner unit running, so unless Junie looks out the window and spots my truck, she won't know I'm here."

"Cass," Mitch growled. "Get away from that house."

"Petchard is in there."

"What?"

"You didn't give me a chance to tell you before. Petchard's truck is here. He must be inside. And as much as I'd like to leave him to her – or him, or whatever she is – I can't. If I can isolate their location, we'll have a better idea of how to proceed when the backup units get here."

"Cass –," he began, but she talked over him.

"Gunshot, Mitch. Imminent danger. There are overgrown bushes by the road. Tell the officers to use them for cover. I'm turning my ringer off but I'll call the lead officer when I know more. Who's running point?"

"Munk, but Cass –"

She snapped the phone shut and turned the ringer to mute. Eyes still scanning, Cass stepped out into the open and darted for the house.

CHAPTER 138

MITCH STARED AT HIS silent phone. He opened his mouth to speak and looked up. The conference room was almost empty. Upon realizing that Junie Archer was probably Calvin Whitman's son, Sheriff Hoffner ordered the officers to her house, instructed Kado to get ready to process a crime scene, and sent Elaine to the reception desk to organize more officers for backup. Only scruffy Englishman Bernie Winterbottom remained with Mitch, golden head stretched toward the computer in the corner, comparing the photographs of Junie Archer and Calvin Whitehead and Calvin Whitman.

Mitch's vision blurred as he recalled a mad dash down an overgrown, rutted trail several weeks ago. With just that image, the metallic bite of panic coated his tongue and his heart rate increased. His last attempt to help his partner ended with himself incapacitated and Cass left alone to face a violent cult. He wouldn't desert her again. He blinked away the memory and cleared his throat. "Bernie?"

"Yes, Mitchell?"

"Can you drive over here? I mean, in the U.S.?"

"Of course."

"I need a ride to the Archer house." Mitch dug his keys from his pocket. "My truck is parked out front."

Bernie turned to him. "Are you sure that's wise?"

"It's pure stupidity. But I have to get out there. I can't let Cass deal with this alone. Not again." He drew a deep breath. "Either you drive, or I do. Are you game?"

Bernie stood, smoothed down his rumpled safari jacket, and crossed the room to take the keys. "We'll go out the back door so Elaine doesn't see us."

Mitch's smile was thin. "Subterfuge. That's good. We can use a man like you on the force, you know."

"Thank you, Mitchell," Bernie said, maneuvering the wheelchair through the conference room door. "But your job requires interaction with the living. I prefer dealing with the dead. It's much less complicated."

CHAPTER 139

KADO DASHED IN FRONT of Truman's truck with his forensic kit raised. Squad cars squealed around them and out of the parking lot, sirens blaring. Truman slammed on the brakes and Munk jerked forward against the seat belt. Kado ran to the passenger side and yanked opened the door. "Move. I'll get in the backseat."

"This is not a good idea," Munk grumbled as he unfastened his seat belt. "Are you armed?"

Kado climbed past him. "Got a spare?"

Munk slammed the door and slapped his seat belt back on as Truman sped out of the parking lot. "Have you ever shot one?"

"I carried in Oklahoma. Old Comfrey didn't, so Sheriff Hoffner saw no reason to issue me a gun. Do you have a spare?"

Still watching the road, Truman reached down and fiddled with his ankle holster. He passed it over the seat to Kado. "Be careful with it," he warned. "My mom gave it to me."

"Not your dad?" Munk asked.

An eyebrow arched above Truman's mirrored shades. "Mom's always been the more practical of the two."

"Do either of you know the area where Junie Archer lives?" Kado asked.

Truman nodded. "It's kind of remote. There aren't many houses around."

"Any ideas on how to handle a hostage situation?"

Munk and Truman exchanged a glance. "We've only had one here in the last ten years or so," Munk explained. "And that was some serious redneckery."

"What happened?"

"A bubba took his girlfriend hostage after she set his restored Mustang on fire."

"Ouch," Kado said. "Why'd she do that?"

"He'd tossed her clothes, shoes, and bags into the pen where he fattened up wild hogs."

"Moron. How did you end it?"

Truman cringed. Munk sighed. "We didn't."

"What do you mean?"

"Somehow, she ended up with a shotgun and killed him."

"That's not promising."

"On the plus side, she rid Forney County of one righteous asshole and saved the taxpayers a load of money," Truman said.

"How's that?" Kado asked.

"We suspected he was moving drugs and weapons, but couldn't catch him at it. She did save us the cost of a trial," Munk conceded. His phone rang. "Mitch?"

He pressed his free hand against his ear. "Say again?... She isn't?... Bernie? Mitch, that's not a good... I know, I know. Fine. Just hang back, okay?"

Munk snapped the phone shut and leaned into the headrest.

"What is it?" Truman asked.

"Cass says one shot was fired from Junie Archer's house. She's out of her truck and scouting the place to see if she can figure out where it came from."

Kado paled.

"And Mitch?" Truman asked.

"He convinced Bernie to drive him out to Junie's house." Munk shook his head. "A cross-dressing murderer, a nitwit cop who doesn't realize his date has a dick, a cripple, and a forensic anthropologist. This just keeps getting better."

CHAPTER 140

JUNIE SHIFTED HER ATTENTION back to Emmet. "There are things we need to clear up before you die. Are you ready to talk?"

He nodded.

"In another life, we would've made a good team. How many have you and your friends killed?"

Emmet's glance involuntarily flew to Officer Petchard, who sat with his head cradled in his hands.

"Don't worry about spilling the beans in front of Hugo," Junie said. "I'm the only one leaving here alive."

"Maybe we can talk about that," Emmet said.

"Doubtful. You killed Arlin Ross in Tennessee," she stated.

Emmet nodded. "It was dumb luck that we killed Ross while you were on patrol in that area?"

"I'd just found him and started scouting him, but yes, it was luck that we were in that area at the same time."

"When you pulled up behind us at that stop sign, did you know what we'd done?"

She shook her head. "I saw you pull out of the blacktop road to Ross's house and that made me wonder. Very few people travel that road. I almost stopped you to find out what you were up to."

"Why didn't you?"

"It wasn't until after his murder was called in that I made the connection." Junie hesitated, and then seemed to reach a decision. "I knew somebody else was killing the people that I was after. At the time, I was grateful for the help. Did you kill Eric Jackson and Jimmy Holland?"

Emmet nodded. "What gave it away?"

"The bullet wound through their legs, but more importantly, the swastika."

"That was risky. But I didn't figure any of the locals would be smart enough to match the details to another crime."

"They weren't," Junie said. "The only reason I made the connection was because they were on my list. I managed to get copies of Jackson's and Holland's autopsy reports. It pissed me off at first, but I decided it didn't really matter who was murdering them. The important thing was that they died. The brutality was a nice touch."

"Why were you after them, Junie?" Emmet asked.

"They were part of a longer list. After my father 'died' – and we'll come back to him in a minute – I landed with Boyd Dudley."

"Did you kill him, or was his burning to death an accident like the investigation concluded?"

There was genuine pleasure on her face. "I wanted to save him for last, to see if he could figure out that someone was coming for him, and who it was. But in the end," she giggled, "I couldn't help myself."

Petchard stirred. His green eyes burned when he looked up at her. "I should arrest you for murder, you bitch."

"Language, Hugo," Junie admonished. "And if you speak again without being spoken to, I'll put a bullet through your brain. Understand, *lover?*"

The room had grown chilly from the chugging air conditioner, and Petchard shivered. Slowly, the fire in his eyes died. Joseph remained perfectly still, sitting on the edge of the sofa with his hands hanging near the carpet. Emmet willed his friend to remain silent.

"Why the long list?" Emmet asked.

"Dudley didn't think he was getting enough cash to compensate for his trouble in taking care of me, so he sold me."

"Whored you out?"

"Every man on that list was a pervert who found some bizarre way to abuse me. They treated me worse than their dogs." Petchard flinched at her words. "That's right, Hugo, the mouth you so desperately wanted to kiss has given many a blow job."

The officer stared at her.

"I was nine when my father died. Or disappeared, as I know now. He left me with that degenerate, Dudley. Nobody listened when I told them what was happening. Not the school principal, the doctors who stitched me up over and over, the welfare people. Nobody." Junie adjusted her grip on the shotgun. "So, I decided that when I was old enough, I'd take care of them myself. And with your help, I'm almost there. Three more to go."

"We helped each other out, right?" Emmet asked.

"Up to a point, yes. But why? Why were the three of you after these men?"

"The three of you?" Petchard blurted, shifting to look at Emmet. "You were working with two other people to hunt men down and kill them?" He glared at Joseph, who didn't move. "You're a cop, man."

Junie pressed the Glock's barrel to Petchard's forehead while keeping the shotgun leveled at Emmet. "What did I tell you, Hugo?"

His murky green eyes rolled up to look at her. "To keep quiet."

"That's right. I know you're curious, but you'll just have to listen to the grown-ups talk. I'm sure even your little brain can put all the pieces together if you try hard enough." She bumped the gun against his forehead hard enough to leave a raspberry and then eased back, studying Joseph who still gazed at the floor. "Go on, Emmet."

"There were five of them. They murdered our fathers."

Junie's blink was slow in coming and Emmet wondered if whatever drug she had taken was finally kicking in. "What are you talking about?"

"Can I show you something? In my wallet?"

"Slowly, or Moses dies. Understand?"

He pulled the wallet from his hip pocket, opening it to take the copy of the article out. He held it up for Junie to see. She shot Petchard a warning glance and leaned in to read. "Dudley used to crow about this," she said, her voice thoughtful. "It happened two years before I was born. There were other lynchings, but this is the one he was most proud of." She stepped back. "So you're done now."

Emmet put the article and wallet on the floor. He nodded.

"My father was the last of them."

Again, he nodded.

"How did you find him?" Junie's eyes had taken on a soft look, and the hand holding the shotgun drifted from side to side as if caught in a gentle tide.

"Luck again. I stopped to get gas at his store and thought he looked familiar. It took me a day or two to figure it out. I had a photo of your dad, from his time as Thayerville sheriff. He was a good looking man."

Junie's eyebrow arched.

"Your dad was handsome. Not in a movie star way, but even in his old age he had an air about him. Authority, maybe."

"How long did you plan it?"

"Months," Emmet said. Joseph remained motionless. Petchard was following the conversation, turning his head slightly as each of them spoke. "Donna and Moses went out to see him, and we checked his background. We decided Calvin Whitman was really Calvin Whitehead once we hit 1979 and couldn't go back any farther."

Junie drew a sharp breath. "He died in 1978. Christmas Eve."

"Faked his death," Emmet clarified. "He must've taken some time to change his identity and maybe lay down a false trail if anybody came after him. It wasn't until mid-1979 that he bought the store out here."

"I didn't know," she whispered. Junie's dark eyes were fixed on Emmet, but their glassy gaze stared through him. "It never even crossed my mind that he abandoned me. Not until I saw his corpse outside that store."

Emmet thought he understood. "And we took him away from you."

Her gaze refocused on him. "Yes."

"That's why you're after us? Because we killed your father?"

"Yes."

"We got him, Junie. He's dead. We didn't deprive you of anything."

"Yes you did," she growled, the feminine façade fading. "I would've given him a taste of what I got from Boyd Dudley and his sick friends."

"But you didn't even know he was alive, Junie. Without us, you wouldn't have known to look for him. And he would still be alive. But he isn't."

"I would have found him," she whispered. The shotgun pointing at Emmet steadied and he saw the muscles tighten in her forearm as she applied pressure to the trigger.

CHAPTER 141

CASS CIRCLED THE HOUSE in a crouch, reaching up to test the curtained windows. None budged. Noise came from two ancient window unit air conditioners, one upstairs and one down, and from a groaning water well behind the house. As she rounded the front corner, the late afternoon sun glittered on the patchy grass at her feet. Cass squatted and spotted glass shards, then looked upward. A single pane was missing from a wide window. She studied the shards and saw no blood. Not a guarantee that no one had been shot, but some small comfort nonetheless. She eased toward the house and tried to listen but the air conditioner covered any other sounds.

The house had only two entrances – a back and front door, which were probably locked. Given its proximity to the shot out window, she would by-pass the front door. Cass crept along the house and quietly walked up the concrete steps to the back door. She grabbed the knob and caught her breath when it twisted in her hand. She drew a deep breath, acknowledging that she was violating Sheriff Hoffner's direct order by simply being out of the truck. Going into the house without backup was another matter entirely. Could she put her ego aside and wait the few minutes it would take for backup to arrive? John Grey took a chance to bring her back to work and she appreciated his trust in her. She had to do his decision justice. Reluctantly, she released the doorknob and backed down the steps, wiping sweat from her forehead.

For once, she would prove to Sheriff Hoffner that she could follow an order. No matter how hard it was to wait.

CHAPTER 142

TRUMAN DROVE PAST THE farmhouse at a steady speed. Two pickups were in the narrow driveway. "I don't see Cass or Petchard."

"Where is she?" Kado asked. He pulled his phone from his pocket and dialed. "No answer."

Munk and Kado twisted in their seats as they passed the farmhouse. "I didn't see her," Munk said. "Truman, pull over up ahead. Me and Kado will cross this pasture and come in behind the barn. I want you to drive back past the house and park on the side of the road out of sight of all windows, understood? I'll call Elaine and have her contact the other officers to tell them to wait for further instructions."

The young officer applied the brake and nodded.

"See if you can work your way to the tree with the tire swing in the front yard. It's wide enough to provide good cover. Put your phone on vibrate and call once you're in position, or if you spot anything. Got it?"

"Yes, sir," Truman replied. Munk and Kado slipped out of the truck and through a barbed wire fence. Truman performed a three-point turn and resumed the same steady pace. He parked on the verge once the foliage grew thick enough to shield his pickup from the house. Reaching over, he unlocked the glove box and took an extra magazine for his department issued weapon from inside. He also withdrew another revolver in a holster and strapped it to his ankle.

"Thanks again, Mom," he whispered, then left the truck and crept back toward the drive.

CHAPTER 143

WITH BARELY A MOVEMENT, Joseph tensed beside Emmet.

"You're right, Junie," Emmet agreed quickly. "You would've found him and it would've been much better if he'd died at your hands, not ours." His eyes pled with hers. "But we didn't know you were out there. We had no idea you or anybody else would want him dead. He murdered our fathers."

"He murdered *me*," she said, releasing tension on the trigger. "He abandoned me and picked Boyd Dudley to raise me. He had to have known what a monster Dudley was, that the man would use me. All this time? *I loved my father.* I excused him, tried to believe that he did what he thought was best. That it was bad luck that Dudley turned out to be a pervert. But he knew. My father knew what he was doing."

"I understand why you'd want to kill him yourself, Junie. But we didn't know about you. We just wanted our own revenge. So why would you want to kill us now? It's done. He died a horrible death." Emmet cocked an eyebrow in Petchard's direction. "I understand why you'd want to kill him. But you've got nothing to fear from us."

"No loose ends," she said, aiming the 12-gauge between Emmet and Moses and pointing the Glock at Petchard's chest. "They might be able to trace me back to Tennessee and then on to Alabama, but it's doubtful. Arcadia was only a temporary stop anyway. No one knows you're out here. Once you're dead, I'll hit the road and that will be the end of Junie Archer." She smiled. "Unless I decide to keep her."

She drew a breath and leveled her aim.

"Fine. Kill me if you have to. But leave Joseph out of this. He wasn't involved. In any of it." Emmet was barely aware of a change in Joseph's breathing. *Be still, Joseph. Trust me and stay still.*

Junie blinked several times. "What are you talking about?"

"This isn't Moses, Junie. You killed Moses Wednesday night, not Joseph. The papers got it wrong."

Petchard jerked back to look at Emmet and then Joseph. "You liar," he said to the motionless man, his broiled face turning a deeper shade of crimson. "Impersonating an officer. You used the police department to try to keep tabs on the investigation. You'll go down for this."

"Quiet, lover," Junie said almost absently, waggling the Glock at him. She snorted. "Good try, but it won't work, Emmet."

He was silent for a moment. "I don't know how to prove it to you. Moses and Joseph were identical twins. I can tell them apart and so could their mother. Others," he rolled his eyes at Petchard, "obviously can't."

"What do I care who this really is? It's just another bullet to me."

"No, Junie, it's not. You have a strong sense of right and wrong."

"She's murdered how many men in cold blood, and you call that a sense of right and wrong?" Petchard bleated.

"I told you to be quiet, lover." In a swift movement, Junie took aim and fired a single shot at Petchard.

Over the ringing in his ears, Emmet heard the blond officer howl.

CASS DROPPED AT THE sound of the second gunshot and swept the yard with her weapon. A man's shriek cut through the still afternoon air. Cool adrenaline flushed through her body and she was surprised to find herself at the top of the stairs, gun in one hand, doorknob in the other. She drew a deep breath, acknowledging that she was taking a huge chance by going in without backup and wondering how long Hoffner would suspend her this time. The fact that she might save Petchard's sorry life again would carry no weight with the Sheriff.

She pulled her phone from her pocket, pressed a speed dial button, and lifted the phone to her ear. At least she could let someone know what she was doing. A second scream sounded and Cass turned the still ringing phone upside down and shoved in her back pocket. She focused on the door and what might wait beyond, and pushed into the house to another wail.

"YOU'RE TRYING MY PATIENCE, Hugo," Junie said to the man writhing on the couch. Petchard groaned as blood trickled through the hand covering his left ear. Emmet strained to hear her over the ringing in his ears. "It's a flesh wound. Take it like a man and shut up before I put a bullet between your eyes."

Emmet saw Joseph's left hand moving toward his leg, but all motion ceased as Junie turned her attention back to them.

"Good shot," Emmet said.

"One of you got me in the ear last night," she said, turning her head slightly. "It does hurt, but I didn't squeal like a girl."

"And you don't have it in you to kill an innocent man," Emmet said. Although he had flinched at the sound of the gunshot, Joseph remained still. "Let him go."

"You're boring me," she said, but the shotgun wavered.

"This whole process has been about vengeance for you, Junie, like it has been for us. Righting a wrong. Seeking justice on your own, because the system couldn't or wouldn't provide it for you. Joseph didn't have anything to do with this. He was in jail in New York when we started. Moses never even told him what we were up to. Joseph didn't find out until after Moses and his mother were dead. I told him, but only because I thought he'd leave me alone to get on with it."

Junie's gaze shifted fully to Joseph. "What's wrong with him?"

"Mild concussion, I'd guess. Maybe shock over all this. He's had reservations about coming after you. Even though I offered to do it alone, he's been trying to keep up. But he doesn't have the stomach for it." Emmet returned his attention to Junie. "You're not the kind of person who can kill an innocent man. You haven't hurt anyone else while you've hunted them, have you?"

"No."

"Then don't start now. The men you've killed, the men I've helped kill, every single one of them deserved to die. And maybe you can justify killing me, but there's no way you can kill Joseph and live with it. Let him go." She blinked slowly. "Let him go so we can get on with this. Do what you have to do, then disappear. Joseph won't come after you."

"He's a hacker, if I remember correctly. He'll find me."

"You said you'd change your identity and he won't know where to start," Emmet said, growing desperate. "All he does is break into banks and steal their money."

"You're right, you know," Junie said. "Every kill has been righteous. Two of the men I've murdered had families, but I made sure they were away from the house when I did my business. They didn't deserve to be hurt because of what their husbands and fathers did to me. They were innocent, and I've never killed someone who wasn't guilty of hurting me." She looked straight at Emmet and he could swear he saw glee in her eyes. "But there's a first time for everything."

Junie leveled the shotgun again. Next to Emmet, Joseph tensed. A barely audible ding sounded, signaling that someone had entered the house. Junie backed up several paces and switched the groaning air conditioner off. "Who knows?" she asked in a whisper.

Emmet shook his head and glanced at Officer Petchard, whose murky green eyes were liquid with pain. Junie waved the Glock at him. "Nobody," Petchard whimpered. He swallowed hard. "I swear."

She positioned herself behind the door to the living room, keeping the shotgun pointed at the men on the couch. Emmet watched as she shook her head and drew a quiet breath. *Clearing the drugs*, he thought. He glanced at Joseph to see the other man cut his eyes in Junie's direction, as if gauging her position relative to his. *What have you got up your sleeve, Joseph?* Emmet wondered. *And who the hell is walking around Junie's house?*

CHAPTER 144

MUNK FUMBLED THE PHONE from his pocket. "It's Cass," he told Kado, and the forensics man felt a tangible wave of relief wash over him.

The men were on the edge of the pasture that butted up against Junie Archer's farmhouse yard, preparing to crawl between two strands of rusty barbed wire. A bony cow with long, twisting horns had galloped across the rain-thirsty pasture and now stood bellowing at them. Kado pulled the borrowed revolver from his ankle holster and aimed it at the animal. Munk waved at Kado to put the gun away. "There's no grass out here. It's hungry. Go open that gate and let it eat some hay. That'll shut it up."

Kado hurried to an enclosure protecting several moldy-looking bales of hay. The cow trotted behind him, mooing her urgency. He opened the gate and stood aside as she rushed to the nearest bale, rubbed it with her forehead, and then started eating.

Munk had made it through the fence by the time Kado got back to him. "Cass?"

"She's not talking."

"Did she hit a button by mistake?"

Munk shook his head. "She has a flip phone. It cuts the call as soon as she shuts it. The sound is clear. She wants us to listen."

THE AIR CONDITIONER WENT silent. Heart thudding, Cass wondered if it had switched itself off, or if someone knew that she was here and was listening. Without the unit's rattling hum, the sounds of water sluicing through pipes made sense of the well pump's groaning outside.

She stayed close to the walls and tested each step before putting her foot down. Living in an old house as a teenager had taught her how to creep past her father when he was sober. When he was drunk, she could dance a conga line of elephants past him and he wouldn't wake up. And while her older brothers had explained the concept of silent sneaking to her, it was down to Cass to perfect the mechanics. Some skills had to be learned through experience.

The farmhouse was two stories, and Cass eased up the stairs. Three rooms, only one containing furniture. An empty bathroom with the shower running. On the ground floor, Cass worked her way in a circuit through the kitchen, laundry room, and foyer, to a hallway with two doors, one on either side.

The house was sweltering and a drop of sweat rolled down her cheek. She wiped her face against her shoulder and studied the door that led to the room at the front of the house. The room with a window missing one pane. She hesitated. This was moving way too fast. Cass pulled her phone out and checked the screen. Still on an active call to Munk. She had to know where he was; how far out backup was. She lifted the phone and prepared to speak.

A thump, followed by a yelp, came from the front room. Cass twirled the phone so the microphone was exposed, shoved it back in her pocket, and opened the door.

CHAPTER 145

EMMET WATCHED JUNIE SMILE as the door swung inward to create her hiding place. Moments before, she had taken a featherlight step forward and smacked Petchard on his injured ear. The man barked a scream. As the door opened, Emmet realized that Junie had drawn her opponent in. He saw the flash of confusion on the attractive redhead's face when she spotted Emmet and Joseph sitting on the couch next to an agonized and bloodied Officer Petchard. But that confusion cleared in an instant and she spun before Junie had a chance to swing the door closed. The two women faced off, the redhead with a 9 mm pointed in a double handed grip at Junie's chest, Junie with a shotgun leveled at the couch, and her own Glock aimed at the redhead. It took Emmet a moment to realize that this was Cass Elliot, the detective who had been in the newspapers for the last few weeks over that whole cult mess. He appraised her steady breathing, her level gaze at Junie, and decided that they might have a chance to get out of here alive.

The room had quickly grown warm without the air conditioner's steady stream of damp air and each face glowed with the heat. Junie's attention was split between Cass and the men on the couch, and she took a small step back to give herself a wider angle.

"How nice to see you, Detective Elliot. I never thought we'd have a chance to spend time together as girls."

"Nice to meet you, Calvin," Cass said.

Junie's dark eyebrows shot up. "Really? You figured it out?"

Cass nodded.

"I'm impressed. How?"

"You look very much like your father, Calvin, when he was a young man."

"I do not," Junie snapped. She turned a fraction more to face Cass, and the hand holding the shotgun trembled. From the corner of his eye, Emmet watched as Joseph slipped a revolver from a holster on his ankle and slid it under his thigh. He caught his breath and indicated with a slight movement of his finger for Joseph to pass the weapon over. Joseph ignored him. Emmet glanced back at the two women and saw an awareness in Cass's eyes. She'd spotted the gun. Suddenly, the situation looked less grim.

"You can't fight genetics, Calvin. You look like your father and you act just like him. Coming to Arcadia to kill these people when their only crime was to have their daddies stolen by your father. That's something Calvin senior would do."

"They've killed, too," Junie shot back. Color crept up her neck and Emmet realized that the slight tremor in her hands was gone. *Adrenaline*, he thought. *Not so good for us.*

"Perhaps. Someone killed the men who lynched their fathers. These were some of the same vermin who abused you, I'd imagine."

Junie's eyes narrowed. "What do you know about me?"

"Enough to know that Boyd Dudley turned you into a little girl when you were only nine years old." Cass's expression softened. Her body shifted and Emmet spotted the open clamshell of a phone sticking out of her back pocket. *Dear God, this is one smart woman,* he thought. "I can't imagine what you went through, Calvin. How many times you were raped, what that did to your self-esteem."

"I said that's not my name," Junie growled. Her voice fluctuated in timbre between a man's and a woman's. "Shut up before I kill all of you."

"The house is surrounded, Calvin. You won't kill all of us. You might wound some of us. But then you're done. There's no escape."

"Bullshit."

"You waited one day too long, Calvin. We figured out who you were this morning." Cass flicked her eyes at the bloodied officer. "If Petchard over there was any kind of cop, he'd have the connections to know what was going on with the case. But he's not, Calvin. You chose badly. He's a terrible cop. Everybody knows it and nobody trusts him."

Junie licked her lips. "Why haven't I heard sirens?"

"They came in silent. Pull back the curtains and check. And then put the guns down, Calvin. It's over."

CHAPTER 146

MUNK AND KADO HUDDLED together behind the barn with their heads tilted over Munk's phone. Kado pulled away and looked at Munk's sweating face. "It must be a front window if Cass wants Junie to check for patrol cars," he whispered.

"Call Truman and asks what he sees."

Kado turned away to have a murmured conversation with the young officer, then ended the call. "He's in position behind the tree and can see a window in the front of the house with a pane shot out."

Munk covered his phone's mouthpiece with a hand. "Can he hear anything?"

"No. I told him that if he has a clear shot at Junie when she opens the curtains, to take it. He's calling two patrol cars to come up the driveway and park on either side of the pickups. Lights on, sirens off. They'll take cover behind the car doors and wait."

"Good," Munk said. "Meanwhile, you and me get close to that house. I'll take the porch and front door. You go around back in case Junie tries to run."

"The only way that's happening is if Cass is down."

"That's why you're going around back. The last thing I need is for the man who loves her trying to go in to get her." Kado flashed him a surprised glance. "It's written all over you, man. The only advice I can offer is to grab her while you've got a chance. Life's too uncertain to wait."

CHAPTER 147

MITCH POKED AT THE truck's instrument panel and breathed a sigh of relief as cool air rushed through the vents. Bernie Winterbottom backed out of the courthouse parking lot, checked traffic, and punched the accelerator. The truck flew around the square and cleared a yellow light, barely missing the curb and a fire hydrant. A smile creased the Englishman's face. "I've always wanted to drive a big truck like this. Lights? Siren?"

"Lights," Mitch answered, and flipped the appropriate switch. "We'll go in silent so we don't jeopardize whatever Munk has going on."

"How's the leg, Mitchell?"

Mitch glanced down at his brace. The fabric around the heel and ankle was gone, ripped off when Bernie spotted Elaine coming out of the courthouse and panicked. Mitch was trying to finagle his leg into the truck and Bernie had shoved it past the door frame. His leg throbbed now, and he wondered if they'd moved any of the pins. "It's a little boogered up, but I don't see why it matters. The brace comes off next week."

"Good. Now, on to more serious matters." Bernie paused while Mitch directed him to the highway. "What do you plan to do once we're at this Junie person's house?"

Mitch flipped open his phone and dialed Munk, but got sent straight to voicemail. Then he called Kado but got no answer. Same with Truman. "No idea. We'll weigh it up when we get there. My crutches are in the pickup's bed?"

Bernie nodded, then paled. "Darla. Should we call to tell her that you're not at the station?"

"Hell no," Mitch said. "She'll torture somebody until they give up my location and then she'll come out to get me." He paused. "That's not a bad idea, actually. Darla'd be so mad she could probably take Junie down with a single shot."

CHAPTER 148

CASS WATCHED AS JUNIE blinked, almost in slow motion. The woman gave a slight shake of her head. "If there's no way out, Detective, we might as well all die right here. I'm not going to jail in Arcadia. Three worthless souls will live, but I've got nothing left to lose. Do you?"

An image of Kado flashed through Cass's mind and a fist of longing slammed into her gut. Yes, she did have something to lose. But fear was what this strange creature wanted and Cass refused to give it to her. The hostages had an edge. There was a fourth weapon in the room, well hidden from Junie. Cass smiled. Kado and Mitch were right that Joseph was still alive. Moses couldn't have kept this quiet or still. But she was glad to have Joseph here. He might not be a cop, but he had street smarts. "Everybody dies some time, Calvin."

"That's not my name," Junie growled, face contorting as her forefingers tightened on each of the guns she held.

Time slowed. Cass saw Emmet and Petchard shrink from the shotgun aimed in their direction, but Joseph didn't seem to notice. He sat straighter now, having edged himself to an upright position. His hands rested on the sofa, near his thighs. His breathing was slow and even, and Cass could feel his attention focused on Junie.

Cass drew a slow breath and put pressure on the trigger. Without warning a man in a scarlet robe materialized in her mind. Twin dots pierced his chest and he flew back, arms wide, robe billowing. He landed on his back with a thud, a rush of air knocked from his lungs. Cass blinked the vision aside. *Easy, girl*, she thought. *You told Maxine you could take another life if you had to. Five pounds of pressure on the trigger. Let's hope it doesn't come to that.*

Junie's eyes were focused on Cass with an eerie intensity when a small dark figure darted from beneath the sofa and twined between Junie's legs. The woman stumbled and deafening gunshots sounded. A bullet slammed into Cass's body. She felt no pain, only a vague astonishment that she had been hit. Reflexively, she released her two-handed grip and squeezed the trigger, adjusting her aim even as she spun away. The blow twisted her body toward the curtained windows and she lost sight of the men she had hoped to rescue. Her head smashed into the windowsill and a searing heat sucked the breath from her as she hit the floor.

CHAPTER 149

GLASS EXPLODED ONTO THE front porch and Munk ducked, then climbed up and onto the cool concrete and twisted the front door's knob. Locked. Heart racing, he stood and lifted a pudgy leg to kick at one of the panels. Once, twice, and then the old wood splintered. Munk yanked his leg out of the jagged hole and reached up, feeling for the interior knob. He twisted the thumb lock and then found the deadbolt and unlocked it. The door stopped as he shoved, caught by a security chain. With a growl, he threw his shoulder into it and the chain popped free. He moved into the foyer in a crouch, gun sweeping the dim area.

TRUMAN CROUCHED BEHIND THE wide oak tree. When the gunfire subsided, he yelled to the four patrol officers, "Two of you, circle to the back, watch the windows for shooters. Two stay in front. Call for an ambulance."

And then in a burst of speed he hadn't put on since his high school football days, he darted across the yard and up the porch steps, racing across the glass strewn space with two long strides. He stepped into the dim interior behind Munk and shadowed the older man as he inched toward a hallway.

AT THE SOUND OF gunshots, Kado shoved open the kitchen door, blood pounding through his veins, the borrowed revolver in his hand. The kitchen was clear, but he was faced with two closed doors and a choice. The sound of splintering wood came from behind the door to his left and a man's furious screams from the door to his right. Kado chose the right hand door. Panting, he pushed it open and hid behind the door frame.

When no fire came, he stepped into a dark hallway. Movement caught his attention and he pivoted, revolver aimed at Munk and behind him, Truman. The older officer's glance shot to the door on the left at the far end of the hall. A man's angry voice and a strange thudding sounded from that direction, followed by a sputtering cough and Cass's shouts. Kado moved forward but Munk stopped him and stepped in front, motioning for Truman to follow him. Tamping down the frustration swelling in his chest, Kado stood aside.

MUNK REACHED ACROSS THE door for the knob, glancing at Truman behind him. In most situations, Truman would be on the other side of the door, allowing them each to see half of the room before they entered. In this case, the door was in the corner of the hallway and only Munk would have a view into the room. It was awkward at best; dangerous at worst. He drew a breath, thinking *hand, no hand*, turned the knob, and shoved.

Munk entered the room and faced a wall bearing a fireplace. He took two mighty steps forward before stopping short. Truman bumped into him and gaped at the devastation. A bloodied Petchard sat astride someone, slamming their head on the floor over and over, muttering under his breath. Mojo was on the couch, a hole in the left side of his chest whistling as he sucked air through it. Emmet Hedder's right arm was punctured in several places and streamed blood in narrow rivulets. Mojo's eyes were fixed on Emmet's face, and as Munk watched, his lips peeled back in a bright red grimace. Mojo spoke and droplets of blood peppered Emmet's cheek.

Kado pushed between Munk and Truman, his gasp startling them into action. Before they could stop him, Kado hurdled over Petchard and the body on the floor and rushed to the far side of the room. Petchard blocked his view so Munk pushed the door against the wall and stepped forward, relief making his knees weak. Cass was on the floor, gun aimed at Petchard as she struggled to sit upright. Her face was covered in blood and a dark stain spread across the left side of her torso.

Truman shouldered Munk aside and grabbed Petchard by the neck of his uniform, yanking the smaller man aside. Munk stooped and checked for a pulse. Finding nothing, he looked closer at the face. Unbelievable. When he squinted, he could see both Calvin Whitman Jr. and Junie Archer in the features. Gingerly, Munk pushed against the chin to display a battered skull and a dark pool of blood.

"What a mess," Munk breathed. He pulled a phone from his pocket, disconnected from Cass's call, and dialed 911, requesting an ambulance and telling the dispatcher to contact John Grey and let him know that at least one body was on the scene.

Munk turned to check on Truman. The young officer had handcuffed a red-faced Petchard and left him in an overstuffed chair in a corner. The man's uniform was smeared with blood and he still muttered to himself, glaring at the body on the floor. Truman was now working on Emmet Hedder, using his belt as a tourniquet around the man's upper arm. Truman glanced up at Munk, then down at Mojo. He met Munk's eyes and shook his head.

Munk turned to check on Kado. He had pushed Cass onto her back and was applying pressure to her left shoulder. Munk hurried to her side. "How is she?"

"She's pissed off," Cass hissed through clenched teeth. "Is that freak dead?"

Munk nodded.

"Guess that means I'm suspended again."

Munk grinned. "How's the wound?"

"She's hit high in the shoulder. The entrance is clean, but the exit wound..." Kado was as pale as Cass. He moved her body to check her back, and she groaned. "Well, maybe it's not too bad, but there's a lot of blood."

"Full metal jacket?" Munk asked.

"Let's hope so."

"And her face?"

"It's a gash near her eye. She'll need stitches, but I think that wound is manageable."

Munk turned at the rattle of handcuffs to see Petchard stretching upward in his chair, chin jutting toward Emmet Hedder. "Arrest him. He's killed a bunch of people. And that's not Moses, man. That's Joseph. Arrest him for impersonating an officer."

At the sound of Petchard's voice, Truman whirled. "Keep your mouth closed, you idiot. Not another word, do you hear?"

Petchard flinched back, his murky green eyes wide, and then started to cry. "She screwed with me, man. How was I supposed to know she was a dude? She had tits and everything."

"Shut up, Petchard, or I swear I'll put a gag in your mouth. Understand?" Petchard wiped his nose on his shoulder and slowly nodded. Truman looked down at him. "Are you injured?"

"She shot me in the ear."

Truman examined the wound. "You'll live, unfortunately. Just sit there and keep your mouth shut."

Truman turned, his jaw set, and saw Munk watching. "Good job," the older man said. "Keep an eye on Emmet. I'll go get a medical kit."

THIS WASN'T HOW I *imagined it happening,* Kado thought. His fingers trembled as he unbuttoned Cass's blouse. "Sorry," he said. "I need to get a better look."

She nodded and closed her eyes. He peeled the saturated fabric back from her shoulder, surprised to see that she wore a jogging bra. He tugged at the shoulder strap and then gave up and called to Truman. The young officer zinged a pocket knife across the room and Kado sawed through the stretchy material. He peeled the blood-soaked bra away to expose Cass's wound.

The shot had struck below the collar bone and left a neat hole oozing blood. Kado lifted her again and saw that the exit wound was larger than the entrance wound but not by much. The bullet probably was fully jacketed and had mushroomed only slightly on impact.

Because the shot was fired from such close range, the bullet's velocity and jacketing would've helped minimize tumbling and mushrooming. Whether intending to or not, the shooter had undoubtedly saved Cass a far more serious injury and provided a shorter recovery time than if he had loaded even partially jacketed rounds.

He gently wiped the blood from her face. Cass's complexion had gone waxy and her skin was cool to the touch. "Cass?" Kado asked.

Her violet eyes fluttered open.

"We need to get you horizontal and raise your legs. You're going into shock."

She helped him as best she could and he propped her feet on the fireplace's hearth. Her eyes slipped closed as he opened her shirt again and gently wiped blood from the entry wound. Kado stopped, a wad of gauze hovering over her chest. He wiped again, but it was still there. The thin tail of a pale scar started at her collar bone then circled and loped along the swell of her breast and disappeared beneath the edge of her jogging bra.

Talk and I'll cut them off. I'm watching.

Tears stung his eyes. A lone siren sounded and he willed the paramedics to hurry.

CHAPTER 150

MITCH WATCHED AS THE paramedics eased Cass onto a stretcher and wheeled her out of the front room. He lowered himself to the overstuffed chair Petchard had vacated only moments earlier and called Darla and then Abe Elliot, watching as Truman ushered the still cuffed Petchard from the room. John Grey knelt beside Junie Archer's body, answering Kado's questions about entry wound angles. The forensic man was in the corner where Cass had fallen. Truman hurried to stand near the couch and help figure trajectories, avoiding Porky, who squatted in front of Mojo, his head bent and lips moving silently.

Sheriff Bill Hoffner strode through the door and stopped, removing his Stetson and taking in the carnage. He hesitated at the sight of Porky and Mojo. A series of expressions flickered across his face before finally settling on something that looked more like constipation than regret. Mitch watched, wondering how much effort it took the man to figure out how grief should appear on his face.

He spotted Mitch in the corner and gingerly made his way across the room. "What are you doing here?" he whispered. "And why was Petchard cuffed?"

"Was cuffed?" Mitch asked, anger worming into a cold knot in his gut. "What did you do with him?"

"I uncuffed him and put him in an ambulance. That ear wound looks nasty."

Mitch lifted an eyebrow. "It didn't occur to you that he was cuffed for a reason?"

"What reason would that be?"

"He was in a room where two people were killed and two others wounded, including one of your detectives. When Munk and Truman got to the scene," Mitch motioned across the room, "they found Petchard attacking one of the victims, slamming his head, or her head, into the floor. It didn't occur to you that he might have shot someone in this room?"

Hoffner blinked. "Kado will clear him. Besides, Hugo Petchard's not a flight risk. His entire family is here in Forney County. His father's well-established in the community."

"Daddy's checkbook can send Hugo anywhere Daddy thinks he should go, Sheriff," Mitch said softly. "By sending Petchard to the hospital, you've robbed Kado a clean chance of testing him for gunshot residue. But you've also made sure those campaign contributions continue, which I suppose trumps ensuring justice is done for the dead and wounded."

Hoffner's face bloomed crimson. "How dare you?"

"How dare *you*, Sheriff? Kado managed to process Emmet Hedder before the paramedics took him away. He found light concentrations of GSR on Hedder's right pant leg. Grey arrived shortly after and they began processing the bodies, trying to figure out where the shots came from. There are seven guns in this room. Five nine millimeters, a sawed-off twelve gauge, and a revolver. If Petchard fired one of those weapons –"

"It'll have his fingerprints on it," Hoffner interrupted, nostrils flared.

"Maybe," Mitch said. "But he's the only person who was mobile when Munk and Truman arrived. If anyone wanted to destroy or plant evidence, such as fingerprints, he's the only one capable."

Hoffner deflated a bit, his eyes shifting to study the room. "And Cass? Any GSR?"

"Yes. Heavy concentrations on her right hand and arm."

Hoffner snorted. "She's too damn hot-headed for this job."

Mitch looked up at the man, incredulous. "Do you have any objectivity left, Sheriff? You turn one suspect loose without checking with the officers on the scene, and you condemn one of your detectives without having a clue what actually happened." His voice rose. "For all you know, she was saving Hugo Petchard's worthless ass again. It wouldn't surprise me. The moron didn't even know his girlfriend was a man."

All five men swiveled to face Mitch and Sheriff Hoffner. Color drained from his face and he shooed them back to work. They turned slowly to their jobs, voices muted.

"I don't like your tone, Detective."

"And I'm sick of your attitude toward your team, Sheriff. Cass is a damn good detective and all you can do is find fault with her. You brought Kado all the way from Oklahoma, only to run him down after one problem with corrupted DNA. Evidence is compromised all the time. Yes, possibly by the forensics department but also by anyone else who handles it. There's no proof that Kado did anything wrong. But the rest of the force picks up on your attitude and mimics it. I haven't been around for the last few weeks, but I've heard about the kind of hassle he's taking from the men over that DNA problem. Fed by you."

"I have no idea —"

Mitch sighed wearily. "No, you don't. You don't have any idea how you demoralize the very people who work so hard for you. I've had six weeks to think about things and you know the biggest problem with this force?"

Hoffner stared, mouth agape.

"You. You tolerate incompetents like Petchard and harass your strongest people. There's something wrong about that. I'm not sure what exactly, but I do know it's backwards. And I know that people like Cass and Kado are mobile. They don't have to stay here. And eventually they won't. They'll give up trying to work around you to do their jobs and go elsewhere."

Hoffner bristled. "If it's so bad here, why haven't you left, Stone? Surely you're a good enough detective to work anywhere. You don't have to work for me, do you?"

"No, Sheriff, I don't. I've had several offers to move to other counties and even other states over the years, the last one about six months ago. I choose to stay because this is where Darla's family lives. Being close to them is important to her. That's the reason I'm here."

Hoffner's gaze darted to the other men, who were studiously avoiding them. "Why are you bringing this up now? Here?"

"Because Cass fired her weapon and that means another Firearm Discharge Board investigation. You'll suspend her with pay and drag your feet about signing her back on again. I'm about to come back to work. And as much as I respect Carlos, I don't want him as a partner. I want Cass. And really, I want you to change. I want you to go home tonight and come back a different man tomorrow." He scratched absently at the top of his brace. "Maybe I need to change some, too. And I'm willing to do that, if you'll tell me what you want that's different than what you already get. But I doubt that you're capable of change, so I'm giving you some home truths now, so you can think before you act on Cass's situation."

"And Petchard?" Hoffner's gaze was icy. "Your recommendation?"

"Fire his lazy, cowardly ass and go find campaign contributions from somebody else. Hell, you've run uncontested for years. It can't cost much to mount a reelection campaign without an opponent."

Hoffner glared at Mitch and slapped his Stetson back on his head. "Good work, gentlemen. Carry on."

No one looked up as he left.

CHAPTER 151

CASS FROWNED AND TRIED to open her eyes. They were stuck shut and she struggled to pull them apart. But the effort was too much and she slid back toward a comfortable darkness.

"I think she's waking up," a familiar voice said. A cloth gently rubbed her eyes. "Cass? Can you hear me?"

"Mmm," she answered.

"Get Dr. Rambo." A chair scraped and footsteps sounded. "Cass? Wake up. I'm not working on the kitchen by myself."

Cass recognized Bruce's voice and her lips flitted upward. *It's about time you did some work*, she wanted to say, but the words wouldn't come. She tried again to open her eyes, but was just so tired. She heard a soft whooshing and footsteps, and then a cool hand was on her forehead.

"Detective Elliot, wake up, please. This is Dr. Ramasubramanian. We're all anxious to see you."

Obediently, she tried. The cloth wiped her face again, and she managed to pull her lids apart only to squeeze them shut. "Turn off the overhead lights, please," Dr. Ramasubramanian said in his lilting voice. "And close the blinds. Thank you."

Cass tried again and managed to keep her eyelids open long enough to see the kindly Indian doctor smiling down at her. "Ahh, there are those unusual purple eyes. Welcome back. We've been waiting for you. It may take a few moments, but please keep blinking. Your eyes will adjust."

Mustering a reply, her tongue clicked against the roof of her mouth and Cass tried to swallow.

"Mr. Elliot, there is a cup next to the bed," Dr. Ramasubramanian said. Something touched her lips and she parted them, allowing a straw to slide in. "Sip slowly, please. It is only water but it will ease the dryness in your throat. You may still feel the effects of your last shot of morphine. Gentlemen, five minutes only, please. I will be back shortly."

She heard light footsteps and the whoosh again. Obediently she sipped, fighting the drifting tug of the drugs in her system. At last she pulled back. "Happen?" she croaked.

A hand stroked her forehead and she opened her eyes to see her father's troubled face, his eyes still bloodshot from Friday night's binge. "Don't worry about that now, Cass. Just rest. You'll be fine," Abe promised.

She cleared her throat. "What happened?"

Bruce's broad, handsome face appeared beside her father's, and Harry's bobbed into view on the other side of the bed. "You were in a shoot out, Cass," Bruce said to her father's frown. "Involving Junie Archer, Emmet Hedder, Mojo, and Petchard. You got hit in the shoulder."

Fragments of the event materialized in her mind and she closed her eyes, trying to fit them together.

"Shut up, Bruce. She's not ready," Harry whispered.

"It's a flesh wound. She's fine."

"Boys," Abe warned. "Let her rest."

"No," Cass groaned. "Was anybody else hurt?" She fought to keep her eyes open as the men exchanged glances. "Who?"

Bruce drew a deep breath. "Emmet Hedder got hit with some buck shot. Dr. Rambo's picking it out and stitching him up. Mojo was hit in the chest. He died, Cass. Petchard got away with a nick to his ear."

She blinked, her lids heavy. "And Junie?"

Abe took her hand. "That's enough for now."

"What happened?"

"She was shot and killed, Cass."

"By who?"

Bruce shifted. "They're not sure. She was hit with more than one shot."

"By me?"

Harry scowled at his brother. "They don't know. Kado's out at the house now trying to figure it out."

"Hoffner suspended me?"

"Not yet," Bruce said. Harry jabbed him in the arm. "I mean, it's like Harry said, Kado's still looking into what happened. Do you remember anything?"

How can eyelids feel so heavy? Cass thought, submitting to the warm pull of the drugs. "It was the cat."

"What?" the men asked in unison.

"The cat did it," she whispered, and drifted off to sleep.

CHAPTER 152

IT IS A STRANGE truth that tragedy can cause even the most cautious of people to drop their inhibitions and take extraordinary risks. Maxine Leverman punched the treadmill's 'stop' button and stared at the text message. For an instant, she was furious that Cass would've given Mitch Stone her phone number. Then the message sank in and Maxine flew for the door, grabbing a pair of oversized sunglasses, a baseball cap, and her purse. Her defensive instincts were so well honed that she punched the 'away' button on the alarm keypad without thinking. But beyond that security measure, Maxine lost all sense of precaution. She stepped outside without first checking for stalkers and slammed the door, leaving it unbolted.

THE THREE ELLIOT MEN hovered outside Cass's room until an ER nurse shooed them into a private waiting area. Bruce was reaching for the door, heading for the cafeteria to find coffee, when it banged open and a thin woman stepped inside. She was in sweaty workout clothes with a cap on her head and a pair of movie star sunglasses in one hand, a purse slung over her shoulder. Her green eyes were clear and wide.

"Where's Cass?" she demanded.

Bruce stopped short, a tickle of recognition in his gut. "Maxine?"

"Bruce? Dear Lord, you turned out nice." She squinted. "What happened to your cheek?"

The curve of her lips rendered him speechless. He watched, dazed, as she said hello to Harry and hugged Abe. It was a well-rumored fact that Bruce Elliot had bedded most of the eligible, and some of the not-so-eligible, women in Forney County. While it was true that he had dated far and wide, his sexual exploits were not quite as extensive as legend might lead one to believe. For the simple reason that once he mastered the almost uncontrollable urges of his youth, he realized that sex without some sort of intellectual connection wasn't very satisfying. For him, anyway. It was rare these days that he met a woman who made him look twice. But his sister's best friend, once knock-kneed and gap-toothed, had turned into a stunning woman.

He started at the sound of his name. "Yeah?"

His father stifled a smile. "You'd better make that four coffees and some pastries. Can you handle all that?"

"Of course. Be right back." Bruce fled, pulling the door shut behind him. He leaned against the hospital wall, somewhat amused to find that he was so attracted to the skinny woman that he was wondering where she'd like to go on their first date, while his only sister lay recovering from a gunshot wound just down the hall.

A NURSE TURNED AT the sound of the door opening and nodded Maxine to a chair, then continued fiddling with the bedside equipment.

"How is she?" Maxine whispered, clutching a cup of coffee and a bear claw in a napkin.

"She's a hard one to keep down. She keeps fighting the drugs."

"That's Cass."

"Well, if you care about her, fuss when she wakes up, would you? She needs rest so her body can heal." The nurse peeled Cass's gown back. "This is one of the strangest scars I've ever seen. Do you know what happened?"

Maxine's mouth went suddenly dry. She tightened her grip on the coffee cup as the nurse removed the gauze covering Cass's gunshot wound. And there it was. A narrow, silky line swirling from Cass's collar bone and along the swell of her breast, disappearing beneath the faded hospital gown. Following the same path as Maxine's. She suspected that the cut meandered beneath the breast and ended at her areole. The scar was so faded that it almost disappeared into Cass's skin; only a faint sheen was visible, and that only in the right light. *So that's what it will look like in another five years*, she thought. *True body art. I wonder if the mental scars will have faded so well by then, for both of us.*

"Do you know what happened to her?" the nurse asked again.

"No," Maxine lied. "But it is unusual, isn't it?"

"At least the injury was superficial and won't interfere with how the gunshot wound heals."

Superficial, Maxine thought. *If you only knew.*

CHAPTER 153

MUNK AND MARTINEZ STOOD outside the exam room and took turns peeking through the small window in the door. Celia Hedder sat by the bed, holding her husband's hand as Dr. Ramasubramanian talked to them and left a bottle of pills on the counter. He met them outside the door.

"Mr. Hedder already has a wound in his right arm that was very poorly stitched, but is healing well," he told them. "Perhaps it is a blessing that the buckshot caught him in the same arm." He glanced into the room. "He asked me to tell you to wait, please, while he speaks with his wife. He would like to talk to you next."

"Thanks, Doc," Munk said. "How's Cass?"

"Surprisingly well. The morphine has put her to sleep. Do you need to speak with her?"

Munk nodded.

"Check with the nurse's station. I will leave word with them when she is awake again."

"The damage to her shoulder?"

"It is a mercy that the bullet did not mushroom as it entered her body. Nor did it fragment once inside. There is muscle trauma but the bullet missed her scapula. A minor miracle."

"Range of movement?"

"That will depend upon how much scar tissue develops and how her physical therapy progresses."

The three men started as the exam room door opened and Celia Hedder stepped out, wiping her cheeks. "Keep it short," she instructed.

Dr. Ramasubramanian took her arm and led her toward the waiting room. "You have had quite a shock, my dear. Can I get you a cup of coffee or a soda?"

"I need to run an errand, Dr. Rambo, but I could use some coffee first."

Martinez watched until they rounded a corner, and then looked at Munk. "It's going to be a long one, despite what Mrs. Hedder wants. You take the lead."

———

EMMET HEDDER EYED MUNK'S rust-streaked uniform. "Some of that mine?"

"I think I got some of everybody's blood on me. It was quite a scene."

Emmet's eyes closed. "That it was."

"You ready to give your statement? I'd like to tape it, and Detective Martinez is here to take notes and act as witness."

"Yes, sir," he said, putting Emmet the Marine into play.

Munk switched on a small tape recorder. "Tell us about Junie Archer, Mr. Hedder."

"Call me Emmet, sir," he began. "You're not going to Mirandize me?"

"Should I?"

Emmet chewed his lip. "No, sir," he said. And then he explained how he and Joseph worked together and used the investigation to identify the shooter. "It was Moses who figured it out. Junie was at his house for the wake, and she mentioned that whoever replaced the head on the rooster did a good job. Moses realized there was no way she could know that the rooster tile was shattered unless she'd seen it down the scope of a rifle, or someone had told her about it. Officer Petchard never went into the kitchen after the murders, not until everything was cleaned and repaired. And Moses checked the case log; Petchard didn't access the photos of the kitchen."

"So you started stalking her?" Munk asked.

"Tracking her," Emmet corrected. "Using a cell phone. We didn't figure Junie for the actual shooter. Moses saw a photo of Calvin Whitman in the man's murder file, and made the connection to her. We thought she must be working with his son."

"Why?"

"Why what?"

"Why would Calvin Whitman's son come after you and Moore and the Franklins?"

"I don't know, sir," Emmet said.

"We know your fathers were lynched the same night in Thayerville, Alabama. Is that the connection?"

"I don't know."

"Why would the son of the man who murdered your fathers come after y'all?"

"I have no idea. Maybe to finish what his father started? To put an end to our blood lines?"

Munk examined him and Emmet waited. Finally, the pudgy officer spoke. "After the shooting at your house," Munk motioned to Emmet's upper arm, "why didn't you come to us?"

Emmet blanched. "The cops?"

"Yeah, why not?"

He shook his head. "I started running, sir. It never occurred to me to dial 911. Maybe it was a throwback to Libya or Panama."

"But you hooked up with Moses, a cop. You violated your little circle and called him. Why?"

Emmet's mind raced to make the connections. "You have Donna's phone."

Munk nodded. "And we got a look at Moses' call history by mistake. What were you three up to?"

"We were friends."

"Since when?"

This was why he wanted to speak to Celia before talking to the cops. *Be as honest as possible*, she advised. *The fewer lies you tell, the fewer chances they have to trip you up.* "Since Moses responded to a call at her office and they realized how they were connected."

Munk sat in a chair near the bed, and Martinez leaned into the wall "How did they make the connection?"

"He asked about her paintings and drawings. Have you seen them?"

Munk nodded.

"They're bits of what she remembers from the night our fathers were lynched."

"She was there?"

It was Emmet's turn to nod. "She didn't tell Moses what they were, exactly, just that something bad had happened and this was her way of working through it. He found out she was from Thayerville and the pieces kind of fell into place. Moses introduced me and Donna, and the three of us hung out occasionally."

"Why the call circle?"

"Me and Moses had such variable schedules, sir. When one was available we'd make the rounds and see if the other two could meet up."

Emmet held his breath while Munk digested this. "Tell me what happened at the house today," the officer finally said. "Start with how you got out to her house."

"We drove my wife's car. You'll find it on County Road 819."

"You snuck up behind the house?"

"Yes, sir. We wanted some answers, but thought that checking the place first, finding out who was around, was the safest way to proceed." He swallowed. "She caught us snooping and managed to get both of us inside."

"Did you bring weapons?"

"Yes, sir. We each had a nine millimeter, and I didn't know it at the time, but Moses had a revolver in an ankle holster."

"Why come armed?"

"We weren't sure who we would find or how they would react, so we thought it was best to be prepared."

"Junie Archer?"

"She took our nines, but she had one of her own and a shotgun."

"How did Petchard get messed up in this?"

Emmet actually chuckled, the Marine façade slipping. "I'm not sure, but the dude's got some serious problems." He explained about the notification system Junie had rigged over the doors. "We heard the chime and Junie hid behind the door into the living room. This police officer comes creeping into the living room, locked and loaded, and she disarms him in a heartbeat. Seems he had no clue she was a man."

"No," Munk agreed, "I don't think he did. And Cass?"

"She came in after Junie fired the second shot." Emmet carried on at Munk's frown. "Junie got irritated with Petchard and fired a warning shot through the window and told him to shut up. He couldn't stay quiet and she shot his ear. That's when Detective Elliot entered the house."

"Junie shot his ear? Was she aiming for his head and missed?"

Emmet shook his head. "No, sir. After she shot him, she told him that she'd put a bullet between his eyes next time."

"Junie caught Cass the same way?"

"Detective Elliot was too quick for her. They ended up facing off, guns pointed at each other, Junie's shotgun aimed at us."

"What caused the gun fire?"

"A cat, of all things," Emmet said. "It must've been hiding under the couch and for some reason, it went for Junie's legs. I guess she lost her balance. And she was taking drugs, I think."

"Why?"

"She acted like she had a headache, kept pressing her hand to her temple. And her eyes were a little fuzzy." He shrugged. "It made me wonder if she had migraines and had taken something for them."

Munk motioned for Emmet to continue.

"The cat bolted out and then all hell broke loose." His eyes slid closed and then slowly opened. "While Detective Elliot had Junie distracted, Moses managed to get the revolver out of its holster and hide it beneath his leg. I know he fired once at Junie, and she got us with the shotgun. She must've hit Detective Elliot, too, because she went down fast." He replayed the scene in his mind. "I think Elliot might've fired her weapon, but I'm not sure. The shots were all close together."

"Where was Moses when he fired?"

"Next to me on the couch."

"Sitting?"

"Yes, sir."

"How did Officer Petchard end up on top of Junie?"

"I'm not sure, sir. The shotgun blast threw Moses into me, and I lost track of what was happening."

Emmet shifted position on the bed and winced. Munk asked if he had anything else to add, then stopped the tape. Emmet thought about Joseph's whispered request and decided to honor it. "Can I tell you something, off the record?"

Martinez and Munk exchanged a glance, then nodded.

He took a deep breath, all sign of the Marine gone. "I don't think it matters now, but that was Joseph who died today. Moses was murdered Wednesday night."

"We wondered," Munk said. "Why are you telling us now?"

Emmet touched the wound Joseph had stitched up. "Joseph was a pretty honest dude. Despite the hacking and impersonating an officer. Before he died, he asked me to make it right to protect Moses' memory. What will you do with it?"

"I don't know. Like you say, I'm not sure it matters." Munk almost smiled. "From your description of the shot he took at Junie Archer, I wondered how Moses could have made it. He didn't have that kind of aim."

"It was close distance," Emmet protested.

"Moses couldn't have made that shot at any distance," Detective Martinez said. "But Joseph? He seemed to have a gift."

"Then maybe I shouldn't have said anything. Just let Moses go down as a hero." He glanced up at them, wondering how black and white their view of the world was. "Maybe he still should."

"Maybe he should," the pudgy officer said. "Maybe he should at that."

CHAPTER 154

LIGHT HAD BLED ALMOST completely from the evening sky, painting faint sienna streaks through the blinds and across the white blanket. Maxine finished her coffee and snaked a hand beneath the sheet to find Cass's hand. The monitors beeped rhythmically although Cass stirred more frequently now.

Maxine studied her friend's face and felt a strange pride. She'd rushed to the ER to find half of Forney County's police force clogging the waiting room and hallway. She had managed to overhear a few comments about Cass's role in stopping the man who had brought such death to the county these past few days. Or perhaps it was a woman. Opinion was unclear. What was perfectly clear was the consensus that Cass had acted bravely to protect a fellow officer whose life was in imminent danger. Although a few muttered that he wasn't worth saving.

"I'm so proud of you, Cass," she whispered, releasing her friend's hand to stroke a strand of hair off her forehead. "I know you hoped you wouldn't have to shoot anyone else. But you wiped another worthless cretin off the face of the planet, girl. It's practice for when we find the beast that did this to us. He's an animal and needs to be put down like one."

Maxine saw a narrow door in a corner. She crossed the room on tiptoe, relieved to find a toilet. When she finished, she opened the door to see Cass's eyes open, gazing at her with a confused expression.

"Max?" she croaked.

Maxine hurried to her side. "It's all right, Cass."

Cass blinked and tried to lift her head, falling back onto the pillow with a soft grunt. "Water?"

Maxine held a glass with a straw to Cass's lips, stroking her hair while she drank. "Better?" she asked when Cass turned her head away.

"Thanks." Her eyelids slipped closed.

"You remember?"

"Some." Cass touched the bandage over her cheek. "How bad is it?"

"That Indian doctor said you'll be fine. You won't even have a scar."

She looked at Maxine in horror. The beeping from one of the monitors quickened. "The scar. Maxine, who's seen it?"

"It's okay." Maxine snagged Cass's free hand and held it tightly. "A nurse, the doctor, and me. That's all I know about. I was with your dad and brothers a little while ago and they didn't mention it."

Her voice was frantic. "Anybody at the scene? An officer? Paramedics?"

"Maybe Cass, but calm down, honey. There was bound to be a lot of blood, right? Your scar's not very big; the blood probably covered it completely. With all the worry about getting you to the hospital, I doubt anybody even noticed. And if they did, so what? What are they going to say? And to who?"

Cass's breathing slowly returned to normal and the beeping subsided. Maxine's smile was gentle. "Besides, if anybody does say anything, use my line and tell them it's body art. Men will think you're totally hot and women will line up to get one of their own. Hey, maybe we could start a business. Tattoos, piercings, and scars. We'll be rich."

Cass managed to roll her eyes before the hospital room door opened. Dr. Ramasubramanian peeked inside. "May I come in?"

Maxine stood but Cass gripped her hand. "Stay. And wash my face. It feels disgusting."

She waited as the doctor had Cass move her fingers and hand, and watched as she lifted her arm about a foot off the bed. Cass was panting and her face was coated with sweat by the time he finished with her.

"You are very fortunate, Detective Elliot. The bullet traced a narrow path between your collar bone and scapula. Neither was injured. You will need some therapy, but will heal very quickly."

"My face?"

"I've asked a plastic surgeon to look at the wound and my stitches. I hope my work will be satisfactory." He told her where the button was so she could self-administer morphine.

She managed a brief smile. "I've got a budding opium habit already, Dr. Rambo. I can't afford heroin on a cop's salary, so I'd better kick it now."

He patted her hand. "Try to get some rest. If that involves morphine, we will find a discount drug dealer on some street corner when you are on the outside again, okay?"

Cass raised an eyebrow. "Was that humor, Dr. Rambo?"

"Yes," he said, chuckling as he headed for the door. "Yes, I believe it was."

CHAPTER 155

JOHN GREY PUT HIS scissors aside and looked at the contraption wrapped around Calvin Whitman Jr.'s chest. "So that's how he did it," he said.

"Did what?" Mitch called from the corner.

Bernie Winterbottom looked over from his position near the fireplace, where he held a piece of string next to a bullet hole in the plaster. Bright halogen lights on poles lit the small room. "That's quite a harness."

"A what?" Kado called as he shut his phone. He and Truman moved to the body. "How did he do that?"

"Do what?" Mitch asked again, struggling to his feet.

Bernie knelt beside Grey and with his approval, poked at the garments, peeking inside the bra. "He used cutlets inside a strapless brassiere to push his pectoral muscles up and together, and some sort of contraption over the brassiere to help boost the effect." He slipped a finger under the strap. "The shoulder straps are tight, very uncomfortable I would imagine, but the total impact is one of cleavage creation from a normal-sized man's pectorals." He turned to Grey. "May I?"

The medical examiner nodded and Bernie fiddled with the clasps and peeled each layer away. A man's well-muscled chest was revealed, along with two entry wounds and small smears of blood.

"That's not fair," Truman said, and then blushed. "I mean, if a man can do that and look like a woman, imagine what a woman could do. That's sneaky."

Mitch finally looked over Bernie's shoulder. "Dang. I missed it."

"It's a common practice for cross-dressers and even transvestites to use various means of enhancing their breasts and cleavage," Bernie said.

"You are full of fascinating facts, you know that, Bernie? And sometimes, they're a little scary." At the Englishman's blush, Mitch turned to Kado. "Well?"

"Give me a minute. Grey?"

John Grey slipped plastic rods into each wound, then unfolded himself and stood, snagging one earlobe between his thumb and forefinger and rubbing. "That clears Cass."

"How?" Mitch said. "Hoffner will challenge it, so let's get the story down now."

"There's no story to get down," Kado said. "The science says it all. Junie was standing about here." Kado straddled Whitman's torso, his body facing between the couch and window. "According to Munk's interview of Emmet Hedder, Moses was seated on the couch to Junie's left when he fired his weapon. That must be the shot that penetrated the heart, upward and from left to right. The shot to the left shoulder is almost straight in." He looked down at the rod in the wound. "Well, maybe with a small upward angle. It makes sense that Cass fired at or near the time that she was shot." Kado motioned for Truman to stand where Cass had stood. "Aim at me." Truman lifted his right hand, and Kado lifted his. "They had guns in their right hands and shot each other in the left shoulder. It holds water. She's clear."

"Thank God for that," Mitch said. He peg-legged back to the chair and collapsed into it. "He'll still suspend her."

"He has to," Truman piped up, "department regs."

"There's an exception to every rule," Grey said, and turned to help Porky maneuver a gurney into the room. He looked at his assistant's bloodshot eyes. "Are you sure you can handle this?"

Porky's chin quivered but he nodded.

"We'll make a separate trip for this one," he said, looking at the body on the floor. "He's caused enough grief for the Franklin family. I don't want him in the same wagon as Moses."

CHAPTER 156

DARLA STONE WAVED TO Maxine and closed the door to Cass's hospital room. She turned to her husband. His face was a pale wasteland but there was peace in his eyes. "They don't come tougher than an Elliot," she said.

Mitch drew a ragged breath. "I know. But there's nothing like seeing for yourself." He tucked a stray strand of hair behind her ear. "I wish I'd been there for her."

"The best thing you can do for Cass is concentrate on rehab and beat her back to work. She won't stay down for long."

"Hey," Mitch said, heading for the waiting room. "You owe me fried chicken."

"What?" Darla laughed.

"You bet that Junie Archer was Calvin Whitman's kid. You were right. That means you have to pay up."

"Ahh, Mitch. That's not the way it works with bets. If I was wrong, I'd have to pay up. Since I was right, you can take me to that new winery outside town."

His face fell. "That's the way it works?"

"Afraid so, sweetie. But that was a good try."

They found a group of officers huddled in a corner, whispering. Wally Pugh hovered nearby, notepad in hand, nose twitching as he scented for a story. Sheriff Hoffner stood in the middle of the room, face stoic as he listened to a report from Kado. Truman stood beside Kado, offering the occasional nod.

"He's going to suspend her again," Mitch said.

"Does he have to?" Darla asked.

560

"Probably," he admitted. "At least until the Firearm Discharge Board clears her. But there were two witnesses to this shooting –" He pivoted on his crutches. "Where's Petchard? Was he admitted?"

"He's gone," Darla answered. Mitch had called his wife as soon as he learned that Cass was wounded and asked her to wait at the hospital. It was now quarter past ten. She'd been here for almost five hours. "I saw him come into the ER on a gurney, but he walked out on his own steam. His ear was bandaged but that was all the damage I saw."

"I'll bet nobody took a statement from him, did they?"

She shrugged.

"First thing tomorrow morning, Kado," they heard Hoffner bark. "And I mean first thing."

The tall man spun and nearly collided with Wally Pugh, who had edged close to the threesome. The sheriff recovered and offered a smile. He took Wally's arm and steered the smaller man toward the exit. "What can I do for you, Mr. Pugh?"

Kado and Truman walked over.

"How was it?" Mitch asked.

"He listened," Kado said, "but he thinks I'm skewing the results in Cass's favor."

"I think he's looking for a reason to fire Cass," Truman added. "He doesn't seem very partial."

"Is that why he wants the paperwork by tomorrow morning?" Mitch asked.

Kado nodded and yawned as a big black man in scrubs hurried through the emergency room doors. He spotted the small group. "I heard Detective Elliot got shot," Jerome said, concern in his dark chocolate eyes. "How is she?"

"She'll be fine," Mitch said.

"And you found Emmet? Is he okay?"

"A few shotgun pellets in his hide, but he'll recover. See for yourself."

Jerome turned and spotted Emmet and Celia at the billing desk. "Thanks," he said, and joined the other couple.

"Are we just going to let Emmet leave?" Kado whispered. "What about the murders around the country? What about Whitehead's murder?"

"Truman," Mitch said. "Very quietly, tell Emmet not to leave the county. We'll have more questions for him. Don't tell him about what."

They watched as Truman waited for Emmet to sign the last of the hospital's paperwork, then pulled him aside. Truman leaned in close and Emmet made eye contact with Mitch, then nodded.

Kado drew a deep breath. "I might as well get to the station and start pulling the data together for Hoffner. He told me to stay away from Cass until the Firearm Discharge Board hearing is over. Tell her I'll be thinking about her."

"That is such nonsense. Why don't you tell her yourself?" Darla asked. She lifted a chin in Jerome's direction. "I'll bet he's up for a little undercover work."

———————

JEROME WHISTLED SOFTLY AND nodded at the young officer standing guard outside Cass's room. Truman checked the hall and then pushed the door open and stood aside. With a grunt, Jerome pulled the laundry cart inside but then jumped as a woman's voice said, "Clean sheets? At almost ten-thirty?"

Jerome's breath caught in his throat. "Wrong room," he mumbled, preparing to wheel the cart back out.

"Jerome?" a soft voice called. "Is that you?"

He turned to find Detective Elliot flashing him a tired smile. A skinny dark-headed woman sat beside the bed. "It is. How you feeling?"

"Not bad, considering. Are you moonlighting for the hospital?"

"Not exactly. Is this a friend?"

"My best friend. Jerome, meet Maxine. We've known each other forever."

Maxine wiggled her fingers at Jerome. He relaxed and jostled the cart. "It's clear."

Kado popped up from beneath the sheets and towels. Cass and Maxine started to giggle.

"Men have done wild things for me, Cass," Maxine said. "But none ever snuck into my hospital room in a cart full of laundry."

Kado plucked a wash cloth from his head and tossed it in the bin, then leaned in and grabbed a paper bag. "Thanks for throwing clean stuff in here. I'm not sure I could've handled riding with bodily fluids."

"My pleasure. If you don't need anything else, I'll take my cart and be going." Jerome smiled over at the women. "Glad to see you're okay, Detective. And thanks for getting Emmet out alive."

"I'm not sure how helpful I was, but I'm glad he's okay."

Maxine stood. "I think I'd better head out." She bent and kissed Cass's forehead. "I'll see you in the morning, if you haven't convinced Kado to break you out by then."

She followed Jerome from the room, asking about his marital status.

Kado pulled pudding cups and plastic spoons from the brown bag. "I promised you dinner," he said, ripping the foil from one cup and handing it over. He sat in the chair next to her, opened another cup, and took a bite. "I hate hospitals."

Cass licked her spoon. "Me, too. My brother Bobby had leukemia. We spent a lot of time in doctor's offices and waiting rooms. The smell…"

"And the sounds. How can they expect anybody to get well while all this equipment beeps and staff are in and out of the rooms at all hours?" He finished his pudding and sat back, watching her.

"You shouldn't be here," she said.

"*You* shouldn't be here," he clarified. "Whitman's dead. So is Joseph Franklin. What do you remember about the shooting?"

She told him.

"That ties with the evidence. Joseph's shot killed Whitman, not yours."

"Where did I hit her? I mean, him?"

"Shoulder. Almost the same place as where he wounded you. If Joseph hadn't been there and fired, your shot would've incapacitated him."

"It's funny, but I can't help but think of him as Junie Archer."

"He created an excellent illusion. The makeup, the clothes. Whitman even wore this contraption that squeezed his pecs together to make cleavage."

"A bra?"

"Kind of, but with a bunch of other parts. Bernie can tell you about it." His tired gray eyes twinkled. "Apparently he's seen one before." His smiled faded and his voice was quiet when he spoke. "I saw the scar, Cass."

Her eyes closed. "Secrets. They have a way of coming out, don't they?"

"You were raped?"

She nodded.

"The note. Is it related to the scar?"

She slowly opened her eyes. "Yes. But not mine."

"He did this to someone else?"

"At least two other women. He left the note for Maxine."

"I guess I understand why she didn't report her rape, but you didn't report yours?"

"No, I didn't. I was young and dumb and thought it was my fault. I was careless and gave him the chance to roofie me."

"It doesn't matter how careless you were, it wasn't your fault." He took her hand and glanced at the clock. "I have to finish some reports tonight for Hoffner. But we'll talk more about this later, okay?"

"What's there to talk about?"

Kado looked at her. "About what you'll do when we find him."

"*If* we find him."

"We will. And then you, and probably Maxine, will have some decisions to make."

CHAPTER 157

MOONLIGHT PLAYED ON THE low, drowsy waters of the Sabine River. It was early May, and the mercury was already well above normal levels and the rainfall well below. The old timers who gossiped in the shade of the great trees around the courthouse projected that this would be East Texas' driest summer in nearly a century. Celia drove across the bridge with the windows down, listening to the soothing snick of the tires over the concrete seams. She promised herself that they would put Emmet's little black pickup in the shop next week to have the air conditioner fixed. Then she corrected herself: they'd put his truck in the shop once the police were finished with her green Camry.

She looked over at her husband and wondered how they would put their marriage back together. He was a murderer, no two ways about it, but she understood why he had done what he had done. She wasn't sure whether she could release the hurt of the last several years, but she intended to give it a try. Emmet had taken a huge step by telling her about the murders and his role in them, and Celia honored him for that. She only wished he'd placed his trust in her sooner.

Celia checked for headlights and did a u-turn, heading back across the bridge. Stopping near its middle, she touched Emmet's shoulder. "We're here."

He woke slowly, groggy from the pain medication she'd demanded he take before leaving the hospital. "Anyone around?"

Celia shook her head. Emmet reached for the door handle, but she stopped him. "I'll do it."

"Asking you to take the bags from the trunk of your car was enough. That's tampering with evidence. Destroying it is mine to do. For Moses and Donna. For Joseph." He looked across the truck at her. "And for me and you."

He slid out of the car and Celia pushed the two duffel bags across the seat to him. With difficulty, Emmet unzipped each and dumped their contents into the lazy current. Bloody towels, new and used medical supplies, changes of clothes. He thumbed the ammunition from two spare magazines and then tossed it and the duffels over the bridge. Their guns were with the police, evidence taken from Junie Archer's house. The only thing he kept from the bags was the cash.

Emmet let Celia buckle him back in, then sat with his head leaning toward the open window, breathing in the wash of muggy night air as she drove away.

"That's it?" she asked.

"It's the best I can do. There are no records to prove that we killed those men. Or that we were together at the times they were murdered. No physical evidence to tie us to those crime scenes."

"It's over?"

"As over as I can make it. I figure the cops will poke around for a while and try to link us to those killings. But they can't."

She sighed then, a soft sound that was whisked away by the wind. He held out his good hand and she took it. "Home?" she asked.

Emmet nodded, his eyes tired but at peace. "Home."

CHAPTER 158

"WHO KNOWS?" KADO ASKED.

Truman, Munk, and Martinez exchanged glances. They were seated around the square evidence table in the forensics room, faces grim. Paperwork was scattered across the table, the scant evidence linking Moses Franklin, Donna Moore, and Emmet Hedder to the murders of three men around the country and Calvin Whitehead in Forney County.

"Us," Munk said. "Cass and Mitch. Darla."

"Porky, probably," Truman piped up. "I heard him telling Mitch that Moses was singing bass at the church service, and that Joseph was the one with the lower voice. Moses sang tenor."

"Anybody else?"

"Porky might've told Grey. And Bernie."

"Petchard," Munk added. "Although nobody would believe him."

"He's got no family left. Why does it matter?" Kado asked.

Martinez stirred. His brown eyes were bloodshot, his steely crew cut wilting. "There's a lot of money at stake. Moses' will leaves everything to a little girl named Amelia. For her college."

"Technically," Kado said, "that will was forged."

Martinez glared. "What is it with you?"

"I think the kid should get the money, Carlos, but this is serious business. Let's walk through it. When Moses and his mother were killed, their estates passed to Joseph. So legally, he would've received Moses' death benefits, right? Then Joseph could leave them to whoever he wanted. Since he died without a will, the state decides how his estate is distributed."

The men nodded.

Kado's tone turned reflective. "If Moses died Wednesday night, he wasn't killed in the line of duty, so Joseph wouldn't receive any extra benefits. But if *Joseph* died Wednesday and Moses died today…"

"Then his heir gets the extra benefits and he's a hero," Munk said. He yawned until his jaw popped. "I can see the headline in the Forney Cater, 'Hero Cop Sacrifices Self to Save Others'. We could use a little of that around here."

"Any objections to leaving things as they are? With Joseph dead on Wednesday and Moses dying today? Will Cass or Mitch have a problem with it? Grey or Porky?"

"I can't imagine they will," Munk said. "They loved Moses as much as we did."

"Okay, how about pursuing Emmet Hedder for the murders in those other states?" Kado asked. "And for Whitehead's lynching?"

"There's no real evidence that he was involved. And do you think anybody cares?" Martinez asked. "Child abuse? Prostitution of a child? Sounds like every one of them needed killing."

"I hear you, Carlos, but we've got Whitehead's murder to clear."

Truman leaned forward, his hazel eyes sharp. "That gas plant explosion in Watuga County was lucky for us, because the press hasn't put any time into these crimes. But the Forney Cater will run more stories. What if we helped Wally Pugh with a few anonymous details?"

"What are you talking about?" Munk asked.

"Not lying, exactly, but leading him in the wrong direction. This is some juicy stuff. A man living in Forney County for over thirty years is really a violent, corrupt cop from Alabama? And his son shows up in Arcadia, dressed like a woman? All that's true. What if we nudged Wally a little?"

Munk snorted a laugh. "In the direction of thinking that Junie Archer, a.k.a. Calvin Whitman Jr., killed his father?"

Truman nodded. "Why not? He did shoot Donna, Mrs. Franklin, and both the Mojos. And he tried to kill Emmet."

Kado rubbed his temples and looked around the wide forensics table, his face grim. "You realize what we're doing, guys? We're talking about committing fraud and condoning vigilante justice."

Munk shifted in his chair. "Who would know?"

"We would," Kado said. "But I don't think anybody else would dig into the Moses-Joseph thing, or try to link Emmet, Donna, or Moses to those murders."

Martinez sighed. "Of all of us, I've got the most to lose. I'm closest to my pension. But I don't have a problem with leaving the Mojo situation as it is. As for the vigilante stuff, I've got enough cases to work in Forney County. Hoffner won't care about helping other jurisdictions, that's for sure. Anybody got a problem with dropping it?"

"No," said Munk.

"I don't, but what about the food mashed in Moses' shoes? And the gas on his clothes?" Truman asked.

Martinez snorted and looked at the equipment on the counters. "I guess you and Hazel the sniffing machine were right. One of the Franklin twins was involved in Whitehead's murder. Good work."

Kado dipped his head.

"But the evidence," Truman protested. "The tomatoes and strawberries and gas."

"What tomatoes and strawberries? What gas?" Kado asked.

"The food from the storeroom and Mojo's clothes," Truman said, then stopped. "You never loaded that in the system, did you?"

"What tomatoes and strawberries? What gas?" Kado asked again.

Martinez nodded. "There's hope for you yet, *hombre.*"

CHAPTER 159

THE QUIET MAN IN the cowboy hat walked down the hospital's corridor, nose twitching at the stinging antiseptic scent. A janitor pushing a floor buffer moved the whirring machine from his path. Hitch carried on, golden eyes watchful.

It was nearing midnight. Visiting hours were long over. The nurses were updating reports and watching the late news. The guard stationed outside the detective's room had either been reassigned or was on a break. Either way, Hitch was grateful. He peered in the window of one room; the bed was empty. In the next, a man put his fishing magazine down and struggled to reposition himself, fighting his leg cast and the apparatus that held it suspended.

Hitch moved on, seeking the flame-headed woman. The old man had sent him to the emergency room to hear firsthand what had happened out at the little farmhouse. It had taken several hours for an accurate picture to emerge of who was alive and who was dead. Hitch had stayed in and around the ER waiting room eavesdropping, trading one tattered magazine for another, drifting through the clusters of officers and the few reporters, and sipping dreadful coffee until the information flow stabilized and repeated itself.

Once people began drifting away, Hitch stepped outside and called the old man. After Hitch delivered his update, the old man's pipe clacked against his teeth in a way that Hitch had come to recognize as satisfaction. He allowed himself a brief moment to wonder why the old man was so interested in these people, and then pushed the thought away. The old man told him to head home, that his work was done for the night.

But Hitch hadn't left. Instead, he'd waited and watched until the last of them had gone. A nurse stopped by occasionally to ask if he needed anything, and he would shake his head with a smile. It was only now, when the hospital was as silent as hospitals ever got, that he looked for her. It was a compulsion he didn't understand or question. Hitch simply needed to find her.

He checked the last two rooms, then turned and walked back along his path on the opposite side of the hall. He found her three doors down. A lamp shone from one corner, its outer edges providing scant illumination. But it was enough. She was sleeping, deeply from the look of her breathing. Hitch checked the hall and then pushed into her room, crossing silently to the bed.

Her red hair was a dark mass against the white pillowcase, lustrous in the low light. Her skin was pale but her features were peaceful despite the bandage near her eye, and her long lashes lay like soft wings against her cheeks. A corner of gauze was visible from beneath the sheet and Hitch was filled with an intense longing, an emotion he had never felt before. It made him want to cradle this woman, this stranger, in his arms. To offer healing, protection. Reaching out a finger, he stroked her cheek. She frowned and her mouth twitched.

Squeaking footsteps hurried past and Hitch stole to the door, peeking through the window and checking the corridor. It was empty. He turned back to the beautiful detective and wondered why she attracted him so. He allowed his gaze to travel over her features one last time, then Hitch settled his hat on his head and trod quietly to the exit.

His thoughts were troubled as he moved across the quiet parking lot. She was the one who had uncovered the old man's cult back in the spring, and she had enough tenacity that without the break due to her suspension, he suspected she would have found him. The old man wasn't done with Hitch and his unique gifts, and therefore he would cross paths with this woman again.

As adversaries.

The old pickup's engine purred to life and Hitched slipped onto Forney County's dark back roads. He gazed through the windshield up at the sparkling sky, and wished upon a star that he wouldn't have to kill her.

THE END

ACKNOWLEDGMENTS

They say that writing is a solitary endeavor, and to a great extent, I'd agree. But the inspiration and ideas that underlie my books spring from a variety of sources, and the support I've received while writing *Avengers of Blood* has been invaluable. Martyn, thanks once again for your faith in me. You waited with infinite patience while I worked my way through the plot for this story, then chuckled and said 'a-ha!' at all the right places while you read that first rough draft. You are a gift, and I treasure you more every day.

I'm blessed with an amazing family whose lives are full of the wonderful and weird. Special thanks go out to my niece Lydia and my nephew, MacGreagor. They allowed me to liberate the incident of the mouse fart and Froggy from their original circumstances and twist them for use by a little girl named Amelia.

Lark. What can I say? Even with my devious, creative mind, never in a million years could I have come up with the story about the green Army men heads. Truth is stranger than fiction, indeed. Thank you for that bizarre tidbit and letting me incorporate it into Cass's childhood.

Jerry, o brother of mine, your advice on how a badly abused leg would heal and the various devices with which I could torture Mitch during his recovery was fantastic. As was your repeated demonstration (without actual bullets, thankfully) of what could happen if Cass was shot in the shoulder. She was, and hopefully, I've done your explanations justice. If not, the fault and any errors about the medical stuff and anatomy are entirely mine. And Terry, o other brother of mine, thanks for your help with my questions about handguns. Yes, yes, any screw-ups with the weapons are mine alone. Both of you, stop laughing like that. You'll get a hernia.

As for you, Kathy Shelton, it's been an absolute delight to work with you. Your candor and eye for detail have made this a much stronger read. I can't wait to finish the next book just to hear what you have to say.

And to Lillian, thank you so much for pointing out my errors regarding twelve-step programs. You are a strong, courageous woman, and I thank you for making contact and letting me know where I'd gone wrong. You're the kind of reader every writer longs for, and I'm so glad to know you.

Many, many thanks to those who read the first Cass Elliot novel, *The Devil of Light*, and waited with much impatience for the second book. Your pushing and shoving and encouragement have kept me going, and I appreciate you greatly.

For you brave souls who have picked up this book by an unfamiliar author, you have my sincere gratitude. Diving into a world created by an unknown author can be a bit scary. I appreciate your willingness to risk your hard-earned cash on a book of mine and hope you've enjoyed reading *Avengers of Blood* as much as I enjoyed writing it. I can't wait to see what terror reigns down on Forney County next.

If you'd like to know more about the real-life events that led me down the path to *Avengers of Blood*, check out this blog post: **Genesis of a Novel: The Horrific Death of James Byrd Jr.**

Gae-Lynn Woods
February 2013

www.ingramcontent.com/pod-product-compliance
Lightning Source LLC
Chambersburg PA
CBHW030535020726
47494CB00005B/1381